the
GRAVITY PILOT

TOR BOOKS BY M. M. BUCKNER

Watermind
The Gravity Pilot

the
GRAVITY PILOT

a science fantasy

M. M. BUCKNER

a tom doherty associates book

new york

THE GRAVITY PILOT

A Tor Book
Published by Tom Doherty Associates, LLC
175 Fifth Avenue
New York, NY 10011

www.tor-forge.com

Tor® is a registered trademark of Tom Doherty Associates, LLC.

Library of Congress Cataloging-in-Publication Data

Buckner, M. M.
    The gravity pilot / M.M. Buckner.—1st ed.
        p. cm.
    ISBN 978-0-7653-2286-9
    1. Skydivers—Fiction.   2. Virtual reality—Fiction.   I. Title.
PS3602.U29G73 2011
813'.6—dc22

                                                        2010036537

First Edition: March 2011

Printed in the United States of America

0   9   8   7   6   5   4   3   2   1

To Jack, my constant hero
and
To Rhyan, who will dream the future

This is love, to fly toward a secret sky, to cause a hundred veils to fall each moment. First to let go of life. Finally, to take a step without feet.

—Jalal ad-Din Rumi

ACKNOWLEDGMENTS

My primary thanks go to Jack Lyle, who has made over 1,200 skydives. His experience as a former jump master, instructor, and relative work competitor has been immensely helpful to me in researching and writing this novel.

Additional thanks go to the many friends and colleagues who advised and supported me through this project, including, in alpha order: Rita Bourke, Sue Bredensteiner, John Bridges, Mary Helen Clarke, Frank Cunningham, Joe DeGross, Mary Bess Dunn, Susan Eaddy, Phyllis Gobbell, Doug Jones, Jan Keeling, Thomas Longo, Bonnie Parker, Nathan Parker, Wil Parker, Kathy Rhodes, Martha Rider, Rick Romfh, Janet Schreibman, Jason Sizemore, Carole Stice, Shannon Thurman, and Ava Weiner.

Much appreciation goes to Stacy Hague-Hill for her valuable suggestions, and most particular gratitude goes to my editor, David G. Hartwell, whose wise advice helped me envision a broader horizon for this novel. Finally and always, heartfelt thanks go to my agent and friend, Richard Curtis.

first

THE ETERNAL SPIRAL CURVE

See him glide into the blue dance. Watch him soar on thermal swells. Feel the crosswind skew him sideways through drenching Arctic clouds, and he steers, banks, treads the shining air, till down down down the eternal spiral curve he falls...

1

AAD. Automatic activation device, opens parachute in emergencies.

Orrpaaj Sitka lay stretched on his back, visualizing his skydive. Light gray eyes. Windburned skin. Stinky gym socks. Clean soap in his ears. High up in a geodesic dome, he rested on an I-beam and squinted through the glass at Alaska's winter sky. Forty meters above the concrete, one leg dangling free, his body made small twitches as he practiced the moves in his mind. Twenty-two years old, and how he could narrow his focus. The sun, the clouds, the shaping forces of the universe all centered on one event: his skydive that day. No other notion could stick in his head. Not on that day, surely not. He swore to himself that nothing else mattered, but he was lying.

Squirming on his steel beam, he wadded his gloves for a pillow. Mentally, he sorted his gear. Yet his girlfriend's voice repeated, *Why do you throw yourself away for nothing?*

Last night, because he couldn't list his reasons, everything between them ended. Today while Orr braved the stratosphere, Dyce would leave for Seattle to take a library job.

He sat up and straddled the I-beam, plagued by the memory of her hair. Last night while she packed, her long braid came loose, and her hair smelled of candle smoke. He'd never been with anyone else. He'd never wanted any other girl. Seattle was a myth to him. All his hopes lay in completing this stratosphere dive. He sat in his high dome chanting an old Aleut prayer. He hadn't yet learned what vapor dreams were made of.

Smog rolled around the base of the dome. Noxious fumes had buried the long chain of Aleutian Islands where he lived. Only the highest volcanic peaks emerged above the haze, and from space, the ancient land bridge resembled the broken spine of some great fallen bird. Acid storms immersed the cliffs as predictably as tides, and the rivers ran so yellow, any possible salmon had long since expired. Who can say how the Aleut people endured those islands for nine thousand years? Yet endure they did, even to the day in 2068 when Dyce left for Seattle.

Orr loosened his collar. The glass dome focused the sun like a lens. Built at the summit of Mount Shishaldin, the seedy old Unimak Air Base had long since been abandoned by the United States government and taken over by the tribe. Still, its dome rose above the smog right into the blue January sky, and Orr ached to be up there. Up in the stratosphere.

On the launchpad below, loud sirens blared the ten-minute warning, and he refocused. He got to his feet, drew on his frayed gloves and whispered the Aleut war cry.

"*Yio'kwa*. Let's do it."

From the I-beam, he dropped into the gantry tower, then slid down the metal ladder, skimming his gloves along the rails, barely touching the rungs with his feet. His limbs seemed to flow like music. At the capsule level, his quadriceps pulsed and contracted. He felt so ready for this dive.

The air in the dome seemed to crackle with static. The usual loiterers lounged by the hangar doors, trading friendly insults and passing around a sack of fry bread. Orr waved to them, breathing in the heady smell of grease and engine oil. Then he spotted his cousin, Gabe Lermontov, crouching over their gear bag like a chubby bear.

Orr snuck up and goosed Gabe in the ribs.

Gabe's shaggy eyebrows merged into one. "Do you realize what time it is?"

"No worries. We've got plenty of time." Orr twirled his electronic helmet on his fingertip, dodging back and forth to keep it in balance.

Gabe unzipped the gear bag. "You're worse than my five-year-old."

Ah, but what tenderness the two young men displayed toward their gear bag. They reached in and lifted out their Celestia Sky Wing. Most of their gear was patched and faded, but the Celestia was new, virginal. It dazzled them. They glanced at each other and grinned.

"Today we do it," Orr whispered.

"Don't push." Gabe wiped his damp hands down his beard. "You've gotta see how this Wing behaves."

Orr clamped on his helmet and visualized the stratosphere, thirty kilometers above the Earth. Lots of people jumped from that height, but Orr never had. Eight years he'd been working part-time at the tribal seafarm, collecting equipment, practicing, saving his money. He wanted to earn his instructor license. And today, he would do it. He felt feathers tickling his insides. He had to stamp his boots to keep from singing out loud.

Warm winter sun radiated through the glass dome. Gabe climbed onto a step stool to drape the new Celestia over Orr's body like a tent. Light as air, its transparent micromesh could withstand a nuclear explosion, but Gabe coddled it like wedding lace. He hunkered underneath its folds and jacked its control leads into Orr's helmet. Then he climbed down off the stool, stepped back, and pretended to beat a drumroll. "The moment of truth."

Orr chinned a toggle in his helmet, and the Sky Wing came alive. Energy sang through its gauzy folds, and from inside, Orr watched the veil shimmer when he touched it. He felt like dancing. But every eye on the launchpad was trained on him, so he stood a little straighter, and his baritone dropped to bass. "Let's see if she'll furl."

He nudged his toggle, and a mandate surged through the mesh. Within its warp and weft, billions of microscopic sacs released spiraling polymer chains of nano-resins which combined and reacted. The Wing's material memory realigned, and with a waffling snap, the mesh rolled up into a tight cowl around Orr's helmet, so thin it might have been a wreath of glitter. Despite Orr's resolve, a note of involuntary bliss hummed out of him.

The final minutes were speeding by, so he strapped on his parachute rig. The Celestia would sail him aloft, but he would need his parachute to land. He couldn't stop grinning. Fully geared up, he felt almost too excited to breathe, so he circled their rented rocket, eyeing the new seams he and Gabe had welded.

He'd sold many things of value to make this day happen. His health card. His transit pass. The one good shirt Dyce bought him for job interviews. Along the rocket's flank in runny yellow spray paint, some previous owner had scrawled a name, *Mister Missile*. Drone rockets like this were easy to retrofit for sport diving. They were cheap, too, since the U.S. liquidated its arsenal.

Gabe got out his wrench and retightened the mosquito cameras mounted under the fins. His pride, those cameras. Gabe claimed his videos of Orr's skydives would earn mind-boggling sums of money one day. Both cousins had a gift for pipe dreams.

When the two-minute warning blared, adrenaline hammered Orr's rib cage. He ran up the tower steps, fondling his silvery cowl to make sure it was really there. Then he swung into the tiny cockpit, snapped a salute to Gabe and closed the hatch. But an ache rippled through his mind. Dyce. He rolled his shoulders to shake off the gloom.

Dyce wouldn't leave him. Not today. After the dive, he would smooth things over. He always knew how to make her smile. But as the prelaunch sequence began, misgivings rose through his blood like bubbles.

A leisurely Montana drawl rumbled over the radio com link in his helmet. It was Pete Hogue, the fixed-base operator. "Aye, Orr. I'm showing high pressure in your fuel tank. Could be a glitch."

Orr checked the heads-up display in his helmet visor. "My readout looks good."

Screwy indicators were common at the air base. Pete leased the operation from the Aleut Tribal Council, and his control tower gauges were nearly as obsolete as his rust-colored rental rocket. For today's launch, he'd let Orr and Gabe install an oversized fuel tank scavenged from a junkyard. No one but Pete Hogue would allow the old buzz bomb to take off. The flight was illegal. But Pete used to be a skydiver himself, so he understood their need.

"It's nothing," Orr said after a pause. "Don't mention it to Gabe. I think he's having his period today."

Pete chuckled. "When is he not?"

Orr squinted out his side portal to make sure Gabe was safe inside the hangar. Gabe's three little sons were pressing against the plate-glass window, throwing him good luck signs. Ilya, Nick, and Yanny, his fan club. He waved to them, then switched on the air supply in his pressurized jumpsuit as the final pulsing siren announced the opening of the dome.

With a loud boom, the dome split across the middle, and metal squealed against metal as its two halves retracted. Alaska's toxic smog gushed in like a dozen yellow wind-devils, warmer than it should have been for January, though the temperature seemed to go higher every year. Orr watched the smog spiral around the tower and mushroom against the sealed hangar doors till the whole dome filled with unbreathable haze. Inside his pressure suit, he gulped recycled air. Sure, tonight, he would convince Dyce to stay. But now he needed to focus. Pete was calling the countdown.

"Five . . . four . . . three . . ."

At the mark, Orr ignited the main engine, and fire exploded through the aft nozzle. Thunderous vibrations rocked the hangar windows, and *Mister Missile* lifted on a thick column of exhaust. Acceleration flattened Orr deep into his vinyl seat. His stomach tightened as the rocket shuddered upward through the long jolting climb to the tropopause, the highest reach of Earth's blustery weather.

When he broke through the cloud tops into the sudden calm, the quiet engulfed him. Black silence, as pure as ice. His interior spaces opened wide, and he released his grip on the yoke. He was rising into the stratosphere, higher than he'd ever been. Even through a thick scarred window, such a view clears a young man's mind. He rocked forward and bit his lip to keep from singing.

Pete's slow drawl crackled over the radio com link. "Check your velocity, son."

Orr scanned the rocket's old-fashioned console dials. "I'm still accelerating. That's funny."

Pete said, "You're climbing too fast to exit. You gotta slow her down."

Orr flipped a switch to override the rocket's cranky onboard computer. He punched keys to cut fuel and close off the oxidizer flow in the combustion chamber. But the engine didn't respond. Maybe a valve was stuck.

"Firing retros," Orr said. He felt a slight jerk as the side-mounted verniers expended their short burst of fuel. He slowed for an instant. Then the acceleration resumed.

"Little firecrackers ain't worth shit," Pete said.

Orr accelerated straight up through the stratopause, the roof of the stratosphere. He knew better than to exit. If he popped the hatch, the speed would rip his body through the metal wall before he was halfway out.

"Orr, this is Gabe. Abort the jump. I repeat, abort the jump."

Pete came on. "Just ride her up and down, Orr. See the sights. That fuel pressure warning must've been for real."

Gabe's voice rose an octave. "Fuel pressure? What's this about fuel pressure?"

Orr gripped the helm and rotated the deflectors in the exhaust nozzle, trying to reduce speed and force the rocket over into a flat trajectory. He'd worked too hard to get this chance. Raking kelp. Fixing machinery. Washing out tanks at the seafarm.

Why? Dyce's voice echoed.

He flipped keys to reposition the rocket fins, but the engine fought back. He heard it detonating inside like a ruptured heart, and he climbed through sixty kilometers, sixty-one, sixty-two. He soared above the stratosphere, into the freezing mesosphere. The temperature outside read minus forty degrees Celsius.

At last, the engine sputtered out, and he knew its chambers would never fire again. His velocity dropped. In a few seconds, the old bucket of bolts would pitch over, exactly as it should have done in the stratosphere. And Orr would feel that instant of weightlessness—his one chance to exit. After that, *Mister Missile* would drop like a bomb till its glider 'chutes deployed for a splashdown in the Gulf of Alaska.

He had to make a decision now. Exit, or stay with the rocket. But he was so high, almost at the edge of space. His pressure suit wasn't rated for this altitude.

"Ride the rocket down," Pete said, as if reading his mind.

"Don't jump, Orr. We'll find another engine. We'll try again." Gabe's voice cracked. "I'll sell the bus." Gabe supported his wife and sons flying his bus around the Aleutians. The offer was desperate.

Orr checked the altitude, and his mouth went dry. Sixty-four kilometers. Nearly forty miles above the Earth. The thought of leaping into that frigid void made his balls retract. But a Wing dive from that height would set a new world record. He tried to imagine what Dyce would say. A world record. She couldn't call that nothing.

The rocket pitched over, and he floated up in his seat. Against all reason, he felt lucky.

"I've gotta do it."

"No," Gabe whimpered.

"*Yio'kwa!*" Orr slugged the ejection switch and exploded from the cockpit.

Above ground level. Altitude referenced to drop zone level
instead of sea level.

Orr and his rocket hung side by side in the mesosphere. Cold bit through his pressure suit, and Dyce's face seemed to waver before him like a ghostly reflection. The sun blazed to his left, too bright to look at. On his right, he saw a swell of yellow haze, but he felt no connection with that vague contour. He drifted in a separate place all his own. Measureless. Mute. Eternal.

He chinned his radio. "Can anybody hear me?"

No answer. The com link in his helmet had always been fickle. Dyce fussed about his unreliable gear. But his GPS was almost new, and that didn't work either. Maybe he was too high for satellite relay.

Though he seemed to drift weightless, he knew he had to be falling. One side of his body felt on fire where the sun hit, but the other side felt bone cold. His suit couldn't equalize the energy loss, and shivers whipped along his spine. Quick, he had to unfurl his Celestia Sky Wing before it froze.

He chinned a toggle, and the cowl around his helmet brightened. Nano-resins formed elastic pairs. Molecular bonds realigned. The micromesh began to unroll. In seconds, it stiffened out and snapped into a clear pliant cone, open at the rear, with Orr swinging free inside, attached only at the helmet. The funnel-shaped airfoil was so glossy, it looked wet.

Almost vibrating from cold, Orr slipped his icy hands and feet into the Wing's sensitive pilot braces. His slightest movements would alter the shape of the flexible cone so he could steer. For a test, he bent his right arm, but in the thin mesosphere, the Wing barely skidded left. Then it started tumbling. He couldn't stabilize in such rarefied air. Just holding a straight line took all the skill he had. His teeth chattered, and the Wing made unpredictable moves. It was like learning to fly all over again. He felt the giddy edge of mortal terror.

Gabe's four mosquito cameras separated from the falling rocket and ze-roed on his helmet signal. They swarmed into his draft to begin recording, and he wondered if Gabe would receive their transmission. He angled his body inside the Wing and checked his speed. He was plummeting into the stratosphere now at a rate of—could that be right? Five hundred meters per second? That was over eleven hundred miles per hour, an inhuman speed. Yet he felt no resistance, no sense of falling. Instead, he felt luck riding on his shoulders.

Below him, the rocket spiraled down, glinting in the sun. He saw it disap-pear into a yellow cirrus cloud bank where lightning arced wide enough to span mountains.

". . . got your . . . calling . . ." Voices crackled in his helmet.

"Pete? Gabe?"

Still no answer. The silence went to his head like a drug. He felt as wide open as the universe. What name could he give to such a feeling? He found himself humming.

When he blasted into the denser air of the troposphere, heat rippled the Wing's leading edge. The pilot braces felt hot through his gloves, and Gabe's cameras shot sparks. He steered the Wing to shield them. He'd never cared about video before. Just doing the dives was enough. But today he would set a new world record. He pictured Dyce running to greet him, leaping into his arms.

"Sitka, you blamed fool . . ."

"Pete? This is Orr. I did it. The view's unbelievable."

"You've got . . ." Pete's voice broke up in static.

Orr felt the wind now. It moved at terrific speed, driving him due west into the sun. He darkened his visor as the airy tops of smog clouds rushed over him in a blur. The acceleration intoxicated him. When his horizontal speed maxed out his gauge, he hooted, *"Yio'kwa!"* He'd read about the hot new greenhouse jet streams that swept down from the Arctic and tore holes in the sky. Now he'd caught one by the ears.

Sailing the high-altitude current, he lost track of time, and he chuckled aloud like a happy fool. He gazed down at the amber cloud banks as if they were continents he might claim. If only he could share this view with Dyce. He imagined guiding her, arm in arm, through his kingdom of clouds. But . . . skydiving scared Dyce.

Rain streaked his Wing as he passed through hollows in the smog. His GPS was still fritzed. He kept trying to contact Pete and Gabe, but their silence didn't worry him. Here in the thick brown air, he flew the Celestia as he was born to fly, by reading the wind and feeling his way through the currents. The Wing was so swift and responsive, she moved like his own body, and the physical action stoked his senses. He felt the liberating confidence of sinew and bone. All he needed now was a thermal to ride till he sighted a few landmarks.

"Come in, Sitka. You're . . ."

"Pete? Come in, Pete?"

The radio signal cleared. "You're two thousand kilometers off course. Do you read? You're halfway to Japan."

Orr chinned a switch, and the GPS map finally popped up on his visor. He was cruising due west over—what? The North Pacific Basin?

Gabe's voice buzzed over the com link, talking to Pete. "Didn't I tell him to wear a jet pack? No artificial power, he said. Keep the dives pure, he said." Gabe sounded ready to weep.

Pete broke in. "We're calling air-sea rescue."

Orr squinted down through the auburn clouds, trying to spot the Pacific. His display showed him dropping fast over the Chishima Islands, and a bright, red warning popped up on his visor. Those waters were infested with box jellyfish. Sea wasps, the Aleuts called them. Lately, their venomous blooms had spread all over the northern seas. If he landed anywhere near, their long silky arms would trap him and drag him under.

No time to think. He needed to gain altitude. His lips wetted the radio mike. "Check the weather, Pete. Find me a storm I can surf."

"Be careful what you ask for, boy."

Pete's weather map flashed on Orr's display, but before he could read it, he saw the cloud swirl dead ahead. A category seven cyclone was building over the hot Kuroshio Current. It was cycling two hundred kilometers per hour, chewing up the eastern coast of Japan.

He chinned for graphic display, and his interface morphed the storm into a panic-stricken jet stream coiling and biting its own tail. Orr breathed through his teeth. Storms like that never used to hit Japan, but the North Pacific was changing. The display showed a column of hot air boiling up from the cyclone's eye, and that would give the lift he needed to fly home.

Reaching that eye, though, would be tough. Those wind shears could rip him out of his Wing. But the challenge engaged him. He imagined Dyce watching, and he felt his luck rise. So he flexed his limbs and focused on what he had to do.

"There's a ship, Orr. We're trying to contact a ship." Gabe's voice always broke when he was lying.

"Did you get your video?" Orr asked.

"Sure I did. A new world record." His cousin sounded frantic. "The boys are with me. We're watching you now."

Orr waved to the cameras. "Show this to Dyce, okay?"

"I will, Orr. We'll show her together. I'm calling that ship."

"See you soon." Orr shut off the com link. Then he flew toward the storm.

The outer winds buffeted him counterclockwise around the outer cloud swirl, and downdrafts thrust him lower. He needed to cross through that swirl to reach the rising air at the center. So he forced the Wing onto its side to carve through the current at an angle. His horizontal speed picked up fast, but the Wing started fishtailing. He felt like a child riding a paper kite.

When the Wing began to spin, he reacted fast and rolled it upside down. Runaway spins could kill. He tried carving into the windstream at different angles, but each time, the Wing started bucking. He made a mental note: the wingtip needed a flatter edge. When he got home, he would text the designer.

Wind shears were intensifying, but he kept trying to slice through. At last, the current caught him, and he spiraled toward the center. The vortex was sucking him in. Only two of Gabe's cameras still trailed close in his draft, and he glimpsed them over his shoulder. When Dyce saw this recording, surely she would admire his skill. She'd be waiting. Surely, his sweet girl would wait.

Out of nowhere, a rogue gust knocked him sideways, and he felt a force like hard vacuum tearing his body out of the airfoil. He lost his hold on the braces. Only his helmet wires held him in the Wing. He felt them tugging, straining. Then one wire snapped. It lashed across his visor, grazing the clear ceramic with a starburst of hairline fractures.

But he was rising. No doubt about it, he felt the buoyant upsurge of air. He grabbed for the pilot braces and chinned the toggle for his readouts. Nothing. His helmet display was dead. He was flying blind now, soaring back up toward the cloud tops. At last, his Wing tumbled over and bobbed upside down in the boiling upper reaches of the storm. He'd made it to the center. His eyes leaked tears of pure elation.

Inside his suit, he felt soggy with sweat, out of breath. His oblique muscles burned when he flipped the Wing upright. Filtered sunbeams drenched every surface in bronze. As he surfed the storm's crown, he looked for the cameras. Only one had survived. Its lens irised wide to gather the metallic sunlight. Brass, silver, copper, the clouds heaved and tossed. An arc of mist geysered upward and hung suspended. It glowed like platinum, edged in white gold. Orr watched it shimmer.

He grew calm watching the clouds. Gradually, he became aware of a riveting joy. The sky seemed to billow and pulse with unspeakable poetry, and Orr's chest swelled. Dyce felt very present, very close beside him. He could almost sense her hand in his.

Around him, the cyclone whistled. His limbs ached from holding his position in the boiling uplift. He couldn't stay in the storm's eye, exhausting his strength. He had to cross out and fly east.

He took one last glance at the geyser of mist, haloed against the sunset. It was dissolving and falling, a crimson spiral curve, fringed in black.

"Let's do it," he whispered.

He flew into the swiftest inner wall of the cloud swirl. His worn-out muscles sang with pain, but he gripped the braces harder, willing himself to stay strong. Winds jetted around him like furies. All at once, the Wing stood on end, and Orr's head smacked the airfoil.

He woke under his parachute canopy. Silence. Smog. Drifting. He had no memory of opening his parachute. His automatic safeties must have kicked in. The side of his head raged, and it took him a few seconds to realize his Sky Wing was gone. Gone? The storm had ripped it away.

He turned and squinted through his scarred visor, but in the murky smog, he couldn't see the Wing anywhere. He knew the laser signal in his helmet still worked, because that last tenacious camera still buzzed beside him, documenting everything. He imagined Dyce watching. Maybe this would be the video to make his cousin rich. A new world record. Orr drew a breath. He was about to complete the highest pure skydive any human being had ever made.

Why do you throw yourself away for nothing?

The sky felt cottony quiet, dappled in golden light. Stratus clouds parted below, and he glimpsed the yellow Pacific. He was lower than he thought. He could see the bubbly foam on the wave crests. He would hit the water in seconds. No time for recovery. His mind screamed, *This can't be.*

Time whistled past. He switched on his locator beacon and activated the CO_2 cartridge to inflate his life vest. The ocean rushed up. *Not yet. I'm not finished.* He checked his canopy to make sure the cells were inflated and the lines were clear. He spun to face the wind, but before he was half ready, the waves engulfed him, and his own weight carried him down.

2

Accuracy. Competition in which Wing divers attempt to land on a ground-based target.

Orrpaaj Sitka had always been a skydiver. Dyce understood that. Knees in the breeze, he lived to soar. Who knew better than she did?

As Dyce boarded the freighter to the mainland that day, she agonized over her choice. She almost got out of line. Yet when the purser called for tickets, she hoisted her pack and made her way down the ladder to the third-class deck. Already, she felt his absence.

Her earliest childhood memory held two bright sounds—the whoosh of air when Orr dove headfirst off the school roof into a pile of sand, and her own shrieking voice begging him not to do it. He was five years old. She was four. He broke his arm, and she made him a crayon drawing of an angel with wings.

From the first, her mother warned her to keep away from Orr. His clothes were dirty. He didn't belong to anyone. He was supposed to live at the tribal orphanage, but he roamed the village like a stray pup. Dyce obeyed her mother, though sometimes she left bits of muffin in the alley where she knew Orr would find them.

The following winter, a sickness hit Unimak Village, and all the medicines failed. Dyce lost her brother and both parents. The next time she saw Orr, she was huddled under a table in the orphanage, squeezing her brother's old Game Boy that no longer worked. Orr stole batteries for her from the teachers' supply room, and she rewarded him with the only gift she had, a kiss.

After that, she stuck close beside him. She missed her family, but she felt safe when Orr was nearby. Many nights they slipped out of the orphanage— Orr knew all the exits—and they would lose themselves in the dark village, running through the alleys and hooting like freed jailbirds.

Orr knew a bell tower where they could climb and peek out through the dusty steeple windows at the stars. Back then, stars still came out at night, and cold winds rattled the glass panes. The Russian priest claimed dead souls dwelled underground, which made Dyce weep for her little brother. But Orr said it wasn't so. He taught Dyce to search high up in the eastern sky where Agugux, the Creator, lived. That's where her family waited, he told her.

And Dyce taught him the names of the constellations. Cassiopeia. Draco. Hydra. She looked up star charts on the web. Orr didn't know the constellations had names. Funny boy. His empty head made her laugh.

Sometimes they visited old Mr. Bobby Tangaagim, who lived in a shipping crate in the alley behind Connie's Pub. Mr. Bobby called himself the shaman of the Unangan people, the real name for Aleuts, and he told them old stories about the days of miracles. Orr's favorite was the one about the boy who cut the sky with his knife to set the wind free. He liked to hear it over and over. But only Orr believed Mr. Bobby could speak with spirits. Everyone else called Bobby a gin head.

The young pair loved to ramble. They played chase through the fire escapes and made pets of the feral cats. But the village was small, and some busybody always dragged them back to the orphanage. Each AWOL brought repercussions, separations, and sermons from the Russian priest. So when Orr turned fourteen, he decided to run away. Dyce was thirteen. The wardens scared the breath out of her. By then, though, she needed Orr like Earth needed light.

So they absconded. They hid in Gabe's basement at first, but later, Dyce found a dirt-cheap rental in one of the old concrete project houses. Orr scrounged a couple of respirators and took her climbing above Bechevin Bay. She signed them up for vaccinations. He rebuilt an old bike and taught her to ride. She got him steady work at the seafarm. He took her hiking to the top of Mount Shishaldin. She wiped tables in Connie's Pub so they could eat.

She called him "Lagi," the Aleut word for goose. He called her "Berry," because he said her eyes were as blue-black as the tiny round fruits that once grew on their island.

She spent every minute earning, saving, and planning ahead, while Orr spent all his free time on sports. Running, swimming, scaling rock walls, anything to work up a sweat. She couldn't keep up with him. He moved too fast. He took reckless chances. Early on, she began to worry.

That first afternoon when he came home from Pete Hogue's air base crooning about parachutes, she knew she'd lost a part of him. He was going to be a skydiver, he told her. Only two things he needed, his girlfriend and his knees in the breeze. That night, she made him add up their household expenses by hand. She knew how he hated doing sums, but she'd been working all afternoon at the cannery while he . . .

Dyce felt evil sometimes. Way too judgmental. She knew Orr deserved a sweeter girl. Softness didn't come easy to her, but she did try to be a good mate. She took web courses on computer hygiene, technical writing, and library science. She saved up for an ocular so she'd have a constant clear-air link to the web, and she applied for every possible job. She wanted . . . so much.

For a long time, she'd been waiting and hoping for luck, but on the eve of Orr's stratosphere dive, she received a message that unmoored her. Orr stayed out late, helping Gabe install the oversized fuel tank on the rocket. He came home after midnight, filthy and tired, and when he opened the door, she was dancing on their mattress, waving her arms in the air.

He stood quietly in the door with that small tightness in his lips that showed he was smiling inside. She knew he liked the way her long black braid swished down her back. Sometimes he said her beauty hurt his throat.

But Dyce was no geisha. She had her mother's Asian eyes, but her mouth was too wide and her nose too short. She said, "Before you come another step, take off that grimy coverall."

This wasn't how she meant to start. The message she'd received still hissed through her head like a joyous stinging fire, but she had no idea how to tell him. She watched him kick off his boots and shed his greasy coverall. Underneath, he wore ragged long underwear, and his copper skin gleamed through the torn places.

His gray eyes got that wide amorous shine. She glanced down and saw the top of her blouse had come undone. Between her breasts, a golden locket dangled. His love gift. She fingered the metal disk, and he moved toward the bed.

"Raggedy man." She laughed and threw a pillow.

But then he stopped, and his face closed down. Dyce saw him examining her right eye. Oops, she'd forgotten to take out her ocular. For reasons she would never understand, Orr hated her oc.

She bent her head, tugged her right eyelid and popped the silver contact lens out into her hand. Its three tiny wires thrashed like spider legs when she pulled them loose from her cheek, and Orr made a face. Then she saw him looking at her duffel. It was gaping open on the floor, half packed.

She stepped down off the mattress and pulled him into her arms. "I got a job," she whispered. Inside, she was dancing, burning, kicking her heels. But she buried her face in his chest and whispered, "It's what I've dreamed of. I'll be helping to build a free web library for people around the world. Only . . . we have to move to Seattle."

Before he could react, she yanked him down in the pillows and stifled him with kisses. Hardly breathing, she listed all the benefits of her rosy new job. A startup had hired her. She'd be working with top-notch librarians.

"We'll create the first truly accurate archive." She tried to instill each word with weightiness. "You know how fast garbage multiplies on the web. People docudramatize rumors and repurpose statistics, and the underlying facts get wrinkled and squeezed. Before you know it, the truth goes unstable. So we'll evolve specific criteria to sift out the misinformation. We'll finally stabilize a knowledge base people can trust."

"You're leaving?" Orr's voice split like a reed.

"You're coming, too, silly."

Their room felt too small. Their bed took up most of the space. As usual, Dyce had lit candles to cover the moldy smell, but now she felt their smoke bogging down her lungs. She nestled beside him in the blankets.

"We'll rescue obsolete media, you know, like video games, iTunes, printed books. We'll transcribe everything to full immersive web space. So you'll be able to watch a silent movie in an authentic reenactment of a 1920s movie house, complete with the smell of popcorn and the player piano."

"How soon?" Orr's mild baritone always dropped an octave when he was stressed.

She rolled into the crook of his arm. "I leave in the morning. You'll come a few days later, after I'm settled. You'll find a job, too, and you can finish school. And then we can start our family."

His light-colored eyes clouded, and she wondered what bothered him more, Seattle or family. Of course, she knew how he felt about Seattle. People in the city lived half a kilometer deep in the ground, and he'd seen pictures. She knew their bruised eyes and pale subterranean skin unnerved him. Still, she honestly believed she and Orr would find a better life in Seattle.

She slid her hand under his T-shirt. "We'll do this together, babe."

Orr's thumb made a trek along her collarbone and down her sternum. He touched the plate-gold locket he'd given her, and its two halves clicked open. Inside, its thumbnail screen came alive and played the quick-movie they'd recorded at last year's tribal potlatch. Laughing like first-graders, they'd crammed into the tiny stall, clowned for the camera and crooned the karaoke song, "I Will Always Love You."

The quick-mo ran ten seconds. When it stopped, Dyce closed the locket. "So you'll come, right?"

He didn't answer.

Then she felt the energy drain out of her. She got out of bed to finish packing. Orr sat up and watched. She had to step over his big feet to reach the metal locker where she kept her clothes. In her mind, she asked, *What's happening? We can't be breaking up.*

After a while, Orr searched under the pillows for his blue socks, the ones she always stole from his drawer to sleep in. When he handed them over, her eyes stung. *He's letting me go.*

She stuffed the socks in her bag, and her loosened braid hid her face. Shining raven black, it fanned across her cheek like a wing. He reached to touch it.

But she was angry now. "You had the grades. You could've graduated."

He didn't answer. She hated his sulky silence. She saw him spread his fingers as if gauging the direction of the wind.

"You're a skilled mechanic," she said. "You could fix bicycles or skateboards or wheelchairs. If you just weren't stuck on one note all the time, that good-for-nothing sport."

She saw his face go still. She hadn't meant to nag. It just boiled out. But this was an old argument, one neither of them could win.

He got up and massaged her shoulders. Under his touch, she stopped packing. His hands felt as familiar as her own skin. When his thumbs found the knots in her deltoids, he rubbed small circles round and round, the way she liked. Then he kissed the back of her neck.

She said, "I'm not a genius, Orr, but this job, it's useful work. And that's all I want, just to be of use. If I can help one person see through the bogus crap on the web . . ."

She felt his tongue exploring her hairline. *Say something, Orr. Stop me. Keep me.*

"You'll be brilliant," he said.

She swiveled in his arms. "You promised we would always stick together."

When he finally spoke, his voice shook. "There isn't any sky in Seattle."

She turned and smashed a wad of shirts into her duffel. Then she crushed makeup in a side pocket and brutalized a pair of shoes. "Is the sky a better fuck than me?"

"Berry," he whispered.

Her duffel wouldn't zip, so she flung the bag to the floor and kicked it. Then she backed away, clenching fistfuls of air. "I love you, Orr. You're killing me."

3

Airspeed. Velocity of object moving through the air.

K illing me," Orr mumbled.

His lips felt blistered. He came awake slowly in a place that was all white. The air lay stagnant. A smell of chlorine bleach burned his nose, and nearby, a cyberdoc dripped fluids through a tube into his vein. Sometimes a face would loom over him like a cinnamon-bearded moon. Gabe. When the moon sank out of view, Orr saw the hospital meter staring from the foot of his bed, ticking up what he owed for his medical care.

Half dozing, he dreamed of surfing his Celestia Sky Wing through a vortex of whirling scrip coins. Each round metal token was minted with his tribal logo, the face of the goddess Aleut, wife of the Moon. When he tried to gather the coins in his hands, they slipped through his fingers. Sometimes the goddess changed into Dyce, and his pulse quickened.

He might have dozed for minutes or decades, but the meter counted thirty-one billable hours by the time he spoke his first clear sentence. "Gabe, did you find my Wing?"

"You're alive." Gabe jumped up from his chair and overturned the blood-flow monitor.

Orr said, "Is Dyce here?"

Gabe spilled chipped ice on the bed trying to pour a cup of water. "You feel okay? Are you thirsty? Want me to call the nurse?"

Kriis was there, too, Gabe's wife. She plumped the pillows and brushed away the melting ice. Gabe's three sons were playing handheld video games under the bed. Kriis patted Orr's face with a damp cloth, and her large bosom brushed his nose. She was almost as round as her husband, pregnant again with another surrogate child for some mainland parent wannabe. Her enormous silver ear studs knocked against her jaw when she spoke. "You could've died up there, dimkus."

"Let the boy rest." Gabe squeezed next to Kriis by the bed, and they filled the narrow space like a pair of balloons.

Five-year-old Yanny climbed onto the bed. "I saw you turn a somersault. Waaooow!" He tugged at Orr's drip tube till Kriis plucked his little fingers loose.

Nick, the middle boy, jumped on top of Orr's legs. "I wanna skydive, too. I'm old enough." He spread his arms and dove. Gabe caught him just before he landed on Orr's mending ribs.

"No roughhousing." Gabe swung his flyboy in an arc, making him giggle, while Ilya, the grave eight-year-old, scanned the room with his Batman watch.

Ilya spoke with the soberness of a judge. "I drew a map of your dive, Orr. You can see it if you want to."

"Thanks." Orr's eyelids drooped. Things went a shade whiter. When he woke next, Gabe was snoring in a chair.

Six hours later, the cyberdoc pronounced Orr well, and Gabe helped him dress to leave. But every time Orr asked about Dyce, Gabe skittered to other subjects. Arm in arm, they pushed out of the clinic into the lively streets of Unimak Village.

Unimak was a layered town, a federal project built over the sunken winter dugouts of the ancestors. Lately, newer nanoform structures had webbed around the old concrete row houses. The knobby new bulbs swelled half a kilometer up the Isanax River valley to shelter the growing populace. Thick sheets of plexi covered the streets to seal out smog, and from satellite view, the village looked like an insect nest made of saliva and mud.

Stepping off the curb, Orr felt the wind of passing bicycles. He smelled cave mold and deep-fried kelp, the blessed aromas of home. Pedicabs and pushcarts wove among street vendors and off-duty seafarmers. A schoolteacher led a daisy chain of children holding hands. Skateboarders raced down the center lane, and little boys squatted in the gutters poking sticks at the bright orange millipedes that fed on the slime. Air ducts hammered, and a light-cable snaked overhead, casting bluish light. Vending stalls blared Alaska's rowdy mishmash of Texas swing, Russian mazurkas, and Native American blues. Outside, seasonal Pacific storms lashed the plexi roof panels. Orr and Gabe headed for Connie's Pub.

But when Gabe unlocked a little three-wheeled rented tractor, Orr grabbed his arm. "We can't afford this. Let's walk."

Gabe fiddled with the seat adjustment. "You've been through hell, cousin. Take it easy. Just for today."

No denying it, grouchy old Gabe had a marshmallow heart. Today, Gabe wore his Hawaiian shirt, and not only that, he'd tied his long hair with a string and oiled his beard. He looked fancied up for a funeral. When he fired the electric tractor, Orr straddled the seat, and they rollicked down the corridor at a breathtaking five klicks per hour. But Orr felt uneasy. Gabe wouldn't tell him anything about Dyce. Something had to be wrong.

Money, he knew it had to be money. The clinic bill. The rocket. The lost Wing. He figured the air-sea rescue must have cost a zillion dollars. And the debt would fall on Gabe. Orr couldn't imagine ever having that much cash. Orr, the trade school dropout. Dyce called him irresponsible. He tightened his hold on the tractor, and his face burned.

As they bumped down the covered street, he thought about Gabe's sons. Would the boys have to go without shoes or vaccinations? He should've thought about that sooner. No, he wouldn't let the boys suffer. Clinging to the tractor, he tried to think of ways to earn money, though it wasn't a subject he knew much about.

Gabe was acting cagey. He didn't wave at anybody, and when the tractor jolted against the curb, he ham-handed the joystick and almost turned them over. Orr began to suspect really bad news. But the scene at Connie's Pub confused him. People were spilling out the front door and lining the street in both directions. The crowd began to cheer.

"You slammed it, Orr!"

"Banners, man!"

"Yio'kwa!"

Orr grinned as a gang of his seafarm coworkers grabbed at his vest and slapped the seat of his jeans. He brushed tangled hair out of his eyes. He'd always kept quiet about skydiving. Few people at the seafarm even knew he jumped. When someone sailed a good-luck origami bird at his head, he caught it and cupped it in his hand.

He said, "What's all this, Gabe?"

"Party!" his cousin shouted. "Man, I sold the video!"

Orr wove and nearly stumbled. This news was so different from what he'd expected. Gabe bear-hugged him, bruising his tender ribs and almost lifting him off his feet. "The XS Channel paid for everything. They sent their corporate aircar to fly you home from Japan."

Before Orr could respond, Gabe yanked him into Connie's Pub. Dozens of people jammed among the metal tables. They stood three deep at the polished copper bar in the back. Kelp chips sizzled in the fryolator, and greasy smoke layered the air. Everyone was hollering at Orr.

He saw guys from his gym, and his landlord, Shep Innoko, who dunned him every week for overdue rent. He scanned the crowd for Dyce's face. There was his secondary teacher, Mrs. St. Paul. She'd expected so much from him. He felt a tingle of pride to see her lift a glass in his direction.

"Someone I want you to meet," Gabe shouted over the noise. As they moved toward a corner table, people pressed from all sides, congratulating him. Orr hadn't realized so many people cared about skydiving. But he didn't see Dyce.

Gabe yelled in his ear, "Orr Sitka, meet Cho Sen Yao. The newscaster."

Orr saw a thin mousy person with a face as white as a street mime. The newscaster's short black hair and sharp angular bones gave no clear hint of gender. Cho Sen Yao wore all black, including high-gloss black gloves that fit like spray paint. He or she sat at the table rolling an illegal cigarette and appraising Orr with gloomy feminine eyes. "Hail the conqueror."

Orr glanced around to see if anyone had spotted the forbidden tobacco, but Connie's general credo was to live and let live. He noted Cho's mannish clothes and midrange voice. As an experiment, he said, "What channel do you work for, sir?"

Cho lifted his/her upper lip and bared one eyetooth. "I freelance."

Then someone clutched Orr's shoulder and swung him around. Suddenly he saw himself, huge on the wallscreen, flying his Celestia Sky Wing. It was Gabe's video, computer enhanced, hastily edited, and framed in splashy graphics. XS, the extreme sports web channel, was broadcasting his skydive at the top of every hour.

"Sshon, you did it." Pete Hogue sloshed a glass of beer in the air. "We're all famoussh. Now you gotta make us rissh."

"Can I be rich, too?" A woman reeking of floral perfume embraced Orr from behind. She was his overhead neighbor, Anna Smersk. He turned and gave her a sheepish greeting. Then Shorty Wethluk, his credit broker, stepped on his foot and shoved a beer mug in his hand. Everyone was talking.

A harsh voice broke through the racket. "Come back here, Sitka. We have things to discuss."

It was Cho, the newscaster. Potent lungs for such a small body. Cho had to be a guy. Orr found a bar stool and scooted up to Cho's table.

The newscaster balanced his hand-rolled cigarette in his gloved fingers, took a deep drag, then twisted his lips to blow smoke at an angle. Felonious nicotine fumes drifted around the bar. Cho said, "I'll pay three thousand for an exclusive first interview. That's fair, so take it. You're just a sports byte. Remember that."

With all the party noise, Orr couldn't hear well, but Gabe answered for him. "Are you aware my cousin just broke a world record? Three thousand is *not* acceptable."

Cho's eyes stayed fixed on Orr.

"Are you aware," Gabe went on, "that eight other web channels have already asked for exclusive interviews? And that's just so far. We're still—"

Orr said, "I don't want a lot of media hype."

Cho tapped the table with one long black-clad finger. "Hype you've got. The question is, how will you use it?"

The commotion in Connie's Pub grew deafening as more people wedged in. Orr heard something crash. A girl whispered in his ear, and he turned. But the kiss he received square in the mouth did not come from Dyce. It came from Connie Nujuat, the bar owner. Orr drew back and almost wiped his lips, but he stopped in time. Connie suffered from a disfiguring allergy. It would have pained Orr to insult her.

An unsteady hand fell on his shoulder, and when he turned, there was Mr. Bobby Tangaagim. The red-eyed old alchy was so drunk, he could barely keep his feet, and Orr put out a hand to steady him. Bobby's worn-out voice rustled, "Iidigidix stirs."

Orr stared at the drunken shaman, not sure how to respond. Iidigidix? The spirit of destruction.

Mr. Bobby's pungent stench made people back away, until Connie Nujuat caught the old bum by the elbow and led him out. Not for the first time that night, Orr wished he were safe at home in his room.

Pete Hogue got piss-drunk on the bar's weak beer, and he jerked Orr bodily to his feet, overturning the table. "All my chips on Orrpaaj Sitka!"

Orr couldn't hear what anyone said next, because Pete launched into a chant. "World Champ! Sitka Sitka Sitka!" Pete hoisted Orr up like a bale of kelp, then staggered and almost dropped him. Other hands joined in, and Orr, who until that moment had believed himself virtually invisible, was tossed up on someone's shoulders like a hero.

His head bumped along the ceiling as the crowd spilled out of the bar in a spontaneous parade. One of his boots got torn off. Someone ripped his best silver earring from his earlobe. Every part of his body was slapped and caressed, and he felt a wild instinct to break free.

But he suppressed the wish. These people were happy for him. Their faces gleamed with sweat and drunken exuberance and another emotion that surprised Orr. What he sensed was their need. He felt their need pulling at him like a tangible force. Maybe they needed to believe one of their own could make good. And for all Orr's recklessness, it was not in his nature to let people down. So he drew his elbows tight to protect his ribs, and he smiled inside at the irony. He could face a Pacific cyclone, but he couldn't hold out against his neighbors.

Angle of attack. Angle at which Sky Wing enters the apparent wind.

Only when they ran out of beer sometime after dawn did the merrymaking die down. Long before that, Orr slipped off to the air base at Mount Shishaldin. Dyce had not come to his party. Gabe finally admitted she'd caught the freighter to Seattle. She left a good-bye text, but Orr didn't want to read a text.

Alone at the top of the gantry tower under the dusty dome, he watched low-hanging contrails widen across the sky. Mainland air freighters made them, not as many now because of the carbon tariffs. On a nearby ridge, Pete Hogue's faded orange windsock luffed in the breeze.

For once, Orr skipped his morning habit of swallowing light. Mr. Bobby had taught him how to greet the Creator each dawn, standing to inhale the rising sun. *I do not sleep. I am alive. I face you, Agugux, life-giver.*

But the old Aleut prayer didn't fit Orr's mood. Instead, he wet-nursed his anger. He'd broken a world record, risked his life in the mesosphere, and Dyce couldn't put off her trip to watch? Righteous snorts puffed out his nose, and he searched the sky for a star.

Dawn came late in the Alaskan winter, and on this rare morning, the smog had thinned to gauzy translucence. His trained eye picked out high cirrocumulus clouds, a sign of cold convection winds aloft. Pete Hogue had taught him what the cloud shapes meant. He recognized them automatically now. With teachers like Pete and Mr. Bobby, who needed a girlfriend?

Better to be footloose. Single. Free to follow the one pursuit he understood. He lay on his back and listened to the breeze whoosh over the dome. How could she ask him to give up skydiving? He pondered his secret name. *Wakinyan Tanka*. Thunderbird.

Mr. Bobby gave him that name when he turned thirteen. Mr. Bobby said he carried the energy of thunderbolts in his hand. "Be humble in your power," Mr. Bobby said. "Don't question your luck. Accept it, because you have *asiriyuq* riding on your shoulders."

Orr squirmed on his roof beam, remembering the madness in the old man's red eyes. *Asiriyuq* had two meanings, Mr. Bobby warned. It meant good luck, or maybe right luck. But it also meant right *doing*. The two values had to stay in balance, or there would be hell to pay. It was not a light thing to have *asiriyuq* riding on your shoulders.

January clouds raced above the dome, and different layers moved at different speeds. Orr's copper-brown face softened. Not long ago, he'd been up there, soaring at the edge of the universe. He shut his eyes and pictured the luminous colors. They kept changing into Dyce. Her lips. Her eyes. Her sweet hard little body.

He told himself she would get tired of Seattle. Maybe she needed to see the city lights, but after a few weeks, she'd come back, and everything would be the same. His young ego grew so feverish denying the possibility that she was gone, he failed to hear the steps of a stranger climbing the gantry tower. He didn't notice till a shadow fell across his face.

"Magnificent view." The woman's voice rang like a bronze bell.

Orr sat up and balked. Her appearance startled him. Sculpted Caucasian face, emerald eyes, voluptuous curves swathed in a clingy suit of pure shimmering white, she looked like an angel, or an actress. Either way, she looked utterly out of place in his rusting tower. As she approached, he caught a whiff of perfume. He sprang to his feet.

She said, "You're Orrpaaj Sitka?"

Her musical voice echoed under the dome. Orr stared at her high-heel boots. He didn't know where to look. Not at her sultry eyes. Not at her glossy mouth. Not at her rich wavy red hair. A city woman, a mainlander, what was she doing here? Yet something about the way she fidgeted with her belt purse made her seem in need of reassurance. When her boot heel twisted in the metal grid, he caught her elbow to keep her from falling.

"Thank you." She touched his fingers, and he noticed old wounds on the back of her hand. She said, "Some of your friends told me you'd be here. I saw your skydive on the web. Impressive."

She blinked as if the light hurt her eyes, and he moved automatically to shield her from the rising sun. He'd never seen anyone more beautiful. Her perfume made him dizzy.

"I'm Vera Luce," she said in her rich velvet voice. "My company's Grupo Mundo. We market the Celestia Sky Wing."

"The Celestia?" Orr stared. So many thoughts streamed through his mind, he didn't know what to say first. "I was going to text you. Um, I mean your designer."

The woman's green eyes shimmered. "Yes? Go on."

"The leading edge," Orr rushed his words, "it needs a sharper profile."

She fumbled a small wafer of clear material from her purse and pressed it into his palm. "We intend to redesign the Celestia, make it all new and improved. Tell me what you think of this beryllium alloy."

He held the clear material up to the light, as fine as spun silk, as flexible as stiff plastic.

She said, "It's more resistant to heat."

He twisted it between his fingers. "Too rigid."

She took the chip back. "We want you to test our new design."

Orr held himself very still. Had he heard right?

The woman touched his hand again. "Say yes, Orr. Join our team. You'll have alpha-grade equipment, a professional crew. My company will sponsor everything if you'll wear our logo when you dive."

He wanted to sing. Yes. Unconditionally yes. He would tattoo the Celestia brand across his forehead to get this chance. "My cameraman," he said aloud, "Gabe Lermontov. We're partners."

"Your cousin deserves handsome compensation for his work to date." She put her lips close to Orr's ear, and the figure she whispered raised his pulse. "Understand," she said, "from now on, we'll own full rights to your skydive recordings."

Orr turned to face the east, and his gray eyes caught the sunlight. His pectorals twitched. He could not believe the enormity of his luck.

The woman's bell-tone voice kept pulling, tugging, coaxing—as if he needed more persuasion. "You won't have to leave home. We'll build our new drop zone here on Unimak Island," she said. "We'll purchase your tribal contract, and as for your salary, you can name your own price."

The last thing on Orr's mind was salary. He put out his hand to feel the moving air, and he said, "You'll let me skydive for free?"

4

Angle of incidence. Angle at which a Sky Wing sails through the air.

If Vera Luce had known what a pushover Orr would be, she might have chosen different tactics. She might not have tuned her body mods quite so full or worn such a binding quu-suit. She might have gone easier on the hypnagogic perfume. The boy's bashfulness put her off guard, though. She was afraid he might not like her. And Vera Luce needed Orr to like her. She had cogs of justice to set in motion.

Three weeks it took her to transform those first bald lies into reality. Three weeks of mind-numbing web fests with bankers, lawyers, and Indian chiefs—because Vera didn't actually own Grupo Mundo, or the Celestia Sky Wing. She'd spun that little tale out of necessity.

Did someone once scribble that the universe began with light? Vera didn't believe it. Creation began in the crushing black womb of gravity. For more than a year, she'd lain holed up in her condo in subterranean Seattle, browsing extreme sport sites and dreaming up content for a new web project. Skydiving was a fading sport, out of fashion, almost obsolete. But she thought its very obscurity might make it appear fresh to young viewers. Early on, Orr's videos caught her eye. The boy had an uncouth style—self-taught, naive in the purest sense, and full of grace. She watched his replays for hours. When his record-breaking mesosphere dive hit the web, she knew he was the star she needed.

Before seeking him out, though, she'd ransacked his profile on the web.

She absorbed every public record about this part-time seafarmer with the dismal lack of schooling. This boy had an athletic gift, for sure, plus a deliciously photogenic physique. Oh yes, she needed him to look good on the web.

But at their first live meeting, in his work boots, torn jeans, and native vest, with his flushed cheeks and exotic gray eyes, she found him—gentle. That surprised her. There was a muscular poise in the way he balanced on his toes that made her feel safe. Vera was not accustomed to feeling safe. Why this backwoods jock gave her such a rush of hope, she couldn't analyze. But Vera Luce needed hope.

After acquiring Grupo Mundo and its celebrated Sky Wing—at a hugely inflated premium—she blew another full week buying land on Unimak Island to build a drop zone. Next, she spent seven tedious days in parley with the Aleut Tribal Council. She traded water rights to a small Martian ice field to get her hands on Orr's contract. It was necessary.

After pushing, pounding, smiling till her cheeks quivered, she finally finished the negotiations, and her crew began building the drop zone the third week of February. A lifelong resident of Seattle, she'd never spent so much time out of doors. The sunlight made her woozy, and the winter wind gave her headaches. She'd almost forgotten the feel of weather.

She flew back to the city half anesthetized, and when she stumbled through her condo door, all she wanted was to turn off her implants, swallow more meds, and drift off into sweet inebriation. But someone was waiting in her bedroom.

"Where've you been?" The familiar snarl crimped her neck hairs.

"Hello, Daddy."

Her father, Rolfe Luce, was sitting at her dressing table, playing with her lipsticks. His face in her mirror looked dead white. He hadn't been out of Seattle in ages. "Why do you keep all this junk?" he said.

Makeup was Vera's religion. She collected face paints like some people collected art. Rolfe had already broken two of her hard-to-find shades, and he was using her favorite Prima Mauve to scrawl a question mark on her mirror. She bit the back of her finger.

"What the hell is Grupo Mundo," he said, "and why did we pay twice its value?"

"Petty cash." Vera chirped her cheerleader laugh and shrugged off her white jacket.

"'Petty fears and petty pleasures,'" he quoted, "'are but the shadow of reality.'"

"Henry David Thoreau," she replied with a yawn. Rolfe's famous quotes bored her hollow. He'd made her memorize dozens of moldy old phrases. When she stooped to peck his cheek, she smelled ketosis on his breath. He'd been starving himself again, and that always played hell with his mood. "Why not come see my project for yourself?" she asked. "You'd like Alaska."

Rolfe opened a jar of liquid concealer and sniffed its fragrance. "You're running some con as usual."

She knew he wouldn't visit her construction site. Rolfe had a dread of disease. He hadn't left his antiseptic compound in years, though he was always threatening to. He looked decades younger than his eighty-seven years, but he'd had so many facelifts, his overstretched mouth didn't quite close over his teeth. His bald head gleamed like bone.

She fumbled through her purse for her pan. "I have a surprise for you, Dad. This is guaranteed to soothe your itchy palms."

He said, "You didn't ask about my fir trees. We just planted our first saplings."

Vera kicked off her boots. His darling firs, she had zero desire to know. Another eco-fad. Another total misuse of company funds. He'd spent more than the sovereign wealth of several small police states to buy acreage in the North Cascades. Allegedly, he was cloning a forest inside a huge glass bubble. Frankly, Vera found her father's obsession with the past a little embarrassing.

Noises boomed through her bedroom walls. Her Seattle condo lay deep underground, and though her rooms were large, dampness was forever rotting the tapestries that masked her concrete walls. No matter how high she turned up the dehumidifier, her bedroom always smelled muggy. She switched on her pan and cued up Orr's skydive.

"Watch this, Dad."

Her panoramic projection flared around them, a phantom globe of three-dimensional light and sound. Unfortunately, she had only Gabe Lermontov's video to display. The recording opened as a flat 2-D pane floating on the panorama's 3-D surface.

Rolfe snatched the pan from her fingers. "You bring me video? Who asked you to scout content? I develop content, not you."

For ten seconds, the 2-D image flickered across Rolfe's pale features. Its light illuminated the clutter on Vera's bedroom shelves, bits of wood, shells, dried flowers, dead birds, all childhood gifts from Rolfe. In the shadows, his thin body shifted like a sack of nails.

Then he lobbed the pan at the wall. "This is bullshit, Vera. You should be tending my web servers, that's your function. I don't recall promoting you."

Luckily, the pan didn't break. She got down on her knees and groped behind her dresser to reach it.

He said, "From the ground up, that's how you learn a business. Be patient. You'll get your chance when you're ready. I want you to be brilliant, kid."

Patient? Vera clawed the carpet. Too many fricking years he'd made her wait. For her own good, he said. Flattening herself on the floor, she teased the pan out from under her dresser. Condensation dripped from her ceiling and pooled along her baseboard. Her carpet felt tacky, and mold smudged her white quu-suit.

She said, "You can't ignore the boy's talent. I've watched a hundred sky-divers, and Orr has a radical new style."

Rolfe dabbed some of her perfume under his chin. "Who wants to watch skydivers? What goes up must come down. End of story."

Twice, she had to restart the pan. She hated how Rolfe's presence made her fidget and fat-thumb the control disk. She was too agitated to try subvocal command. A loud noise whirred through her bedroom wall as heavy machinery switched on next door.

When she finally called up the Nielsen global ratings, the numbers glistened in midair. Orr's video had gone viral. People were spreading it around the web like a pop tune. To date, nearly a billion unique users had viewed his record-breaking skydive—a twelfth of the human race. And the media was going berserk.

Rolfe eyed the numbers, and Vera pursed her lips. She knew how he hankered for media attention. She launched into her pitch. "Skydiving is so old, it's new again. Imagine sailing the proverbial *blue sky*. Trust me, Dad, this is the content we need to launch our new season lineup."

Rolfe tapped his front teeth together. "Is the sky still blue up there?"

When he replayed the video, Vera's hope rose. She kept selling hard. "We'll license merchandise, beverages, serialized graphic updates. I can do this, Dad. Trust me."

The muscles around Rolfe's nose twitched, and she knew he was smelling money. He said, "Have you noticed how truth is like a horizon? The closer you approach, the farther it recedes."

Rolfe and his platitudes. She performed the obligatory smile.

As he watched Orr plunge into a wall of storm clouds, he kept tapping his front teeth together with a soft dull click. "The boy needs a brand. Cloud Surfer, Gravity Pilot, something catchy. Do a trademark search."

"Oh Daddy, thank you." She plopped into his lap and flung her arms around his neck. "I'll make you a pile of cash, I swear."

For a few seconds, Rolfe let her nuzzle and hug him. Then he pushed her away and watched the video again.

5

Apparent wind. Wind direction as viewed by an observer.

Meanwhile, Orr packed his gym bag. He whistled while he balled up his socks. He couldn't wait to escape the barren rented room. Dyce had taken the lamp and the batik bedspread. She left behind dust bunnies and empty shelves. It didn't matter. Orr was going away, too—if only to the far side of his island.

For a while, sports reporters and gear manufacturers kept pinging his inbox, but their attention made him nervous. He didn't return the calls. He paid off his few debts and closed down his account at Connie's Pub. He slept on Gabe's couch those last three weeks, horsing with the boys and making believe he felt ecstatic. No, he didn't miss Dyce—he refused to admit how often she crossed his mind. He had his own perfect job. He was going to help design the new Celestia Sky Wing.

But denial is a drug that frags its victim in pieces. Orr raced around the village on Gabe's rented tractor, seeing friends and talking about his plans. He climbed the rainy cliffs above Bechevin Bay and watched the cool February squalls move across the water. Long hours he spent in the roof structure of Pete Hogue's glass dome, counting the lightning bolts and pretending every moment he was the luckiest man alive. Yet even the most deadening anesthesia wears off.

Why didn't Dyce call?

She didn't text or vmail. She didn't tweet. Where the heck was she?

Orr haunted the tribal library, checking the communal web link for messages, and he grew more sullen with each passing hour. On the last night, he finagled the library's padlock, broke into Miss Tompkin's secure file, and looked up Dyce's new unlisted vone number.

The library was dark and humid. Miss Tompkin, the senior librarian, turned the AC off at night to save power, and the air barely stirred as Orr tiptoed through. LEDs winked from the four public computers perched on the center table, and they made a nervous ticking sound, like metal warping back and forth. Orr smelled Miss Tompkin's sour cologne. Her old-lady fragrance gave him a crawly feeling, like she was still there in the room, criticizing him.

He sat down at one of the computers. He didn't use the web very often, so he fumbled through the touchscreens. He entered the vone number and waited uncountable microseconds for his call to go through. He'd never bothered to learn how the web-based vone system worked. It had something to do with air waves ricocheting against satellites. He visualized a jet of wind zooming straight down to Seattle and drilling through the Earth, air-blasting through layers of rock, blowing white-hot sparks and boring down down down to Dyce.

The computer screen brightened. And there was her face, framed in his monitor. "Berry," he whispered. The first thing he noticed was her hair. She'd cut it.

Her voice buzzed through the tiny speaker. "Orr, thank God you called."

His deltoid muscles tensed. "What's wrong?"

"Nothing. I . . . I miss you." Her voice came out strained. She was swiveling around on her workstool, reaching for objects he couldn't see. She sounded light-years away.

"You could've called me," he said. "I thought we were mates."

For an instant, she stopped moving. "I hope we are." She sounded out of breath. She started swiveling again, brandishing her arms. "My boss has a policy against personal calls. And I've got a wicked deadline. I'm working late again tonight."

She explained that she was sorting virtual documents in the web library. Orr didn't listen to every word. Her appearance disturbed him. Fatigue lined her young face, and she'd lost color. Her black eyes darted back and forth, and one of her eyelids kept jumping. At least she wasn't wearing her ocular.

A blight, that thing. Orr didn't believe in planting machines in the body. He thought they ruined a person's reflexes, like using backup jets in a skydive.

"We're indexing live performances," Dyce said. "We've got thousands of real-time RSS feeds, and I'm simplifying the search syntax so people can find what they need and . . ."

While she talked, Orr scrubbed his cheek with his knuckles. He couldn't get a read on her mood. When her voice got that hard flinty edge, it usually meant she was frightened. He resented the intervening frame of the monitor. He wanted to hold her.

"Look, I've got a wireless oc." She widened her right eye so he could see the tiny sparkle of her transparent contact lens. Her old ocular had been solid silver. This new one was see-through, and there were no threads snaking across her cheek. Orr hadn't realized oculars could be wireless.

She said, "The company supplied it for free, isn't that amazing? It's way more vivid, and you won't believe how much faster I move through the web."

He clenched the edges of the white library table. "I hate being away from you."

Again, she paused, and he got a close-up of her sallow cheek. "Orr, I didn't mean to be so bitchy. Please forgive me. I adore you, you know that. But . . ." She resumed her work, and her voice sounded muffled. "I . . . I've been thinking. Maybe this little break is good for us. Maybe we both need a chance to grow up."

Grow up. Orr clamped his jaw. Accept responsibility, her favorite phrase. It all came down to one demand, she wanted him to quit skydiving.

He said, "You're not the only one with a new job." Then he told her about the Celestia Sky Wing project.

"You did good, Lagi. I saw your skydive on the web. I was proud of you."

"Yeah?" He blinked. She had a knack for pushing him away, then pulling him back. He gripped the monitor with both hands. "When are you coming home?"

The skin around her eyes tightened. "Not for twelve months. It's in my contract."

He saw the downward sag of her shoulders, and for the first time, he sensed that maybe she did miss him. Maddening, this distance keeping them apart. He wanted to bend the laws of space and time—and hold her.

On screen, she kept swiveling and reaching for bits of invisible data, and when she spoke next, she sounded urgent. "Come see me before you start your job, okay? This weekend. Say you'll come."

She made it sound easy. Did she forget he'd sold his transit pass? He said, "I have to report for work tomorrow." But when her face went stony pale, he said, "I'll come soon. I promise."

She pressed close to the screen so her nose and chin looked out of proportion to her eyes. "Orr, don't forget me. You know, I'm not really alive without you."

6

*Aspect ratio. Proportional relationship of a Sky Wing's
width to breadth.*

Me. This is all about me." Vera Luce wriggled her cramping fingers. "I have to do every fricking thing."

She'd been working nonstop for a month, living on caffeine and ampalex and other less licit medications, losing weight and serenity in equal measures. What did she know about drop zones? She had to learn everything from scratch. The bowl-shaped caldera she'd purchased at the top of a volcanic peak lay far out on Unimak's extreme western coast. Her crew needed eight days to scrape a level construction site. Cargo freighters couldn't land, the terrain was too rough. They had to lower equipment on cables from hovering buses. And the wind never let up. Late winter gales walloped Unimak's western shore. The crew used robots to snap the first prefab shelters together. She dubbed the site "Mundo Mountain."

Circling in her aircar, she documented the work in progress. Late February winds blew hot and cold, ping-ponging her against the window frame and making her airsick. She'd chosen this site because the remoteness gave her better security than a Chinese firewall. But it also caused delivery delays and cost overruns. She had her crew pulling twenty-four-sevens to finish the launchpad.

She'd never liked flying, and after a while, she shut her eyes to ward off the view. For Orr's skydives, she'd ordered a decommissioned space shuttle from government surplus. Mothballed back at the turn of the century, the rickety old wreck still came at a vicious price. She had to draw way down on her expense account. And only after the purchase did she discover its main engine had to be revamped and its interior totally remodeled. Thank you, NASA.

In two months, if the rebuilt shuttle arrived as promised, they might feasibly conduct their first stratosphere dive and make holographic recordings for the web. But Rolfe expected her to shrink that schedule into four weeks.

Rolfe wielded due dates like a whip. Everyone in the company felt him pushing. Sure, Vera knew he needed cash for his cloned forest. He had to buy more peacocks. More fricking frogs. His legacy to the world, that forest. It was supposed to make him immortal. She gnashed an antacid tab. Four weeks! With all the rain, they hadn't finished pouring concrete yet. And to crown everything, she had a royal case of colitis from eating too many stimulants.

As soon as she landed and cycled through the airlock, she tore off her respirator and jogged to the design lab. She'd scheduled a meeting with the two design engineers she'd acquired, along with the other detritus of the Celestia Sky Wing project. Her rush-rush takeover of Grupo Mundo had left the usual messy trail of alienated employees, missing assets, and corrupted files. Already, she felt tired.

She sprinted through the passage, reminding herself how much she needed these designers. The reek of fresh construction glue made her nauseous. Today, she wore loose business attire instead of cling-wrap, and she'd tuned her body mods to normal size. She really wanted them to like her.

As she approached the lab, she heard the designers talking. Elsabette Rimini and Alejandro Vere. Bettie and Al, they called each other. Vera called them the Prune and the Bird Beak, though not to their faces. The steady whine of earthmovers muffled their voices, so she tuned up her earbuds and peeked through the plastic door.

Bettie, the Prune, was griping. Baggy bosoms, copious hips, gray cloud of hair held back with a dozen mismatched combs. Bettie's dark skin had ripened to coarse wrinkles. No sense of aesthetics, that woman. Had she never heard of plastic surgery? A wireless ocular glinted in her left eye, and a memory pod dimpled the side of her neck. Vera flagged the Prune as a troublemaker. Bettie complained about the facilities, the remote location, the fragged data, the lack of decent tea. But the main thing she griefed about was her new boss, Vera.

That was plain unfair. Vera had made a genuine effort to win the Prune's friendship, and the Bird Beak's, too. But Vera suspected nobody ever liked her, not really.

"Hard power," the Prune was saying. "It's the only thing jacks that woman off. She'd sell her own organs to get more control."

Al whistled and wheezed through an asthma mask that covered his mouth and nose. Apparently, Al suffered numerous allergic reactions. Couldn't wear an oc. Said it chafed his delicate cornea. Evidently, he was sensitive to silicon.

He said, "We only met her once, Bettie. She seemed civil enough."

Prune tugged at her waistband. "Yeah, she played it coy, but every time she turned her back, those mods in her ass nearly slapped me down."

Vera raked her fingernails across the back of her hand—and kept listening.

"I liked her ass," Al said. He fine-tuned a setting on his handheld pod. With his white hair, wireless web spectacles, and beak-shaped mask, he reminded Vera of a myopic dove.

She watched his long fingers twiddle his pod, and he seemed so absorbed, she wondered what he was up to. So she triggered her ocular to piggyback his web signal. Her oc streamed continuous multiple inputs—her calendar and clock, incoming texts, security views of her home office, various queries and feeds. But Vera had learned long ago how to view more than one image simultaneously. Aha, so Bird Beak was role-playing a magician in EverQuest XXIII. Wasting her valuable work time.

He wielded his pod with gusto, fending off invisible spells and bewitchments. He said, "It's not her fault someone sabotaged our data. Anyway, you've got eidetic memory."

"Yeah, photographic recall." Bettie tapped the pod in her neck. "But she expects us to use this cheap beryllium shit."

On and on, the hussy droned, while Vera stood outside, scraping the back of her hand. At length, she relaxed her jaw and reconfigured her smile, then unzipped the plastic door. "You two look serious. I hope you're planning our celebration after the first stratosphere dive."

Bettie cinched her lips. She gave Vera's glossy white outfit a once-over, then swiveled away in her extra-wide ergonomic chair.

"I'll buy the vino," Vera said, straining to keep up the cheery tone.

The design lab reminded her of a vacant garage. Gritty new concrete floor, celluloid panel walls, concentrated smell of bonding cement, and one triple-thick plexi window facing the future launchpad. Two computer workstations sat on tables made from sawhorses. In one corner, pipes and hoses snarled down from the ceiling like loose ganglia. Eventually, her ceramic kiln would connect there—if it ever arrived. The only decent furniture in the place was Bettie's ergonomic chair.

The Prune spoke with her back turned. "Your schedule's psychotic. We'll never make your dates."

Vera wanted to punch her in the kidneys.

Al croaked through his plastic beak, "We shouldn't take too many short-cuts. It wouldn't be safe."

I'll show you what's not safe!

Vera swallowed the words before they emerged. Her bowels burned. Such whiners. Hadn't she kept them on the job, even raised their pay? Why couldn't they warm to her? Every trivial detail required damage control.

She gazed through the window. Outside in the February downpour, ten humans and a score of miscellaneous robots were excavating a seventy-square-meter pit to sink the equipment under the launchpad. They were also building forms for the reinforced concrete flame trench that would deflect the space shuttle's exhaust. Soon, Vera hoped, the crew would erect the crane that would Lego their geodesic dome together. Arching over everything, the re-tractable dome would seal out the weather and make it easier to move around the launchpad.

And Rolfe expected her to finish this construction in four weeks? His deadlines made her want to spit fire. She snatched Al's pod from his hands and dropped it in the waste chute. "Rule one. No gaming on company time."

7

Astral edge. Leading brand of ceramic micromesh used in the manufacture of Sky Wings.

That same afternoon, Orr climbed aboard his new employer's aircar in high spirits. Vera had sent the driverless car just for him, wow. Only the super-rich could afford aircars. Orr's friends gathered to send him off, and they made jokes about his cushy limo. Everyone marveled at the leather seats.

Orr had flown Pete's antique Cessna. Once, he'd ridden an aircar from Japan, but he'd been unconscious. This time, he stayed glued to the window. Incredible as it sounds, he'd never flown the entire length of his own island. But now as he approached the storm-blasted western coast, his saw volcanic mountains shearing straight down to furious ocean breakers, two thousand meters below. There were no roads or seaports at this end of the island, only pinnacles, crevasses, and blasting surf. He hadn't realized how isolated the drop zone would be.

Rain gusted against his windshield, and swathes of nimbostratus clouds masked the low valleys. He twisted in his seat and gazed back in the direction of his village. It lay a hundred kilometers away by air, but the wicked mountain topography made it ten times farther by land. He felt a twinge of unease. He'd studied enough maps to know crossing the mountains by foot would take three weeks of hard climbing. And no hiker could carry enough air for three weeks.

He faced forward, and his trapezius ligaments tightened as he pictured what lay ahead. The city lady. He dreaded meeting Vera Luce again. What if he couldn't do this job? She expected a lot. What if he blew it?

He pinched his lip between his teeth. It wouldn't take her long to see he was just a common seafarmer who happened to break a skydive record by accident. Sure, he had luck, but luck could change. He slid his hand over the empty seat beside him, imagining how Dyce would argue him out of his nervousness. She always urged him to believe in himself, but she was the one with the brains. He felt her absence like a missing rib.

The rain dwindled, and the sun made a vague white smear in the sky. He used its light to gauge the direction of Seattle. But there was nothing to see that way, only brown vapor. He felt the car decelerate. Below, through a break in the clouds, he glimpsed a black and red volcanic crater, like a pockmark where the mountain's peak should have been. Earthmoving drones were gouging raw wet tracks in the pumice. The handful of thrown-together huts in the crater looked like an outpost on the Moon.

He kept telling himself this was his own Unimak Island. He wanted to revel in his new job. He wanted to believe he was Thunderbird, king of the sky. Yet as the aircar hovered to land, he felt cut off from everything familiar.

The car touched down in a welter of muddy gravel, and Orr squinted through the mist at the new hangar. It stood twenty meters high, a hulking quonset of ribbed sheet metal, darkened by the rain. A large yellow IN marked the airlock door. Farther off, he saw smaller buildings, linked to the hangar by what looked like clear pipes, large enough for people to walk through.

He tugged on a respirator and sat still for a moment, trying to buck up his confidence. Then he got out and sprinted for the airlock. The wind almost lifted him off his feet.

But Vera Luce was not waiting in the hangar. Two strangers met him instead. A plump dark-skinned lady with gray hair introduced herself as Bettie Rimini. When he realized who she was, he nearly tripped over his feet. Elsabette Rimini was one of the two original designers of the Celestia Sky Wing.

Bettie had a beautiful weathered face and a welcoming smile. Before he could stop her, she took his gym bag and linked her arm through his elbow. "Let's find you a bunk and get you settled. Are you hungry?"

Her pint-sized companion had thick white hair and wore a strange-looking respirator that covered the lower half of his face. When Orr heard the man's name, he wanted to bow down and kiss his knobby fingers. Alejandro Vere was the other legendary Celestia designer, the one who invented micromesh. Al said, "We saw your mesosphere dive. Brilliant."

Orr tried to stammer some kind of respectful reply. Before he could speak, Al waltzed forward, flourished his slender hand and said, "Imbue air!" Suddenly, a bouquet of purple silk flowers snapped out of his sleeve, and Orr laughed in shock.

Bettie's eyes twinkled. "Al thinks he's channeling Harry Potter. Don't encourage him."

Orr took the silk flowers and said, "Wow."

Al and Bettie chatted nonstop as they led Orr out of the hangar through one of the clear flexing pipes. Bettie told him the tubes connected all their structures like an oversized gerbil habitat. Al explained the petroleum-based sheeting came at a steep price, but it was the best for sealing out toxic smog. Bettie said it smelled exactly like new luggage.

Orr had never smelled new luggage. He'd never had anyone carry his bag, and he didn't know what a gerbil habitat was. His attention swung from the gracious Bettie to the white-haired Al, and he wondered what planet he'd landed on.

Al said, "We've been studying the video of your dive. That fishtailing when you sliced into the wind? We need to fix that."

"Yeah," Orr said. "That was wild."

"We think a deeper camber might do the trick."

Orr said, "Maybe . . . um . . . a sharper leading edge?"

Al's spectacles caught the light. "I have some drawings in the lab. I'll show you when you're settled. We'd appreciate your feedback."

Orr blushed. Happiness choked his power of speech, so he simply nodded.

8

Backslide. To freefall backwards.

Vera Luce had planned to welcome Orr in person. She'd restyled her makeup. She bought a new white blouse. White, the purest absence of color; she always wore white to enhance the redness of her hair. For days, she'd been looking forward to meeting Orr again. But at exactly the wrong time, her father tied her up in a web conference call.

Damn the old man! Micromanaging already, like she knew he would. While she sat listening to Rolfe critique her business plan, her skydiver was probably getting an earful from Bettie Rimini.

Vera raked her fingers over the rough concrete floor of her "private office." Her tiny cube was a glorified box made of soundproof panels bolted inside the hangar wall. No furniture yet. She sat on the bare floor, hugged her knees and watched Rolfe through her ocular. The tiny lens spiked his image straight through her optic nerve to her cerebral cortex, so the old man seemed to prance back and forth in front of her, gesturing like a candidate for office. Rolfe expected Orr to do a freaking promo tour.

"We need media buzz," he said. "That's how you build the crave for new content. You should know that."

Without even consulting her, he'd already assigned his publicity chief to "help out." Mrs. Ara Jadri. Vera broke a fingernail scratching the concrete floor.

Mrs. Jadri stepped into the web frame, all smiles. She had short black hair, high bouncy breasts, and an unfortunate weakness for red lipstick. Who dressed the woman, Vera wondered. Poor thing, like a streetwalker. "Jadri, you look ravishing," she said.

Mrs. Jadri didn't return the compliment. The red bindi dot between her eyebrows glowed laser sharp as she laid out her marketing plans. *Her* plans? Pushy bitch. Vera played with her oc interface and painted Jadri blue.

Already, Jadri's people were steaming up the web with rumors about Orr-paaj Sitka. A notorious womanizer, fluent in the twelve principles of sexual practice, father of illegitimate twins, and other vapid myths. Jadri had also lined up interviews with sportscasters around the globe.

Vera bit her little finger till it bled. "He's *my* discovery. *Mine*. Let me do this, Dad. I'll tell you if I need help."

"I'm watching you," Rolfe warned. "You haven't convinced me you can handle this project."

After the vone call ended, Vera inspected her ceiling. Had the old man installed cameras? She made rude gestures with both hands, just in case. Then she texted the security service to debug her cube again.

It wasn't until the next morning that she finally met Orr. She found him talking in the lab with Prune and Bird Beak. Rain drummed the roof, yet the glare coming through the window nearly blinded her. She saw their silhouettes. They were joking like three close chums. Perfect.

"I'm so glad you're here, Orr." She offered her hand, squinting to see him. He wore cut-off jeans and a vest. When he shook her hand, his bronze skin felt warm.

"We're calculating lift coefficients," he said. "This new beryllium alloy—"

Vera cut him short. "Let's go for a walk."

He followed her out through the clear plastic tube, and she blinked till her eyes adjusted. An early March gale was barreling through the caldera, splattering their tube with mud, and it was a mystery to her how so much sunlight could filter through a rainstorm. She glanced back at Orr's brawny legs.

She tried to engage him by pointing out where the fixed and rotating towers would go and where the crew would install the tanks, umbilicals, and platforms for their refurbished space shuttle. He kept a wary distance, though, saying little and never quite meeting her eye. Considering all she was doing for him, his aloofness pissed her off.

But nothing was ever fair. That backstabbing Bettie must have poisoned his mind with gossip. Damage control, Vera's endless task. She moved close and nudged Orr with her hip. "Did Bettie say something to upset you?"

Orr stepped away, knocking into the plastic. His hair fell in his eyes, and he didn't push it back. This annoyed Vera out of all proportion. Why the freaking hell did her body language repel him?

She said, "If something's bothering you, ask me. I'll tell you the truth."

He turned and played with a seam in the plastic tube, flipping the edge of the plastic back and forth. Tongue-tied yokel. She was beginning to find his shyness too damned frustrating. After a minute, though, he surprised her with a question.

"Why don't my calls go through to my girlfriend?"

That caught her unprepared. "Girlfriend?"

"Yeah, I can't get through to my cousin either. I tried vone, vmail, text. Nothing works."

"I'll have a tech look at your web link," Vera lied. For the success of her project, she'd restricted communications. That wasn't going to change.

"You promised me a new transit pass," he reminded her.

She lied again. "It's being processed now. You'll have it soon."

"Are you cold?" he asked.

"What?"

"You're shivering."

He took off his vest and draped it around her shoulders. Warm March winds crackled the filmy tube walls, but yes, Vera did feel cold. When he buttoned his vest under her chin, she noticed the pale color of his eyes. Light gray, shot with azure.

"It's all right, Miss Luce. Don't be afraid."

Afraid? What did she have to fear? Certainly not his pesky girlfriend. She realigned her smile. "Call me Vera. I want you to feel perfectly at home here. Anything you need, just ask."

He poked at the plastic tube wall. "Um, can I make a skydive today?"

"Today? But—" She gestured at the sheeting rain. "Do you have a death wish?"

He flashed his rare smile. "Storm diving is awesome."

Sheepishly, he admitted he'd already picked out some gear from the Celestia inventory. Since the space shuttle wouldn't be delivered for a while, he thought maybe he could fly up in the aircar, if she didn't mind. The car wouldn't reach the stratosphere, but the autopilot could take him high enough for fun maneuvers.

Talking about the sky, he rocked on his boot heels and cupped handfuls of air as if it were real solid stuff. Of all the skydivers Vera had scouted, no one moved the way Orr Sitka did. She enjoyed how his shoulders rolled and dipped, as if he were already dodging through rain clouds. He was such a kid about his sport, he made her feel lighter. This kinetic energy, this was why she'd chosen him for her game.

"Go for it," she said. "Take anything you need. I want you diving every day."

He lit up like a babe in toyland. "Want to join me?"

Vera's first thought: *Not on your life*. Wide open spaces petrified her. But as she watched Orr leap up and bat the plastic tube to make the water droplets fly, she recognized an opportunity. Again, she squinted out at the glittery glaring rain. "Okay," she said, "if the storm lets up, I'll make one skydive with you."

His slap-happy grin told her she'd pronounced the magic words. He was so pleased, his eyebrows dimpled. And she laughed. More than anything, she wanted this simple young man to like her.

Bag. A deployment device which contains a parachute before it opens.

Vera ordered the crew to clear a hasty drop zone in the half-flooded construction rubble, and for the rest of that stormy day, she hid in her soundproof cube and watched Orr make body dives from the aircar. She sent holocams to record him, and she shunted the real-time feed to her oc so she could control the light level. She felt more comfortable in her soundproof cube, less exposed to the great outdoors. She set up a folding cot, burrowed under the sheets, and watched him fly.

First he would freefall from about four klicks and do aerobatics, using only his body to steer and cartwheel through the gale. Then he'd open his parachute, make a hook turn, and scream low across the muddy construction site for a fast swoop landing in the wet gravel.

He was a wonder to watch. Even the crew paused in their work when his parachute dropped through the cloud ceiling. Of course Vera used high-resolution optics to record his jumps. These storm dives would make fabulous webcasts.

Cocooned in her cot that evening, she replayed the close-ups of Orr's face. Had he believed her about the vone? No way could she admit how many calls she'd jammed. Hundreds of reporters asked for interviews. Scores of companies offered sponsorship deals. Everybody wanted a piece of Orr Sitka. Cousin Lermontov voned several times a day, and the girlfriend called, too. Dyce Iakai. What a pest. Vera couldn't afford to let her skydiver lose his focus, so she phuxed the web link and locked everyone out.

Deeper she burrowed into her blanket. The silent cube felt like a refuge. She intended to sleep and eat there, when such things were possible. Yet already, Rolfe wanted her back in Seattle. She had to launch the Orr Sitka sportswear collection, plus an energy drink and a line of male jewelry. And she was running out of time. Mrs. Jadri had just trademarked their new brand: Gravity Pilot.

Vera wasn't sure if she liked that name, but she needed a few million chumps to love it. Otherwise, her righteous game would fall flat. Nights like this, even Vera needed someone to confide in. On a whim, she voned her surgeon, Dr. Leo Mandragora.

"You love novelties," she said. "Come take a sneak peek at my new rising star."

Leo purred, "What's in it for me, darling?"

The two of them popped into Leo's web den. He'd done up his virtual décor in plush cherry and saffron. Very retro. While Vera cued Orr's skydive, Leo sprawled in his imaginary sofa cushions and yawned. "You want me to watch *sports*? I'd rather watch mold breed."

Dr. Leo's gold-threaded scarves and gauzy orange skirts accentuated his pink freckled skin. A perpetual cross-dresser, Leo was. Also, he dealt quality drugs, and he gave amazing massages. But his claws were sharp. Along with his friendly bedside manner came a cash-register heart. Vera had paid Leo's way through med school back when they were lovers, yet he always had his hand out for more.

She subvocalized a command, and as they cozied up in their make-believe sofa, Leo's den dissolved into a three-dimensional view of the stormy Alaskan sky. Orr sailed around them, unaware that anyone was watching.

She said, "This is the guy I told you about. He's my ticket to glory."

Leo arched his back, made a lazy stretch, and settled his orange veils over his knees. The harem getup was just a costume, not a religious statement. Leo didn't believe in anything. Still, he was the closest Vera had to a friend.

"So what do you think?" she said.

He rolled his liquid brown eyes. She could see him weighing and judging—not Orr's athletic prowess but his likely position in her game. "What does the old man say?"

"Rolfe's totally on board," she lied, squeezing a sofa cushion to her chest. "He sees the same potential I do. Can't you feel it? The magnetism?"

Leo watched Orr spin and play in the storm. "I see a boy-toy with thunder thighs. When are you coming back to Seattle? Everybody's meeting at Lethe's tonight for cocktails."

Vera hugged her cushion. "When I'm ready."

"Take care, love." Leo pulled the cushion out of her hands, and his languid eyes reflected the phantom clouds. "Don't stay away too long. Things fall apart faster than you realize."

She tensed. "What have you heard?"

Leo adjusted the golden coins dangling across his forehead. "Nothing definite. Just a slight weakening of confidence in Rolfe's solvency. They say he's blowing his wad on a bird habitat."

She relaxed. "You're such a gossip. Daddy's pockets go deep." For a moment, she mused over Leo's words, calculating how she might use the information. "Listen, I need you to express my usual order to Alaska. I'll text you the local address."

Leo moistened his lips. "Rush orders cost triple, lovey. Cash in advance."

Leo had a date with friends, so after he took her payment for the drugs, Vera left his web den, and for the next hour, she sat alone in her soundproof cube watching Orr's replays. She knew she was right about Orrpaaj Sitka. He had a powerful gift, and before long, the entire worldwide web would feel his charisma. Her game was unfolding just as she'd planned. That night, she streamed every breathtaking visual to Seattle. Rolfe expected daily reports.

9

BASE jump. A skydive made from a ground-based structure.
BASE stands for Bridges, Antennas, Structures, Earth.

Orr still couldn't believe Vera Luce wanted to skydive. He'd asked her in fun, never guessing she'd say yes. She surprised him. But she did look fit and strong. He found his thoughts circling back to her, maybe a little too often.

Early the next morning, she appeared in the hangar dressed in a gray coverall borrowed from one of her crew. She usually wore white, but in the darker color, with her hair tied back, Orr thought she looked younger and smaller, more like a gym student than the ruthless entrepreneur Bettie had described. She kept fidgeting with a pair of tinted glasses, trying to adjust the setting, and again Orr noticed the scars on the backs of her hands. He didn't understand city people. He didn't know how to judge Vera's behavior. All he knew was, she showed up to make a skydive. He liked her grit.

He'd already been outside to check the air. The storm front had passed in the night, and the air felt smooth at ground level, smooth as silk, good for landings. Winds aloft might be sketchy though. Unimak's western coast was not the ideal school for beginners. Still, he'd taught people before, and he loved sharing the finer points of his sport.

Inside the hangar, he trussed Vera in his parachute harness and made her hang from a scaffold to practice opening the canopy. She took instruction well, although she refused to part with her tinted glasses. Okay, she was nervous.

He reassured her that her first skydive would be an easy hop-and-pop, not a Wing dive. A person needed hundreds of parachute jumps before even thinking about flying a Wing.

"Hop-and-pop. Sounds explosive." Her Caucasian cheeks dimpled. "You really like to flirt with death."

"No, honest. It's fun." He scooped up three random lag-bolts off the concrete floor and tossed them into the air. To put her at ease, he started juggling them. "Hop-and-pop just means you hop out of the aircar and pop open your parachute right away."

Her perfume had a sweet spicy scent, but he could smell her perspiration, too. He stooped and spun the lag-bolts on the floor like children's tops. He had to work fast to keep all three spinning in balance. He glanced up to see if she was watching.

All morning, he coached her. Over and over, he made her grip the parachute release handle and count: "One, two, three, pull!" Hundreds of times, they rehearsed yanking the toggles to steer, and they went through the landing drill ad infinitum. He thought she was getting the hang of it.

Next, he spread a tarp on the concrete floor and made her lie facedown. "Belly to the Earth," he said. "Spread your arms like this, and arch your back. This is called the box."

While Vera stretched to hold the position, he adjusted her elbows and lifted her chin. She had strong shapely calf muscles and good biceps. He didn't want to admit how much he enjoyed being near her. "Memorize how that feels," he said. "You have to hold that arch no matter what."

He warned that she might tumble out of control the first few seconds after she stepped from the aircar. She said, "That should be entertaining."

He lifted her left leg higher, and his hand lingered on her ankle. "If you hold your arch no matter what, you'll eventually stabilize facing the Earth."

"Staring straight down at oblivion," she said. "Marvelous."

He kept holding her bare ankle, feeling the hard tendon under her skin. "Once you're stable, that's when you deploy your parachute. If you open while you're tumbling, you might get twisted up in the lines."

"Yeezes God. You do this for fun?"

He shrugged. "That's the excuse we give. We'll make our first dive right after lunch. Do it like we practiced. It's easy."

Someone dropped a crowbar, and the hangar walls rang like a gong. Vera shouted over the ringing, "Sounds like my death knell."

Her jokes cracked him up. She showed way more backbone than he'd expected. But she had some kind of medical problem. He saw her swallow a bunch of pills when she thought no one was looking.

They broke for lunch, but he noticed she didn't eat. Her skin had a clammy sheen. Yet when he asked if she was ready to skydive, she gave him two thumbs up and said, "Let's take cameras."

Yeah, the city girl had nerve.

That afternoon, they flew up to three thousand meters, not quite two miles above ground level. The plan was, Vera would step out, count three to stabilize, then open her 'chute. Piece of cake.

When the aircar reached altitude, Orr felt his usual charge of exhilaration. They put on their helmets, and he switched on their laser optics. Then he opened the door and put out his hand to feel the rushing air. It felt cushiony fluent and cool. Slide air, he loved it. The current spread his fingers apart.

"Exit exit exit!" he sang through his helmet radio.

Vera hesitated, gripping the door frame and staring down. Then she stepped out and fell into the vapor. Orr dove after her, followed by sixteen rolling holocams. As predicted, she went turvy at first. He watched her flip-flop through the yellow haze, and he counted off seconds, waiting for her to arch her back. But she didn't. She was tumbling, spinning, thrashing. Static blurted through his helmet radio, and she screamed, "Save me!"

He pressed his arms to his sides, tucked his chin and steered toward her. He saw her body clenched in a tight fetal curl. She was panicked. That happened to new students sometimes. Vital seconds ticked by as he coaxed her over the radio. "Stay calm. Arch your back. Belly to the Earth."

But she couldn't unclench. Wheeling head over heels, she yanked out the pilot 'chute to open her canopy, and true to form, the lines wrapped around her legs.

Faster than breath, Orr zoomed straight down to overtake her. Already, she'd fallen more than a mile, wasting too many precious seconds. When he gripped her waist, their combined weight whirled them in a bipolar spin. Blindly, he tore at the webbing to free her from the malfunctioning 'chute. He found the release ring and pulled. Her main 'chute cut away, and their spin changed to a violent somersault.

He saw the ground rushing up. No time. He found her reserve handle and yanked. Her spring-loaded reserve parachute fired off like a gun, rapidly towing the bright red canopy out of its bag. The canopy snapped open and slowed her descent, and Orr dropped below her like a stone.

Less than a hundred meters above the knife-edged peaks, he popped his own 'chute and caught an updraft. Sixteen holocams recorded his spiraling flight as he fought to hold altitude while she drifted down. Wind currents sailed her east, away from their volcanic crater, and Orr studied the mountainous wasteland below. There were few good places to land on Unimak Island. Their only safe bet was the clearing in the crater.

"Vera, you have to turn. Do you hear me?"

"Uh-huh."

"Pull your right toggle. See where my hand is pointing? That's it. Easy. Very easy. Now hold it. Now let up. Pull your left just a little. That's good. Just ride it. You okay?"

Steadily, he spiraled around her, guiding her across thermals to gain lift and talking evenly to help her relax. Seconds ripped by. They were so close to the mountain tops, he could see the grain in the rock. He manhandled his 'chute to stay with her. Even if they reached the caldera, landing a high-performance parachute took good concentration, and Vera had seized up like a ball of ice.

Practicing in the harness, she'd made cavalier jokes, but now she was sailing over the peaks at a horizontal speed of seventy kilometers per hour. She couldn't land at that speed. Time was running out. She had to flare and slow down.

He'd taught her how to pull hard on both toggles with perfectly balanced force, but altitude was critical. If she braked too high, she might stall and crash. Too low, she might fly straight into the ground at full speed and plow her own grave.

He tried to keep his voice steady. "See the launchpad? It's not far."

"Yeah."

He could taste the fear in her voice. He said, "That's a big area. Bigger than it looks. You'll land on tiptoes with that parachute. Nice and soft."

"Soft," she said.

"First we'll turn into the wind, okay? Pull your left toggle. Now let up. Easy, easy. Now give the right a tiny tug. Good girl."

Seconds whirled away, and the hot spring winds blew grit and haze, clouding the view. He could hear her uneven breath through the radio com link. He kept one eye on his altimeter display.

"Vera, you're lined up fine. Just before you touch down, I'll tell you to flare. You're going to pull both toggles at the same time, remember? That'll slow you down for a nice fluffy landing."

"Um-hum."

She overshot the clearing.

"Flare!" he bellowed. "Pull the toggles now!"

She must not have pulled hard enough. Her parachute drove her against the jagged rim of the crater. Then a gust filled her canopy and dragged her over the brink, where the mountainside cleaved apart in steep lava cliffs. Orr saw her gloves clawing at the loose rock of an outcrop.

He swept down fast, cambered his 'chute, and hit the rim hard, letting his thighs take the impact. Then he flung off his rig, scrambled down to the outcrop and threw himself on top of her to pin her down with his weight.

They sprawled together on the narrow outcrop, panting in their helmets, waiting for their hearts to stop dieseling. Her wind-filled parachute kept tugging at her shoulders, trying to haul her away. He pulled the release, and with a sibilant swish, the parachute swept off into the mountains. He clutched her to his chest, bumping their helmets together, and he felt her gripping him just as hard.

After the first stunned moments, he ran his fingers over her arms and legs, checking for fractures. "Are you hurt? Do you feel any pain?" When she shook her head, he boosted her up over the rim and half carried her back to the hangar.

Inside the airlock, he took off their helmets. He could feel her trembling. He pressed his forehead against hers. "You're safe."

In a shuddery voice, she said, "That was some fun, Orrpaaj."

Bearing. Horizontal direction of Sky Wing flight expressed in compass degrees.

Vera couldn't stop the quaking in her chest. As the airlock ticked through its cycle, she heard the vents rattling. She smelled the ozone and chemical cleaners. Alive, she was still alive. She tried to speak again, but her heavy breathing echoed out of harmony.

"It's my fault," Orr said. "I should've put you on a static line. I might've killed you."

Vera sank against him, unable to think.

"Forgive me," he said.

Her mouth tasted like battery acid. She could feel how tenderly he patted her back, but she still didn't trust herself to answer.

"I pushed you too fast." He spoke into her hair, and she could feel the moist warmth of his breath. "After a few more days of drill . . ." He seemed to hesitate. "Maybe we could do it over."

She gripped the seams of his jumpsuit. *Never.*

Sixteen holocams buzzed inside the airlock, recording them from every possible angle. Then all at once, Vera's brain kicked in. Rolfe would see this recording. She wrestled out of Orr's embrace. Rolfe would see it all.

She said, "Let's go back up for another try."

Orr shook his head. "Not today. You need—"

Her voice cracked. "Now!"

Orr went stony quiet. Vera couldn't tell what he was thinking. She bit her lip. Maybe he didn't like direct orders, but she absolutely could not let Rolfe see her fail. Possibly, her plummet down the gravity well had frapped her wits, but it also brightened her instinct for survival. She resorted to lies.

"Orr, what you said about the sky, I understand now. When I was up in the air, falling free, it was like channeling pure bliss. I've never felt so liberated. Please let me try again."

Orr slung hair out of his eyes. "Do you mean that?" He searched her face. When she fumbled with her helmet, he caught her shaking hands. "Tomorrow," he whispered.

Vera jerked free. She didn't need to activate false tears. Her eyes were streaming. But her brain wheels were spinning again. She said, "I need to face this down. If I don't go now, I may be too scared tomorrow."

After a moment, Orr squeezed her shoulders and nodded. "I understand."

This time, though, he insisted on using a static line to open her canopy, and he spent another hour going through the safety checks. Her legs nearly buckled as he rigged her with a fresh parachute harness. Again, he made her hang from the scaffold to practice. Again, he grasped her ankles and pressed the small of her back. "Feel that?" he said. "Hold the arch. Trust your body."

She stiffened to hide her jitters. Somewhere overhead, she sensed Rolfe's satellites stalking her. Why had she trapped herself this way? Was this game worth dying for?

Through her filmy quu-suit, she felt Orr's hand supporting her abdomen. His warm fingers imprinted her skin. He said, "Your lips are chapped. I'll get some salve."

When he let go, she twisted in the air like a hanged felon. The parachute harness felt like an implement of torture. Why couldn't she simply win Orr with sex? Didn't she have body mods tunable to any preference and a face as perfect as any surgeon's scalpel ever carved? She absolutely required Orr's trust, but what a hellacious way to win it.

Orr dug through his gear bag for lip balm, but his stuff was so jumbled, he couldn't find it. Outside, the smog thickened to burnt umber, and the sky looked bruised. Another storm was building. A bitter taste welled at the back of her throat, and the palms of her hands ached. She didn't know what bothered her more, letting Rolfe get an edge—or letting Orr down.

After they went through the drill at least thirty more times, they walked out to the aircar with the holocams whizzing around. She slapped at them, then marched ahead with a gutsy swagger, counterfeiting a smile for Rolfe's satellites.

Her second jump was tame compared to the first. She counted off the seconds and made blunt mechanical moves. Not elegant, but she lived through it. Rolfe couldn't make fun of her now.

When she slid to a stop in the gravel, Orr cheered over the headset. He landed right beside her and helped her to her feet. Then from the way he laughed and hugged her, and from the proud look in his eyes, she realized she'd gained much more from this death-defying stunt than she'd expected. A new intimacy united them, the bond she'd longed for. Worth the price, oh yes. She giggled like a child. But only after she'd gathered up her parachute did she notice the salty pang in her mouth. She'd bitten through her tongue.

Body dive. Skydiving without a Wing.

Orr's whole body shed tension after Vera's second dive was over. That night, he shared a ready-meal with her in the breakroom. He shoveled down a bowlful of green stew. Nothing ever hindered his appetite. Al and Bettie were modeling Wing profiles in the lab, and the crew had eaten earlier, so he and Vera had the breakroom to themselves. A leftover smell of microwave dinners flavored the air, and someone had accidentally dropped an earbud down the sink. Caught in the drain, it hummed like a tiny muffled banjo.

He watched Vera push food around her plate without tasting it. She kept raving about the pleasures of skydiving, but he saw her shiver. Her hands moved as she talked. "It's like you're totally alive, like superhuman. You feel so . . . unbound."

He caught himself staring at her throat. Her skin glowed a paler, creamier shade than he was used to. And her small straight nose . . .

His face burned when he realized he was comparing Vera to Dyce. He seized his tea mug and balanced it on the back of his hand. When it was perfectly steady, he snatched his hand away and caught the falling mug by its handle before the tea spilled. Only a few drops splashed on the table. Vera clapped.

Orr crinkled his lips. He didn't know much about women. Funny, though, he knew twelve different names for the air. Ribbon, slide, electric, lax, dry . . . He reminded himself how much he owed Dyce. Who else would put up with his thick-headed ways?

But he could feel Vera's body heat. She was describing a view he'd seen thousands of times, of lemon cloud mountains. Her voice shook as she talked, and he knew exactly how she felt, that soul-swallowing bliss. He wanted to add something meaningful, but he was so lame with words. He balanced a spoon straight up on his fingertip. Dyce called him "the speechless wonder."

Dyce. Her voice whispered through his mind, *Don't forget me.* She must have known the sky would steal his attention. He dropped the spoon and glanced at Vera's scarred hands. "When will the vone be fixed? I really need to make a call."

Vera hid her hands in her armpits. "I meant to tell you. Turns out we're in a satellite dead spot."

"A what?"

"It's like this weird Bermuda Triangle for vones," she said. "There's a wave interference pattern that blocks certain frequencies. I've ordered a special antenna, so you'll have to be patient till it comes."

Orr mulled that over. He'd never bothered to learn how vone calls bounced around the worldwide web of satellites. Vera's explanation sounded like geek speak, a language he could only take on faith.

Then Vera started asking questions about his life, and he wished he had a more interesting story to tell. Parents unknown. Basic tenth-level education. Since age fourteen, he'd worked at the Aleut seafarm, tending his tribe's communal kelp beds to earn money for skydiving.

Vera laughed. "You don't care about money. You've never even asked what I'm paying you."

He balanced the spoon across the salt shaker and set it spinning like a helicopter blade. He was too embarrassed to raise his eyes. Dyce always handled their finances. He said, "You're covering the cost of the dives, so . . ."

"You thought that was all? Orr, brace yourself. You're about to be drowning in riches."

Vera whipped out her handheld pod to display his contract. He scrolled down through the dense legalese—till he spotted the amount of his advance. When Vera explained the royalties he stood to earn if their marketing campaign succeeded, his earlobes flushed.

She shut the pod before he could read the rest. Why was she always so anxious, he wondered. At least her hands weren't shaking anymore. Small dainty hands. Fragile. He winced at how she'd bitten her nails to the quick. And there were scars along her knuckles, faded scars, like tiny animal bites. She put up a brave front, but something behind her smile chilled him. He wanted to warm her. He almost reached out, but he stopped himself.

She wet her lips. "Shall we go for a walk?"

Five minutes later, Orr was guiding Vera along the path he'd made up over the caldera's rim. When they reached the highest point, he loosened his respirator and pushed back his raincoat hood to feel the warm breeze blowing off the Pacific.

One day, Vera told him, when their project succeeded, he would skydive through the mesosphere again. He would travel all over the world and break all the records. The engineers would keep improving the tech, and one day, he would freefall from the Moon, she said. From Mars, maybe even from Pluto.

Orr tried to see the picture she was painting, but all he could do was laugh. He took off his glove to feel the ribbon air. Silky smooth, it sang through the dried husks of last year's Canada thistle. Lately, foreign weeds had sprouted everywhere over his island. He glanced up at the sky. The haze had thinned, but not enough for stars to peek through.

On impulse, he told Vera about Polaris, the North Star. She'd never seen it, but he had, a few times when he was small. He pointed out its approximate location, and they both squinted at that patch of sky for several minutes.

Farther on, they sat down in the rocks, and Vera said, "I understand why you love this island. The scenery's spectacular."

He lay back and crossed his arms behind his head. "When you look up and see all that space out there, you know, it—it makes you realize what a big thing we're part of."

"Big." She chuckled at his word, though he hadn't meant it as a joke.

He felt like a fool. Still, he struggled on. "We think we're smart, trying to explain everything. What we know about the world can't cover a pinhead." He cupped his hand and caught the breeze in his fingers. "We're like . . . like gnats trying to guess what causes weather."

She asked, "So how did you get into skydiving?"

Well, that was his open sesame. For twenty minutes, he told her about hanging out at the air base as a kid, doing chores for Pete Hogue, and sometimes stowing away on planes to watch the old-time jumpers do their tricks. Talking about the sky revved him up. He described storm fronts and wind shears and the hushed stillness of the stratosphere. He tried to explain the quality of the quiet.

Vera kept urging him on, so he told her the skies were clearest near the poles. That's why most skydivers lived in Antarctica, Chile, Finland, places like that. Australia held an annual "boogie" which he described as a combination liar's tournament, gear sale, skydive marathon, and round-the-clock beer bash. He'd always wanted to go. He said the skydive clubs in Australia had the best web sites. In fact, the only reason he cruised the web was to watch skydive vlogs and find cheap gear. He never posted vlogs himself, although he once traded texts with a Finnish title holder named Juho Fagerholm.

Vera's deep bell-toned laughter echoed through the night. "Forget the Aleuts. You belong to the skydiver tribe."

That's true, he thought, gazing at her face. Talking to Vera came easy. He enjoyed the play of light in her green eyes.

She said, "I can't wait till you dive the stratosphere again."

He tugged off his respirator and brushed his hair back, remembering the times he'd tried to tell Dyce about skydiving. Finally, he said, "It's just a pastime. Using wind and gravity to turn your body a certain way, it's a frivolous skill. I know it doesn't have any practical value."

"Not true," Vera said. "It's like music."

He cocked one gray eye open. "You think?"

Vera lifted her chin, and he saw her eyes shifting back and forth. She said, "Music doesn't feed anybody or cure disease. It's just vibrations in the air. Is it pointless?"

He didn't answer, but he sat up straighter in the rocks.

She carried on. "Some people are born with a gift for physical movement. It's a special category of IQ, did you know? They call it athletic acumen."

His gray eyes blinked. He'd never heard of physical IQ.

She said, "Everybody loves to watch a master perform. We worship our sports stars. Here, put this respirator back on before you catch cancer." She tilted his head and slipped the band over his hair. "Orr, every culture in history has held athletic contests. Why do you think that is?"

"Why?" He sat like an obedient schoolboy, letting her jerk the mask over his nose and ears, waiting for her answer.

She said, "You show us the best we can be."

He studied his boots. Her words sounded too high-flown for him. He knew he wasn't anyone special. "You know what I sense when I'm up there?"

Vera adjusted his head strap. "Tell me."

He gazed in the direction of Polaris. "Like, when I have to work really hard to make a move, and I come out on top of the clouds, I'm out of breath, my chest is going boom boom boom, you know, from the effort. And then everything goes quiet. And it's shining. And I feel, for just one second, that I have the whole universe inside me. My body doesn't exist. My name, who I am, all that sinks away, and I'm everywhere."

He glanced at her, blushing to his hairline. Then he added in a darker tone, almost to himself, "I'll do whatever it takes to feel that again."

Vera sat quietly for a moment, apparently lost in thought. "You'll never quit skydiving, will you?"

"Never," he said. "Why would I?"

All at once, she bounded to her feet. "Teach me to fly the Celestia, Orr. I want to see the stratosphere."

"Yeah?"

"Yes, I want to fly like an angel."

His happy grin lifted his respirator five centimeters up his cheeks. He stood and showed her how to touch her knuckles against his, the skydiver salute. Backlit by the night, she seemed luminous.

10

Boogie. A meeting of skydivers for fun and competition.

O rr didn't like the web, though he sometimes used it. He was fifteen when Dyce taught him how to cruise. They shared the same chair in front of a desktop computer in the Unimak tribal library. He didn't like "schoolwork," as he called it. Nevertheless, he felt a pressing need to learn about thermal currents.

Pete Hogue had sold him a surplus military parachute, but he hardly ever had enough money for airplane rides. So, he'd been throwing himself off the cliffs above Bechevin Bay. But every time he ran off the precipice, sea breezes brained him back against the rocks. He needed to find out what he was doing wrong.

Dyce set him up with a free web account, and she taught him how to research wind science. The tribe's communal desktops clustered on a round white table that took up most of the library floor space. The room always smelled of dust and carpet cleaner and stale cologne. And the hum of fluorescent fixtures competed with the noises of children at the daycare center next door. It was a clean dry place, a sanctuary from the crowded village streets.

In the evenings after work, Dyce showed Orr how to organize a list of his favorite skydiver sites. At first, she browsed the vlogs with him, and she got jazzed every time they found a new one. In fact, Dyce was sitting beside Orr the night he texted Juho Fagerholm.

They were alone in the tiny room. The senior librarian had stepped out for tea. Dyce nudged Orr with her hip. "You have a legitimate question. Why shouldn't you ask an expert?"

Orr tucked his chin into his shirt collar. "Juho's a world champion. He's too busy to talk to me."

She scratched the old-fashioned stylus over the touchscreen to cue the text header. Her moves were always brisk and efficient. She didn't believe in wasting time. When the screen was set, she handed the stylus to Orr. "Worse case, he'll delete your message. No loss."

Orr stared at the blank message box, and his fingers knotted. The CPU whirred. The cursor blinked.

She tickled between his shoulders. "Did you forget how to write?"

She tugged his hair. She blew in his ear. He dropped the stylus and put his hand between her thighs.

Some while later, after they'd made love among the boxes of inkjets in the library storage closet, he did sit down and compose his question to Juho Fagerholm. The Finnish hero replied a few days later with useful advice about the total idiocy of BASE jumping off a low cliff directly into an onshore breeze. So Orr started saving his money for airplane rides.

Stretched in his bunk at Mundo Mountain, Orr went mellow, reminiscing about Dyce. She helped him find information on the trade winds. And the jet streams. And the aurora borealis. Smart as she was, she did her best to stuff knowledge into his head.

Several times, she hiked up to the air base to watch him dive. She'd bring a tote bag of snacks and cold tea and a blanket to spread on the hangar floor. Usually she'd have a bookreader checked out from the library. She was always on some new kick, trying to learn Spanish or Zen or oceanography. Waiting in the packing area between jumps, watching grown men kneel together and fuss over the best way to fold nylon, that couldn't have been the most thrilling of pastimes.

Yeah, but every detail entranced Orr, from the reek of the turbo fumes to the salty jokes of the old jumpers. He threw himself at the sport. He practiced single-mindedly, every night, every weekend. Forget the cuts and bruises, the broken bones, the cost. Skydiving filled him up. Sure, maybe he got a little addicted, like Dyce warned, but how else could you learn something that complicated? How else could you get really good?

He remembered her wide Asian eyes watching through the hangar window. She'd wave and blow a kiss as he loaded into Pete's airplane. But it must have been boring for her to wait in the hangar twenty or thirty minutes while the small plane spiraled up to jump altitude. No one to talk to. Nothing to do but sit on her blanket on the hard concrete floor.

Finally, Pete would announce jump run, and the spectators would press against the smudged windows, trying to see straight up. Dyce was small. She would've needed a crate to stand on. And even on a clear day, even if you wiped the steamy window with a towel, there wasn't much to look at—just a handful of specks in the sky. By the time you could make out who was who, they were landing. No wonder she lost interest.

Orr turned over in his bunk and wadded his pillow under his chin. As soon as they were together again, he would be more considerate. He would. His bunkroom felt stuffy. The air was stale, and the only light came from LEDs on the climate control panel. Still, he could see the clutter around his bed, gear and shoes, his enormous shoes. His lockers were so full, they wouldn't close. He could hardly walk through the mess. Dyce would freak.

Still, she was fearless in her own way, moving to Seattle by herself, but skydiving had terrified her. More than once, he'd offered to teach her, but after a while, she got snappish at the very mention of the sport. When he tried to tell her about a cool maneuver or a new piece of gear, she would talk about some lame book she was reading. There was, like, a block. Maybe she was afraid he might hurt himself. Sometimes he thought she might be jealous.

He twisted in his bunk. He wasn't used to sleeping alone. He felt lopsided. He needed to see her. The new antenna had still not made an appearance, though, and neither had his transit pass. Over a month had gone by since he'd held Dyce in his arms. For almost twenty years, they'd never been apart that long.

Bounce. A fatal skydive crash.

Around 2:00 A.M., Orr jolted awake. Some noise had roused him. Maybe he dreamed it? He lay for a minute, listening to the soft sough of the air blowers. He got up and tiptoed into the dark breakroom in his briefs, then strolled out through the clear tubing under the Alaskan sky.

Early March, the days were almost as long as the nights now. Sharp breezes rattled the plastic tube, and outside under a security light, he saw fresh green kudzu sprouting through a crack in the concrete. A lone robot was chopping at the vines with a hand tool. Alaska had changed a lot in his short memory. He'd heard there used to be trees on this island, before the permafrost melted and smudged the sky with methane.

People said the winters used to be cold, and there used to be large animals living in the air. Seagulls, terns, osprey, Dyce showed him pictures. But now, only small animals made their homes in the sky. Gnats, wasps, mosquitoes, way too many mosquitoes. Yet clear winds still washed the Aleutian Islands in early spring. That night, the smog had thinned, and he strained to see the stars. Maybe that pale smudge in the east was Venus?

Often he wondered about infinity. Worlds without number, distances too vast to measure. The night sky reached into his chest and pulled. He wanted to lift off and explore the galaxy in his bare skin. The plastic sheeting blurred the view, though, and after a while, his neck began to cramp from looking up. He wandered to the lab.

Inside, the air lay quiet. The lab smelled of primer paint and foam insulation, and somewhere a pipe dripped—a steady slow ping like a sonar bounce—plumbing installed in too much haste. Only one screen still glowed, lighting the lab walls a soft powder blue. He saw a blinking dialog box asking for his password. That was odd.

He sat down, picked up the stylus and scratched the four-letter code, D-Y-C-E. The monitor took longer than usual to cycle through its protocol. Then, a face materialized on the screen. A bearded face as round as a moon. Gabe said, "It's about time you answered."

"How the heck—" Orr scrubbed his jaw. "I thought I'd never hear from you again."

"Whose choice was that? You know my number." Gabe's cheeks had a dark aggravated flush. "I thought we were partners."

"We are. It's great to see you, but how—"

"Yeah? What about this?" Gabe played a webcast from Channel XS.

". . . Fans go wild for the Gravity Pilot," the commentator raved, while on-screen, a heroic Orr Sitka swept down to save a distressed damsel, entangled in the lines of her parachute.

Orr didn't realize Vera had posted the clip on iTube. He hadn't seen the recording yet. He studied his moves with a critical eye, but the scene gave him déjà vu anxiety when he saw how close Vera came to biting it. Someone had scored music to the action. Sequences ran quick-mo and slow-mo, and the colors were brighter. Orr pleated his lips.

One close-up caught his face through the visor, just at the moment when Vera overflew the drop zone. In his rush to save her, his expression turned savage. The montage continued, repeating sequences from different angles and drawing the action out much longer than the real dive had lasted.

Gabe's glum face reappeared. "So?"

"I signed over recording rights to Grupo Mundo," Orr said. "You know that."

Gabe lifted his hands. "It's not about copyrights. Why didn't you invite me to watch? I used to watch all your dives. You used to need my help."

Orr didn't know how to answer that question. He was still trying to understand how this call got through in the middle of the night, just when he happened to wake up. The timing couldn't be a coincidence.

Gabe said, "Kriis made a web album about you. I'm supposed to play it."

Orr shrugged. "A web album. Cool."

"Here it comes." Gabe streamed a series of short clips from various webcasts. Footage of Orr's dives was showing up on every major channel. He'd become a sports byte, sure enough, a jock hero du jour. Browsing the clips, he learned that fans had created over eight hundred web sites dedicated to the Gravity Pilot.

What surprised him most was Banda Ratulangi. Banda Rat, president of the Australian Skydive Club. She said, "Sitka has some new moves. I respect what I've seen so far."

Banda was a famous freestylist. Orr had watched her championship skydives for years. And she was complimenting him? He felt light-headed.

The screen split into six frames simulcasting live vlogs. In one frame, a crazy-looking blond man was speaking, and Orr dialed up the sound: "The Gravity Pilot flings his vitality at the void and creates himself as he falls. He pursues a fiction of up and down. Events and people orbit the line of his strange attraction . . ."

Gravity Pilot. Vera had told him about the pseudonym they'd created for promo ads, but Orr didn't understand what the vloggers were saying. Could all these strangers be talking about Orr Sitka from Unimak Island? Well, so much for his five minutes of fame. He knew it wouldn't last.

A rough cut brought Gabe back on screen. He was still bristling his eyebrows and flattening his nose, though Orr knew he wouldn't stay mad forever. Orr twirled the stylus between two fingers.

After a while, Gabe said, "You look tired, cousin."

Orr rolled the stylus back and forth under his palm. "Things here are— not what I expected." He decided not to divulge how much fun he'd been having, jumping every day with his pick of new gear. Instead, he asked, "Have you talked to Dyce?"

Gabe's eyebrows lifted. "Sure. Haven't you?"

"No, I . . . We're in this satellite dead spot. It messes up our vone signal."

Gabe grunted. "Dead spot, huh? I've been calling you every day. Why this call got through, now, at this hour, how do you explain that?"

Orr said, "I was going to ask you."

Gabe leaned close to the screen. "That freelance newscaster, Cho Sen Yao? He called me today, gave me a code, told me when to punch it. Middle of the night. You know anything about that?"

Orr shook his head. Cho Sen Yao. He remembered the reporter's chalky white face and illegal cigarettes.

Gabe said, "I guess he's still angling for an interview. It was his idea to play you the web album. He said you don't get the XS Channel. I thought the whole solar system picked up the XS Channel."

"No, we don't get it," Orr said, "but how was Dyce? Was she okay?"

Gabe knuckled the bridge of his nose. "She works too hard. Spends hours in some wikiverse thing. Said she's having the time of her life. You're a pair of fanatics, both of you."

Rain misted the windows, and Orr watched beads of water collect and dribble down the glass. The time of her life?

Gabe said, "Yanny has a poster of the Gravity Pilot hanging in his room. I told him, 'It's your Uncle Orr,' but he wouldn't believe me. He thinks you're a superhero."

Little Yanny. Orr pictured the boy climbing into his lap, demanding a ride on his shoulders. He picked up the stylus and balanced it on the very edge of the counter. He watched it start to tip.

Gabe said, "That Grupo Mundo, you don't need their money. I can get you a hundred better deals."

Orr gave the stylus a nudge. Gabe always exaggerated.

"Come home and see us, Orr."

"I want to."

Orr thought he meant those words, but he was lying. He could've asked for transport home. But the crew never got time off, and he didn't want special treatment, that's how he rationalized. In truth, he was having too much fun to stop and examine his choices. Better to glide and let gravity steer his course.

He teased the stylus another fractional millimeter over the edge. "We'll test our new prototype soon. I'll let you know when, so you can do a flyby and maybe shoot a video for the boys."

"Your word used to be good, Orr. Don't promise what you've already sold."

Orr felt strangled. Gabe was still angry.

"It's your call now," Gabe said. "You're the Gravity Pilot." Then he leaned forward to fidget with his keydeck.

The screen went dark. The vone link died. Orr smashed his fist on the countertop, and the stylus rolled off.

Brakes. Parachute steering lines pulled simultaneously
to reduce airspeed.

Over the next two days, Orr tried repeatedly to call Gabe back. He tried Dyce's number, too, and he sent dozens of misspelled text messages, but he couldn't reach anyone outside the caldera. Vera kept reassuring him the new antenna was on its way, and he made up his mind to believe her.

Here he was, helping redesign the Celestia Sky Wing and getting paid every single day to dive. He'd reached the highest pitch of happiness, right? He didn't want to see any negatives. Dyce was always there, haunting the underside of his mind, but meanwhile, spring rains had set in, and he loved diving in fierce weather. Sometimes he came down from the sky drenched. He would stand in the hangar and shake himself like a wet pup. Then Vera would towel him off and listen to his stammering descriptions of the air's bumps and swales.

In the lab, Al and Bettie were struggling with the new design, trying to work out some glitches with the beryllium alloy. Orr thought he might be useful, but Vera kept pulling him away to teach her skydiving. She wanted to learn all she could before she had to go back to Seattle, so how could he turn her down? He loved teaching his sport.

Evenings, the two of them worked out in his makeshift gym, lifting free weights, practicing tai chi chuan, and doing isometrics on a floor mat in the hangar. Next they had "classes" where Orr scrawled diagrams on a white-board. Wrinkling his brow and gesturing with his marker, he tried to explain the chaos of the winds. He said you had to sympathize with the currents and understand their moods, not to control them, nor to be at their mercy, but to bond with them. Usually, he just demonstrated.

He did "dirt dives," lying prone on a wheeled dolly and rolling around the hangar floor to show Vera the maneuvers. Then he let her try it. While the crew tromped through the hangar, whispering, Orr would adjust the position of her hand or foot. Small things mattered, he told her. And although he usually steered clear of computers, to help Vera out, he hunted down a sky-diving tutorial on the web.

Whenever the rain let up, they dove. In those last two days, Vera made four low-altitude parachute dives from the aircar. Her nervousness did not go away, but she refused to quit, and he saw she was totally obsessed. Well, that's what it took to learn skydiving. He loved how she understood that. When she finally got the knack of stabilizing, he was so pleased that he grabbed her hands in freefall and spun her in a wild dance.

Then he taught her how to move horizontally, how to brake, hold position, and turn left or right. He flattered her about her progress, but she got angry every time she made a mistake. Sometimes, he had to remind her they were doing this for fun.

Late at night, after their lessons were over, he prowled around the caldera watching the crew work under the mercury floodlights. Sometimes he would slip off his respirator and let the sea breeze dampen his face. The crew was forever pouring concrete. Seven men, three women, he didn't count the robots. They worked freelance, and like all migrants, they had a million stories. He liked to lend a hand and listen. They were working people like himself.

After a while, though, he would wander away from the floodlights and climb over the caldera rim, hoping to see a star. Most nights, the smog hung thick, and he had to be careful of his footing. There were fissures in the mountains, steep cliffs and sudden drop-offs. Also feral cats were every-where, digging in the volcanic rock for millipedes. Orr heard their mating cries in the distance. The breeze toyed with his clothes and pushed against his back. He heard it shushing through the peaks with a sound like laughter.

Often during those two days, he ruminated about Vera. She didn't eat enough. He wondered if she ever slept. Maybe he thought about Vera more than he should have. Everything felt upside down. He was supposed to test the new Sky Wing at the end of March, but with construction behind and design snags and still no space shuttle, he felt guilty pestering Vera about the vone. He couldn't help but notice, though, how she hemmed and hedged when he asked.

On the third and final evening before Vera had to leave, they were lifting weights together in his improvised gym, and he was thinking about the Matanuska wind. Vera lay on the mat beside him, lifting her wobbly barbell and clenching her teeth. With every move, her breasts shifted under her thin white shirt, and he glimpsed her silky shorts riding up her thighs.

In a rush, he started explaining the names of the Alaskan winds. The Matanuska. The Taku. The Knik. Dyce taught him their meanings. Dyce, his constant teacher. She also taught him about Aeolus, the islander who held the winds in his hand. By opening his fingers, he could set loose a zephyr, a mistral, or a tempest.

Orr's pecs swelled as he bench-pressed a hundred kilos. "Dyce is ardent. You know that word? It means 'to burn.'"

Vera lifted her own ten-kilo barbell toward the roof. "Did you look that up in Wixionary?"

Orr didn't see Vera's frown. He glimpsed her ankles, though, and her dimpled calves. He heard her soft panting breath close beside him on the mat. Again he started talking, as fast as his lips would move, about the time he got sick sleeping in Gabe's damp basement, and Dyce traded her Game Boy, her only precious possession, for meds to bring down his fever.

Vera grunted. "Saint Dyce."

"That's not all," he said. When Gabe's mother discovered them and threatened to call the orphanage, Dyce completely changed her mind and coaxed her into fostering them so they could attend school.

"Clever." Vera's lips twisted.

"Yeah, she has a way with people." He told how Dyce waited tables in Connie Nujuat's bar in exchange for free meals. Every night, she snuck half her food home in her pockets for him. Then she took an extra job at the kelp cannery when he needed new boots. See, during his teenage years, his feet grew like bean sprouts. He needed a larger size every couple of months.

He got so involved in his serenade, he didn't notice the sullen change in Vera's breathing. Maybe it was the exercise that increased blood flow to his vocal cords. Maybe he wanted to believe that, any time, he could step back into his old life at Unimak Village, and there would be Dyce and Gabe and all his friends waiting at Connie's Pub, just the same as when he left.

So he told Vera about the day he rented a two-person kayak to take Dyce down the Isanax River. It was a real Aleut *baidarka,* he said, although the frame was aluminum instead of whale bone, and the fabric was not sealskin but synthetic fiber.

Dyce loved the kayak trip, but her respirator didn't fit well, and she got a lungful of burning smog. By the end of the day, she was hacking up blood, and Orr thought she might be dying. Three kilometers to the village clinic he ran, carrying her in his arms, totally forgetting to tie up the kayak, which drifted out to sea.

Dyce was young and hale. She recovered fast from her short-term toxic exposure. But the purchase price of the lost kayak ran them deep into debt. Of course, Dyce didn't waste her breath lamenting. What she did, she took a third job—this time at the tribal library. From then on, she swore the lost kayak revealed her mission in life.

"Stop. I give up. She's a goddess," Vera said.

Orr should've stopped. If he'd understood himself better, he would have. Instead, he kept reenacting old memories. Dyce's work on the junior counsel. The preschool class she started. Her batik quilts. "She's a good person," he said.

Vera dropped her barbell on the rack. "You two probably skydived all the time, right? Soaring through the clouds hand in hand, that must have been pure bliss."

Orr's arms shook a bit as he lowered the bar to his chest. He felt Vera watching the plexus muscles in his face. He didn't trust himself to answer.

She said, "Too bad Dyce had to rush off to Seattle. Me, I hate the city. Wish I didn't have to leave tomorrow."

He lifted, lowered. "Maybe you'll see her."

"Dyce?" Vera snorted. "Seattle only has eighteen million people. We're sure to cross paths."

He tried to imagine eighteen million people. A person could get lost forever in a crowd that large. He watched Vera gather her things to leave, and like a wrong note, he realized how much he would miss her.

She said, "We'll pick up our lessons when I come back, okay?"

"Yeah," he said.

Long after she'd gone, he kept exercising. He used free weights, did a routine on the parallel bars, ran the treadmill. He moved from one set to the next, pausing only to gulp a little water. Sweat drenched his shorts and T-shirt, and he pushed himself harder, faster, farther, building stamina and strength. His breaths came even and slow. He took every muscle group to the burning edge, while his pulse beat to the unstable memory of Dyce.

11

Break off. To move a safe distance away from other divers before opening a parachute.

Rolfe Luce valued the words of wise men, and for years, he'd tried to instill that value in his daughter. His personal favorite was Socrates. "An unexamined life is not worth living." Often, he reminded Vera that the more people hid from themselves, the more they needed to. That truth was the source of his wealth.

Vera always agreed, but her sweet talk never fooled Rolfe. Vera's favorite quote: "What goes around comes around."

Too bad, his daughter had no real grasp of karma. She didn't dare examine her own life, and Rolfe faulted himself for not instructing her better, though he did try. After all, she was part of him.

He was just finishing up a laser skin treatment with Dr. Leo when Vera pinged at his office door. Oh yes, Rolfe used Dr. Leo's services. The obliging little surgeon carried on a wide practice, and Rolfe liked to keep in shape for the triumphant public appearance he would make. Any day now, he would rise up into the spotlight again—as soon as he knew it was safe.

Leo had him lying facedown in his fur-lined hammock, nose buried in the hide of an extinct wildcat, while a sharp laser needle seared precancerous cysts off his back. The fur made him sneeze, and the treatment hurt like the dickens, so when Vera pinged for entrance, he sat up with relief, drew on his robe, and shooed the surgeon away. Leo arched his neck and did a little parting toss of the head, then trotted out through the private back door one microsecond before Vera's boot heels click-clacked through the front.

Palatial, Rolfe's suite. Cavernous. He enjoyed the way his massive arched doorway dwarfed his visitors. Jade-colored stone tiled his walls in a mosaic of sine curves meant to suggest waving fields of grass. Overhead, his rotunda curved up to a faceted central skylight, and behind his hammock, a gilt-framed window opened onto a vista of the Congo Basin wreathed in orange fumes. The live webcam view changed every half hour, bringing him scenes from all over the globe.

In reality, his compound lay deep in subterranean Seattle, and every gadget in the place was designed to sip energy. Rolfe had been a Green from way back. He helped develop Seattle's smart grid. In fact, he wrote the code.

The frosty filtered air in his office carried a scent of germicide, and the tinkle of a dripping stream came from an audio speaker. The six potted orchids clustered under his imitation skylight were dying, though. Every month, he had to replace them with new ones from his private greenhouse.

He didn't glance up when Vera circled behind his hammock. He pretended to ignore her. Nearby on a small table lay a pile of mud-caked fossils needing to be cleaned, so he chose one and began working at it with a little wire brush. Yet he watched every move Vera made through microscopic mote cameras he'd sprayed over his walls.

The motes streamed her image through his ocular, and long practice made him adept at multivisioning. So while he paid tender care to his petrified sea urchin, he also watched his daughter sashay behind his white marble desk and casually tug at each locked drawer. She seemed in a wistful mood. That made him suspicious.

He said, "Do you know why the universe re-creates itself over and over again? From expansion to collapse? Cycle after cycle?"

"No, Daddy."

"It's trying to master its guilty memories by repeating them."

He dropped the brush and chose a metal pick to dig at his fragile fossil. He worked with quiet intensity. Most people considered him charming, but the motes caught Vera wagging her head in mockery. He half expected her to stick out her tongue.

Screw her judgmental soul. He saw her checking out the remnants of his morning meal scattered on a tray. Yes, he'd eaten breakfast. She didn't approve of his fasting. But Rolfe loved being thin. He also enjoyed the psychedelic effects of extreme hunger, but he wasn't fasting today, he had work to do. He polished the fossil with a cloth and said, "You're over budget and behind schedule. Did you set up the promo tour?"

"No, I—"

"Do it."

She tried another drawer in his desk. "Interviews are boring. Jadri's running a teaser campaign with Orr's body dives. Have you seen them? No one else can do what Orr does. He's—"

"Sod your body dives." Rolfe picked up another fossil to clean. "Sometimes, I wonder if you're really my seed."

He watched her bite the side of her hand. At times, he actually enjoyed sparring with Vera. Once, he made her submit legal genetic proof of their kinship. Didn't she hate that! Ah, but there was no denying Vera sprang from his loins. She was too much like him.

He said, "Get your boy talking on the web. Show off his divine anatomy. How hard can that be?"

"Sure," she said. "Easy."

She crouched on the ottoman near his hammock and reached under the furs to massage his toes. She seemed distant and dreamy. What was she after? At bottom, Rolfe felt proud of his princess. She could be brilliant, if only she would let him mold her. Ah, but she was so impatient.

They streamed the usual morning spreadsheets to each other's ocs. Rolfe browsed a few key numbers, then shunted the data to his implanted memory pod. He'd scheduled the webcast of Orr's stratosphere dive for Saturday, March 31. That was less than three weeks away, and he had a hunch Vera was nowhere near ready. She'd been hounding the coders, though, and dogging the suppliers. He knew she worked like a fiend. The people rehabbing her space shuttle had invented new obscenities to describe her zeal.

As for her Mundo Mountain hideaway, Rolfe spied on everyone via the same mote cameras Vera used. Sure, he'd let her shoplift a spray can of motes from his inventory. He knew she would spritz them everywhere around her worksite, and he was an old hand at hijacking mote signals. He enjoyed watching Vera exert herself. She'd ordered her crew to use off-the-shelf parts and skip safety checks. How many hours did her people work without rest? Not as many as she did. Yeah, she was her father's daughter.

What amused Rolfe most was how her pretty flyboy crooned about his girlfriend. Veritable sonnets he gushed. Lovelorn goose, Orrpaaj needed his sweetheart like gravity needed mass. And whether Vera admitted it or not, she was jealous. Rolfe recognized the signs. Jealousy didn't mix well with business.

She rubbed his feet. "Count on me, Dad. I'm going back to Alaska tonight to take care of everything."

"No," he said, picking at his fossil and watching her face through his motes. "I've decided you need to stay here. Your priority is still maintaining my web servers."

"But Dad!"

"A capable exec can run a project from anywhere in web space."

She pooched out her lip as if he'd taken away her favorite toy.

He said, "I'm not your enemy, Vera. I never have been." He turned his fossil to catch the light, and its interior crystals glinted like tiny rock-bound stars. He said, "With so many tragedies in the world, it's easy to miss the approach of your own downfall."

"Everybody falls down sometime, Dad." She twisted one of his toes.

"Stop it."

She pinched his Achilles tendon.

"Ouch! Little hellion." He grinned and threw his fossil at her.

Uh-oh, she didn't dodge quick enough. It grazed her eyebrow. In retaliation, she dumped him out of his hammock, and next thing, they were laughing and tussling on the floor.

12

Bridge. Transitional wire leads connecting skydiver helmet to Sky Wing electronic controls.

O rr felt the force of Vera's deadline. Her time limits drove everyone at Mundo Mountain a little bit berserk. But rain slowed the construction. The feisty warm Pacific kept pummeling the Aleutian Chain with squalls, and raw pumice mud caked to everyone's shoes like cement.

Orr celebrated the weather. Time pressure aside, the crackling air levitated his mood. Leaping from the aircar, he sang through the currents like a high note. He waltzed. He bebopped. He wore out three pairs of boots landing in the abrasive gravel.

Meanwhile, Bettie and Al camped in the lab and worked. When Orr wasn't diving, he loaded their inkjets, boxed up their printouts, microwaved their lunches. He massaged their stiff necks. He hand-walked across the countertop to make them laugh. Also he kept tabs on the experimental beryllium micromesh cooking in the kiln for his new Celestia Sky Wing.

Al's asthma flared up. Late one afternoon, as brown rain hammered the lab windows, a smell of sulfur leaked through the caulk. Orr tromped in, fresh from a dive, and found Al hunched over his desk, buzzing like a band saw.

"You okay? Should I get your inhaler?"

Al couldn't answer. His eyes watered so much, he took off his specs and rubbed his eyelids.

Bettie unhooked his breather and pulled it loose from his cotton-white hair. "Sweetie, your gas mask needs cleaning."

Orr didn't often see Al without his breather. The engineer's face looked like something unhatched. White wrinkled skin. Broken capillaries. Al covered his naked mouth with a handkerchief and said, "Thanks, Bettie."

As she moved past, Al patted her tuchus, and she bumped him with her hip. Orr enjoyed the comfortable way they treated each other. Al had lost weight working such long hours, but if anything, Bettie had gotten plumper. She kept alert by chain-chomping red chocolate bars, and now her lab coat stretched tight across her middle.

Orr rubbed Al's back while Bettie ran the mask under the lab faucet. "Filthy," she said. "This dust is grotesque. This is supposed to be a science lab. I ordered another HEPA filter, but did it come? No. We get rebar, steel trusses, concrete, not one single air filter. I ask you, where are the priorities?"

"No vone antenna?" Orr said.

Bettie blinked, and Al sneezed. Orr saw them trade looks. Outside, lightning flashed.

Al asked in a mild voice, "Did you order a vone antenna?"

Orr slid his thumbs down the engineer's knotted rhomboids. "It's for the dead spot, you know, the satellite anomaly that blocks our vone calls?"

Bettie started to say something, but Al shot her a negative sign. Orr saw it. He flushed dark brown. "There isn't any dead spot, is there?"

Bettie scrubbed the mask with her fingers. "The imperious Ms. Luce censors our web link. We thought you knew."

Al cleared his throat. "She's probably guarding you from the paparazzi. And stalkers."

Orr looked out the window. Lightning flared again, and distant thunder moaned. Paparazzi? He didn't want to think about what that meant. After a moment, he pulled a folded sheet of printout from his back pocket, smoothed it out and laid it on Al's desk.

Al squinted at the pencil drawing. "Is this for the Wing?"

"It's, like, a belly strap." Orr leaned over Al's shoulder, and his blunt fingertip rubbed along the sketch he'd made, as if that might make his scribbles more clear. "I was thinking, if there was, like, an attachment point."

"At the belly?" Al tried to help.

"My belly to the Wing's belly, yeah. More control."

Bettie came over, drying the wet mask with a towel. She gave Orr's drawing a critical browse. "Explain."

"Well, uh." Orr stepped back to get more elbow room. He bent his knees, crunched his ab muscles and curved his torso inward like a bowl. "This is what I do to flare the Wing."

The two engineers studied his posture. Orr held the pose, letting them get a good look. Bettie kneaded her chin. When Al started wheezing, she snugged the damp breather over his face and hooked it.

"You're a peach, Bettie."

"You're welcome, Al."

Orr liked them. In his mind, they were both world-famous geniuses, and why they treated him like an equal was more than he could grasp. But he was getting red in the face from holding the pose. "So if, you know. A belly strap?"

Al took a photo of Orr with his handheld. "I'll load it into the model."

Orr nodded and went back to his isometric yoga behind the kiln. The storm rattled the walls. Dead spot? He didn't want to think about Vera's lie. He knew she was under some complicated work pressure. Who was he to judge Vera Luce? Hadn't she built him this drop zone? Hadn't she introduced him to Bettie and Al? He felt grateful.

But Dyce never lied. Or soft-pedaled. Or sugar-coated. Dyce always said exactly what was what, whether you wanted to hear it or not. Well, Dyce was a better person than he would ever be. He couldn't hold everyone to Dyce's standards.

He remembered how she used to spread his workshirts on the bed and press out the wrinkles with her hands. He could still see her rapid little fingers squaring the seams. She folded his shirts like love notes. The memory made him lose count of his pushups.

Between sets, he drifted over to take a peek at the diagram evolving on Al's screen. There was his belly strap, a thin transparent loop attached inside the cone. He, Orr Sitka, had added his mite to the Celestia Sky Wing.

But he could not forget that Vera lied.

Burble. Turbulence created by an object moving through air.

The satellite dead spot, Vera should've known that zeppelin wouldn't fly. She'd observed Orr's conversation through the mote cameras she'd spray-painted on the lab ceiling. Damn it. He'd caught her in a bald-faced lie. She needed to smooth things.

So she violated her father's direct order and left her post. Such a gamble—she didn't want to think about the consequences if Rolfe found out. But even the great Rolfe Luce couldn't be everywhere at once. She still had means to elude his cameras.

Mid-March, the equinox was near, and dawn's pink fingers were already streaking through the plastic gerbil tubes when she arrived at Mundo Mountain. Surprise, she'd actually missed its wide-open summit. The view didn't scare her as much, and she'd gotten used to the light. She'd even missed the shock of freefall. There was something about the toe-curling thrill of whipping through the sky that a person could get to like.

She found Orr tapped out in Bettie's chair in the lab. He'd been finessing his belly strap design, drawing sketches with a stubby pencil on recycled printout. He awoke when she turned on the desk lamp. His cheek showed a pattern of creases from resting on the countertop.

She stood over him, cradling her helmet in one arm, still pulsating from her rushed flight, still uncertain how to proceed. She touched the small wound over her eye, the love tap from Rolfe. The bruise throbbed viciously, but her cosmetic patch seemed to be holding.

She said, "Suit up. We're going for a ride."

In the aircar, she told Orr how many millions of people had downloaded his body dive holos. She thought this news would please him, and when he didn't answer, she suffered every genus and species of doubt. A distance had opened up between them. Maybe he hated her. Maybe he was planning to quit.

She'd never driven an aircar much, but over the last few weeks, she'd gotten used to the feeling of control. So as soon as they cleared the caldera, she killed the autopilot and steered down a valley with her own hands.

Golden sunrise filtered through the vapor, and the shadow of their car raced over the rocks like a shape-shifting spirit. Abrupt cliffs zoomed by, and grit whirled up from the valley floor. Atmospheric sediment had decorated the rocks in shades of olive, ochre, and clay, and canyon winds had marbled the colors into sand paintings. Orr pressed close to the window glass.

Rounding a bend, they saw sweeps of pink thistle flowing down the mountainside, mixed with purple loosestrife and yellow dandelion. Morning breezes set the flower stalks dancing, and fleets of black wasps spiraled above. But Vera didn't care about the invasive weeds. She wanted to see Orr's face.

They dove lower and dropped into a pocket of clear air trapped below the smog. A temperature inversion must have created it. Vera slammed to a hovering stop and locked the brakes, slinging them both forward in their seatbelts. Orr braced his knees against the dash. He still wouldn't look at her. She absolutely had to make him trust her again.

So she tried the one ploy that always worked. She asked how his skydives were going. He answered readily enough. Using his hands, he described the turbulence of colliding air masses that tumbled him like a windborne seed. His fingers drew invisible lines in the air. The raindrops felt like nails, he said. Sometimes, the rain hit so hard, he thought the drops might pierce his jumpsuit. Frankly, he'd been having a blast.

Vera watched his eyes. She'd tuned her mods up to the irresistible zone, and her smoky sweet perfume filled the car like burning spice. She didn't trust her charms alone. This time, she brought hypnagogic nerve gas.

After a few minutes, Orr got loopy on the gas. His speech slurred, and his expression morphed to a comical joker face. He started telling her some screwy native legend about a bird. She watched his eyes lose focus. Apparently some monster whale was killing all the other whales and stealing the people's oil. The Aleuts were starving. Then this bird showed up. Orr shaped the air with his hands, describing his magical bird, and Vera slid closer.

So this supernatural Thunderbird plunged into the ocean and caught the monster whale in its beak, then soared up to a great height and dropped the beast in the waves. The ocean flung itself over the land and sky in a terrible storm, and all the elements got mixed up together. Orr elaborated this by flapping his elbows. He said Thunderbird was dashed to the ground. He lost all his feathers, and from then on, he had to walk the Earth naked, as a man. But the people were saved.

"Thunderbird, huh?" Vera toyed with the curls hanging in Orr's eyes. "You better not dash my new Celestia Sky Wing to the ground."

When Orr's eyelids drooped, she thought she had him. She wet her lips and subvocalized a command. Instantly, their seats reclined, and they rolled together. She lounged against him. "You smell sexy."

He draped his arm around her and pressed the small of her back. His nose nuzzled her cheek. He fondled her hair. Then he sat up and scooted away. He practically flattened himself against the door handle. This was not the reaction she'd planned.

She sat up, too, trying to play it casual, to cover her embarrassment. "So everything's A-OK for the stratosphere dive? The prototype's good?" She was smiling too hard, forcing herself to pretend he had not just blown her off. But she could feel her mouth quiver, and she knew he noticed.

He spoke soberly. "We'll do our best, Vera."

"Do you have everything you need?" Talk about Pandora's box, she flung it wide.

He said, "The vone's still blocked."

Sparks of pain arced across Vera's forehead. What a fool, to leave herself open like that. She gathered her wiles and mothered inventions. "Yeah, I was wrong about the satellite dead spot. It's really a problem with our firewall."

Her eyes shifted, she couldn't help it. She felt him flaying her bare. This backwoods jock, this stupid boy, she imagined he could see right through her. If he recognized who she really was, how could he ever like her?

She kept fabricating new fibs. "Sorry I misremembered. Sometimes I have lapses. It's a memory disorder. It runs in my family."

"Don't," he said, just that.

He flipped a switch and brought their seats upright. His calmness unnerved her. She had no idea what he was deciding. Was he planning to quit? If he did, her grand game would collapse.

"One day, Orr, you'll skydive higher than anyone. You'll dance with the northern lights. You'll sail the aurora borealis. Picture it, can you? The galaxy in your arms. Infinity for your foot cushion. That's what I want for you." A salty tear dropped down her cheek, a real one. "Stick with me, Orr. You can't conceive how much I need you." Then she hid her face. Telling the truth shamed her worse than lying.

After a while, Orr said, "You hired me to fly your Sky Wing, and that's what I'll do." Then he activated the autopilot, and they zoomed back to the drop zone. Ten minutes later, he got out and waved good-bye.

She owned him still. He loved skydiving more than anything. He wouldn't quit. All her game pieces stood exactly where they needed to be. Didn't they? Vera had not felt so unsure of herself in years. She wiped her wet face and soared back over the Alaskan Gulf to sneak into Seattle.

*Call. Time remaining before skydivers board the
next departing aircraft.*

Orr watched Vera's car disappear in the morning smog. Then he unzipped his raincoat and tromped off through the mountains, letting the wind comb through his clothes. His head felt full of steam. He'd almost lost control with her. Had he made the first move? He must have. What would she want with a bum like him? But nothing happened, nothing that mattered. He raced up a slope, then skidded down the other side, trying to outrun his qualms.

Dyce, his best friend. Sun-washed clouds reflected her saintly face. But the clouds kept shifting, wrinkling, changing, till all he could see was the curve of Vera's throat. He stamped his boots in the grit, wishing these lustful stirrings would leave him. Did Agugux create all females as witches? He scowled up at the eastern sky, almost accusing his maker of treachery.

Okay, so Vera told lies. She meant to protect him. She wanted him to skydive through the northern lights.

But Dyce would never mislead him, not for any reason. She always told him straight out when he was acting a fool.

He lay back in a bed of kudzu and closed his eyes. The golden daylight came filtering down, softened by the haze. It brightened the insides of his eyelids. Wind fluted through rocky crevices, piping chaotic half-notes. And as the sun-warmed current flowed over his outstretched body, he remembered the first time he and Dyce made love.

They weren't lovers when they first left the orphanage. Just two good buddies seeking adventure, fourteen and thirteen years old. Orr rubbed the tops of his thighs, remembering how innocent they'd been. Those first nights on their own, they clung to each other for warmth.

They slept on a rank mattress hidden in Gabe's basement, which even Gabe's mother didn't find for two weeks. Water seeped through the walls, and insects rustled in the corners. Floor joists creaked overhead. Orr didn't like that basement. He could never sleep through the night there, and he hung on to Dyce's promise that it would not cave in.

Gabe snuck them bowls of soup, and they supplemented that diet with scraps begged at the back doors of restaurants. A few times those first two weeks, Orr stole. In the damp basement, they huddled together to fend off each other's nightmares.

Maybe if things had been different, they would have grown up brother and sister. What happened though was the tribal potlatch. Every winter, Unimak Village turned upside down for one week of merrymaking. Adults wore carved animal masks and handed out small gifts. Children ran rampant. Much gin was consumed, and the streets became stages for dancing, singing, and magic shows.

Dyce made Orr a costume out of kelp bags, but she was a nut for cleanliness. Usually, they bathed at a faucet in the public alley, but two nights before the festival began, a cold snap hit, and the faucet froze. Disaster. Dyce couldn't wash her hair.

Never underestimate the wiles of a teenaged girl. She'd made fast friends with Gabe's mother by then, so she asked Mrs. Lermontov to lend them a bucket for a real indoor bath. That day, Orr fixed the exhaust fan at Connie Nujuat's Pub to earn money for a brick of vegetable soap. He knew Dyce enjoyed soap.

When he brought home the surprise, Dyce held the brick to her nose and inhaled its fragrance. The soap smelled like old potatoes, but she pretended to cherish it. And Orr noticed, not for the first time, how her smile creased the corners of her eyes.

"Guess what I found." She sprinted to the back of the basement. Dyce never walked like an ordinary girl.

The basement was large, dark, and cluttered, with many small rooms and lots of junk to trip over. In a musty recess under a dilapidated coal chute, Dyce lit a candle, and what should appear but a galvanized tub. Dented, its drain plugged with glue, three of its legs missing and the forth twisted flat—she had dragged it out of the rubble and scrubbed it clean.

Then, what a production. Up and down the steps they trooped, carrying water from Gabe's mother's tap. Dyce was in her glory. At least ten trips they made to fill that old tub. Cold water, too. They couldn't afford to heat it, but the climbing made them warm.

Dyce lit a dozen stubby votive candles stolen from the Russian church, then stood them in their own wax around the tub. Hot melted paraffin scented the air. Dyce undressed and got in the water first. She shuddered at the chill. Orr had seen her naked lots of times, though not for a while. He noticed how her skin dimpled above her hips. He wet the soap and rubbed sudsy bubbles down her shoulder blades. She'd always been slender, and now she was downright thin. She lifted her arms to be washed.

Orr made a show of lathering the soap, rubbing it between his palms and letting it slip away so he had to hunt through the water to catch it again. But when his sudsy hands glided down Dyce's ribs, he winced. She needed more to eat. He said, "We'll get a hot meal at the potlatch."

She said, "Can we afford it?"

He mentally counted the coins left in his pocket. There would be foot races. Maybe he could win a prize. After he lathered her hair and shaped it into a coil on the top of her head, she dipped under the water and came up with purple lips.

"I'm freeeezing."

He put his hand under the water and made spurts with his fist. "Let's find a place above ground to live."

"With hot running water," she said, "and a kitchen, and a lamp, and a locker to keep our things."

"And things to put in the locker." He laughed.

"One day." Her teeth chattered. "One day, we'll have a real home with lots of family all around us. Our children, Orr."

"We'll get Mr. Bobby to marry us," he said, their oldest joke.

"Wash my front. Quick. I'm getting frostbite." She handed him the soap, cunning girl.

He reached around, and his lathery hands slid over her chest. He heard himself breathing. She was breathing deeper, too. And the water was so cold. She was shaking.

He undressed and slipped into the tub behind her. He clasped her slick wet flanks between his legs, and they played with the soap. When they were both bright red with cold, they splashed out of the tub, wrapped themselves in their one borrowed blanket and tumbled onto the mattress. Two virgins, fourteen and thirteen. Orr thought he heard harps.

The truth was, they created each other. Like binary stars, they circled and warped each other's magnetic fields and traded fire. It wasn't random sex or teenage loneliness or even near starvation that drew them together. It was gravity.

13

Cascade. The point where two parachute lines merge as one.

Twenty-four hours after Vera's attempt to seduce Orr, her intestines were still snarled in a wad. She felt sure he despised her now. Would he quit? She would've rushed back to see him again, but her father kept her tied down in Seattle overseeing his web servers.

Fricking hardware. She kicked one of the rack-mounted units. The old man didn't trust web clouds. Wouldn't store his graphics in the ether like everyone else. Stuck in the past, he wanted his own hard boxes. Solid chunks of plastic and metal that he could touch and take apart and put back together. Vera tugged at a cord. Maybe she should have felt pleased that he trusted her to guard them. But she hated those boxes. She yanked loose a pin connector. Rolfe had just taken away the keys to her aircar. He was sending Mrs. Jadri to Mundo Mountain. Mrs. Jadri!

Vera slammed out of the server vault and fled to her condo next door. "Jadri, my eye!" The publicity chief claimed she needed fresh images for her ad campaign. Vera wanted to eviscerate her. Who knew what the red-lipped vixen might say to rile up her skydiver.

Already, so many images of Orr were circulating on the web, Vera wondered if there was anyone left on the planet who didn't know his face. She could not replace him now if he quit. Late that night, sleepless and overmedicated, she fired up her oc and voned him through the lab's censored web link. She needed to gauge his mood.

His first question when his sleepy face brightened her retina: "Why can I talk to you and not Dyce?"

Yeezes, the boy chapped her patience. Who knew the girlfriend would be such a fixation? She studied his brown face. Keeping him incommunicado at this stage was still crucial to the game, yet somehow she had to mollify him.

She'd memorized the skydive tutorial, so she blitzkrieged him with questions about steering a parachute in strong headwinds. Orr listened in moody silence, but eventually, he answered.

He warned her not to dive in strong headwinds until her skills improved. He explained how wind speeds could vary at different altitudes, so she always needed to check the forecast for "winds aloft" before a jump. One trick he learned from Pete Hogue was how to make a wind-drift indicator. Basically, you weighted a strip of paper at one end with a thickness of Kevlar tape. Then you dropped it out of your aircar to see how fast the wind was blowing. Very high-tech.

As for him, he loved strong headwinds. Heavy weather had been walloping Unimak Island all day, and he reveled in it. Pacific storms were blowing up from the tropics this time of year, bringing thunder and lightning. The air came at you like a fist, he said. It could punch you flat.

"This morning, we had hail. And these amazing straight-line winds."

He told her about steering his Wing through convective gusts that blew ninety kilometers an hour. Better still, there were pockets of hot and cold air scattered through the storm that created random updrafts and downdrafts. Wild flying, he loved it. He'd been hoping for tornadoes.

Vera curled up in her clammy Seattle sheets and watched him frisk his shoulders like he was steering. Good, she thought. He was having too much fun to quit. Whatever he felt about her personally, he wouldn't give up his glorious job. Still, as she listened to him wax lyrical about the Alaskan wind gyre, her feelings seesawed. She'd never felt compunction about conning someone before, never. Could it be she'd developed a scruple?

"No way," she said aloud.

But Jadri, that bitch. Rolfe relied on Jadri to handle his market campaigns, and it was true, Red Lips knew her ad space. Vera sometimes joked that she carried the media rates in the little red bindi dot between her eyes. But Jadri could be way too direct.

Vera squirmed in her sheets. Should she warn Orr about the photo shoot?

No. Better to keep him blissfully uninformed as long as possible. She shifted in her Seattle pillows. Everybody in the fricking world would be at that photo shoot, everyone except the project leader. Damn Rolfe, she needed to be there.

After she said good-bye to Orr, she sat chewing bits of skin off her thumb. As a fallback, she decided to send her own personal agent on site to safeguard her skydiver. She needed someone subtle and perceptive, discreet, utterly reliable. She called Dr. Leo.

She found him lounging in bed with three friends, watching a rugby game on the web. He'd swathed himself in a glittery purple head scarf, gold hoop earrings, and a tangerine sari. She said, "I'll buy you a kilo of figs if you'll take care of a little matter."

Ripe greenhouse figs were Leo's favorite treat. "Whom do I kill?"

"Rescue, darling, not murder." She blew him a kiss. "Have you ever been to Alaska?"

14

Ceiling. Distance above ground level to lowest cloud layer.

O rr watched Dr. Leo wander around the hangar, nosing into things. Orr usually liked people, but Dr. Leo gave him the jeebies. Under the white surgeon's coat, Leo wore a hot pink blouse and a pair of billowing puce pantaloons, but Orr barely noticed his clothes. It was more Leo's creepy way of slinking behind people, listening in on conversations. He picked up a pair of Orr's hand weights and sniffed them—what was that about? He seemed especially interested in the construction robots. Orr overheard him asking the foreman how much each one cost.

Orr liked Mrs. Jadri much better, at least at first. The pretty young Pakistani wore ruby red silk, and she hurried around calling out orders in a lilting soprano. But it was hard for Orr to follow her quick movements. A couple of makeup artists were poking little brushes at his eyes.

Mrs. Jadri's people had invaded Mundo Mountain at daybreak. They were throwing up scaffolding, cueing microphones, and mounting lights. They yelled at the construction crew to move toolboxes out of the way. Meanwhile, the makeup artists argued about Orr's hair. They crimped his locks with a curling iron, then spritzed him with cloudbursts of hair spray because Mrs. Jadri vetoed the wig. She preferred a rowdy "all-natural" look.

The Gravity Pilot costume fit Orr like a coat of paint. There was no shirt, only skintight pants that rippled from lavender to lime green. Quucloth, the costumer told him. The colors and patterns were programmable.

The construction crew stood around wisecracking, and Orr felt trickles of sweat running down his bare chest. He felt like a mutant on display.

After he'd been standing on the improvised stage wearing almost nothing for what seemed like an hour, Dr. Leo and Mrs. Jadri crouched before him to discuss the shape of his knee. Mrs. Jadri poked his kneecap. "When I'm done, these legs will be more famous than Krishna."

Leo picked up a staple gun and pulled the quu-cloth tight around Orr's upper thigh. "Yum, what a quad."

Mrs. Jadri circled, evaluating the effect. Then she jerked the fabric from Leo's fingers and stretched it tighter. "Do it this way. I want to see every muscle."

Leo cocked his staple gun. "Get outta my face, candy lips."

She said, "Bite me, Leoretta."

It seemed Dr. Leo and Mrs. Jadri had met before.

Caught in the key light, Orr closed down his feelings and held his body still. From inside his quiet shell, he peered out at the invaders. He didn't want his quadriceps to be more famous than Krishna. Mrs. Jadri kept checking the wall clock while Leo stapled the cloth. Orr wanted to shove Leo's hands off his leg. He wanted to fly straight up through the roof and disappear. He endured the ordeal, though, because Mrs. Jadri said his contract required it.

Sometimes, but not often, Orr wondered when the authorities had stopped letting workers read their own contracts. Was it after the weather changed? After the sunshine states turned to desert? After the United States government defaulted on its bonds?

He blinked at the spotlights and wondered who the authorities were. He had a vague idea how his tribal council elected their chief. He knew cities had sheriffs and startups had CEOs. The news had its editors. The web had its masters. Far across the continent, there were delegates sitting on a hill. So which ones were the authorities?

Dyce told him about a city in Australia that dwarfed Seattle. A clean progressive city open to the sky, with universities and symphony orchestras and city parks. Melbourne, it was called, a tribal place governed by the elders of the Kulin Nation. She told him scientists in that city had divided and recombined the smallest particles of reality to telegraph instant messages across the multiverse. And ordinary people still controlled their own contracts. But Orr half suspected she was making it up.

"Quick now. The boots." Mrs. Jadri chewed her fingernail and appraised Orr's naked chest. "She'll be here in three minutes."

"Jadri, dear, you'll tear yourself a new aneurism." Leo ripped open a box and drew out a pair of shiny silver boots with little bird wings attached at the ankles. "Aren't these clever. Can I have these when you're done?"

Orr sat down on the stage to put the boots on. They fit tight, and without socks, they wouldn't slide over his bare skin. The animatronic wings flapped and fluttered. He tugged with both hands. Then Leo startled him by dropping a heavy silver necklace over his head. He glanced down at his chest and touched the medallion. It was made of dark metal, with some kind of carving at the center.

Mrs. Jadri's black eyebrows pinched together. "Idiot. You forgot to oil him."

"My favorite part." Leo knelt and lifted the medallion so he could slather Orr's chest and shoulders with ointment. When he leered and made licking motions with his tongue, Orr flushed dark brown.

"Stand up. Straighten your shoulders. Face me." Mrs. Jadri tousled his hair with her fingers and teased a wavy mass down over his forehead. She twisted the ends into coils. Then she pursed her bright carmine lips. "Good. Now, left foot back. Right forward. Turn."

Orr obeyed, and Mrs. Jadri backed away, scrutinizing him. Her close attention almost made him trip. The light level shifted as technicians adjusted settings, and the air smelled scorched.

"Roll cameras," she said.

Thirty-two self-propelled holocams moved in and hovered. Each one was a nickel-plated sphere the size of a golf ball, with propeller fins buzzing too fast to see. They intruded way too close into Orr's personal space. They zipped under his arms and circled his chin. They ran rings around his legs. Their synchronized motors whirred, and Orr felt ambushed. He saw the construction crew poking each other and pointing at his winged boots. He studied the hangar ceiling.

"Move, boy." Mrs. Jadri snapped her fingers. Somewhere in the audience, Leo made a joke, and everyone tittered.

Mortified, Orr began to go through the complex dance Mrs. Jadri's choreographer had taught him that morning. A lot of the moves were based on tai chi chuan, which Orr already knew. He turned from one pose into the next, trying to ignore Dr. Leo's razzing. But he felt exposed, and the cameras distracted him. His hair itched.

"This is silly," he muttered, too low for anyone to hear.

He was balancing on one foot, slowly stretching his other foot toward the ceiling, when everyone in the hangar fell silent. He turned and saw a shimmering apparition. It was Vera.

People hurried out of the way as Vera's holograph glided toward the stage. Her projected signal ricocheted through every pod, pan, and oc in the hangar, also the teleprompter and the sound engineer's mixing board, but Orr didn't care how the technology worked. Her beauty stunned him. Her hair radiated dark fire, and her diamond-studded white tunic splashed around her knees. Subtle reverberations enriched her voice.

"Are we on schedule?"

Jadri clenched her hands behind her back. "How can you doubt it? We're running twenty minutes ahead."

"And I helped," Leo said, yawning.

Vera clicked her teeth. Orr saw her emerald eyes twinkle as she appraised his costume. She stepped onto the stage and leaned to examine his medallion. When her holographic shoulder grazed his chest, he felt a slight shock. She spoke in an intimate whisper. "You hate this, I know. Just remember, you'll be back up in the sky soon."

Orr swallowed and nodded.

"Keep your focus." Her phantom knuckles passed over his real ones. "In a few hours, this'll be over."

Then she called Dr. Leo and Mrs. Jadri into her private cube. When they emerged a few minutes later, the publicity chief kept her eyes down. In a subdued voice, Jadri ordered everyone out of the hangar except the essential staff. Then she threatened to fire anyone who harassed the Gravity Pilot. Leo curled up in the director's chair, while holographic Vera stood in the background, observing.

The session lasted all day, into the night, with only a couple of quick breaks for food and water. Vera glimmered in the shadows like a guardian angel, or maybe a gargoyle, so no one dared crack another joke about Orr's costume. Nevertheless, Orr wanted to flee.

But he couldn't run away. He had no transit pass, no money, no means of escape. More, he'd been skydiving every single day, amusing himself on company time, and he felt indebted. He had no gauge to measure the scope of his obligation. Then, too, there was his ego. Twenty-two years old, he wasn't about to turn tail because a few strangers stared at him.

By midnight, sweat ran in rivulets down his ribs and soaked his waistband. He felt sure they'd have to cut the tight boots off his feet. The worst part came when he had to say his line. One short sentence, the Gravity Pilot advertising slogan. He tried to inflect the words a dozen different ways, but nothing satisfied Mrs. Jadri.

"You're mumbling." She pressed her fingers against her temples. "This is our trademark line. It has to be stellar."

He said, "The words don't make sense."

"Ignoramus. Do it again."

He felt throttled. He repeated the line, straining for volume if not feeling. "Come chase the perfect sky with me."

Jadri smacked her forehead with the heel of her hand. "Worse and worse. My coffee machine could do better."

"Time's up, Jadri."

Everybody jumped at the sound of Vera's amplified voice—everyone except Leo, who'd fallen asleep in his chair. Vera's deep bell tones echoed through the hangar. "Pack your cameras. The session's done."

Orr sat down on the floor and closed his eyes like a man released from torture. Then he felt a sharp tingle in his arm, like electric current. He glanced up and saw Vera's holographic fingers stroking his biceps. Angelic rays streamed from her face. She was just about to speak when something like a shadow whisked across her glowing field and erased her.

15

*Cell. Open fabric rib in a parachute pressurized by
air rushing through.*

R olfe Luce. Renowned inventor, wealthy entrepreneur, notorious
con artist. Who among us is entitled to weigh the sediments of his
heart? It was Rolfe who phuxed Vera's holographic signal, but he
had his reasons.

Rolfe was born in 1981, the same year the first crude graphics lit up the
early Internet. That coincidence formed him. A bright lonely little kid, he wor-
shiped the visual metaphors that exploded from his computer screen. He dwelt
in a world of combat troopers and battle tanks, where victories were easy to
measure. It was a saner world in every way than his two upper-class homes in
suburban Chicago.

His divorced parents, both surgeons, shuttled him back and forth like a
sack of laundry. They were too absorbed in their own busy lives to notice
how he spent his time. As long as he made decent grades, they let him play
all the computer games he wanted, so his dual bedrooms accumulated head-
sets, earbuds, joysticks, and wireless consoles.

When he began to gain serious weight, his chagrined parents argued over
remedies, but not until morbid obesity threatened his health did they take
action. Naturally, they wanted a perfect son. So his father prescribed diet
drugs and a stomach staple, and his mother disciplined him with a bamboo
cane. Rolfe didn't understand. He was only a boy. In the seventh grade, he

was arrested for scorching a classmate's hair with homemade napalm, so they shipped him off to military school.

Cloistered through the night in his dorm room, buzzing on Ritalin and Phentermine, he opened accounts in social nets and virtual worlds, impersonated heroes and government agents, lost his virginity online. He stole media clips from random web sites, then spliced and posted his own grisly dramas. His plots ranged from sleazy to sophomoric, but his graphic effects improved with practice.

Needing a more visceral interface, he skipped college and taught himself advanced programming skills. While other kids learned history and law, he built his first massively multiplayer online role-play game. Death Count. He made so much money from that game, he sent both his parents complimentary Kevorkian kits.

Glorious, those years. Live interviews. Celebrity parties. The media couldn't get enough of him. His youth ended long before he was finished being young. Now, eighty-seven years old, patched and repaired with cloned organs, he slumped in his leather chair, spritzed his desk with germicide, and browsed his balance sheet.

Vera was clamoring for attention as usual. She was down in his server vault, going fissile. "Unfair," her constant catchword. "You had no right to black out my holograph!" Sometimes Rolfe wanted to pinch the damned ocular right out of his eye.

Of course Vera would rather waltz off to Alaska and carouse with her pet athlete. But Rolfe needed her close beside him. They had serious legal issues. They'd aired Orr's mesosphere dive in a promo ad, and the XS Channel sued for copyright breach.

Worse, his forest needed moss and lichen, and he was getting itchy for cash. One solid season hit would put him in the clear, and it was high time to pump up the Gravity Pilot crave.

"Vera, chill," he said. "We've scheduled a public appearance for tomorrow night."

She screeched through his oc, "Impossible. The stratosphere dive is one week away."

"Right, it's perfect timing."

"Orr needs to train!" she yelled.

He watched her career through his fragile web servers. She took her boot to one of his AC units. She blitzed his oc with digital flames till he thought his eyeball might explode. But he'd witnessed Vera's tantrums before.

He spoke to her with calm gravity. "Vera, use your brain. Our boy needs live face time on the web. We'll parade him through some local Seattle venue to captivate the paparazzi. I know my business. Trust me, I've done this before."

"Go get your own face time," she snarled. "No, you're too afraid of catching herpes."

Rolfe watched her seize one of the server cords like she might yank the plug. "Enough," he said. "I've assigned Mrs. Jadri to handle logistics."

Rolfe waited patiently. After a moment, Vera wiped her sullen cheeks and yielded, just as he knew she would. She was no rebel. She was his own crown princess.

"That's right, listen to your old man. I want to see you do well, kid." He sent her a stream of loving emoticons and said, "Remember, we're on the same side. We have to stick together."

He'd chosen Klub Kamikaze for the Gravity Pilot debut, and Vera couldn't object. What she did, though, she connived to stage the public appearance without disturbing her precious skydiver. Rolfe saw it all through his oc, and he was furious.

First, he watched her pilfer some of his advertising graphics and cobble together a clumsy sim. Bad anime. She lacked his artistic gift. After that, she made a secret visit to Klub Kamikaze to lay groundwork. Oh, Vera had a passion for groundwork. Rolfe followed her plot with growing rage, and also curiosity.

Vera's antics fascinated him in a depraved sort of way. Always this game, tit for tat. He tried to rise above her childish feud, but she drew him in. When the evening arrived, she sealed herself into a binding white quu-suit. It fit so tight, she had to lie flat on the floor to zip up. Through his motes, he watched her prance around in her bedroom, checking herself in the mirror.

Next, she sat down and slathered on her face paint. Lately, she hadn't slept much. He spotted tiny grooves around her eyes and mouth. Her mirror kept fogging, and the dampness made her hair frizz. Heavy pumps were clattering so loud through her walls, he had to turn up his volume to hear her humming. She was twisting her hair into a clip when he tiptoed into her room.

Her condo felt unclean. She never took time to sweep for microbes. He always had to wear a full antiviral suit when he came here in the flesh. Quietly, he stepped up and kissed the back of her neck. Her face paint smelled like camphor. She smiled at his reverse image in the mirror, and when he massaged her shoulders, she wriggled luxuriously under his touch.

She said, "Mmm, that feels good."

Trickster. Let her play her spiteful game. He examined the objects lying on her bed. Half a dozen medallions were arranged in a row. They appeared to be dark polished metal, each about the size of a scrip coin. The carvings showed a black Cyto sun, their company logo.

He said, "This is our new jewelry?"

Vera did up her hair. " 'Holy Lodestones.' Orr found them at the roof of the world when he dove through the divine flame of a sacred Himalayan volcano."

Rolfe knew the ad copy as well as she did. He said, "Himalayan volcanoes went extinct ages ago, but no one reads geography. Travel is dead. We're raising a generation of slugs."

"Exactly." Vera tugged on her glitter-white spandex hood, then teased out a few red curls.

He grasped her chin and turned her head this way and that, wrinkling his nose. "Beauty's a precarious thing, Vera. A simple change of light can wilt it."

She jerked away. "Orr's body dives are selling like opium. Did you see the numbers?"

"Chump change." Rolfe pinched a rhinestone off her hood and rolled it between his fingers. Then he tossed it aside. "Mrs. Jadri needs to buy more ad space. I'm reallocating half your budget to marketing."

He watched her mouth open and shut. Ha, he'd scored his little revenge. He glimpsed himself in her mirror. The antiviral suit coated his skin like spray-on plastic. It even coated his wig. He liked wigs. They were easy to clean, and when they lost their perfection, you ditched them.

He said, "Aren't you going to ask about my news?"

But he didn't wait for Vera to ask. He flicked his handheld pan, and a three-dimensional model blossomed in the air. It was his magnum opus, the great work of his life, the botanical habitat he'd built in the North Cascades. The sight of that lush green foliage warmed his corpuscles.

After decades of struggle and sacrifice, his dream would soon come to fruition. He flared the pan around Vera's room so she could admire his handiwork. "It's opening ahead of schedule. How about that?"

He zoomed in on a little blue-feathered chanteuse with a bit of white fluff for a chest. The mountain bluebird, recloned from preserved DNA. So fragile and light, so full of grace, its sweet ballad enchanted him. Only in his safe, hermetically enclosed habitat might such a songbird thrive.

When he caught Vera turning up her nose, he switched off his pan.

She shifted sideways in her chair. "You waste too much goddamn money on those vermin."

"Vermin, my birds? Have you never understood me?"

"What good are they? Useless." She painted her eyelashes.

In a fit of pique, Rolfe raked every object off her dressing table onto the floor. He hated losing his temper, but she pushed him. He saw her staring down at the mess. All her exotic shadows and highlights, her tiny scissors and blades, smashed in a welter of reds and flesh tones on the carpet. He gripped the back of her chair. "Where's my season hit?"

"You'll have it." She produced something like a laugh. "Trust me."

Watching her false expression in the mirror, Rolfe felt old. Sometimes, this combat exhausted him. He drew his thumbnail along her eyebrow and down the curve of her cheek. Very tenderly, he tugged her mouth open and touched the wetness inside.

"Sweet Vera, this is your chance. Don't blow it."

16

Center point. Point at mid-torso around which a skydiver centers
his or her body positions.

Klub Kamikaze was already blaring three different styles of cacoph-
onous music when Vera arrived. She entered through the roof of an
abandoned air-exchange tank buried under Seattle. The rusty old
tank ran twenty meters deep, and cave crickets swarmed under its ceiling.
The club owners had added little more than ladders, power cables, Porta-
Johns, and FM projectors.

FM, "full immersive," the vibrant technology of sims. Those projectors
could transform the tank into a fantasyland of sight, sound, touch, taste, and
smell. "A group sim room," Vera mused. "I want one."

Vera knew the Klub inside-out. She'd stopped by earlier that day to rig her
magic show. Now she hung on to the ladder and gazed down at the clientele
filling the bottom of the tank. The venue attracted party-hardy juveniles who
found web social nets too lightweight for the full display of their egos. Under
the purple blacklights, their faces bobbed like a stew of goblins. She covered
her nose as she descended the ladder. The air stank of armpits. Someone was
reading text poetry through a loudspeaker.

Over her shoulder, she carried a heavy bag of free giveaway medallions.
She shifted the bag to her other arm and scanned the crowd. The UV lamps
gave off eerie lumens, and youngsters gyrated on the dance floor. Their shadows moved up the walls like black flames. A few kids sported "eyelights," the

cut-rate contact lenses that flashed primary colors. Most wore cheap Tyvek unisuits, and the youngest kids huddled together trading homemade armbands braided from product packaging.

Vera looked on, appalled. Jadri picked these raggedy kids as their target demographic? No way could these urchins pay the magnitude of fees her company needed to break even. But Jadri convinced Rolfe to hook customers early and lock in their brand loyalty at a formative age. Later, when their earnings increased, she said they would stay loyal. Vera scrutinized the crowd and wondered.

If it weren't for Rolfe's damned botanical habitat, she wouldn't have to be in this smelly tank. She pictured his cloned birds. Feathered vampires, that's what they were, sucking her company's lifeblood. Of course Rolfe's habitat was running ahead of schedule. He funded his own manias to the max. No shoestring budgets for him. He was so hooked on green scenery, he actually dreamed he could turn back time. Vera's nostrils fluttered. Doddering old bugger, stuck in the past. Elderly people never could accept change.

Something was happening near the center of the tank, and the kids closest to the action began yelling and jumping. Their motion spread through the crowd like a wave. Vera slung her heavy bag and forced her way through the wriggling bodies. When she asked what was happening, someone beamed her the code for the FM simulation, so naturally, she connected.

Voila. The real Klub Kamikaze materialized around her—not the slummy old air tank but a sumptuous revolving penthouse overlooking Puget Sound. She'd landed in the fricking Space Needle. What's more, the kids wore glamorous quu-suits and jewelry, and they were all as sexy as hell.

On stage, a band keyed a style of music that was new to Vera. The vibrating tune set her teeth on edge, but it made the crowd go ecstatic, so she recorded it for possible later use. More kids were arriving by the minute. A lovely young boy leaped onto the stage and clapped his hands over his head to start a "body rhyme." She'd seen these performance poems on the web. The boy struck an incredibly contorted pose and held it, waiting for someone to accept his challenge.

Soon, a beautiful girl danced up beside him and dropped to one knee. She made impromptu cutting gestures with her left hand. Then four more kids clustered around the stage, bending and posturing. One girl balanced in a handstand. Their interlaced figures created spatial poetry—"body rhymes."

When a score of kids joined the rhyme, Vera decided to act before the poetry spread too far. She whispered a string of voice commands, and deafening feedback squealed through the musician's instruments. The melody died, and the confused performers stopped playing. The poem unwound.

In the silence that followed, a huge apparition shot up and hovered over the crowd. It was the Gravity Pilot, complete with lavender pants and winged silver boots, ten times life size. His oiled chest shone like brass, and his curly black hair glistened. Talk about eye sweets, around his head glowed a circlet of flashing stars, and his Cyto medallion shot prismatic sparkles. He extended one finger, and spicy incense filled the Space Needle.

In the real tank, Vera's hypnagogic nerve gas spewed from the ceiling, drugging the kids. The gas jets had been easy to rig. The tank was practically a killing jar. As her nerve gas diffused through the crowd, most of the kids sank down to the floor and got quiet. She clipped a small rebreather into her nostrils, though in the Space Needle, it didn't show.

Stoned on gas, the kids viewed the giant figure in awe. Most of them recorded the event live and voned it to friends. Good, the more recordings the better. Vera beamed a free Cyto coupon to every active vone.

Orr's computer-gen voice ricocheted through the tank like a thousand drums playing out of time. The sound touched the kids at a subliminal level. They felt his words humming through their marrow, and the nerve gas heightened their receptivity.

"Come chase the perfect sky with me in Cyto Cyto Cyto."

The juves whispered, "Cyto?"

The phantom hissed the refrain, "Cyto Cyto Cyto."

Everyone joined the mesmerizing chant. Their voices set up a rhythmic oscillation that reinforced the hypnotic effect. Yeah, Vera used every advertising trick in her bag.

Of course, her hypnagogic spell didn't affect everyone with the same intensity. Some people didn't respond to the gas. Still, the kids were dazzled, and well over half fell into a shallow trance. Even Vera, who stood behind the proverbial curtain working the levers, even she found it tough to resist the pull.

The show lasted ten minutes. Then the gas dissipated, the vision vanished, and the Space Needle sim shut down. Everyone dropped back into the drab old air tank. As the kids shook off the last traces of inebriation, Vera hopped up onto a scaffold and switched on a laser beam. Every face turned toward the light.

Vera amped up her voice. "I found these holy lodestones, exactly like the one worn by the Gravity Pilot himself. These medallions concentrate the celestial forces."

She tossed a medallion high into the air, and its glossy surface tumbled through her laser beam, arcing over the crowd. A melee erupted as scores of kids reached to catch it. She flung the rest like piñata prizes.

The kids stampeded. Everyone wanted a medallion. Vera dropped to the floor and curled in a tight ball to protect her head and limbs. Juves shoved each other and argued over the treasures. Somebody kicked her. When fights broke out, she crawled toward the ladder. "The things I do for Cyto," she muttered. "Daddy, do you see me now?"

Chute assis. Freefalling in a seated position.

Vera's daddy did see. And Vera quickly discovered he was not pleased. She was still trudging home from the Klub when he called her into a mandatory meeting. She entered Cyto's private web zone with her sensors flipped to orange alert. Mrs. Jadri was already there.

Blast the woman! Jadri wore a cross-your-heart red wrapper with a deep V gaping down her midline, and her breasts poked up like baked muffins. The bindi dot between her eyebrows blazed, and it took her all of one minute to unsheathe her talons.

"Tonight's comedy was a cheap trick, Vera. Your protégé has still not made a single live appearance. I've had to fabricate everything out of thin air."

Vera glued on her innocence. "You're so good at that."

"Yes, but the news flacks don't like holographs. They want *live* interviews. And what you did tonight has not helped one bit."

When Rolfe logged into the conference, Jadri gave him a flirty sweep of her eyelashes, which Vera did not fail to notice. The woman kept flapping her scarlet lips. "Sports reporters need to press flesh, Vera. And you know, with the money we've sunk, we can't afford to miff the media."

Jadri waxed effulgent about target audiences, cross-market tie-ins, and worldwide gross rating points, all the while flipping gant charts through their shared view, showing off her metrics. In real life, Vera was still walking through the tunnels of Seattle toward her condo. It must have been around 3:00 A.M. Municipal lights had minimized, and the day's musk of air freshener hung like a dying song. Not many people were out. And though Vera's boots made loud echoes, the stone tiles gave her no sense of stability.

Jadri kept boasting that her own promotional brilliance had drummed up the Gravity Pilot crave. Her ads had increased Cyto blink-throughs by 74 percent—she had a slew of evidence to prove it. She flaunted her spreadsheets. Fat cow, she was half Vera's age.

Rolfe said, "Show me results, Vera. I want people foaming at the mouth for the Gravity Pilot. I want a promo tour."

"No problem. He dives the stratosphere this Saturday. How about next week?" Vera was all smiles.

"That's too late." Jadri flounced her arms over the virtual conference table and showed Vera her shoulder. "She has not been cooperative, Rolfe. Since the photo shoot, she hasn't once let me speak to the skydiver in person."

Vera opened her hands. "You can see him anytime. Let's go right now."

Jadri scrunched up her roly-poly cheeks. "Humph. Maybe I will."

Rolfe groaned. "I'm dealing with preschoolers. Are we done?"

Jadri pawed Rolfe's arm, and Vera realized they were sitting side by side in the same room. Two against one, they were teaming up on her.

Jadri said, "Let's review the arrangements, Rolfe, shall we?"

Without a by-your-leave, Jadri had already scheduled Orr's worldwide promo tour for that very Wednesday—three days before his stratosphere dive. She'd booked him in all the northern capitals: Sapporo, Changchun, St. Petersburg, Stockholm, Reykjavik, Quebec. Obviously, the tour would occur in web space. With so many competing carbon tariffs, only the super-rich could afford world travel. Vera would've argued for a digital Orr look-alike, but it was true, savvy reporters would spot the fake, even on the web.

Vera lowered her eyes. "So Dad, will you join the tour, too? You're always threatening to come out of hiding."

Jadri said, "Oh yes, Rolfe, would you? The media would eat you with a spoon."

Rolfe fluttered and basked. "Someday," he said, "when the time is right." He patted Jadri's hand, and Vera noted how they rubbed shoulders and nudged knees. Bile lurched up her esophagus.

Jadri wanted Orr to do the interviews in a professional FM studio in Seattle. But no way would Vera let Red Lips snatch her skydiver. "Mundo Mountain has a sim room," she invented, "with top-of-the-line FM projectors. You can stage the tour there."

Rolfe said, "I didn't approve any sim room."

But at the same time, Jadri materialized a folder. "Here's his speech. I wrote it myself."

Vera looked over Jadri's libretto. Well, the trashy tart did know marketing. She'd written a heroic homily, dripping with romance, passion, and subtle product endorsements, although Vera spotted Rolfe's heavy edits.

Jadri rubbed noses with the old man. "Remind her about the sneak preview."

Rolfe's cheeks creased like old leather, and Vera imagined she could hear his skin crackle. "Right," he said. "We want to air a sneak preview of our new sim on April 1, just before the season launch."

Orr's dive was scheduled for March 31, and Rolfe expected a fully produced sneak preview the very next day? Vera improvised, "That's Fools' Day. Bad luck. We'll jinx the launch."

"What crap." Rolfe winked at Jadri. "Don't play your games now, princess. We all depend on the success of this project. Remember, we rise or sink together."

"We?" Vera felt so incensed, her face mods shifted. "Sorry, I'm not up for a threesome tonight."

Rolfe sighed. "You wear me out." Then he tickled Jadri under the chin. "I'm afraid we had to cancel your space shuttle. It's just too expensive right now. You can rent a jumpjet for a day."

In the dark Seattle street, Vera smacked into a lamppost. The bump barely registered, though. In web space, her father's green eyes nailed her.

"I put my faith in you, Vera. Show me the payback."

Vera punched the virtual kill switch and terminated the conference. She wanted to yank the lamppost up by its roots, but there was no time. Not enough fricking time. So she called Dr. Leo.

"Do you know where I can get some FM projectors fast? I have to build a sim room."

———

Cinch. Device used to tighten a parachute harness.

That same night, in another chamber deep under Seattle, Dyce Iakai opened her eyes. She'd fallen asleep at her desk in the new library. She sat up and rubbed her cheek. Her narrow cube smelled musty, and the partitions showed water stains. Eighty-odd cubicles divided her department into a grid. She coughed quietly into her sleeve.

Her workscreen still glowed with marbled tints and shades, calling her back. She'd been editing the music archive. Only . . . no, that wasn't right. She'd been cruising a wikiverse called Cyto. It had really cool simulator apps, and she'd been using them to reenact scenes with Orr. Their awful parting in Unimak, she'd revised it, made everything come out happier. Except the new draft felt too good to be true.

When she stood to stretch, backache made her whimper. She'd been sitting too long. She needed to run and jump, get her circulation going. But there was no space in her cube for calisthenics, and this was not the hour for a break. She didn't dare leave her post. The supervisor might be watching. This job was not what she'd expected.

She glanced across the tops of the nearby cubes, where her fellow librarians lay sprawled, draped or fetally curled in their seats. A few of them snored. One or two were awake, though. She noticed tiny quivers in their limbs, raised fingers, mumbled words. In the Cyto wikiverse, they might be battling dragons.

She glanced at the music archive on her workscreen. Figaro's marriage, she'd been trying to decide where to file it. The old-fashioned lyrics didn't make sense, and the characters were not believable. Was it tragedy? Farce? Her right eye felt inflamed. She'd run out of cleaning fluid for her oc, and . . . what kind of half-life had she fallen into? She needed relief. Maybe if she dropped back into Cyto for just a minute . . .

"No. Think." She scratched her greasy hair.

Lately, she'd been riding Orr's skydive sims, and the beauty of his blue world surprised her. The simple clarity of the wind, the liberty of sun-warmed air. She understood his obsession now. Why had she ragged him so hard? Cowardice, that was it. She'd been afraid of losing him.

Now she stretched her arms and knocked her hands against the damp stone ceiling of the library. Somewhere, hundreds of meters above, the sun might be shining. Maybe the moon. Orr showed her the stars once. Hydra. Draco. She could re-create them in Cyto. All she had to do was . . .

"No," she said aloud.

A white millipede inched across her desk. Fat and sluggish, its legs moved like fringe. She watched it stop to lick a drift of dust collecting under her workscreen. The creature was seeking its daily food, dead human skin cells.

The exit door was two steps away. She limped toward it and shook the lever. Pointless. Her department would be time-locked till the next break. She'd been told their project was highly sensitive, and the security was for her own protection. She returned to her cube, sat down in the horrible chair and tried to vone Orr. She knew the call wouldn't go through. It was just a game she played with herself.

While she watched the white worm feed, she sent texts to Gabe and Kriis. She even streamed a note to Miss Tompkin, but her messages no longer escaped Cyto's firewall. They ricocheted in her skull like tiny screams.

Inside the wikiverse, she'd re-created Gabe and Kriis and Miss Tompkin. She'd made other people as well. A whole family of boys and girls with curly black hair and blue-gray eyes. She could go there now and play with her imaginary children. They would welcome and soothe her with sweet loving kindness. Orr would be there, too. In her oc, the Cyto icon beckoned—a shining black sun.

"Wait," she told herself.

She blinked her right eye and made a snapshot of the time-lock on the department door. Then she streamed it into the local area network seeking guidance on picking the lock. A few coworkers fired back instructions, but she had no cyber tension tools, no gamer skeleton keys, not even a magic rune. Nothing but . . . her stylus.

She scanned the nearby cubes. No one paid attention. She knelt at the door and poked at the timer. Scratch, scratch. The tip of her stylus etched the yellow metal. Cheap obsolete tech, this mechanical timer. Her efforts had no effect, though, and her awful headache blurred her vision.

"Do you need assistance?"

She turned and saw her supervisor glaring from her workscreen. The artificial brain manifested as a beautiful young boy with dappled pink skin and tiger eyes. Its expression never varied.

Dyce got to her feet. Her head felt on fire. "I don't feel well. I need a doctor."

"At your next break, you can visit the health clinic."

"Yes, fine." There was no arguing with the AI.

She kicked at her chair. Implement of torture. The millipede kept licking up dust, and her thoughts strayed to Cyto Cyto Cyto . . .

Already the black sun was swelling in her oc. She imagined sailing through the clouds, hand in hand with Orr. All she needed was to speak her password. Those two syllables would fling open the gates of paradise. Blessed reunion with her true love. Release from all sorrow. Sweet inebriation. She could taste the password on her tongue.

She pressed her lips tight. "Stay alert," she said aloud. She rolled her shoulders and slung her hands. She kicked her heels against the chair. Break time had to be soon.

When the door opens, you'll run.

Her password throbbed on her lips. She always felt free in Cyto. Smart and powerful in Cyto. Orr would enfold her in his wide beating wings and . . .

"Help," she whimpered.

The supervisor reappeared, and his feline eyes goaded her. "Your systems are functional. What help do you require?"

"Can I get a lumbar cushion?"

"Request noted." The screen blanked out.

She rubbed her aching tear duct. She needed to forget that password. She needed to seal it out of her mind. How could she trick her own memory? Think of something else. Anything.

The black sun swelled to fill her cube. It darkened the top of her desk. Its shade cooled her skin, and its sibilant call seemed to whisper through her soul.

"Shut," she cried.

The logo minimized to a black dot in her oc. She arched her snapping spine. Every three hours, a break. One hundred and eighty minutes, don't fall asleep, wait for the door to open.

She picked up the worm and set it on the floor. Then she tried to focus on Mozart's opera, but the music skipped around, mocking her. Once upon a time, she felt proud of her work in this library. No, that was some other library. All she ever wanted was to follow the rules, respect authority, work hard, be useful.

A whiff of cave mildew drifted through her department, and the living scent brought back scenes of home. She imagined strolling through Unimak Village, meeting friends at Connie's Pub, tossing a Frisbee with Gabe's little sons, and sharing a bag of deep-fried kelp with the one person in the world who made her whole . . .

"Lagi," she whispered.

Her password.

The bright mouth of paradise snapped open and sucked her in.

17

Closing loop. Device that holds parachute container flaps closed.

The evening before the promo tour, Orr saw an aircar land at Mundo Mountain. Mrs. Jadri had come for dress rehearsal. Through the lab window, he watched with sinking spirits as she directed the construction workers to unload her stage lights. He wasn't surprised to see Dr. Leo there as well, pestering the crew with questions and pickpocketing small tools. Orr hated this promo tour. He hid in the lab with Bettie and Al till Mrs. Jadri came and dragged him out.

Lights, holocams, electronic control boards, the new portable sim room sweltered. The crew had worked all day installing it. Orr peeked inside, curious. A plain padded cube, four meters square, the sim room came in modular snap-together panels. Once it was finished, half a dozen suspension harnesses drooped from the ceiling, the type stage actors used to perform wire fu and other acrobatic illusions. Recessed into the walls were the six projectors that created the lifelike illusions needed for full immersive simulations. The sim room gave a much more visceral experience than a mere oc.

Vera texted Orr that she'd installed the sim room to augment his training. She said any time he liked, he could hang in one of the harnesses and swoop through a movie-magic sky to practice his maneuvers. Orr had never practiced in a simulator before, and he wondered how it would feel. Unfortunately, his first trial would be Mrs. Jadri's promo tour.

He took his seat at the improvised makeup table. His face showed the usual subdued quiet, but inwardly, he felt exasperated. One idea preoccupied him: his stratosphere dive. He focused on that and tried not to think about speaking in public.

Leo clutched Orr's chin and wielded the mascara brush with a nasty gleam in his eye. "Hold steady, meathead. Ooh, he's got pretty eyelashes. Ooh, see how he blushes. Look at the red Indian."

Orr clamped his jaw and ignored Leo. He was supposed to wear his Gravity Pilot costume. He hated the stupid superhero suit, but the battle wasn't worth fighting. As soon as his makeup was done, he tugged on the silly green pants and silver boots.

"I covet your footwear." Leo hovered over Orr's boots like he wanted to eat them.

Mrs. Jadri made Orr memorize the two-minute stump speech she'd written, plus a dozen generic sound bites to answer reporters' questions. Bettie helped him learn his lines. He had a quick memory. But when he asked how his scripted sound bites would match up with the reporters' actual questions, Mrs. Jadri brushed him off. The point, she said, was that he should not ad lib.

"It's a crazy way to give an interview," he said.

Mrs. Jadri squared her glossy red lips. "It'll *sound* perfectly spontaneous."

He raised his hands and backed off. Mrs. Jadri was a nice enough lady, maybe a little short-tempered from working too hard, but why she wanted to keep him on a choke chain, he couldn't figure.

While Al microwaved faba burgers in the breakroom, Bettie role-played scenarios and fired questions so Orr could recite his canned answers. The words were right, he had good recall. But his tone—dismal.

He said, "You know, I'll never be any good at this."

"Too true." Mrs. Jadri stalked in, carrying a full-length mirror.

She propped it against the breakroom wall and made him stare at his reflection and rehearse his speech while everyone sat around and gave feedback. Performing in front of his friends stressed him, but he went at it manfully, raising his eyebrows and lilting the words as Mrs. Jadri ordered. He picked up physical instructions fast, but he knew his limits. He had no gift for sales talk.

Mrs. Jadri holoed his speech against a fake Japanese skyscape. She had a different wallpaper for every whistle-stop on the world tour. Orr watched the playback without much hope, although Bettie and Al both swore later that he gave a decent imitation of a sports star.

The rehearsal finished around midnight, and Orr was leaving when Mrs. Jadri caught hold of his arm. "Tomorrow, no surprises. Sing from our song sheet, yes? It's in your contract."

He nodded. What choice did he have?

Next morning in the make-believe Japanese media room, the sports reporters gathered for simulated tea and rice cakes, while in the real sim room, Orr paced back and forth under the roasting holo lights. He smelled like greasepaint. Leo had overdone the mascara and blusher. Still, his costume was striking. Bettie stood on tiptoes to comb his hair while Mrs. Jadri read out the names of the reporters he was about to meet. He waited, as tense as a plucked string, till Bettie reminded him to smile.

Then Mrs. Jadri clapped her hands. "Cameras! Action!"

In a blink, the sim room filled with brightness. Mrs. Jadri and Dr. Leo vanished. Orr felt disoriented, like he was drowning. He steadied himself against a metal box—a podium. It felt solid and cool. He smelled sweet tea. Exotic language babbled behind him. He turned and saw a semicircle of Japanese reporters who were pointing their vones at him like a firing squad.

Mrs. Jadri had hand-picked twelve friendly faces from the prime Sapporo channels. She'd created a comfy lounge setting with padded benches facing a small dais. Orr stepped behind the podium in self-defense.

The reporters' foreign language intrigued him, until the translation filter dropped in. Then everyone's speech morphed to web English. The newscasters congratulated him and asked for autographs. They got in line to make quick-movies of themselves shaking hands with the Gravity Pilot. This absorbed half the hour.

When Orr gave his speech, he stammered at first: "Skydiving is an . . . old sport. It began in China sometime in the 1100s. . . . Then Leonardo DaVinci designed the first parachute . . ."

His voice came out low, but as he got into the rhythm, he loosened up. Also he managed to reproduce the facial tics Mrs. Jadri taught him, though he felt a lot of his lines sounded sappy. "Everyone asks why I skydive. I say, why do people sing? It's a way to express the human spirit . . ."

Near the end, he described his preparations to test the new Celestia prototype in the stratosphere, and he invited everyone to watch his dive. He repeated the webcast date three times—exactly as scripted. When he finished, the red bindi dot between Mrs. Jadri's eyebrows relaxed its crease.

After Orr's prepared statement, the reporters asked easy questions, and he replied with the prefab answers. He didn't make a single false move, in Sapporo or any of the other stops. For ten grueling hours, he faced reporters, blinking his bashful gray eyes, and between sessions, he worked off his stress by running laps around the hangar. Dr. Leo had to retouch his makeup, but Mrs. Jadri didn't object. She said Orr was doing fine.

At the end of the tour, Al and Bettie threw a party in the hangar to celebrate. The crew streamed Texas swing from their pods, and they moved their equipment to make a dance floor. Bettie found a miraculous supply of frozen pizzas in the food locker. Al wrapped a green silk shirt around his head and did card tricks. Dr. Leo offered face paintings. And Mrs. Jadri poured champagne—not the pricey grape-based stuff, this swill came from fermented sorghum. Still, everybody toasted each other like bosom friends. Orr was in training, so he was the only one who didn't get drunk.

18

Container. Housing for parachute canopy.

After the promo tour, Vera felt more sidelined than ever. Rolfe kept her buried with work in Seattle, while he drooled eulogies over Mrs. Jadri's brilliance. Vera slow-roasted and reckoned her tallies. Her time would come.

Meanwhile, Jadri basked and strutted. Apparently, her latest web poll ranked the Gravity Pilot more famous than the United States president. Big deal. Nobody cared who was president. Vera knew fans swooned over Orr because of his talent, not the ditzy ad campaign. He showed people a brighter life. Jadri didn't get that.

But Vera couldn't take time to educate Mrs. Cow Teats. The last two days of March swirled down the drain, leaving her tête-à-tête with Rolfe's deadline. No more delays, Orr had to dive their new Celestia Sky Wing through the stratosphere, and she had to produce a primo sim. But the prototype Wing was still cooking in the kiln, and its internal pieces and parts lay scattered across the lab. Was it ready? Was Orr?

Whenever she could, Vera linked into her mote cameras to watch him. She wanted to be there with him, in person, but Rolfe gave her too much to do. She couldn't keep her figurative finger on Orr's pulse every minute. Nevertheless, on the last night before the momentous dive, she set up some equipment in her bedroom and convened a conference with the full Mundo Mountain team.

"Her heiny-less speaks," Bettie announced when Vera's conference call rang through.

Orr and the two designers gathered around the flat screen to see Vera's face, while she viewed them through her oc. The wingback chair in her condo had grown a mysterious gray film that rubbed off on her hands. She wiped her fingers on her white shirt and envied their high mountain. Rolfe was leaning on the back of her chair, wearing the stupid antiviral suit that made him look like a shrink-wrapped sausage. Such a coward. He stood just outside the webcam frame so the others couldn't see him.

The Prune came on-screen first, looking savage. She hadn't brushed her wild gray hair in days. "This deadline's insane," she grumped. "Tell us you've bought more time."

Al's plastic beak clogged his voice. "We're worried about Orr's safety. The beryllium alloy needs more checks."

Vera made a fresh bite mark on her hand. She resented those two unspeakably. But Orr seemed anxious. She studied the slant of his cheek, the firm swell of his shoulder. Would he notice the circles under her eyes? She'd concealed them with makeup. But would he worry about her?

Rolfe was breathing down her collar. She said, "The test will go as scheduled."

"But we've no creedy space shuttle." Bettie, such a whiner.

Vera tapped her front teeth together. "We'll do without the shuttle. I've rented a jumpjet."

Al took off his wire-rims, and Bettie trumpeted her objections through her nose. Orr said, "You're not coming to watch?"

Vera glanced up at Rolfe, then said, "I'll monitor from here."

Orr rocked back on his heels. She knew he wanted to ask something, though she wasn't sure Rolfe should hear it. She said, "What's on your mind, skydiver?"

He swallowed. "Vera, you know how much I want this, but the Wing's still in the oven. Give us one extra day to test it on the ground."

Again she glanced up at Rolfe. His gaunt face hovered over her, the color of clotted cheese. He moved his head from side to side, signaling a negative.

Did Orr see the brittle line of her smile? She hadn't planned it, but maybe her real stress came through. She couldn't pretend any of this made her happy, and for once, the truth worked in her favor. Orr said, "All right, we'll make a short test dive in the morning."

His kind voice lifted her up to heaven. Then Rolfe vise-gripped her shoulder and brought her back to Earth. She knew what she had to say. "You'll dive from the stratosphere. We've invested major funds in this project. We need a good quality holo to advertise the new Sky Wing."

Bettie started to speak, but Orr put out his hand to stop her. He said, "All right, Vera. We'll make it look like we jumped from the Moon."

Gentle-hearted boy, she'd conned him again. How bizarre to see her own desperation warped into a scam. When she ended the call, Rolfe released his grip on her shoulder.

"Now that wasn't so hard. You're learning, Vera. Truth is movable. It's all in how you frame it."

19

Crabbing. Steering a Sky Wing sideways across ambient wind.

Cho Sen Yao, the notorious reporter, breached Mundo Mountain security using a counterfeit pass. Often, the simplest tricks worked best. In the wee morning hours before the stratosphere dive, the slippery hermaphrodite stole into the hangar dressed as a black-clad ninja. Softly, swiftly, he/she glided into the crew quarters and found the bunkroom where Orr lay tossing and trying to sleep. Cho knelt by the bunk and laid his black-gloved fingers across Orr's lips.

"Hush. I have news of Dyce."

Orr sat up. In the semidarkness, he recognized the genderless voice. Instinct kept him quiet. As his eyes adjusted, he made out the slim shoulders, the long graceful neck, the pinched features. Also, he smelled the nicotine.

Cho whispered, "She's in trouble. She needs you."

Orr threw back the covers and swung his feet to the floor. "Is she hurt?"

"Shhh." Cho planted a black-gloved hand on Orr's knee. "Listen to my news."

Orr got up and tugged on his trousers. "Where is she?"

"In Seattle. But you can't get there." Cho kicked a pile of dirty clothes out of the way and sat cross-legged on the carpet.

Orr yanked his boots on. The only light in the bunkroom came from climate-control LEDs, and the only sound came from the rustle of his clothes.

He kept a chary eye on the androgynous newscaster. When he was fully dressed, he opened the door.

Cho said, "Sit down. Your keepers won't let you leave."

Orr stood in the door, vibrating with adrenaline and mulling over Cho's words. True, he still didn't have a transit pass. And for all his promised wealth, he had yet to see a single coin. His first impulse was to steal a construction tractor, but that was a capital crime. "What kind of trouble?" he said.

Cho lifted one hip and pulled a handful of sharp metal grommets out from under his butt. Parts of a disassembled high-altitude parachute lay scattered under the bed, along with shoes, dirty socks and several microwave bowls of uncertain content. Rich human aromas mixed with the chemical reek of new paint to create an atmosphere not unlike a high school gym. "Your girlfriend's hooked on a virulent wikiverse called Cyto. That's Latin for a basic unit of life. Or a packet of data. Cutesy, huh?"

"What do you mean, hooked?" Orr peeked out the door into the empty hall. "I thought she was building a library."

"Oh, Cyto has a fat archive. Get comfortable. It's a long story."

While Orr remained standing at the door, Cho narrated in a rolling sing-song, as if he'd recited the tale a hundred times. Cyto was an old wiki, private and heavily encrypted, maybe the first of its kind. Cho had been researching it for years. He said the wiki hired Dyce under false pretenses. From that point on, Orr paid close attention.

Cyto began in the late twentieth century when a few webmasters set up a multiuser environment to share animes, video games, and similar cultish ilk. Their wiki came online almost before the word existed. In addition to pirated media, they also hoarded graphic shareware. Soon, they were producing their own fantasy worlds, and Cyto became their private screening room.

Word about Cyto eventually lured other larcenous story-makers. With no central direction, and no rules except the tech itself, the wiki expanded beyond standard artificial reality into a byzantine universe, where the growing cache of illegal apps gave insiders nearly unlimited powers of creation. In Cyto, whatever they could imagine, they could make.

But the larger the community grew, the more the wiki experienced accidents, intrusions, and severe system noise. It evolved stochastically. Certain biases crept in. Autonomous feedback loops developed kinks. Eventually, the unrestrained creation proved habit-forming. The users couldn't quit.

Orr rolled his shoulders. "Web addiction's old news. Dyce would never fall into that. Even Unimak has web heads."

"True." Cho puffed his cigarette. "You've also got shoppers, masochists, opium eaters. There's no such thing as original vice."

Orr gripped the newscaster's arm. "Where is she? Tell me now."

Cho pinched the inside of Orr's thumb just hard enough to make his muscle spasm. "Don't touch me again, skydiver." Then he opened his pod and turned the small screen so Orr could see. "You like libraries? Check out this reading room. Mocha lattes and cream-filled novellas. Browsing and binging merge as one."

Orr sank in front of the tiny pod, and soft light dappled his face as he watched the ugly scene unfold. People in a web café were pigging on pastries, caffeine drinks, and massive tomes of inflammatory narrative fiction. Orr couldn't watch. He covered the screen with his hand.

Cho lit a fresh cigarette. "Dependency's a lifelong condition. It carves pleasure grooves in your brain that never disappear." He blew a smoke ring and watched it warp through the air. "Thing is, creation's an unusually satisfying drug. If web geeks were the only ones getting hooked, I wouldn't care. But a while back, Cyto went public. They're selling creation time to anyone who can pay."

Orr shot to his feet. He pictured Dyce locked in a trance with that God-blasted ocular, and he wanted to gallop across the ocean to save her.

"Sit down." Cho yanked him back to the bunk and showed him a thin glass band, about the size of a wedding ring. It was clear, almost invisible. "It's a vone." Cho yanked Orr's earlobe and hooked the ring in his flesh.

"Ow." Orr touched his ear and felt a wet spot. A drop of bright blood smeared his fingers.

"You'll feel the earring get warm when I call." Cho dragged at his cigarette, then blew smoke out his nostrils. "No one will hear my voice but you. Answer by speaking normally. Or you can subvocalize if you know how."

Cho's herbal smoke wafted through the silent room while Orr scrunched up his eyelids and pondered. After a minute, he said, "What's in this for you?"

The newscaster tapped ash from his cig with his long black-sheathed fingers. "Call me the agent of justice. You need my help to get Dyce. I need a great news story."

Orr shook his head. "There's more to it. What else?"

Cho cracked his knuckles. In the quiet room, his snapping joints rang like an explosion. "I have a friend there, too."

20

Cross ports. Holes in parachute to allow air flow between the cells.

Deadline day. March 31 dawned in grimy rings of yellow haze around Mundo Mountain. When Orr walked out to the drop zone, the chartered jumpjet was just landing. He darkened his goggles to see it. Wasps buzzed around the construction site and hovered under the hangar eaves. The incomplete dome still lay open to the sky, and in the hot pools of rainwater scattered over the concrete pad, mosquito larvae swarmed.

Today, instead of in a raincoat, Orr was sealed in a pressurized jumpsuit. The prototype Wing circled his helmet in a tightly furled collar, and Vera's new high-res holocams circled around his head. Thick smog rolled over Unimak, and bleary sunlight heated the lava rock, turning the caldera into a barbeque grill. At least, no storms were predicted.

Orr did not want to make this jump. Stratosphere? New Celestia Sky Wing? He'd been dreaming about the dive for days, years, maybe his whole life—but on that spring morning, he felt ready to blow it off.

Dyce was trapped in Seattle. Deep under the faulty cracks of bedrock, she needed him. He wanted to go there, that very instant, as fast as he could fly. But Cho made him promise to wait for a vone call. So he sweated, and ached, and waited.

The earring did not grow warm, but it itched. Orr had his doubts about Cho. The guy showed way too much skill at storytelling. And who smoked leaf anymore? The world's scarce tobacco supply was reserved for sick people. Orr held off judging, though, till he learned more about Dyce.

He waved at Al and Bettie, who watched through the lab window. Then he gazed up at the new docking tower, naked under the dome's steel rib cage. Higher up, the sky glowed like old yellow pearls. Construction debris littered the damp concrete, and beyond the pad lay a bulldozed field covered in crushed pumice gravel. That was his drop zone. In that one-acre space, he would land.

The air lay stagnant. The jumpjet engine raced. Orr focused on his earring, but it made no sound. All his dreams of glory turned to immaterial mist without Dyce. Why did he let her go to that cesspit alone? He should have protected her. He should have . . .

The pilot was signaling him to board the jet. "Just do it," he told himself.

He climbed into the fuselage, slid the door closed, and grabbed the handholds bolted to the deck. The jet made a blistering liftoff, and he sank hard into the bare steel. Al's voice wheezed inside his helmet, reminding him to recheck his data display. That's what he was doing when he spotted the other jumper hiding in the shadows.

The stranger scrambled out on hands and knees, gesturing for silence. In the dim fuselage, Orr needed a couple seconds to recognize the delicate features through the helmet visor. It was Cho. And surprise, Cho wore a Sky Wing. Furled around his neck hung an off-the-shelf Volare Wing, the large slow type a novice diver might choose. None of this made sense to Orr. When Al's voice buzzed in his radio com link, asking for status, Orr failed to answer.

Cho opened a handheld pod and showed Orr the screen. The earring warmed up, and Cho said, "This is your get-away plan." The screen displayed a map of Unimak Island, and Cho pointed to a small cove on the northwest coast, just out of sight of Mundo Mountain. He wanted Orr to skydive into the cove.

Through the earring, Cho said, "Drop into the water, and let yourself sink. Don't inflate your life vest."

Orr blurted, "You're not serious."

Bettie answered over the radio, "What did you say?"

Orr didn't speak aloud again, but somehow, he had to warn Cho. Currents on the western shore were too strong for swimming. Worse, there might be stinging jellies. He tried using hand signals, but Cho said, "Stick to the plan."

No choice. Orr narrowed his focus on the dive. Cho's Volare Wing would never survive the stratosphere, so he chinned his radio and gave the pilot new orders. "Forget the stratopause. Take us to three thousand."

"Three thousand meters. It's your dime." The pilot reset his flight plan.

Al buzzed over the com link, "What's up?"

Orr said, "One quick jump to get out the wrinkles. Then the stratopause." He felt guilty lying to Al, but at that moment, it was necessary.

At three thousand meters above the caldera, the pilot reduced speed and opened the hatch. "Exit in fifteen seconds. Fourteen. Thirteen."

Cho didn't wait for the count. He flung his little body through the hatch and sailed into the blue. Orr followed, with sixteen holocams in close pursuit.

Over the radio, Bettie said, "Who's that other diver?"

The smog hung as thick as mustard gas, so Orr used his laser optics. He saw how ineptly the newscaster steered. Cho's body angle was all wrong. Instead of gaining horizontal speed, he was dropping way too fast, and for some reason, he didn't unfurl his Wing. Orr rifled down and modeled the correct body position, hoping the newscaster would understand and adjust. Another beginner student, two in one month. The coincidence made Orr question his karma.

Mountainous terrain spread below like a thick impasto painting, full of edgy pinnacles and deep grooves. Even with laser optics, Orr could barely see the drop zone inside the thumb-sized caldera. That minuscule gray square presented the only safe landing area in sight, and they were racing away from it, toward the hidden cove.

Time was always in a race with gravity. Orr made hand signals, trying to get Cho to unfurl his Wing. Meanwhile, Bettie and Al buzzed so many questions over the com link, Orr felt tempted to shut it off. Seconds boiled away, and Cho lost altitude fast as they tracked along the coastline. Then two words burped through Orr's earring. "Need help!"

"Unfurl your Wing," Orr shouted. He didn't care who overheard.

Fear serrated Cho's voice. "I can't find the release handle."

"In your helmet. Center switch. Use your chin." Orr zoomed close and pointed to the spot on his own helmet while the holocams swarmed to record.

Back in the lab, Bettie and Al exchanged mystified glances. Bettie said, "Who the heck is he talking to?"

Finally, Cho got it right, and the Volare popped open. With relief, Orr unfurled his own Celestia and checked his altimeter. Then the dive went sideways. Instead of snapping into shape, the prototype Sky Wing encased Orr like wet glue.

Bettie snarled over the com link, "Sodding beryllium. The nano-resins are going fluky."

Orr fell from the sky like Galileo's lead ball. He struggled inside the Wing, but the micromesh wouldn't harden. Parts of the Celestia went stiff, while other areas sagged and clotted. He fought for control.

"Furl it. Use your parachute," Al yelled.

"Right." Orr chinned a switch, and the Wing rolled back up into a tight gummy cowl around his helmet. "It furled," he reported, stabilizing in an arch. "I'll try unfurling again."

Bettie and Al shouted in unison, "No!"

But Orr had already chinned the command. Again, the Wing flapped and flagged, part rigid, part soggy wet. He held his arch and waited, watching his altimeter spin down. "Wait, wait," he whispered, as if words could slow time. The mountains leaped up at him, an effect jumpers called "ground rush." He would crash in seconds.

"Wait," he breathed. He could sense more of the Wing getting hard. Gradually, the nose took shape. Next came the sharp leading edge he and Al had spent so much time perfecting. Fingers of stiffness spread through the mesh. The wobbly cone blossomed and swelled. Finally the Celestia snapped into a stiff conical teardrop.

"Fully unfurled," Orr reported. He saw the Earth rushing to meet him, and he swooped for an updraft.

Bettie said, "Thank God you didn't take that thing to the stratosphere."

Orr rose in the sun-heated wind and sent his silent thanks to Agugux. Then he spun to look for Cho. Deep in a canyon beneath him, the Volare fishtailed like a drunken moth. Cho could not control the big floppy Wing. He kept sweeping left, then veering drastically right to avoid hitting the canyon wall. He was oversteering, fighting the currents instead of riding them. He had no natural instinct for the air.

Orr dove into the canyon. He could see only one way to prevent a crash.

He had to dock with the Volare—to physically connect the two Wings so he could steer them in tandem. Wing docking posed one of the riskiest challenges in the whole skydiver repertoire. Orr had never done it, but he'd seen it on the web. Docking took skill and hours of practice, but he had to teach himself and Cho in the next few seconds.

"Hold your Wing as steady as you can. We have to slide your nose into my aft."

Cho's words came in breathy jolts. "Sounds erotic."

Orr shot out in front and tried to match the Volare's unpredictable flight path. But the prototype Celestia didn't respond the way it should. The new material was too stiff. And the deeper they fell, the more the canyon walls narrowed. Orr gripped the braces and forced the Wing to bend.

The Volare swerved very close behind, and he reacted fast, ballooning his Wing to brake his forward speed. The Volare's nose slammed into his aft opening. It impacted his feet and crumpled his body forward inside the Celestia. For a couple of seconds, the two Wings flew as one heavy unit. Then they recoiled and bounced apart. The blunt Volare nose was too wide to dock with the Celestia. Ahead the canyon was closing in.

Seconds spilled away, and Orr narrowed his thoughts to one pure purpose. Again, he tried to hold the Volare in the backwash of his Wing. When he felt its nose nudging his feet, he told Cho to lie still. "Don't even blink. I'll steer."

The swirling suction behind Orr's Wing created just enough forward pull to hold the Volare in lockstep. Together they glided along the warm south-facing wall of the canyon. When the Volare drifted too far behind, Orr altered his speed to maintain their fragile bond. He had to keep correcting to hold altitude. He couldn't risk a sudden move. But the jagged box end of the canyon came charging toward them. There was no more time.

Orr set a rising angle, and they began to plane upward. He could see the canyon rim. And the bright line of sky above it. Just a few more meters. Hold the lift. Wait, wait.

And they made it.

"Let's head for the water," Cho said.

Orr let out his breath and switched on his defogger. They were drifting twenty meters over the cliffs now, and together, they made a slow wide turn toward the sea. By luck, their precarious union held all the way to the coast.

From the sky, the waves breaking on the rocky shore looked small, like soap foam, but Orr knew they were deadly. Tidal forces pummeled the cliffs, and dingy gouts of spray erupted like fountains. He kept guiding the Volare in his slipstream, keeping close to the thermals rising up the south-facing rocks. Finally, the secret cove came in view.

Cho said, "Remember, don't inflate your vest."

In the final few seconds, Orr tried to tell Cho how to furl his Volare and open his parachute. But there was not enough time to finish. The water engulfed them.

Current. To be up-to-date in skydiving skills.

Through a thousand mote eyes, Vera watched Prune and Bird Beak fly into a frenzy in the lab. "What happened?" Bettie squealed. "Who was that other diver? Why aren't we getting an image?" She bounced around, checking data screens and knocking things over with her hips. Vera would've laughed if she'd been in a better mood.

Al adjusted their holocam feed, but all they could see were enormous gray breakers splashing against rugged cliffs.

"He can't survive those currents." Bettie switched to another view.

Al caught hold of Bettie's wrists. "Calm yourself, dear. I'll call the rescue squad. You check satellite scans. We'll find him."

"You're right." Her plump body stiffened. "I'll search for his locator beacon. He has an air supply. And he's tough and young and . . . oh God."

Vera watched them separate and get busy. Bettie linked through her workstation to query the public satellites, although she kept up a steady drone of fretting. "I should never have agreed to use that crappy beryllium. Cost effective, ha. I knew we didn't fire it long enough."

"We were pressed for time." Al texted the Coast Guard. When his breather clogged, he took it off and knocked it against his desktop to clear its filter.

Bettie whined, "I should never have caved to the red-haired she-devil. Damn it, the web link's jammed. I can't get satellite scans. Crap, my ocular's down, too."

Al took off his wire-rims and blinked his myopic eyes. "My text won't transmit."

He and Bettie traded shifty signals with their eyebrows.

Al glanced upward. "Perhaps a solar flare?"

"Yeah, or maybe a satellite 'dead spot.'" Bettie cranked back her ergonomic chair and flicked her middle finger at the ceiling.

"Bitch," Vera whispered. "As if you could see my motes."

Bettie got up and paced, glaring at the ceiling. "What if he's hurt? He could drown. It's my fault. I should have shot Vera Luce through the head."

Al came to her side. "Bettie, dear."

"Oh, Al. I dote on that boy."

The stout dark woman collapsed against the pasty little white-haired man, and they rocked in a close embrace. Vera curled her nostrils at their touching scene. Candidly, she thought they overplayed it. While she, she was the one who had to explain this fiasco to Rolfe. She. By herself. Alone.

She snarled under her breath. "It always comes down to *me*."

Cut away. Emergency release from parachute.

Orr surfaced in two-meter waves. His canopy floated around him, and he bobbed chin-deep in the oily green brine. Each time a wave swept him upward, he spun to look in all directions, but he couldn't spot Cho. Not far away, the ocean rammed against the cliffs. Undertow pulled at his legs, and he kicked powerful strokes to stay on the surface.

Saltwater splashed his visor, blurring his view, so he ignored the toxic pollution and opened his helmet so he could see. The air felt heavy and wet on his face. Then water flooded in. It tasted like gutter slime. He treaded for twenty minutes, yelling Cho's name and searching for a parachute in the waves, right up to the moment when something very much like a giant squid latched onto his legs and yanked him under.

He plummeted into the murk. Jellyfish, it had to be. He held his breath and snapped his faceplate closed, then turned up the air supply to blow water out of his helmet. Dead chemical brine stung his sinuses and washed through his teeth. He snuffled and spat. Only when he could breathe again did he focus on the creature grappling his legs. It pulled him deep under the grimy gloom till darkness closed over him.

Nightmare. His pulse spiked. The venomous tentacles couldn't sting through his suit, but the jelly could pull him down forever. Orr didn't fear many things, but the idea of being trapped alive under a crushing weight—dare we say it?—he freaked. He twisted and clawed and screamed like a child, but the beastie had him shackled. He could not get free.

The tentacles wrenched him down through a narrow mouth, barely shoulder wide. Its lips scraped his elbows, and bubbles exploded. Turbulence knocked him around, and jets of air poked his ribs. He kicked and punched and knocked his head against a metal wall. Metal? The sea beast had pulled him into—an airlock?

Air jets were forcing water out of the metal tube, the same way he'd used his air supply to clear his helmet. Wedged inside the tube, he counted his breaths and watched the water drain. Next, the floor opened, and he fell to the deck below.

A camera flashed in his face. "Picture for my scrapbook," Cho said.

Orr sat up and felt for his Celestia Sky Wing. The globby beryllium had hardened around his helmet like glass. When he cracked it loose, it splintered.

Cho took the helmet and disabled its locator beacon. The newscaster seemed more willowy than Orr remembered. His tight-fitting black silk pajamas were wet, and his short dripping hair clung to his head like a skull-cap. His skin was so smooth and chalky white, it might have been painted on. And his eyes seemed to be outlined in charcoal.

While Orr peeled off gear and struggled to collect his sanity, Cho rolled an herbal cigarette with his black-gloved fingers, then wetted the gummed paper in his mouth. "Care for a pick-me-up? It's laced with methylphenidate."

Orr shook his head.

Behind Cho, a squat aluminum cylinder with telescoping robotic arms secured the airlock hatch. The cylinder swiveled toward Orr, and its slotted front panel gleamed like a chrome truck grille.

"That's Kof. He drives my submarine." Cho snapped another photo of Orr standing in his underwear, streaming wet. "We're off to see the Wizard," Cho said. "Next stop, Seattle."

second

DOWN DOWN DOWN

1

Data card. Documentation on reserve parachute, including date packed.

These days, it's hard to imagine that Seattle once fronted Puget Sound. Even back before Orrpaaj Sitka's time, rising tides had already swamped large sections of the Olympic Peninsula, and when the big quake of 2042 rewrote the shoreline, the citizens had no choice but to gravitate inland.

At first, they retreated to a behemoth Red Cross tent city just east of the Snoqualmie River. But soon, millions absconded to Canada, and several hundred thousand followed a charismatic Scientologist to the shores of Lake Superior. Meanwhile, the rest slow-poached to a dull fury in the hot acid rain. After ten months, they got royally sick of waiting for federal help. So they pooled their funds and started up their own Consortium.

"Tragedy of the commons. I tell you, it's socialism in disguise." Cho stubbed out one cigarette and lit the next. Tobacco ash whitened his gloves.

Orr tried to pay attention, but the tiny submarine closed around him like a coffin. He had a thing about confined spaces. As they cruised west across the Gulf of Alaska, he sat in the control room with his knees drawn to his chin, fighting an urge to claw the walls.

Cho didn't seem to notice. "Guess how this so-called Consortium decided to spend their common wealth."

"Food?" Orr wiped sweat off his face. "Medicine?"

"They built a farking solar plant!"

Orr eyed the pipes bulging down from the ceiling while Cho explained the concept of a concentrated solar plant. A totally crack-brained idea for the Pacific Northwest. The clouds were too thick, the rain too incessant, the tech too high-priced. But Seattle had always been overrun with dreamers. Within five years, they achieved positive cash flow.

"And what did they buy next?" Cho spit out a bit of leaf. "Hand tools!"

Also they bought mining drills, nanotech and biofab. And they chiseled down through volcanic rock to escape the caustic rain. While most cities were building skyscrapers higher every year, Seattle drilled down. They were in survival mode. They needed all their surface land to grow food.

To date, eighteen million souls had trickled down to the new cave city. Cho stubbed out another butt. "Nobody knows its exact size. The diggers keep digging, hollowing more space. Some claim it runs nine kilometers deep."

Orr put his head between his knees. He felt faint.

Cho poured him a cup of bitter tea and told him about Seattle's problems with water tables. With the perpetual rain, underground flooding was a major hassle till the engineers finally blasted colossal cracks in the bedrock. Now the groundwater drained down through thousands of uncharted faults and crevasses into the underlying strata.

Orr couldn't drink the tea. Cho's description of fault lines made him woozy. He'd grown up in the Aleutians, a seismic war zone. Temblors jolted his island every year, and when he was nine, an earthquake buried him under the orphanage gym. For two days, he lay trapped in the rubble. Blind dark, choking dust, a broken femur, and constant mind-warping worry about his best friend, Dyce. Turned out she was safe, but since that episode, he almost never went more than a few meters below grade. Just imagining Seattle's crazed bedrock fired panic through his nerves.

Cho snickered. "You know what day this is? April 1. All Fools' Day. Maybe it's a sign of good luck." He lifted his tea for a toast.

Orr stole another glance at the pipes. Stowaway cave crickets hid in the shadows, and millipedes rustled in the vents. He consoled himself that every second in this creaky sarcophagus brought him closer to Dyce.

Cho dangled a fresh cigarette between his black-sheathed fingers. "Let's talk about Cyto."

The herbal smoke stung Orr's eyes. He braced his foot against a bulkhead and tried to focus.

"It begins with points," Cho said. "That's how the addiction starts. Reward points buy extra minutes in the Cyto wikiverse. Creation minutes, see?"

"Like healthcare minutes?" Orr recalled the meter in the Unimak clinic. He was doing his best to understand, but the metal cabin felt smaller every time he looked around.

"Yeah, like that." Cho sucked his cig, then blew a smoke ring through his thin lips. "Without points, the users pay extortionist time fees whenever they create new stuff. And every year, the fees go up. So everyone competes for reward points to defray their expenses."

"They compete, like in role-play games?"

The newscaster made a scornful noise in his throat. "Not your ordinary dungeons and dragons, casino poker, none of that shit. They invent their own creative prizes. You can't conceive . . . They . . ." Cho picked a cave cricket out of his hair and squashed it. "They fixate on scoring appreciation points for their artwork. But every game has losers, right, so no matter how hard they compete, they still racked up massive time debts."

Orr said, "Dyce has debts?"

"God, yes. When your sweetheart discovered Cyto, she dove in headfirst. She got so buzzed inventing stuff, she totally forgot to notice the time clock. Yeah, she owes."

Orr arched backward in the immovable metal chair. Dyce had always been good with money. She never liked to get behind. His elbow bumped a lever. He hated this submarine. He said, "How can make-believe be so addictive?"

"Your answer's in the question. It *makes* people *believe*. Everyone needs to believe in something beyond this . . ." Cho gestured at the submarine's gray steel walls. Then he reached for the teapot. "Want more beverage?"

Orr covered his cup with one hand. "Who charges the fees?"

Cho blinked. "You're not as brainless as you look, sports byte. That's the salient question. *Who* do they pay? It turns out, all along, there's been a man behind the curtain."

"A what?"

Cho smirked. "*The Wizard of Oz.* The sly prick who owned the original server back in 1996."

Orr was getting frustrated with too much talk and no room to move. The submarine's hull groaned. Gnats landed on the teapot. He wondered how deep under the ocean they'd descended. "So you plan to expose the guy?"

Cho flicked cigarette ash on the floor. "Fucking predator."

While the submarine creaked and popped, Orr listened to Cho's disturbing portrait of the Cyto wikimaster. He was a drug lord, as cold-blooded as any thug selling heroin, except the lure he offered was not a chemical high. It was creativity. For a certain type of mind, that exerted more attractive force than gravity itself.

Most people didn't want to build a whole world from scratch, though. That took too much head work. So every couple of months, the drug lord launched new simulated dramas to give his users inspiration. Last season, they did pentathlon on ice, extreme pizza eat-off, and Barbie roadkill. Users could expand the backdrops, sketch new characters, add music and dream up merchandise to trade. People could fabricate literally anything imaginable, although they mostly just reenacted the original scenes. The wiki software made collaboration easy, and every time a user embroidered a new detail, the Cyto owner sucked more cash. Some people rode the sims for days.

"With omnipotence at your fingertips, who wouldn't lose track of time?" Cho ground the ashes of his dead cigarette under his boot. Then he rolled a fresh one and slicked it with his small pink tongue. "Word is, the Wizard never uses the drug he sells. He's too smart to ride his own sims. Or too scared."

Orr felt hot water dripping down his collar. An overhead pipe was leaking steam. He couldn't move, though, because his metal chair was bolted to the floor. He pictured Dyce in a deep dark cave, surrounded by maniacs. He said, "The owner lives in Seattle?"

Cho's nostrils expelled smoke. "Correct again, sports byte. I don't know the bastard's name yet, but I'll find him."

Orr slung damp ringlets out of his eyes. Everything evil grew in Seattle. He couldn't help but notice Cho's bitter grip on the tea mug.

"Cho, um." He hesitated. "You mentioned a friend in Seattle. What . . . what happened?"

Cho bared his teeth. Orr had never seen such undisguised hatred. "My only real friend in the world. He turned her into a monster."

Orr knew better than to press for details. He watched the newscaster stub out his half-smoked cigarette as if he were stabbing a knife in the Cyto own-er's heart.

"So our plan," Orr said to change the topic, "first we find Dyce, then we get your news story."

"Actually . . ." Cho poured more tea. "I'm banned in Seattle. You have to go alone." He pulled back one sleeve and showed a tiny scar inside his soft white forearm. "It's a police tracking tag. They won't let me in, so you and I part company at the city gate."

Orr drew in his elbows. Images of Seattle hollowed holes in his mind. He hadn't counted on going alone.

Cho leaned across the table and touched the glass ring in Orr's earlobe. With his gloved fingertip, he teased the ring back and forth. "No worries, sports byte. I'll be your GPS."

2

*De-arch. To flatten out the normal arched body position in freefall,
also called Dead Spider.*

Deep in Seattle, Vera watched Rolfe crack her pan against the top of his marble desk. His shrine to himself, that desk. Her pan split, and she watched the pieces fly.

He said, "This is not the stratosphere. Did you forget our season launch? Mrs. Jadri bought airtime for a sneak preview today. That's good money down the toilet."

Vera was toeing the carpet in his office, shivering in the icy chill and marking down another grievance in her mental balance sheet. The cold made her want to hug her shivering arms, but she kept still. Rolfe always turned his AC to blizzard setting. He claimed he had hot flashes, but Vera suspected he did it to destabilize her confidence.

She reformulated her smile. "We'll be ready for the season launch. No prob."

Could she admit her skydiver had run away? She was stalling. She stepped into the warmth under Rolfe's skylight, and her fingernail skimmed a wilted orchid blossom, soft lavender with a spotted crimson heart.

This time she'd come prepared with a second handheld pan. She fumbled it out of her belt pouch and replayed Orr's docking dive. Alaskan clouds fluoresced around her, filling Rolfe's office with a holographic sphere. Two Sky Wings dipped and bumped through the gusts. If only Rolfe would watch, he might see Orr's aerobatics made for high drama. Forget the strato-sphere. This docking dive could be a winner in its own right.

Sure, she'd edited the footage, camouflaged the defects in Orr's Sky Wing and brushed over the presence of the unauthorized diver. She had to make Rolfe think she'd staged every detail. Naturally, she'd deleted Orr's plunge in the ocean, too, though she never doubted where he would go. Seattle, of course, to rescue the beatific Dyce. In the last few anxious hours, Vera had hacked the city surveillance cameras to watch for Orr's arrival, and she was counting the seconds till she got him safely corralled. But she couldn't let Rolfe know that. The cold numbed her lips and stiffened her peppy smile.

"Look, Dad. Two mismatched Wings docking under hazardous conditions—this beats the stratosphere. It's operatic. No one but Orr could've pulled this off. It's got danger, suspense, heart-stopping action."

Rolfe sat at his desk, transferring a rooty green sprig from one pot of mud to another. He didn't watch Vera's holo. He spoke in a husky tone, without looking up, almost as if she weren't there. "I tried so hard to shape you. I wanted to give you the world."

The germicidal reek of his air spray only gave her a headache, though. She tried another tactic. "When this sim comes out, we'll market add-on tutori-als about Wing docking technique. Imagine the extra fees."

"Weak, Vera. You're off your game." Rolfe gazed lovingly at his limp seed-ling, then stood up and faced her. He'd lost weight. Vera could see the cut of his shoulder bones. He started in with his boxing moves, totally pleased with himself, like he was punching an invisible opponent to the floor. "My bo-tanical habitat is *open*."

She wanted to stab her boot heel through his neck. "Gee, Dad, that's ex-cellent."

He pranced around his desk, punching the air and crowing, "Opened without a glitch. Ahead of schedule."

Out of breath, he dropped into his padded leather chair, still gloating. "We'll regenerate the biomass. Hundreds of species living in perfect symbi-otic balance, can you see it? We'll have Eden all over again."

Vera wanted to tell him, Happiness is a sugar high, Dad. The sweetness won't last. They both knew his forest-in-a-bubble wouldn't pay back its cost for eons. Rolfe's habitat was a rich man's toy, not a legitimate investment. Her father was beggaring their future to feed fricking songbirds.

He splayed his legs over the chair arm. "As Confucius says, 'The superior man seeks what is right; the inferior one, what is profitable.'"

She clawed the back of her hand. Infernal green scenery. Rolfe claimed to worship living things, ha! What about people? How many times had he ranted that humans were the root of all evil? Birth control, his mantra. He probably would have nipped his own daughter in the bud if he'd seen her coming. She eyed his bare chest.

"My skydiver's one in a million," she said quietly. "His sims will reinvent the whole genre of artificial adventure."

Her father toyed with his cat furs. She wanted to wring him by the neck, but not yet. Right now, she needed to buy time. So she plucked her next perjury straight out of the vapor. "Orr's planning to skydive from the ionosphere."

Rolfe sat forward. "What?"

For a split second, Vera faltered. The new beryllium Wing had failed. She had no skydiver, no credible plan. Still, necessity drove her. She brazened it out with a laugh. "The ionosphere, Dad. Two hundred and fifty miles high. It'll be another world record, and we'll own it. Everyone jumps from the stratosphere, it's routine. So we'll skip that. Our Gravity Pilot will sail the aurora borealis."

Rolfe moved fast for an old man. His chair toppled backward, and when he charged toward Vera, she needed all her self-control to stand still. They faced each other, toe to toe, and he rested his hand on her collarbone. "You're lying."

Her vocal cords strained. "We've already set the date. Three months from today." She had no idea what her next step would be. Ionosphere was just a word she'd looked up in Wixionary.

His ketone breath sizzled in her face. "Don't con a conner."

Vera's words came out like parakeet chirps. "We'll use the docking sim for the spring season launch, then publish the ionosphere sim in midsummer—"

"You need three months? Why so long, angel? Jehovah needed only seven days to make the world."

"Seven days, that's bullshit, Dad."

He clutched the side of her head, and his fingers spread around her skull. Up close, his face looked cadaverous. "Time waits for no one, Vera. Go ahead, work your miracle. I give you seven days."

3

Decision altitude. Minimum height for skydiver to begin emergency procedures.

Orr peeked through the submarine periscope at Washington. Stranded by floods, the Olympic Peaks guarded the coast like a row of teeth spiking out of the water. Beyond them, rain fell hard and thick, veiling the view, and the mainland appeared hemmed in by three layers of night.

He studied the obstacle course he and Cho had to navigate to reach shore. A bubbly stew of jellyfish swarmed around the remnant peaks, and a wooly blanket of red bacteria had colonized Puget Sound. Tidal turbines rocked in the breakers, generating power from the motion of the ocean. Closer in, rotted skyscrapers from Seattle's old downtown poked up through a swath of floating green crud. The Space Needle looked like a mossy flying saucer on stilts. Cho said the green crud was genetically modified algae. The Consortium grew it to make synthetic jet fuel.

Along the broken shore, a maze of tanks and pumps stood guard over a vast white pond that used to be Lake Washington. This was Seattle's desalination plant. The enormous membrane assembly stretched up and down the former lake, filtering potable H_2O from Pacific brine.

Cho's submarine glided through the algae scum and nosed under a wharf at the desalination plant. When it bumped to a rocking stop, Cho said, "Wardrobe time."

In the narrow cabin, Orr and Cho bumped together as they stripped to their long underwear. Cho never took off his black gloves. Orr stole glances at his flat chest and narrow waist.

"Looking for something?" Cho handed him a pair of laser goggles. "Maybe this'll improve your vision. Our mainland smog is stout, so you'll need these."

Cho tore open a package and dumped out a long thin garment. "I paid a vital organ for this, so don't get it dirty. It's your quu-suit." He showed Orr how to put the garment on, then how to voice-activate its microprocessor stitched in the lining. The suit had five standard settings, plus customizable options. Orr stuck with basic navy blue. Meanwhile, Cho stepped into ordinary gray sweats. For toppers, they both put on Kevlar hoodie coveralls.

"Take this." Cho pressed a cellulose card into Orr's hand. It was a transit pass.

"Thanks." Orr zipped it in his breast pocket.

"Now this." Cho snapped open a small case about the size of a vone.

When Orr saw the ocular inside, he banged his head on a pipe trying to move away.

"Knucklehead. You'll need this in Seattle."

Orr didn't want to look at the lens. He wished Dyce had never heard of such a thing.

Cho slid the case into Orr's breast pocket beside the transit pass. "You'll want it later. Trust me."

They filled their packs with bottles of water and air, protein tabs, survival kits, and a laminated hard-copy map of the Cascade Mountains. Also machetes. Cho said the long knives were necessary. Last, they strapped on full-face respirators. And when Cho wasn't looking, Orr dropped the ocular down a waste chute.

"How long till I see her?" he asked.

Cho Velcroed his boots. "Soon enough."

On shore, lead-heavy rain closed in, dimming the sun. In those days, the skies never cleared over the mainland. Steaming hot, Orr and Cho slashed their way through a tangled mesh of kudzu. It took them hours to hack a path around the desalination lagoon.

A few kilometers inland, the kudzu shriveled under a weight of punky black mold. So they ditched the machetes and struck due east across the coastal plane. Thistle nodded in the downpour, competing with scraggly

Scotch broom and witchweed. Once the going was easier, Orr set a fast pace, and Cho jogged behind, grumbling. Beetles the size of bricks scuttled out of their way, while curious red cockroaches came up to sniff at their boots. Soon, mosquitoes mobbed them. Orr cinched his hood tighter and sealed the wristbands of his gloves.

By then, most of the old city had been leveled and replaced with new infrastructure. Orr had never seen so many weird contraptions. Rain mills, Cho called them. Steadily, Orr wiped the mosquitoes off his laser goggles to see. At one point, they passed a forest of high-tension cables that stretched up to the clouds. Rubbing together, the cables sang like out-of-tune violin strings, and Orr maxed his laser optics to see what pulled them so tight. Far up in the sky, he spotted solar collector balloons bobbing above the smog.

After fording the sludge-thick Snoqualmie River, they waded through acres of wet dripping switchgrass, gengineered to suck fumes and respire oxygen. "Typical pork-barrel stupidity funded by the Greens," Cho snarled. He said their stupid carbon tax cut freight traffic in half, thus doubling the cost of every nonlocal purchase. And who wanted to eat faba beans three times a day? A person could lose his appetite.

Beyond the switchgrass, they entered low foothills, and the view went massively bizarre. Hundreds of acre-sized white bubbles hovered over the rain-soaked landscape like schools of giant flounder. Where the hills rose, the white bubbles undulated up the slopes. Orr crashed through the tall drippy switchgrass for a closer look, and he almost tripped over the guy-wires staking the nearest bubble to the ground.

Cho caught up with him, irate and out of breath. "They're food farms. You've never seen a food farm?"

Shouting through the rain, Cho condemned the Consortium for wasting all their surface real estate on these collective farms. "Communal victory gardens on every arable acre. Where's the sense of personal ownership? It creeps me out."

Mosquitoes whined, and Cho slapped them away from his ears. He said the tension fabric bubbles sealed moisture in, toxics out, and an artificial climate controlled the veggies inside.

While he griefed about the city's land use policy, Orr poked at the moisture-beaded fabric. "I guess people need to eat."

Cho tromped back to the trail, orating about the hazards of communal food. Forget taste. All the appetizing crops gave up the ghost years ago to monoculture viruses. Now, Seattle's tent fields grew nothing but heirloom varieties of tea, sorghum, pearl millet, and everlasting gut-blasting faba beans.

Orr followed on Cho's heels. "We eat the same stuff on Unimak, only it's canned. Tastes pretty good with hot sauce."

Cho gazed up at the heavens. "Why do I bother?"

At dusk, they located a disintegrating asphalt highway, and they followed the broken yellow lines up toward the mountains till they reached the end of a long queue of refugees seeking entrance to Seattle. Wet soot stained the people's faces, as if they'd been basting on the hot road for weeks. Most of them wore protective raincoats and breathers. Some had only paper masks. There were families, small children, old folks, all exhausted to the point of numb silence. The line stretched ahead through the foothills like a rope made of soggy rags.

After nightfall, the refugees sat down on the asphalt to rest, and cockroaches gathered to mooch crumbs. Mosquitoes stocked up their blood banks. A few freighters continued to rattle the sky, and the occasional low-flying aircar zipped bright red streaks through the burgundy rain.

In a nearby factory yard, a trio of house-sized robots swung mechanical hammers to crush and recycle steel girders. Their headlights gleamed through the wet smoky night like demons' eyes. Orr gripped his knees to his chin and tried to be patient. The mainland weather blocked out any hope of stars. He fretted about Dyce.

A little boy ran by, wailing. A sodden paper mask covered his mouth, but mosquitoes blacked his forehead, and his unprotected eyes streamed. Orr took the boy in his lap and washed his face with bottled water. Gradually, the child calmed down. He was maybe five years old, Yanny's age. When Orr released him, he ran to his mother, and for a while, he and Orr played peek-a-boo. At length, the mother said, "Don't I know you?"

Orr shook his head.

"I've seen you somewhere," she said. "It'll come to me."

Orr turned away and pulled his rain hood closer around his face. When the downpour waned to a sprinkle, he asked Cho, "How much farther to Seattle?"

Cho tapped the asphalt. "We've been walking on top of it all day. People live everywhere under here."

Orr lay down, brushed away a pillbug and put his ear to the wet blacktop. Somewhere beneath him, that very minute, Dyce might be wondering why he didn't come faster. He tried to sleep, but the asphalt radiated heat, and Cho woke him every few minutes so they could move ahead in the line. Through the drizzly night, the refugees inched forward.

Orr stood and stretched. Overhead, the sky foamed brown, and he thought Agugux wouldn't expect him to swallow this dirty light. He said, "First thing in Seattle, we find Dyce."

Cho munched a protein tab. "Yeah, I'm hoping she'll lead us to the Wizard."

"The who?"

"The man behind the curtain. Don't you watch webflicks? Never mind."

Orr rolled his shoulders in the sweltering Kevlar coverall and gazed along the road. Ashy rain sluiced over his goggles, and the protein tab tasted like aspirin. He felt flushed, dehydrated. He sucked tepid water from the flask and imagined Dyce in his arms.

Deployment system. Nanotechnology in a Sky Wing
that unfurls the ceramic micromesh.

The rain thinned, and Orr finally saw the Cascade Mountains in the distance. He brushed mosquitoes off his goggles and stared at the scenery till Cho nudged him ahead. Every twist in the trail brought new surprises. When they hiked along the sudsy north fork of the Tolt River, he saw rainbows of red, yellow, and orange bacteria coating the rocks. The terrain curved up and down, yet not an acre lay fallow. Even the steepest hillsides were terraced and planted with bubble farms, and rain mills dotted the ridge lines.

The remnant highway switched back and forth up the rising topography, and when they passed an air freight depot, the methane stink of synthetic fuel seeped into their respirators. By midmorning, they were climbing the base of Mount Index, and Orr noticed a pale nanoformed structure worming along the bottom of a gorge. He couldn't see a single door or window. Cho said it was a "resomation" center where Seattle's dearly departed were reverently reduced to bone ash in a fully automated, eco-friendly, low-carbon solution of lye.

Just before noon, they topped a pass and met a dazzling vision. They had to cover their eyes because their goggles couldn't darken fast enough. Ahead lay a wide alpine meadow of radiant mirages. Orr blinked and squinted. Over twelve hundred parabolic mirrors stood shining in the rain like a choir of bright angels. Mounted on gimbals, they faced the hidden sun and reflected its obscure light upward to the peak of a central tower. To Orr, their misty rays looked like arms lifted in worship.

"Seattle's gold mine," Cho said. "The concentrated solar plant. See the high-res film mirrors? And that generator tower in the middle? Even in the rain, that tower breeds enough electricity to light the State of Washington."

Orr squinted at the mirrors. Rain made their golden faces waver and break apart, and he couldn't help seeing them as divine beings caught in an act of blind faith. As he slogged on, he kept turning back to see the angels one more time.

The refugee queue wound north, veering away from the solar plant. Twenty minutes later, they sighted a flat-topped mountain where aircars were taking off and landing. At its base, recessed in the side of a cliff, were the glossy white doors of the main Seattle airlock.

At least fifty policemen guarded the entrance. Rain spilled off their cap brims as they sauntered up and down the line checking people's documents. More police watched from a turret by the roadside. Cho said the white doors were made of nanoformed ceramic, impervious to damage. "Like my Sky Wing," Orr said. He listened to the doors grind open each time someone passed through.

His chest tightened. Somewhere under this ground, Dyce waited. He'd come to unearth her, yet he was not ready to go through those white doors. He knew they led deep beneath the mountains, and he knew that territory did not lie still. Subterranean plates buckled and scraped, thrusting up continents and cracking mountains apart. Humans didn't belong under moving rock.

Dyce called his fear of depths irrational. His condition even had a name: *bathophobia*. She'd looked it up on the web. When he was younger, he sometimes woke screaming, and she would hold him and talk him through the tremors. She wanted him to see a counselor. But it wasn't fear of dying that unnerved him. He dreaded the trap of an endless living grave.

Cho nodded toward the uniformed cops guarding the entrance. "Time to say adios."

Orr faltered backward.

"Relax, sports byte. You like thrills. Think of this as a new way to dive."

The newscaster's jokes made Orr crazy. He stamped his feet to calm down.

"Oh, I nearly forgot the cash." Cho stuffed a small purse of scrip coins in Orr's pocket, then faded away through the rocks, leaving Orr on his own.

Way too soon, he reached the head of the line and faced the city doors. Above the lintel hung the bronze seal of the Sovereign Seattle Consortium. Streaked with rain, it bore the profile of a Native American hero, Chief Seattle. The chief's fierce cheekbones and stern hawk nose reminded Orr of old Mr. Bobby Tangaagim. *Iidigidix stirs.* Could Mr. Bobby have meant another earthquake?

At the final security checkpoint, a policeman slid Orr's transit pass through a reader. Several seconds went by. An opaque visor hid the policeman's face, so Orr stared at the bronze image of Chief Seattle. Beyond the white doors, rocks were gnashing together and cleaving. "Dyce," he whispered. His back perspired. Under his coverall, the quu-suit stuck to his skin.

The policeman said, "State your full name."

"Orrpaaj Sitka."

Suddenly Orr's earring heated up, and Cho's voice sirened through his bone marrow. "You can't use your own creedy name. Are you brain-dead? Didn't you read the name on your pass?"

The cop said, "This is not your pass. Let's see your ID."

Orr glanced around in wild panic. He slapped his pockets, but he hadn't brought an ID. Sweat burned his eyes. Should he run? His hand closed on the coin purse. "I have this."

The cop seized the purse and shuffled it out of sight faster than Al could have pulled off a card trick. Then he pushed Orr through the city gate. "You're under arrest."

4

Dirt dive. To practice a skydive on the ground.

The first thing Orr noticed in Seattle was the noise. He threw back his Kevlar hood, and echoes assaulted him. Rumbling machinery, forced air, and nondirectional hammering. Maybe it was only the blood romping through his eardrums, but either way, the noise shredded his focus.

The cop hustled him down a muddy concrete ramp into an alcove, then frisked him head to toe, searching for more loot. Orr stood with his hands clasped behind his head watching thumb-sized termites file across the wall. The cop rifled his pockets, then confiscated his respirator. "In the city, we breathe communal air."

Orr took a whiff. Seattle had a funny odor. Engine fumes blended with air freshener and thick human exhaust. Or maybe Orr smelled the funk of his own stress.

The cop ushered him into the dingy police station lobby, where rain-soaked criminals stood shoulder to shoulder. Water rilled off everyone's clothes and pooled on the stone tiles. Orr stumbled against the other lawbreakers. What if the authorities hooked him to a lie detector? He would fail. Of course he would fail. And then . . .

His throat burned. He wanted water, but the cop had taken his flask. Everyone smelled like vinegar. Or was it him? When his earring heated up, he cursed.

Cho's voice warbled, "Brilliant job, sports byte. You should get a medal."

"Cho? How did you . . . Are you watching me?" Orr rubbed his earring. "Get me out of here."

"Working on it." The earring went cold.

His eyes slanted up to the ceiling, not ten centimeters above his head. The rock seemed to bend downward. And something crusty was dripping down. He reached up and touched wet white nipples of stalactites. This was a cave. And the rock was eroding away every second. How could people trust a ceiling like this? He shut his eyes and stood rigid, clenching his muscles and trying to think of something else, anything at all, except the mountain of unstable rock poised over his head.

Half an hour later, they hauled him into an office no larger than a crypt, where an obese jowly woman sat enthroned behind a rolling metal cart. Her badge read: "Inspector Maalik." Her grizzled hair stuck out in tufts like wet fur, and a glossy black ocular covered her left eye. Orr saw a miniature pod anchored at the side of her neck.

She said, "Name?"

"Joseph Kittinger," he stammered. He was too dazed to remember the real fake name. His chest squeezed. He couldn't seem to get enough air.

She worked her fleshy lips. "Sit down."

He sank onto the low metal stool and waited. On the cart sat a large bowl of deep-fried kelp from which the woman fed steadily. Her double chin glistened. Something in her ocular held most of her attention. Her index fingers ticked through invisible files, and her heavy jowls moved up and down, mouthing silent words.

Finally, she turned her naked eye his way. She rolled her cart aside and scooched her chair forward till they were sitting knee to knee. She said, "Counterfeiting a pass. Assuming a false identity. Illegal transit. You've been a bad boy."

Orr breathed slowly and tried to clear his head. *Keep it together,* he warned himself. He would have told any lie, but his powers of invention fizzled.

She put her hand between his legs. "Sweetie pie, you look familiar. Have I seen you on the web?"

"Not me." He shifted on the stool.

The woman studied him. "Yeah, I've seen you. I'll remember later. Anyway, this isn't your transit pass." She slid her hand up his leg and fondled him. "Tell me the truth now."

"It's a mistake," Orr blurted.

She laughed. "Sweetmeat, if you want me to believe that, you gotta give me some sugar."

She leaned forward and puckered her mouth, demanding a smooch. Her breath smelled rancid. Orr got a close-up view of her greasy purple lips, and the crumbs on her chin, and the hairs. He closed his eyes and kissed her.

"Nice." She leaned back and rolled her eyes. "Using a fake pass is a felony in Seattle. I'm gonna sentence you to one year community service with a quarry team." Then she pricked the inside of his wrist with something like a fountain pen. "This is just so I can find you later."

Dive loops. Handholds built into the Sky Wing for easy gripping.

One year? Orr didn't look at the ceiling. Sharp needles of returning circulation stabbed his limbs as he washed his face in the police station lavatory. A cockroach sat on the sink rim, watching. His Kevlar had dripped dry. He concentrated on the smell of bleach and the water seeping through his fingers, and he tried not to think about his jail sentence. This washroom could be anywhere, he told himself. This could be the men's room at the top of Mount Shishaldin.

His talkative guard looked about sixteen. Caramel skin, dirty fingernails, and a lopsided face that would have been doleful if not for his big toothy smile. "Quarry team ain't so assful. I got uncles do that. They work at the eastern margin. Solid rock through there. Mongo safe, so long as the teams don't undermine each other."

The kid handed him a tube of vegetable soap and a rough fiber towel.

"They got power shovels, core drillers, explosives. They got nanobugs that eat rocks and shit floor tiles. Citizens bring the diggers free food 'cause they do righteous work." The kid displayed his crowded teeth. "My name's Hob."

"I'm Joe." Orr rinsed his mouth and spit.

"You remind me of somebody," the kid said.

"I look like a lot of people." Orr rubbed his face with the towel.

Hob wore a black ocular and a throat pod, evidently standard police equipment. His cloth uniform had been mended by hand, and a faint whine emanated from his vicinity, punctuated with little pops and bursts of percussion. Orr guessed the kid must be viewing a webcast through his ocular.

Now and then, Hob shook his left arm really hard, and Orr noticed the kinetic energy band strapped to his wrist. Back in Unimak, Pete Hogue used one of those to power his Coast Guard radio.

Hob's complexion gleamed with zits. "Only thing, you ain't been assigned to no margin team. You're going underneath the bottom, deeper than I ever been. Make your ears bleed. You're gonna quarry the Underside."

Orr splashed more water in his face. The Underside? He'd heard about rivers of molten basalt flowing under the Earth's crust. Sulfuric lakes, toxic gas, blazing infernos, such rumors stuck in his mind. He worked saliva around his mouth. "What kind of minerals do they quarry down there?"

"Man, ain't no cronky mineral. People need room to live. You quarry space."

After Orr swigged several handfuls of cloudy water from the little sink, Hob gave him a strip of pearl millet jerky to chew, then led him by the elbow through the labyrinthine Halls of Justice. Lounging along the walls were clumps of dirt-streaked men, women, and children. Worn down and hungry, their vacant stares made Orr anxious. He guessed they were newly arrived refugees, caught like himself without the correct documents. Some of the children looked ill.

Orr heard weeping. He turned and saw a tiny girl in a soiled shirt and panties huddled between the outstretched legs of what must be her father. The man was mumbling, maybe hallucinating. He didn't seem to know his daughter was there. Then Orr spotted the wires fanning across his jaw. The man was talking to his ocular.

Orr kicked the man's leg. What kind of father would cruise some stupid web site while his little girl cried? Orr wanted to punch the man, but he had no right. The girl's hollow eyes got to him, though. He dug through his empty pockets. Finally, he gave her his vegan jerky.

At the police station exit, Hob stopped so abruptly, Orr almost tripped over him. The kid embraced the air with both arms and did an odd little gyration with his hips. Orr stepped back, startled. High-pitched music leaked from Hob's earbud, and whatever he was seeing in his oc obviously entertained him. Orr tried to slip past him, but the kid whipped out his stun gun.

"Wait up, Joe." Hob grinned and rubbed his thumb over the wall. Specks of soot came off, and he wiped the grime on his shirt. "Mote cameras. We got 'em everywhere in the city. It's assful to run away."

Dock. A physical connection between two Sky Wings in flight.

The exit doors opened, and Orr found himself teetering on the brink of a trench that channeled through the bedrock like a dry aqueduct. He dreaded looking down, but he made himself peek over the edge. Six lanes of bicycle traffic passed through the trench in each direction. He counted four more lanes for pedicabs, mopeds, skateboards, tow carts, and wheelchairs. Titanium spokes flashed. Electric motors purred. Orr hung on to the rail, dazed by the variety of vehicles. Hob laughed and gave him a friendly nudge with the butt of his stun gun.

Halfway across the pedestrian bridge, Orr was still ogling the heavy traffic when a cyclist stood up on his bike and pointed. "Look, it's the Gravity Pilot!"

The boy swerved and dipped his handlebar. Suddenly, dozens of bikes went down. Two mopeds collided, and someone screamed. Hob clutched Orr's collar and shuffled him over the bridge. "Let's get out of here before the rubberneckers mob us."

A sound like a thousand clanging cymbals echoed from the trench. Orr tried to dodge around Hob and get back. "People are hurt down there. I know some first aid."

Hob pushed him through the milling crowd. "Blood on the spokes. Not our problem."

"What?" Orr wasn't sure he heard right. He kept looking back and listening for an ambulance, but no one in the vicinity seemed concerned.

Hob steered him into a bright vaulted arcade. "You can't wig every time somebody drops a bike. We always got more people."

Orr kept seeing the crash in his head, dozens of cyclists, arms and legs—and he himself was the cause of it. But he soon lost sight of the traffic trench. He knocked the kid's hand off his collar and moved on.

The arcade was huge, larger than the dome on Mount Shishaldin, and never had he witnessed so many humans in one place. Laser-beam ads shimmered through the air. Music echoed from shop windows. Chemical air freshener stung his nostrils. He scowled up at the molded foam ceiling. It was painted pink and festooned with rosy garlands of clouds. Also, mildew stains.

"This is uptown. It's flash." Hob maneuvered him through the crowd in a diagonal path. "Stairwell's not far."

Orr felt more and more unsettled. Thousands of people stood, sat, squatted and sauntered up and down the gleaming courtyard. They wore dazzling clothes and jewels, but he sensed something missing from their faces. He couldn't say exactly what was absent, but it creeped him.

He rose on tiptoes to look for Dyce. When several strangers pointed and seemed to recognize him, he ducked and pulled his Kevlar hood around his face. Then he staggered. The floor felt like a sponge.

Hob gave him another cordial shove. "That's a power floor, chode. Every step we take pumps electricity into the city grid. It's good to be green."

Green? Orr kept picturing those cyclists going down, and green was not the color he saw. Then he halted and knuckled his eye sockets. Ahead stood a creature four times his size.

Was the thing alive? Its dark hulk towered up to the vaulted ceiling, and its colossal headdress seemed to nod at Orr, beckoning him forward. Its thick gnarled body twisted upward, corded with ropey muscle. Knots covered its flaky gray hide. It stood its ground, waiting.

Orr took a step closer. The thing had a dozen feet. Orr saw long coiling toes rooted in the circle of black carpet on which it stood. But where was its head? The monster lifted a hundred swaying green arms toward the ceiling, yet Orr could see no head. Perhaps the branching members were not arms but necks, and the monster's multiple heads were obscured by its wild green headdress.

Orr loosened his collar and studied the creature's crown. Thousands of tiny green spikes waved in the subtle air currents. He watched them nod and tremble, glistening dark where light struck the surface, glowing emerald where light filtered through from behind.

He moved closer, and his nostrils caught a sharp petroleum smell. He took another step, and his boot sank in the black carpet. He lifted his foot and saw damp oily loam clinging to his heel. It wasn't carpet, it was mud. The creature still hadn't moved. Orr advanced boldly into the circle of black mud, stretched out his hand, and touched the thing's hide. It felt rough. A bit of skin came off in Orr's fingers. He sniffed it. Powdery dry. He took a bite.

"Don't eat from that tree. Chode, it's toxic." Hob chuckled.

"Tree?"

"Gengineered western hemlock. It absorbs carbon through its needles. We use 'em to clean the city air."

Orr stepped back. "This is a real tree?"

"Hey, you're tracking mud. That's nas."

Orr glanced down at his boots. He balanced on one foot and scraped loam off his boot sole. Hob found a handkerchief in his pocket for Orr to clean his hands.

"You never heard of carbon-eating trees? They got 'em planted all over Washington. Other places, too. In about a hundred years, they say we'll have a clean sky."

Orr watched the emerald needles wave in the moving air. Clean sky? This city mixed him up.

They walked on, and Orr kept glancing back at the tree, penned in its small circle of loam. But the tree soon receded behind a forest of bikes hanging in clusters on vertical poles. Orr saw streetlamps powered by slowly falling counterweights and coin-operated kiosks for recharging batteries. Everyone's garments kept changing colors. Boots swirled up people's ankles like marbled ink. Belts blazed real-looking fire.

Hob noticed him checking out people's clothes. "It's quu-fabric. Uptown glam. Responds to voice command. Who needs that trash, huh?"

Orr noticed the kid's sour expression. Everyone in the arcade wore quu-suits except Hob. Orr had one himself under his Kevlar coverall, and Cho had warned him how pricey it was. Maybe Hob couldn't afford a quu-suit. Maybe the kid felt outclassed, walking through this luxury arcade in his faded police uniform. Orr had a feeling there were layers and layers in this city.

More than once, he caught himself staring. Seattle played roulette with his focus. Everyone was talking, but not to each other. Some people seemed to dance or wrestle, only without partners. Some gazed at empty space, and others grasped at objects that weren't there. Hob was acting weird again, too, mumbling and bumping into things. Orr saw him pitch forward and crack his knee against a kiosk. "Shit," the kid said, rubbing his leg.

When a young woman tripped and fell against a vending machine, Orr helped her to her feet. Blood trickled from a cut on her chin, and by a chance angle of light, Orr glimpsed the contact lens floating in her right eye. Clear as glass, no larger than a fleck, her ocular had no wires. Orr remembered Dyce had a wireless oc like that. Everyone in Seattle must have them.

He steadied the young woman. "Are you okay?"

She didn't answer. The oc so engrossed her, she seemed unaware that a stranger was examining her face. Orr let her go and watched her wander on.

"Check this." Hob paused at a shop window full of web gear.

Orr could identify maybe half the gadgets. He saw pyramids of handheld pods, pans, and vones small enough to hide in your fist. Some you could wear as jewelry.

Hob sniffed at the miniatures. "That small shit is obsolete. Here's the new slam. Retro." He pointed out boxy desktop monitors, oversize headphones and rack-mounted consoles bristling with big knobs and analog dials. His brown eyes misted. "Lavish gear. I'm saving my pay."

Orr reached out to touch a vone, but his fingers passed right through the case, as if the vone wasn't even there.

"Holograms," Hob said. "See, this is retail. You pick out what you want here at the shop, then it comes to you in the web. Efficient, see?"

Orr waved his hand through the holographic projection. He wondered if Dyce had come to this shop. She might have stood right on this spot and looked at these very gadgets. He slid his big feet back and forth on the spongy power floor.

When Hob queried the display for product details, Orr took a small step backward. Then another. Hob was too deep in dialog with the merchandise to notice.

Door jam. Rehearsing a group skydive exit from an aircraft.

Orr walked away fast, turning steadily left, then right, and memorizing his route so he could find his way back to the exit. He kept his hood drawn and tried not to attract attention, but his Kevlar coverall looked out of place in the city. He searched for some private corner where he could take it off. People barely glanced up as he passed. After a while, he realized they didn't see him at all. He pulled off the coverall in full view of half a dozen urbanites. Underneath, his quu-suit still looked fresh and clean. He dumped the coverall in a recycle bin.

His idea was to find Dyce fast and get out. But the farther he walked, the more every path looked alike. Why didn't this place have signposts? He approached an elderly man with gray lips and ashy circles under his eyes. "Pardon, sir. I'm looking for a company called Cyto."

Orr might have been empty air, the way the man gazed straight through him.

Nearby, a sallow-faced woman squatted on the floor, plucking at her purple tunic. Orr stooped to see her face. Her eyes looked bleached. He said, "Excuse me. Do you know where I can find Cyto?"

The woman squinted. "What did you say?"

"Cyto?" he repeated with a polite nod.

"Can't you see I'm busy." The woman continued scratching at her tunic.

Orr stepped back. The woman gave him the willies. He entered a shop to ask for directions. The counters displayed sweaters and capes in soft rippling colors, jeweled scarves, woven metal belts. He'd never seen such a wealth of clothing. But the garments were holograms, and the friendly cashier was a machine, so he left.

He found another hemlock tree and pressed his back against its trunk. Nuts, he thought. How did anyone survive in this loony bin? At least the tree was solid. He sat down and dug his fingers into the fungus-crusted mud and thought about the poor devils in the traffic trench. Had they been wearing oculars, too? Was every soul in this place caught in a web trance?

A young couple sat on a nearby bench pulling invisible levers. They were leaning forward and knotting up their shoulders with intense concentration. Orr watched their fingers snatch puffs of air. Their faces distressed him. He rested his head against the hemlock bark and lifted his eyes to the pink mildewed ceiling. Gengineered tree needles swayed under the air blowers, and chemical perfume congested his sinuses. Could this really be the height of human civilization?

Cho's glass earring warmed his ear. "Where the hell are you going? Do you have a clue?"

Orr said, "How can you see me?"

"Keep still," Cho said. "The cops are watching."

Orr glanced at the fine inky spray of mote cameras on the nearby bench. "They can't pick me out of eighteen million people."

"Actually, they can. They've got a Geist."

Cho had to explain the concept of the Geist cognitive surveillance network. He said the police injected a RFID into Orr's wrist, and Orr thought that meant some kind of insect. He scratched at the little bite on his arm where the lady cop pricked him with her fountain pen. Then he pulled his quu-suit collar up around his ears.

"These people, are they the addicts?" He watched the young couple work. "They're like the living dead."

Cho didn't answer.

Nearby, a middle-aged woman climbed into a potted yucca plant. She looked crumbly, as if she were made of packed salt. She stood in the pot, trampling the carbon-eating leaves and howling threats. When she accidentally knocked a beverage cup from the hands of a passerby, dark syrup dribbled down the fellow's quu-suit, shorting out his paisleys and sending curls of smoke up his arm. Orr could smell his hair singe. But the man walked on without noticing.

Then the woman turned and pointed at Orr. "Gravity Pilot. I know you."

Orr wriggled around to the other side of the tree. He wanted to blast the lid off this mountain. These Seattlites were sleepwalking through their lives. Anesthetized to pain, couldn't they feel what was slipping away through their fingers? He thought about climbing up in the yucca pot with the crazy woman. Maybe if he shouted at the top of his voice, he could wake them up. But no, they wouldn't hear.

He touched his earlobe. His ear had swollen from the tight-fitting earring. "Cho? Are you still there?"

Cho said, "I've located your girlfriend's oc address. Calling her now."

"You're calling Dyce?" Orr's pulse leaped. He was going to speak to Dyce in person. Almost in person. He closed his eyes, and there she was, framed in his mind, his beautiful black-eyed Berry. He gripped a fistful of mud and waited.

5

Dope run. Slang term for a night skydive.

Half a kilometer deep beneath the tree roots where Orr sat waiting, Dyce came awake in her chair. She'd been riding Orr's new docking sim. When she leaned back, her vertebrae made gristly popping sounds. She didn't try to stand. Her legs felt like concrete. She wiped her eyes and saw rings of white fungus furring the rock overhead.

Cold spread through her chest, and she coughed. The damp had gotten into her lungs. She squeezed her gold locket and twisted the chain till it cut into her neck, just to make sure she could still feel. At moments like these, she recognized that she was dying.

An eternity had whispered by since she last saw Orr. Ten weeks? She clicked the locket open to view his face, but when their love song began to play, she shut it fast. Her coworkers complained about noise.

Inside the sparkling ether of Cyto, she could see him. She could replay his webcasts, listen to his interviews. She could fly hand in hand with him through the azure. By now, she'd learned to zip through Cyto the same way her coworkers did, without swinging her arms like a noob. These days, she performed the most complicated tasks sitting perfectly still in her chair. And she multivisioned constantly. In her oc, she watched Orr sail through his clouds, while she also kept a wary eye on the workscreen tilting up from her desk, in case her supervisor checked in.

She was supposed to be indexing filmographies, but her right eye stung like the blazes. She dabbed it with the corner of her shirt. When had she last changed her uniform? She couldn't remember. But three of Orr's new sky-dives were waiting in her queue, and she no longer pretended to resist. She needed Cyto.

She tugged at her hair. What a weak watery soul she'd become. Thank God, Orr couldn't see the wreck she'd made of her life. Useless, rotten girl. She beat her fists against her eyes. She deserved to poison herself. And she knew exactly how. Cyto Cyto Cyto.

She was about to drop back in when a vone call zinged through her oc. Unbelievable, an outside caller? The first words tinkled inside her ear, distant and distorted. She couldn't get a visual, but there was no mistaking the cherished voice.

"Orr."

He said, "Berry, is that really you?"

She could hardly think. "You feel so far away."

"I'm here," he said, "in Seattle. I've come to get you."

"You're in the city?" She bumped her chair against the cube wall.

"Quiet," a coworker growled.

She got down on the floor and squeezed under her desk. Orr in Seattle? She forgot about the pain in her back and chest. She felt too overwrought to subvocalize, but she kept her voice to a whisper. "Orr, you were right about Seattle."

He said, "Just tell me where you are."

His brave baritone warmed her. Of course he would barge in, not knowing the risk. Hadn't she prayed he would come—and hadn't she begged the angels to ignore her plea? This place was toxic. Orr had to leave.

But first, if only she could see his living face one last time. She closed her eyes, whispered her password, and there was the Gravity Pilot, soaring through the nimbus.

His voice jolted her awake. "I know about your debts, Berry. We'll pay them. I'm earning a good salary, and—"

"You don't know anything." She squeezed farther under the desk. "Get out of here as fast as you can."

"I won't," he said, "not without you."

How could she make him listen? Even if he searched the whole city, he would never find her. This place was too well hidden. And if he tried, these devils would trap him like they trapped her. She couldn't bear that, not her Lagi. She wasn't worth it.

She made her voice harsh. "I don't want to see you. Go away."

Then she terminated the call. Static lashed her ear. Orr was gone.

"Shut up," a coworker yelled, but Dyce could not shut up. Crouched under her desk, eyes wide open, she beat her hands against the stone floor and wept.

6

Do-over. Skydiver slang for the impossible.

Orr sat listening to nothing. Dyce hung up? He couldn't even blink. "Lost the call," Cho said. "I can't reconnect. There's, like, a block."

Orr kept hearing Dyce's voice. *Go away?* Those words came from a language he didn't speak. When he tried to conjure her image in his mind, he couldn't see her. What had happened to his best friend? "Berry," he cried out, yanking at the earring, and all at once, he realized a stranger was examining his face.

"Orr Sitka?" A small girl bent over him, arching her eyebrows. Her brown eyes seemed familiar, but glittery Islamic scarves masked her freckled face, and thick mascara gunked her lashes. "You're the Gravity Pilot, right? I'm supposed to hide you."

Orr was too stunned to think. He felt like he'd been clubbed between the eyes. But the girl's voice had a familiar ring. Before he could place her, she said, "Oops. Here comes your cop." She picked up her long orange skirts and dashed away.

"There you are, Joe." Hob came sauntering over, twirling his stun gun. "Like I said, you can't hide from the web. We got you."

Orr sat huddled against the tree, still trying and failing to understand Dyce's words. When Hob pulled him to his feet, he tripped on the hemlock roots. There had to be a reason she hung up. Of course she wanted to see him. Vones were not the best way to connect. When they met face to face, everything would be clear.

Hob said, "You gotta stay with me now. Word of honor?"

Orr grunted. He tugged his collar high over his ears and followed Hob, watching for another chance to slip away. The vone call made him more anxious than ever to find Dyce in a hurry. Hob led him to a pair of sliding metal doors, then made a funny signal with his thumb, like he was pressing an invisible control panel. The doors opened into a stairwell. Orr had seen stairs before, but Unimak had nothing like this.

Two runs of steps spiraled around each other like a double helix. On one, people were climbing up. On the other, they were going down. The stairs were too narrow for passing, so people went single file. The stairwell had no landings. No handrails, either. Just a support pole running down the center. Orr couldn't see the bottom. People bounced back and forth between the two spirals as if they didn't realize how the whole flimsy structure might collapse and bury them alive. He edged backward.

His earring grew warm, and Cho said, "You have to go down."

Orr whispered, "Is Dyce down there?"

Cho said, "The Underside isn't monitored. It's the only place in Seattle where you can move undetected."

Meanwhile, Hob was narrating like a tour guide. "These stairs are heel-strike generators. Every step you take adds power to the grid."

All Orr could feel was, every step took him deeper under the mountain. Bathophobia fired through his nerve endings. When Hob nudged him toward the descending stairs, his forebrain wanted to go, but his hindbrain gripped the doorjamb and held fast.

Cho spoke through his earring, "I'm trying to help you find your lover. Don't fight me, sports byte."

For several seconds, Orr stood grimly biting raw skin off his lower lip. He watched people spring on and off the heel-strike treads. It wasn't complicated. He drew deep breaths and tried to slow his heart rate. Dyce. He chanted her name in his mind. Then he counted three and lunged for the stairs.

Agile as he was, his phobia made him overshoot the stair tread. He swung both arms around the vertical support pole, but he slid down till his boots knocked into the heads and chests of people below.

"Clumsy idiot. Get your boots off my hair!"

"Who is this yokel?"

"Wait. Aren't you . . . ?"

"I'm nobody." Orr tried to cover his face with his arm.

Hob dropped down and helped Orr find his footing. As soon as he felt stable, he tugged his collar higher and eased down the stairs, one step at a time. Several citizens yelled at him to move faster. He tried to. Following behind, Hob talked to his pod and paid no attention.

Doors slid open, and people stepped on and off the stairs, but Hob kept guiding him down. "Chode, we're not there yet."

Metallic hammering echoed from below—or from inside Orr's head, he couldn't be sure. He would have covered his ears, but he didn't dare let go of the pole.

"This ain't nothing. Wait till you see the Underside." The kid gave him a cube of foam and showed him how to twist off small pieces to stuff in his ears. "Stick by me. I take care of you."

Eventually, Hob waved his thumb, and another door slid open. Orr jumped out with too much force and knocked into a large stranger in a thick yellow coverall.

"Watch it, noob." The large man elbowed Orr aside, then stepped onto the spiral stairs with ease.

On this level, many sections of light tube had burned out, and the stale air made Orr cough. Hob cheerfully pushed him along. Dozens of men and women in yellow coveralls were shoveling some kind of material into carts that rolled along the corridor on rails. Every time a cart whooshed by, Orr and Hob had to flatten themselves against the rock wall.

Hob said, "We take a different shaft down from here to sublevel nine."

Then something in web space diverted Hob's attention. It must have been major news, because when Hob pivoted away to confer with his ocular, several others did, too. Orr waved his hand in front of Hob's face. No reaction. He was about to slip away when one of the distracted shovelers swayed in front of an oncoming cart.

"Watch out!" Orr yelled.

But the cart was moving fast, and the man fell.

Orr rushed over and knelt by the track. One or two shovelers glanced to see what had happened. The man's legs lay across the rail, and his feet had been severed off. He wasn't moving. He was probably in shock.

"Would you look at that?" Hob stood with his hands on his hips, shaking his head, still absorbed in his oc.

Orr grasped the man's shoulders and yelled, "Hob, we have to move him before another cart comes."

One of the yellow-suits said, "It's okay. The Geist will call for cleanup."

"Cleanup?" Orr looked the man in the face. Could anyone be that callous? "Hob," he yelled again. But the kid was totally preoccupied.

No one offered to help. Their blank eyes made Orr feel sick. When a pair of robots showed up with a litter to bear the injured man away, Orr followed them into the stairwell. Just as the door slid closed, he glanced back. Hob never turned around.

Down plane. Two canopies flying together toward the ground.

Up the stairs Orr ran, recklessly springing past other climbers, too panicked to worry about falling. Horror animated him.

Cho's voice thundered, "What the bloody hell are you doing?"

Orr panted. "Did you see what happened? I can't do this, Cho. I can't."

"Maybe you need more encouragement."

Somewhere a switch flipped, and all the stairwell doors closed in unison. Electronic deadbolts locked into place. Then the lights went out. Total darkness, no human eye could adjust. People cursed, and Orr hugged the pole as if he wanted to merge at the atomic level.

Cho spoke through his earring. "Want the lights back on? Go where I tell you, sports byte."

Orr mashed his face against the pole. What kind of technology was Cho using? How could a newscaster turn out the lights? Sweat rolled down Orr's cheek. A tiny, multi-legged beast ran across his fingers and crawled up his sleeve, but he didn't dare move. When the lights flickered on again, a door slid open, and he bounded through. He shook the bug out of his sleeve and stomped it. A white spider.

Cho's tricks maddened him. He glanced down a curving hall. The carpet felt plush underfoot, and soft blue-green halogen glowed from recessed pockets. There were no termites here, no crickets or mildew. A whisper of air circulation blended with a low subliminal thudding. He walked a few meters ahead. Metal doors punctuated the stone walls, and surveillance motes coated the ceiling like fur. He saw no door numbers, no markings of any kind. Every entrance looked the same, and the hall's curvature baffled his sense of direction.

"Looking for the emerald city?" Cho's voice raked through his ear. "In Seattle, all signage is virtual. You need the ocular to find your way, so put it on now."

Orr kept walking. "I tossed it."

Cho said, "I'm not hearing this. You threw away a brand-new wireless oc?"

Farther down the passage, a door whooshed open. Cho said, "Go inside. Hurry."

When Orr didn't obey, Cho's voice grated his ear bones. "Idiot. Your cop is coming. Get inside before he sees you."

Orr heard footsteps, and the young guard's voice echoed around the curved wall. "Hey, Joe. Where are you? This isn't fun."

Orr stepped through the open door, and it slid shut behind him.

The residence Orr entered was sumptuous and ornate, more ornate than the Aleut Tribal Courtroom, the most palatial chamber he'd ever visited until now. Silk curtains swathed the walls, and his feet sank in a thick Persian carpet. Cushions lay scattered over the floor in shades of plush cherry and saffron. Gadgets came alive, and the light level rose, revealing paintings of nudes in ancient hanging gardens. Air blowers spread a subtle scent of jasmine, and stringed instruments purred in the background. At the center of the room stood a circle of upholstered recliner chairs with bright silvery arm and leg restraints.

He took a second look at the restraints. "What the heck? Shackles?"

Cho blared through his earring. "Tell me you're joking about the oc. You didn't throw it away. That would be too moronic for words."

Orr edged around the bizarre chairs. "Who lives here?"

"Do you know what an ocular costs?" Cho's voice sounded throttled. "Forget it. Go to the bedroom. No arguments."

Orr peeked through various doorways till he recognized a bed. The room was also jam-packed with gymnastic equipment . . . or something like that. He studied the steel contraption dangling over the bed. "What is that thing?"

Cho said, "Ignore that stuff. Look in the closet."

Orr studied the grisly steel buckles and belts over the bed, trying to work out the spatial relationship. He eased around the equipment, careful not to touch anything. At the back of the room, he found the closet.

Cho said, "Top shelf. Left."

Orr was getting more and more annoyed. "How do you know about this place? And how do you see every move I make?"

"I'm an investigative reporter," Cho said. "It's what I do."

The answer didn't satisfy Orr. Nevertheless, he pulled a lidded box down from the shelf. Inside, he found a tangle of old cable connectors, adapters, wireless routers and random electronic junk. He sat on the floor and kicked off his boots. His sweaty socks had gotten twisted.

"Specs. You see them? Put them on." Cho sounded impatient.

Orr sorted through the box. Under some pin connectors and three-pronged plugs, he found a pair of sunglasses in a case. "Tell me the truth," he said. "You know who lives here."

Cho snickered. "Hob's out in the hall. He thinks you vanished in a puff of smoke."

Orr bunched his lips. Cho's evasions chapped him. He considered the sunglasses. They looked ordinary enough, but when he held them up to the light, the lenses went opaque. He slid his finger along the temples and inside the nose pads. Smooth plastic, old and worn. He knew these glasses held more secrets than he could detect.

"They're old-fashioned web specs," Cho said. "They won't melt your brains. As if you had any."

With grave doubts, Orr slipped on the glasses. Immediately, the nose pads began to itch, and the smooth plastic temples softened to living glue. Soon the frames bonded to his skin and sank nano-whiskers into his nerve endings. Forty-five seconds later, Orr's world went bright.

A three-hundred-sixty-degree view of the bedroom exploded around him. He could literally see out the back of his head. Good thing he was sitting down. The panorama rotated his senses.

Worse were the semi-transparent panes of text and video that overlaid the entire room. He saw an owner's manual for the cooling system, a directory of movies on demand, and payment notices from a carpet cleaning service. Video images pulsed, and voices babbled. Icons blinked yellow and red.

"Ha! The old tech still works." Cho sounded as if he were sitting right there in the room.

Wherever Orr focused his eyes, more data panes popped up. For a moment, he listened to the user instructions for the device over the bed. Then he yanked the glasses off. They tugged at his skin and came loose with a dry smacking rip. It took a while for his eyes to readjust to reality.

He dropped the glasses on the carpet. "How can anybody see with these things?"

"It takes practice. Put them back on. I'll help."

Orr felt woozy when he stood up. "Whoever lives here is depraved."

"The owner won't be home for hours. Have a seat, and let's try to find Dyce's location."

Orr could not conceive of a person who would own such an obscene bedroom device, but it was useless to question Cho. He returned to the front room, carrying the glasses in his fingertips like something he'd pulled out of a toilet. The circle of chairs repulsed him, so he sat on the wine-red carpet near the door. Clamping his jaw tight, he drew the glasses back on.

Again the room exploded in a three-sixty-wide angle. Voices, text, ring tones, and overlapping videos—every gadget in sight projected its own small claim for attention. Advertising coupons splashed and blinked. Orr felt an urge to crush the glasses to shards. He gripped the frames in both hands. But then, the lenses went dark, and only one small pane opened in the lower left corner. He saw Cho's talking head.

The newscaster blew a smoke ring and chuckled. "You're in my sky now. It's your turn for a lesson."

Very slowly, the room behind the glasses reemerged. This time, there were no confusing overlays. Orr saw only the real objects in subdued grayish colors. But the three-hundred-sixty-degree view made him light-headed. He felt himself toppling over, and his hands shot out in reflex for support.

Cho said, "I think we'd better turn off your pan."

The panoramic view reverted to normal, although the room still appeared dim and colorless. Orr said, "Why does everything look washed out?"

Cho minimized to a small inset pane. "Solid objects are suppressed so you can see the web overlays. It helps improve your multivision."

Multivision? Orr wriggled his fingers in front of his glasses. His hand looked spectral, ashy gray. Near his wrist, a pane popped open with blinking orange text: RIFD: SEATTLE PD. The text glowed much brighter than his hand. It began to scroll, and Orr read his name, date of birth, DNA sequence, and

Aleut tribal membership code. He felt stunned. The cop lady's prickly fountain pen had marked him, but how did she know his ID? As he continued reading, the text scrolled more and more of his personal data.

"The web specs sense the muscular movements of your eyes," Cho said. "You make the text scroll. Try stopping it."

Orr glanced away from the pane, and his life story stopped unreeling. He focused on other objects in the room, and he figured out how to make their panes open and close. Next, Cho showed him the navigation bar, and he practiced blinking his lids to work the icons. A diamond-shaped squiggle flashed in the upper corner, and when he focused on it, a menu dropped down. He browsed the pictograms, then concentrated on one that looked like an old-fashioned book. Instantly, the book fanned and displayed the public Seattle directory.

Cho said, "You're getting the knack of it."

Orr scanned the *I*s, looking for *Iakai*.

"Forget it," Cho said. "She's not listed."

Orr kept looking anyway, until another icon caught his attention, a pulsing black sun.

"Look away. Don't focus on that." Cho sounded anxious. "That's the portal to Cyto. I'll see if I can hide it. Meanwhile, concentrate on something else."

Orr peered through the competing audiovisual overlays and tried to see the real room, but so much motion and sound made him nauseous. When he closed his eyes, chatter multiplied in his ears. With an effort, he opened his eyes and squinted at one particular pane. It happened to be a video about the kitchen counters. Immediately, the other panes dissolved, and the chatter stopped.

"That's it. You're stabilizing." Cho smirked from his tiny inset.

When Orr combed his hands through his hair, splashes of color and noise rocketed around his head again. Focusing on one pane at a time was not a trivial task. "This is hard," he said. He tried staring at a lamp, and briefly, he was able to see its true living color. Finally, he discovered how to unfocus his eyes so that everything grayed to shadows.

Cho said, "You're not a total disaster. Now look at me."

When Orr directed his gaze at Cho's talking head, the rest of the field went dark.

Cho said, "Okay, I hid the Cyto portal in an accessory file, but it might pop up again. It's viral. If you see it, just concentrate on anything else. So, are you up for a real web cruise?"

Orr rolled his shoulders. *"Yio'kwa."*

Then time and space inverted. Orr plummeted through hollow black fire. His senses rang. His skin hairs stood on end. He became conscious of ions pulsing through the porous tissues of his brain, and he wasn't entirely sure he still existed. A minute later, he wrenched off the glasses and hurled them across the room.

"I pushed you too fast." Cho sighed. "You better not have broken those specs."

Orr ravaged his eye sockets with the heels of his hands. The room looked different after his brief jaunt through the web. He caught afterimages of panes, as if they were still hovering over each solid object. He had a feeling things would never look the same again. After blinking and popping his jaw from side to side, he crawled across the carpet and found the dark glasses behind a statue of a nude boy.

Then he leaned against the wall and cradled his throbbing head in his arms. Forty hours had passed since he woke on the wet asphalt outside Seattle. He didn't have a watch, but his body kept track. Every time he closed his eyes, he saw bicycles going down.

7

Drop zone. Skydiver landing area.

Rolfe swept the covers off Vera's bed. "Where the hell is my sky-diver?"

He'd caught her sprawled in her Seattle sheets, spying on Orr through the city Geist. It was late, after midnight, and she was so deeply absorbed, she didn't see Rolfe coming.

Lies popped out of her mouth. "The designers are upgrading our Sky Wing for the ionosphere. We need a heat shield for atmospheric reentry."

Rolfe knew better. Ionosphere, hell. Three days ago, he laid down her deadline. All this while, he'd been surveilling her Mundo Mountain hide-out, and she hadn't even begun preparations for the launch. Her constant deception sickened him.

"Cyto's future is on the line, Vera. This is not the time to settle grudges."

His mouth tasted like antifreeze, and the antiviral suit made his skin prickle. He'd been fasting again, consuming his own flesh from the inside out. Some days, he dreamed of imploding through his navel to seek a braver world.

Vera kept gushing her ridiculous fibs. "My design team's working around the clock. We're planning blockbuster graphics. Thrills, perils, high-voltage action—"

"Liar." He lifted her by the roots of her hair. When her dark red wig came off in his hand, he grimaced and dropped it. He hadn't meant to react that way. He wasn't a violent man, he wasn't. But Vera's scheming provoked him. He loathed how she made him doubt the value of his life's work, his glorious botanical garden. She used to be such a charming little girl. But she grew up vindictive.

He said, "I worked myself to the bone for you."

She picked up the wig, and he watched her hug it to her chest with that martyred gloom in her eyes. Oh yes, she'd perfected her act. He turned away and shut down his oc so he could think. Often, he wondered if his own early traumas had somehow been reenacted in his daughter. But he couldn't see any parallels. Days like this, he felt a million years old.

He said, "Show me what you're doing. Now."

Vera reattached her hairpiece. "Sure, Daddy. I'll show you."

She signaled her pan, and a vista swelled outward like a black globe. It filled the room and darkened her tapestried walls to the deep night of outer space. Near the center, a tiny planet revolved, nested in layers of vapor. Vera cupped the miniature Earth in her palm, then zoomed in for a close-up of the atmosphere. Her room filled with golden clouds.

"This is the lowest thickest layer," she said, "the troposphere."

Rolfe saw the wireframe underneath. "Shoddy graphics. What dickhead built this?"

Vera's eyes watered. "Me, Daddy. I did. It's for our ionosphere sim."

"This scrawl is your alleged blockbuster?"

"It's a rush job. What do you expect?"

Rolfe smelled bullshit. Just a rough first draft, she said, not ready for inspection, yada yada. She roamed through fluffy cloud scenes, and Rolfe curled his lip.

"You stick too close to factuality. Nobody's gonna buy this boring stuff." He poked at her panorama, stirring vortexes and lurid sparkles. He sketched lightning bolts and tornadoes. "That's better."

She slapped his hand. "This is *my* artwork. *Mine*. Don't screw with my realism."

She zoomed the view outward from the planet's surface, and the clouds dissolved to fine icy mist. Tedious emptiness. Rolfe felt a yen to add flying saucers.

"The next layer up is the stratosphere," she said, "because it's stratified with different temperatures. Above that is the cold middle layer, the mesosphere, where meteors explode. Higher, you see the thermosphere where satellites orbit."

Rolfe lost interest. He knew she was hiding something. He prowled into her closet and pawed through her costumes.

She followed him, trailing her panorama like a ball of shade. "The highest layer is the ionosphere, where sun rays ionize rainbow-colored auroras and—"

"Seven days I gave you." He took one of her faux-leather belts off its hook.

She said, "Yeah, we both know that's a joke."

He wrapped the belt around his knuckles. "Don't play with my schedule, sweet Vera. I'll demote you back to the brothel you were born in."

She shut off her pan and glared. He hadn't meant to bring up that ancient history. Sometimes his tongue ran away with him. Goddamn, the girl provoked him.

"Princess . . ."

"You sank too much damned cash in your bubble forest," she said. "Cyto's strapped. Everybody knows it. Cloned arthropods. Polka-dot toadstools. Farking bluebirds."

They faced each other across a rack of costumes, fixing each other with the same flared nostrils, the same green eyes. For that one moment, he saw her naked fury. Their family resemblance could not be denied.

Then she reformatted her smile. "You'll get your money, Dad. The Gravity Pilot's guaranteed to be a smash."

Rolfe held up his belt-bound fist. "There are many ways to fail, Vera, but only one way to succeed. We stand together. Or we take each other down."

8

Elliptical. Sky Wing with tapered leading and trailing edge
for higher performance.

Orr couldn't sleep for long in the strange residence. Dyce's words pursued him. *Go away. I don't want you.* He tossed and shifted on the carpet till he woke himself up.

Again, he tried to summon her image in his mind. He saw her ensconced behind her white desk at the back of the Unimak library. She wore one of his faded blue workshirts stuffed into her jeans, and she'd pinned up her hair in a loose floppy knot.

He was sitting close beside her, watching her do research on the Mekong Delta. Turned out their landlord, Shep Innoko, was a reenactor. Shep liked to play a combat medic in the fall of Saigon, and Dyce was helping him track down authentic photos of leg splints. Orr could still hear the cadence of her voice saying, "The web is an ocean."

The afternoon came back to him, the smell of the library carpet, the whirr of the communal CPUs and the children playing next door. She'd been telling him about the web's scale-free network. Like a free-flowing liquid, she called it, sparkling on top and murky underneath, one continuous body of fluent information.

"It's a force of nature," she said, tripping through Vietnam directories. "Remember how that video of the last polar bear flashed through everybody's inbox in a single hour?"

"I don't have an inbox," Orr answered.

She punched his ribs. "Hermit. You don't count. My point is, that two-minute vlog turned the political tide and put the Greens in power."

Orr didn't follow politics, and the web hadn't saved the white bear's life. Besides, Orr distrusted the ocean. He said, "It's too big. What if you drown?"

"Silly, you learn to swim." She pinched his arm, then checked out another cross-reference. They were squeezed side by side at her minuscule desk, rubbing shoulders and knees. Miss Tompkin shot them occasional disapproving frowns from her throne at the front, and her sour cologne flavored the stillness.

Dyce scrolled her index and called up one of Orr's favorite skydive vlogs. The day's post showed a hundred glossy Sky Wings sailing in formation over Melbourne, Australia. Orr watched the Wings dock together in a pattern that looked like an enormous snowflake. Then one lone diver circled the group, keying each person to break off and spiral apart. The effect was musical, like a kaleidoscopic ballet.

Orr pointed out the lone diver with his thumb. "That's Banda Rat. She's the Australian champion."

Dyce zoomed in for a close-up. "Banda's a hottie. Should I be worried?" She bumped his shoulder and winked. "On the web, you can find everything you need in fourteen seconds or less."

Orr didn't understand her infatuation with the web, but he liked to hear her talk. She said she could swim through a million branching inlets of knowledge because the web set her free from the laws of space-time. While she talked, she raced through photo galleries of injured vets.

Maybe she should have chosen a safer metaphor than the ocean. It made Orr think of crushing entrapment, thousands of meters down. He butted heads with her. "You said yourself, the web's not reliable."

"Yes and no. It's plural." She coiled her braid around her hand and fast-forwarded through the photos of war. "Facts and fiction get wrinkled up together, but I think sharing every viewpoint gives a clearer picture of the truth. It's, like, the ultimate crowdsource."

Orr wasn't buying it, though he loved to watch her eyes flash. He'd grown used to her contradictions. Shifting in her chair, she talked a little too urgently, describing how every problem required many different methods of investigation and many solutions. She scrolled the photos faster. Sometimes, she got way too keyed up. She said the more people linked in a wiki, the better the outcome. Different answers might not agree, but they could all still be correct.

"Like communes and capitalism," she said, "or science and religion, or—"

"Women and men?" Orr tickled her belly. His clowning made her giggle. They started wrestling.

When a lamp tipped over, Miss Tompkin stood and harrumphed. The two settled down. Dyce pretended to work. Orr poked her ribs, but she ignored him. Someone came in to return a bookreader. The clock ticked. They waited till Miss Tompkin went to the ladies' room.

Then Dyce gave Orr a shove and nearly knocked him out of his chair. "What I'm saying is, in the web ocean, every kind of truth flows together."

Orr rubbed his nose against hers. "What you're saying is, I'm a seagull, and you're a tasty little starfish."

He nipped at her earlobe and tried to bite her neck. She hammered him with her fists. Then he pulled her into his lap and squeezed and tickled her till she gave up lecturing. They never did agree about the web.

End cells. Outside cells in a parachute canopy.

Orr woke to an alarm bell ringing in his skull. "Dyce?"

His earring burned hot. Cho was yelling. "We have to move. The cleaning lady's coming."

He shot to his feet. Then he remembered he'd left his boots in the bedroom.

Cho said, "Power down, sports byte. You've got five minutes. Put your specs on."

Orr had come awake so fast, adrenaline boiled through his pectorals and quadriceps. He focused on the scene around him. A sour taste stung the back of his throat. Slowly he bent and picked up the revolting dark glasses. When he slid them on, he felt the plastic lick his flesh, and the room sank under its overlay of data panes. He tried not to move his head, but keeping his balance took effort.

Cho explained how to contact his quu-suit and modify its configuration. Orr browsed his options, then focused his eyes to transmit commands. The garment ballooned around him, then quivered from matte blue to sheeny silver to white, then back again. Its shape warbled and morphed. In an instant, it restyled into a dark blue hooded coverall, close-fitting and streamlined, something like a skydiver's jumpsuit.

Cho added rubies and jet beads around the cuffs. "If it's too plain, people will notice."

Orr doubted if Seattlites would notice the roof crashing in, but he didn't argue. He went back to the bedroom to get his boots. "Did you find Dyce?"

"No, but I discovered who owns Cyto. Get ready for a shock. It's Rolfe Luce. Vera's father."

Orr bumped against the bedroom equipment. Vera's father? The view through his specs obliterated his concentration. Vera's father owned the wikiverse that hired Dyce?

When he clutched at the blinding glasses, Cho said, "Leave them on. You need them. Open the main menu. You remember how?"

Orr focused on the diamond-shaped icon flashing in the upper corner of his view field, and through the chaotic overlays, a menu dropped down.

"Here's your next lesson." Cho pointed at the menu from his inset pane. "See the red ball at the bottom?"

"Yes."

"Look at it, and say the word 'Shut.' You don't have to say it aloud. Just make the motion with your throat."

Orr worked his glottis muscles, and the overlays vanished, leaving behind the mute gray view of physical objects. He ground his teeth. "Why didn't you show me that before?"

"Never mind. The cleaning lady's here. Run."

Orr didn't have time to argue. He grabbed his boots and loped barefoot through the shadowy bedroom, knocking against the equipment. One of the devices sprang to life. The front door was already opening. He rushed out and collided with the maid, who went tumbling.

"Sorry, ma'am." He reached to help her up, only to realize she was an eight-armed mechanical device.

"Forget the maid. Run," Cho said.

"Thief!" The cleaning robot slapped him and hailed the surveillance motes. "Police! Arrest this intruder!"

Orr fled down the curving hall. Sirens pulsed through his specs, traumatizing his eardrums, and so many ads blasted him with coupon offers, he couldn't see where he was going.

Cho said, "Whoa, you need an ad blocker."

As Orr stumbled along, Cho showed him how to filter the advertising feeds and mute the audio. When Orr heard the echo of real police boots following behind, he sprinted.

Cho overlaid a map in his view field. It made him tipsy, but eventually, he figured out how to read it like the heads-up display in his skydive helmet. Once he escaped the residential maze, he yanked on his boots, then found his way to a commercial area and merged into a crowd of shoppers. Inside his clothes, sweat ran down his back and chest. His body craved water and food.

He browsed his web menu till he spotted a blue teardrop, and when he followed the map and located a public drinking fountain, he almost wanted to laugh. The liquid that bubbled from the spigot tasted salty and metallic. He slurped long deep drafts.

After he finished rehydrating, he leaned against the wall to think. Dyce worked for Vera's father? That couldn't be a coincidence. So much concealment. Shells within shells. He slung his sweaty hair out of his face. "Does Vera know?"

Cho's head bobbled in the tiny pane. "You're such a child. Vera hired you on Rolfe's orders. You work for Rolfe, too. It all comes down to Rolfe."

Orr stood dead still. Everything he'd believed about Vera Luce had to be recalibrated. Vera. Dyce. Rolfe. When he tried to connect the lines, his brain fuzzed out. He rubbed sweat from his eyes. He couldn't focus. It was like he'd forgotten how.

Cho said, "Cyto is six levels down. That's where we'll find Rolfe Luce."

"And Dyce?"

"He'll know where she is."

Down again. Fright bloomed at the edge of Orr's mind, but still, he concentrated on using his specs to find the nearest stairwell. When he got there, Cho explained how to open the door, so he did that. Mechanical clanging boomed up from below. He peeked down the shaft.

"Dyce?" he whispered.

He stepped onto the spiral treads, gripped the pole and descended.

Exit weight. Total weight of the diver wearing Sky Wing and full gear.

Orr followed the spiral stairs down, heel-striking the energetic treads and trying not to think about Vera's lies. In hindsight, her behavior seemed as unreliable as the tectonic plates moving below. But Vera did honestly love the sky, he couldn't have been wrong about that. He'd seen the light in her face after freefall.

Every downward step made him feel more bitterly confused. His web specs fogged. His collar felt too tight, and he began to pant. Somewhere, he heard water running. Maybe it was raining outside. He pictured walls of mud sliding down the tunnels, burying everyone.

Were his fears irrational? Probably not, but he tried to believe they were. Hyperventilating made him unsteady. He clung to the pole so he wouldn't fall down the stairwell.

Cho whispered through his earring, "Okay, I just found out why Rolfe Luce hired you. You're not going to like this. He's using your skydives to addict new users."

Orr's foot slipped on the wet metal tread. His skydives? What did his skydives have to do with the web? So many questions, he couldn't focus. Right now, he needed all his attention to edge down the treacherous stairs.

When he reached the bottom, Cho guided him along a passage where the air hung as thick as grease. No uptown glam here. No arcade lights, no hygienic freshener. He wiped his foggy specs to see. Fumes burned his throat, and engine racket thudded through the rock. Something slick and wet trickled over the floor, and fungus sprouted along the gutters. Stalactites dripped from the ceiling, and restless termites enlivened the stone walls.

He compelled himself to visualize clouds. When his heart stopped cantering, he used his specs to gather information. The urbanites on this level wore factory uniforms. He browsed their ID badges. They were working people like himself. Shifts were changing, and traffic coagulated around the tea stalls. Several of the factory doors beamed familiar brand logos. He browsed ads for kelp flour, kelp textiles, kelp milk, and kelp oil. This was where his seafarm shipped their raw produce.

He figured out how to filter the panes so he could view the signage one layer at a time. A walk-up med clinic spewed bright slogans for cancer vaccines, and people waited outside in a docile queue. Nearby, a lackadaisical vendor squatted, slack-jawed, while his pushcart sang the praises of his seaweed tortillas. No one moved fast. The people looked tired.

Their faded clothes suggested low income, yet they all wore oculars. Orr saw wires splayed across their cheeks and heard them chatting with unseen parties. One man performed weird leaps and contortions. Another stood on a barrel, thrumming an invisible stringed instrument. Everyone shared the same glassy-eyed disconnection from the present, and their empty faces made Orr feel more demoralized than ever. He'd thought working people, at least, would be safe from the web.

"Are these the Cyto addicts?" he whispered.

"Keep moving," Cho said.

But he lingered, watching the people who couldn't see him. Unspeakable bleakness settled over him. *They're ghosts,* he thought. *All ghosts.*

He touched his web specs, his own link to ghostland. By now, the plastic frames had bonded tightly to his flesh. He didn't know about the side effects. He believed he could take them off any time he liked. He blotted his forehead with his hand.

"Look who it is." An old man nudged his wife. "The Gravity Pilot. It's really him."

People started to point, so Orr bent his head down and walked away quickly. The old man called out, "I watch your skydives all the time. They're awesome . . ."

Orr was so distracted, he bumped against an arch in the dim passage.

"Check your map," Cho said.

Orr fingered the scrape on his forehead. The directionals in his web specs showed the Cyto compound wasn't far, so he flagged the shortest path and hustled through a cross-cut. Already, the web panes felt more useful to him than the blurry gray outlines of the real corridor.

He moved ahead, craning in all directions for the police, till Cho reminded him about the pan feature to widen his peripheral view. When he expanded the angle to a full three hundred sixty degrees, he could see through the back of his head, but he had trouble walking. Panoramic vision made him scatty. He used it now and then, but mostly he kept the angle set at human normal.

Cyto's entrance looked like all the other doors on this level, a scuffed metal loading dock with a heavy-duty recessed grate. The door was unmarked except for the web pane it transmitted. The pane revealed nothing but a cryptic code: S7YX. Orr scanned the walls in both directions. He saw no other data.

"How do I get in?"

"Give me a minute," Cho said.

Orr ran his fingers around the edge of the rolling grate, looking for a latch or lever. Nothing. He flattened his hands against the grate and shoved, but it wouldn't budge. Then he flicked through the menu in his specs, looking for help.

Cho's pane suddenly maximized to fill his view. "One thing you have to swear, sports byte. When you get inside, don't let anyone talk you into entering a sim. Full immersion is severely addictive. Some people get hooked after just one use."

Orr kicked the grate with his boot. "Don't worry. I want no part of that stuff."

"Stand back!" Cho said. "They know you're here. They're coming!"

Orr heard the metal grate rolling open. His adrenal glands flooded raw alarm, and he turned to run. When he glanced back, he expected a squad of security goons to rush out and nab him. But the only person standing in the doorway was Vera.

9

Fall rate. Velocity of diver in freefall.

Vera stretched out her hand. "What in God's name are you doing here?"

She examined Orr from a distance. He stood in the corridor, half turned away, ready to run any second. She thought he looked exotic in the dark specs and midnight blue suit, older somehow. He reminded her of a male model in an ad. But she saw signs of breakage.

Precious boy, she yearned to rush up and feel his limbs, his rib cage, his shoulders, to make sure he wasn't hurt. She couldn't, though. She had to play this scene carefully. He stood hesitating, cinching his mouth in an uneven line.

She motioned him closer. "Are you okay? I've been worried to death." When he didn't move, she triggered her implants to spray calming phero-mones. Finally, she stepped out and took his arm. "Hurry inside, before the city motes read your ID."

She felt him hanging back, yet he allowed her to pull him through the door into the Cyto compound. Could it be, in spite of everything, he still wanted to believe in her?

When they passed through the antiviral screen, an electric shock of UV light flashed across their bodies, sterilizing their clothes and skin. Orr spun on his heel to defend himself, but the treatment lasted only a millisecond.

"It's harmless," she explained, drawing him farther into the lobby. "Rolfe's paranoid about disease."

He shook off her hand. "You knew Dyce works for your father. Why didn't you tell me?"

His question spiked fire through her gut. Of course she knew. Her game operated on multiple moving levels, and long before she hired Orr, she'd scoped his troublesome roommate. Serious risk. She absolutely had to separate the girlfriend from her skydiver without separating the skydiver from his sky. So, yes, she'd manufactured the library job.

Orr stood waiting for her answer. He needed a credible rationale, and this was her chance to give it. She reached to touch his copper-brown cheek, but he backed away. The specs concealed his gray eyes, that was a blessing.

She said, "I'm glad you've come."

He said, "You've known all along, haven't you?"

Sweaty curls hung over his forehead, and she almost raised her hand to brush them back. If only she could reach the end of lies. She longed to show Orr her true face. Even now, she tried to hope he could forgive her. But not yet. She hadn't finished. The scam had to go on.

So she bent her head away from Rolfe's cameras and whispered, "I'll help you get Dyce out of here."

He moved closer. "You know where she is?"

"She's here. I'll show you." Vera felt his hidden eyes searching her for signs of truth. "I give you my word, Orr. Let's hurry." She took his hand and led him along the corridor. Never in her life had she felt so . . . base.

Rolfe's guards arrived then. Two stumpy robots, they looked like over-sized Swiss Army knives on belt-driven treads. She raised her voice and ordered them away. "Leave us. Go back."

She knew her words would have no effect. She'd already programmed the bots to take Orr captive. He struggled and kicked when they flanked and manacled him. She clutched at their bristling calipers. "Orr, I can't stop them."

The robots marched Orr straight to Rolfe's office, while Vera followed behind, dreading the next move in her game. When they reached Rolfe's massive archway, the guards released Orr and pushed him through. Vera saw him pivot to one side, expecting an ambush, but the office was empty. She stepped in behind him, and the heavy doors closed, locking the two of them alone in Rolfe's lavish rotunda.

She said, "I swear, none of this is *my* doing. I'm just as trapped as you are."

She slumped into a seat, then gestured to the leather ottoman next to hers. Orr didn't sit. He paced. She saw his bronze cheeks harden at the sight of Rolfe's gaudy jade walls. When he glanced up at the skylight, she knew he would spot the fake. That light didn't shine from any sky.

He examined the window. Another fake. It presented a view of Andean peaks blazing in late afternoon sun. Beyond them, the sky burned vermillion. Her father had abysmal taste in décor, but she did enjoy his webcam window.

She hugged herself and shivered. "Not many people see the Andes. I guess we're lucky. This is a live feed."

Orr circled the potted orchids, then touched one of the brown-spotted leaves. Next, he ran his palm over the leopard skins in Rolfe's hammock, roughing up the fur, smoothing it down. The room chilled Vera's bones. Rolfe's AC must've been set at zero.

Orr said, "You're cold. Would you like one of these animal skins?"

That good-hearted impulse made Vera want to kiss his hand. She let him drape the leopard fur around her shoulders. But justice wasn't goodness, she'd learned that ages ago. Justice was balance. Equal weights of beauty and ugliness, sympathy and torment, happiness and black despair. Double or nothing. It was blind, relentless, and necessary.

She watched Orr slide his finger along the enormous white marble desk. She thought he seemed more sure of himself. Maybe the dark specs gave him attitude.

After a while, she couldn't bear the silence. "Al and Bettie will be glad to hear you're okay. They're still searching that cove where you splashed down."

He studied her father's case of dead butterflies like he was making a damned inventory.

"Orr . . ." But there was nothing she could say. She tugged the cat fur closer around her neck, and he ignored the simulated view of South America.

A door slid open, startling them both, and another robot appeared, a servant. This one resembled a vacuum cleaner cross-mated with an espresso machine, and its single articulated limb carried a tray of fruit juice. The juice surprised Vera. It came from Rolfe's private greenhouse. He usually reserved it for political guests.

"Ah, daughter. Who have you brought to meet me?"

They both turned and saw Rolfe smirking in the doorway. He wore plaid boxer shorts, sandals, and no shirt. His emaciation made Orr stare. His ribs stood out like two bent ladders, and his frail legs bowed under his skimpy weight. Yet he puffed out his chest and struck a pose as if he were God's own gift to male beauty.

Before Vera could speak, he said, "Scram, princess. I'll speak with you later."

No doubt, Rolfe knew she'd conned him. Not only had she lied about Orr's disappearance. Her project was hopelessly off schedule, and she would miss the season launch. Yes, her father would "speak" with her later.

Orr's fingers brushed her arm as she moved away. He said, "Will you be all right?"

Dear boy, she wanted to kiss his feet.

"Go," Rolfe barked.

Flare. A means of reducing speed in freefall by changing the shape of an airfoil, such as a Sky Wing, parachute, or human body.

Orr listened to the dying echo of Vera's footsteps. Her sudden mood shifts kept throwing him off balance. He could sense some kind of ache in her, like a hunger. He turned his dark glasses on Rolfe.

Cho had painted the drug lord in such tarry colors, Orr half expected him to snort fire. But Rolfe wore a friendly open expression. He lifted one of the untouched glasses from the tray and took a sip. "Delicious. Sure you don't want some?"

When Orr shook his head, Rolfe took another gulp, then smacked his lips. "The moment of consumption is best. The taste on your tongue, the volume filling your mouth. Then you swallow, and it's gone."

Orr spoke in a rush. "I've come for Dyce. I'll pay her debts, buy her contract, whatever it takes."

Rolfe swirled the amber liquid, clinking ice cubes. "Pity you won't try this. It's damned good grape juice. You don't even know what that is."

Orr stood rock still, watching the old man drink. Not a triple-headed dragon, just an anorexic old rich guy in a toupee. "I want Dyce," he repeated.

"Love's a mighty habit." Rolfe crunched ice in his jaw. "The Chinese have a saying, 'Habits are cobwebs at first, cables at last.'"

Orr observed the man's shrunken latissimus dorsi, his stringy forearm flexors, and his wasted abs. For all his wealth, Rolfe Luce showed signs of illness. His sandals slapped the floor as he padded to his desk. He said, "Love etches lifelong ruts in your brain, did you know that? You can see them under the microscope."

Passing the robot, Rolfe casually dropped his empty glass in its scoop. "I don't blame you for running away from Vera. She had you hopping like a circus clown. Forget her. She's out." Then he whispered some sort of code, and Orr's web specs dilated to a three-dimensional panorama of green.

Rolfe's voice rustled, "Welcome to my bliss."

Orr teetered and spread his arms for balance. The abrupt three-hundred-sixty-degree view messed up his equilibrium. He tried to switch back to normal, but couldn't. Giant ferns surrounded him. Scaly amphibians, furry rodents, animals he'd seen only in pictures. He'd fallen into a maze of trees. Blue streams gurgled, and frogs carilloned through the foliage. He'd never experienced such high-definition effects. The sights and sounds made him turvy.

At center stage, Rolfe floated in a magic leather sofa. He motioned Orr to join him. "Sit. Make yourself comfortable." His implant amped up his gravelly voice.

Orr didn't want to sit next to Rolfe, but under the forest's spell, he slid toward the sofa. He knew the padded seat couldn't be solid, yet it seemed to support his weight. Rolfe startled him by reaching across to connect his lap-and-shoulder harness.

At close quarters, the old man gave off a sweet gingery smell, like rot. Rolfe winked, and a control panel materialized in the air, with large retro buttons and easy-to-read dials. He touched a key, and they glided over the forest canopy, skimming the treetops.

"This is my Eden," he said. "You're witnessing a live webcam feed from my botanical habitat. Biologists all over the world will come here for research, and someday, we'll rehabilitate our ecosystem."

Orr didn't see any biologists, only greenery. He brushed his fingers over the treetops, expecting the sharp prick of pine needles. But this was just a holograph, not a full immersive sim. There was nothing to feel.

He said, "Is this Cyto?"

A doting smile curled Rolfe's lips. "This is what Cyto pays for. My forest is a real place." He worked the phantom controls, and the sofa coasted over a grassy field. "What you see here is a pale shadow of the actual environment. If you visit in person, you'll think you're strolling through Elysium."

Orr knuckled his ear. In the meadow, he caught a glimpse of bird wings. Then the scene changed, and Rolfe seemed to whisper inside his head.

"Let's take a tour."

They drifted over a green city beside blue water. It was Seattle before the earthquake. Orr recognized the Space Needle. But the city dome was missing. The streets were open to the sky. He saw people walking in sunlight and breathing atmosphere. This recording must date back to the 2030s—the last clear days before the sky veiled over.

He spotted joggers running along the banks of Puget Sound. Skateboarders. Children flying kites. He saw a girl with long black hair tearing a loaf of bread to feed seagulls.

"This world is gone." Rolfe's surly voice broke the spell. He ran the recording backwards, making the people jerk and jitter like mechanical toys. "Fucking paradise. We blew it."

Orr agreed, that city must have been paradise. Even in his beloved Unimak, people couldn't live in the open air.

"One day," Rolfe said, "we'll bring this world back. That's my dream. We'll clean up the sky and replant the trees. We'll restore Earth's balance."

Orr rubbed his jaw. This was not the conversation he'd expected to have with Rolfe Luce.

The view flashed to present-day Seattle, the city underground. Rolfe had edited a graphic newsreel of congested corridors, food fights, viral epidemics, and similar scenes of overcrowding. He elbowed Orr. "Here's our brave new world, eighteen million idiots sharing one cave. Whoever said it's better to reign in hell never lived in Seattle."

The glint in the old man's eyes made Orr jumpy.

"When I was a kid," Rolfe said, "we had five billion people living on this planet, and that was too many. Now it's twelve billion. More than double. Can you comprehend that number?"

Orr could not. He looked for an exit. The old man was gripping his arm.

"Twelve billion repeats of the genome. No wonder we get so damned few individuals. It's all 'me too' facsimiles of the same miserable pattern. People can't hold on to a basic self-image."

Orr clenched his fists. He was a skydiver, not a philosopher. He didn't follow politics. Genomes? Facsimiles? He noticed Rolfe's legs kicking against the sofa. The old man was getting twisted up in his seat belt.

"Humans are fucking locusts," Rolfe bellowed. "Force has to be applied. We need wide-scale sterilizations. But I digress." He straightened himself in the cushions. "You, skydiver, you're one of the rare originals. You almost restore my faith."

I doubt it, Orr thought. But the old man kept talking. "When you soar through the clouds, you take people beyond their imitation lives. They lose themselves in you, and for a little while, they fly free and full of grace."

Orr blurted, "Are you using my dives to addict people?"

"Who told you that?" Rolfe spread his fingers and studied his lacquered nails. "Everyone makes their own choices. A few people may form dependencies, but most folks remain light recreational users all their lives." He leaned closer and rested his hand on Orr's knee. "If anyone's addicted, it's you."

In a blink, the panorama morphed to a scene in Connie's Pub on Unimak Island. People stood packed together, quiet and tense. They were watching a webcast on Connie's wallscreen. Orr recognized most of the faces. Pete Hogue was holding an untouched beer. Connie stood behind the bar, vacantly scratching her chin.

Orr rocked forward. "How did you get this?"

"Watch," Rolfe whispered.

At the center of the crowd, Orr spotted his cousin. Gabe had shaved off his beard. Brown pouches sagged under his eyes, and his flashy new suit hung in loose folds. He'd lost weight. He looked like a stranger.

His youngest son, Yanny, perched on his shoulders, and the two older boys, Nick and Ilya, stood on bar stools. They, too, wore fine new clothes and sported fresh haircuts. But what grave expressions for such little boys. They seemed almost frightened.

Orr shifted in the make-believe sofa. He hadn't called Gabe in weeks. He should have tried harder to get a message through. Maybe the boys thought he'd forgotten them. The idea that Rolfe was spying on his family set him on fire. He grabbed the controls, but his hands passed through the airy knobs and dials. They were only a trick of light.

"Watch," Rolfe whispered again.

As if on cue, everyone in the bar went goggle-eyed at some event on the wallscreen. Gabe cheered, and his sons boinged up and down. The entire crowd broke into rowdy applause.

Rolfe swung the sofa so they could view the bar's wallscreen. It showed Orr docking his Celestia Sky Wing with another diver's Volare. But something peculiar had happened to the light. Details seemed sharper. Colors were brighter, more saturated. The recording had been so thoroughly sampled, remixed, and mashed up with fiery music, Orr almost didn't recognize it. He felt Rolfe's hot breath in his ear.

"See? They adore you. They imitate every detail of your moves. You're more real to them than their own neighbors."

Orr wasn't listening to Rolfe. He was watching his cousin. Why hadn't he tried harder to contact Gabe? And the boys, his little nephews, they might think he didn't care about them. He should've insisted on a vone call. But he'd put it off, procrastinated. He'd gotten too wrapped up in skydiving as usual. Selfish to the bone. No wonder Dyce left him. All this was his fault, his stupid mistake . . .

The panorama dissolved, and Orr found himself sitting next to Rolfe in the fur-lined hammock. He sprang up and backed away.

Rolfe curled in his cat furs and massaged his thin legs, like maybe they were giving him pain. He said, "You're a hero, boy. You kick death in the teeth."

Orr backed against the desk. He hated being called a hero. He was just the opposite. The old man was mocking him.

"You pit yourself against the cosmos," Rolfe went on. "You tease the hand of God. People would rather piss their pants than skip your act. And do you know the reason they love to watch you fly? The real true reason they can't even admit to themselves?"

Orr crossed his arms and tried not to let the old man get to him. He seriously did not want to hear the answer.

Rolfe said, "They want to see you go splat."

Orr took a slow breath through his nose, trying to stay cool.

The old man chuckled. "Blood and gore, that's what people crave. And the point is, they pay money."

When he reached for the other glass of juice, Orr exploded. He knocked the glass from Rolfe's hand and sent it crashing to the floor. "Where's Dyce?"

"Ah, it always comes back to that." Rolfe twitched his nose at the spilled grape juice. Then he leaned back in his furs. "I'll make you a deal. See for yourself what I've been telling you. Spend one hour in my wikiverse. Then, if you still want to, you can take your pretty lover away."

Orr didn't hesitate. "Let's do it."

10

Freestyle. Individual acrobatics in freefall.

Light sheeted through the backs of Orr's eyes, and everything fell away. Clouds whipped past, and ice crystals pinged his visor. His visor? Right, he was wearing a helmet, a jumpsuit, a Sky Wing! He gripped the pilot braces. His Celestial Sky Wing felt absolutely genuine, and he was sailing through cirrus clouds. One hour, the old man said. Full immersion, how bad could it be? Orr chinned his helmet to set a timer for sixty minutes.

Then a blast of hot wind rushed through the rear opening of his Wing and slammed him forward. He cartwheeled into a flat spin and fought for control, but the Wing whirled like a centrifuge, spinning the blood away from his brain. His field of vision narrowed. He knew if he didn't stop the spin fast, he would black out.

Urgently, he whipped his body in a violent arc, and when he felt the Wing hesitate, he did it again, over and over, until a cross-wind flipped him upside down in a riotous upwelling current. He hauled the Wing upright and surfed hard to hold his position. His helmet display showed him riding the eye of a gigantic cyclone . . . which looked suspiciously familiar.

Déjà vu, this was his own record-breaking skydive over the North Pacific. Only, everything was brighter, more colorful—and he was not alone. Other Wing divers crowded the sky. They wore outlandish costumes, and their Wings came in bizarre impractical shapes—flying green lizards, yellow butterflies, gray stealth jets. They frolicked and skipped through the unreal storm like children in a bubble bath. Orr's radio crackled to life.

"Nice spin recovery. For a *noob*."

Orr couldn't make out which one of the divers had spoken.

A young boy said, "He who hesitates shall inherit the Earth."

"Whoa," said a little girl. "I know that guy. Hey, that's the Gravity Pilot!"

Suddenly, dozens of flyers converged around Orr. He heard their awed whispers, and he felt like an alien. He gripped his pilot braces and sliced away.

Crossing the storm's eye, he had to jog and veer every second to avoid collisions with other divers. Snowflakes, asteroids, bats, everyone wore a different costume. And none of them seemed to appreciate the storm's danger. He checked his clock. Only one minute had passed. That couldn't be right. Time seemed to lose its force in this simulated sky.

New voices hissed through his radio. "So tell me, if my landing 'chute doesn't open, how long till I hit the water?"

"The rest of your life, bozo."

"Hey guys, watch this . . . Oh shit!"

Orr saw two divers smash together, and the sound of their impact ricocheted through the sky. When their Wings exploded in flames, the divers unleashed bloodcurdling wails. Then the fire blew out, leaving the Wings undamaged, and they hung motionless in the whirling storm till their software reset and their game restarted. Orr muted his radio and steered away. He hated this sky.

The clouds refracted gaudy shades of turquoise, sapphire, and aquamarine, and thousands of divers rode the raucous currents. Old people and young, male and female, they'd turned his cyclone into a merry-go-round. He listened to their hoots and cries as they streamed past. They were having fun.

Lighthearted play, he felt it teasing the edges of his mind. Then a tremendous gladness washed over him, though he knew it couldn't be real. Was this Rolfe's drug? Orr felt whiplashed. He couldn't condemn people for chasing happiness. Truth was, he couldn't keep track of what he was feeling. Intoxicating joy kept washing over him, blurring all other sensations.

"Look, it's the Gravity Pilot," someone else yelled.

He zoomed away and hid in the clouds. Then he checked his clock again.

One more minute had passed. The old man was tricking him, screwing with his timer. His Wing bucked as he carved into the swiftest inner spinstream of the storm.

But instead of meeting resistance, his wingtip cut easily through the wind. He spiraled outward. The air felt smooth. There was no resistance, no sense of weight.

Then a force like hard vacuum sucked him from the pilot braces. Only the helmet wires held him in the Wing. The wires strained and tugged. Then one of them snapped and . . . he recognized the repeat. He'd been through this scene before.

His false joy evaporated. "Stop," he said aloud.

He halted in freeze-frame, and his Wing hung fixed. The cyclone continued to churn, while he dangled motionless and unbelieving.

Around him, scores of other divers went through an identical scenario. Vacuum sucked them loose from their braces. Their helmet wires strained and snapped. Then the storm took control and soared them aloft on a buoyant upsurge of air. Instantly, new divers flocked in to take their places, and the carnival replayed.

Orr hung in dead suspension inside his fake Wing. He checked his timer, and sure enough, it had stopped. How long would this purgatory trap him?

"Go!" he howled. "Start. Play. Resume."

He rocketed up to the stratosphere with a host of other divers. The simulation tossed him high above the jeweled clouds into a purple sky. Moonbeams shimmered above, as improbable as they were lovely, and in the west, a golden sun emanated comforting warmth. When Orr's Wing bobbed upside down on the same storm's eye where he'd started, he checked his timer. It was counting again, barely.

Inside his suit, he felt drained. His abs and obliques burned when he flipped the Wing upright. Though the dive was imaginary, it still demanded physical exertion. As he surfed the brutal currents and tried to catch his breath, the last remnants of his bogus pleasure died away. His timer showed fifty-seven minutes still to endure, an eternity. He loathed this place.

"Orr. It's you." Dyce's voice.

He saw a diver approach through the swells.

"Berry?"

"I'm here."

Funnel. Loss of stability which causes a skydive formation to collide and break apart.

When Dyce spotted the Gravity Pilot across the Cyto sky, she almost fled in the opposite direction. For too long, she'd been yearning for and dreading his visitation. Cyto's greatest celebrity, she knew his sims by heart. But this time, he was not a holograph. He was real. Could this be the boy she knew in Unimak? He seemed like a stranger in his gleaming silver suit and dark visor. She couldn't see his eyes. Surely, underneath the mask, he was still her hero.

But . . . there was something she needed to remember. Something . . .

Right, Orr was in danger. She needed to warn him. *Get out quick. Save yourself. This place is poison.*

Yet as she crossed toward him, dipping and curling through the white vapory puffs, she invented a thousand reasons why it would be all right, just for a little while, if he stayed.

Drawing close, she shot pings to reconfirm that he was not a computer-generated phantom. Yes, positive ID. The real living Orr. She vibrated with bliss. Dreaming of this reunion had kept her alive. She bumped her Sky Wing against his. "I knew you'd come. I knew it."

"You're skydiving?" he whispered.

She saw his surprise. Inside her clear Wing, she twinkled. "I ride your sims all the time. I understand now why you love the sky. It's magnificent."

She dove through a cloud tunnel, then glanced back to make sure he was following. She was quick, lithe—she'd done this simulation hundreds of times, and it amused her to see how Orr lurched and slipped. She was the leader now. Sky Wings moved differently in Cyto, and Orr hadn't learned that. She swooped through the simulated currents, while he fell behind.

"You never liked to do this back home," he called out.

"I've changed," she said. His presence gave her confidence. She flared her Wing for a tail-stand, a tricky maneuver which she'd practiced for hours. Then she zoomed up and hovered at his side. "The world's getting brighter, Orr. Let's go play in the cyclone."

Before he could answer, she did a triple back flip. Then she raced away, daring him to keep up.

"Wait a second! Dock with me," he yelled. "I'll teach you how."

She saw him rotate his Wing so she could dock behind. But she was eager to show off her skills, so she maneuvered in front. "Let me lead. I'll take you someplace special."

She snugged their two Wings together with less effort than stacking a pair of bowls. He said, "Where did you learn that?"

"I told you. I ride your sims all the time. Follow me, Gravity Pilot."

Wings in train, they sailed straight into the cyclone. The wind shrieked at ear-splitting velocity, and it tickled Dyce to see how Orr braced for impact. He didn't understand how forgiving this sky could be. Anyone could play this artificial storm, even babies.

Dyce searched for the usual break in the clouds, and there it was, her own patch of blue. She steered their two Wings through the opening, and they emerged into *surreality*.

A cotton cloudscape enfolded them. No wind stirred. No gravity pulled. The storm had vanished. Soft sounds whispered like xylophone chimes, and from all sides came pattering gusts of rain.

Dyce watched Orr's reaction. She giggled. "Can't you feel it? H-h-h-happiness."

Wobbly blue raindrops washed around them, spiraling in gentle waves. Unchained from the concepts of up and down, the rain embroidered transparent filigrees in the air. The effect was hypnotic. Crests of joy stirred Dyce's spirit as the free-floating rain wetted her lover's skin.

Orr stared down at his streaming chest. He was naked. So was Dyce.

"When? How?" He lifted his bare arms. "I didn't feel my clothes disappear. Where's my Sky Wing?"

Dyce nestled against him. "I've been waiting so long for you to come. This place is my secret haven. I haven't granted access to anyone else but you."

She waved her hand, and the raindrops transformed to liquid jewels. Ruby, amber, topaz, carmine. She caught a few drops and slid her wet fingers into his mouth. Each drop brought a different essence—quiet piquancy, tart impudence, sweet salty brawn. She'd spent days creating these faceted flavors.

She laughed in pure ecstasy. "Anything's possible in Cyto."

As if to prove it, her droplets morphed to tongues of liquid flame, and the sky rained candlelight. She watched Orr flinch when the fire touched his skin, but it carried no sting. She prayed he would adore the sensations she'd invented. Caramel warmth, peppermint elegance, chocolate desire. So vivid, wet, lustful.

"What time is it?" he whispered.

Dyce's smile froze. Time? "Look at my clouds," she said.

And her clouds changed to music. Swirling arabesques of whole tones vaporized into misty semi-quavers, then churned up thunderheads of blue notes with jazzy lightning riffs. The visual symphony blew against them like sound waves. She watched his face. Did he appreciate the grand union of senses? Could he understand how every frame of reference interfaced?

He cocked his head sideways and lowered his eyebrows. His doubt made her timid. She'd counted so much on winning his approval.

"Watch this, Orr." She performed a somersault, then a cartwheel. With no gravity, her gymnastics came easy. She spun and flipped in the flashing rain, yearning to impress him. Then she shape-shifted into a dozen different forms in quick succession—dolphin, seagull, starfish, meteorite. Finally, she rematerialized as a black-eyed ballerina whirling in midair, with her long braid restored and spiraling around her.

Pleasure hummed out of her. "What a rush! You try it, Lagi."

Her performance left her bathed in elation. Such gratifying contentment, surely he would feel it, too.

But Orr waved his hand as if brushing away invisible strings. "This isn't real. You're throwing yourself away for nothing." The words were hardly out of his mouth before he seemed to realize what he'd said.

Dyce shot away from him. "It's my artwork. This week, I won a thousand points in the creativity poll. Isn't that worth something?"

He chewed his lip. One kind word, that's all she needed. One syllable of encouragement. He opened his arms and said, "Come here. Let's don't fight."

She rushed toward him. Their bare chests slid together, and her lips found the pulsing vein in his throat. Between kisses, he murmured, "Let's go home."

"No, Lagi. I can't leave. I'm better here. Cyto makes me smarter."

"Berry . . ."

"It's true," she said. "I can think faster. My vision and hearing are perfect. And I can smell the smallest trace of scent. My fingers, you wouldn't believe how sensitive they are. I can sculpt. I can paint living pictures."

She hugged him tight, and his rain-slick flesh felt as warm and solid as ever. All her lonely weeks in Seattle seemed to vaporize. She kissed his naked shoulder and breathed, "Let's make love."

His face closed down in that sullen distant way she remembered too well. He said, "We'll make love at home, in our own bed, in Unimak."

Her clouds darkened. "Why not here? I made this place for us."

He said, "This isn't good for you, Berry. It's like a drug."

"That's not true." His cruel words confounded her.

He caught hold of her hands, and they floated face to face in the blazing rain. He said, "Look at me. Who am I?"

She didn't understand. "You're Orr Sitka."

"That's right." He drew her closer. "Would I lie to you?"

"Never," she said.

"Then believe me, you have to get out."

His words jolted her. Briefly, she opened her eyes and glimpsed the moldy walls of her work cube. "Oh God, what time is it? How long have I kept you here? This place is not safe. You have to go."

"Right, and you're coming with me," he said.

Kaleidoscopic clouds enfolded her again, blaring bright colors and ringing candy sweetness. "Orr, I can't leave."

"Yes, you can." He turned and searched the sky. "Follow me. I'll try to find the exit."

But the instant he let go of her hands, she drifted backward. "I can't," she cried, receding into the mist. "Get out, Orr. Save yourself."

"Wait!" He swam toward her, stretching out his arms and kicking his legs, but without gravity, he couldn't gain momentum.

She saw him grasping empty armfuls of web space. *Forgive me,* she whispered, but her words made no sound. She couldn't reach him. She couldn't do anything. She could only fade into the dark gray vapor of Cyto.

11

Glide ratio. Proportional relationship of parachute forward glide versus downward descent.

Orr plunged through the cyclone. Lightning forked around him, and he was inside his Sky Wing again, fully geared. He spun in every direction, searching for Dyce. She was nowhere. When he remembered to check his clock, the hour was gone. But the helmet had never existed. His own body was a web-enabled hoax. Gravity ceased. Time didn't matter.

In dark driving rain, he fell toward the sea. His body went limp, and his Wing flapped loose. *Dyce, where are you?*

Throngs of other divers stopped playing and turned to watch him. "That's the Gravity Pilot. He can't be crashing. Can he?"

When he splashed into the waves, the currents dragged him deep. Down through the crushing murk he sank, not bothering to resist. All he wanted was for the evil hour to end. But the sim would not release him. He surfaced full of rage.

"Game over. Let me out, old man!" He shook his fist at the sky.

Gravelly laughter split the heavens. The waves and wind dissolved, and he found himself standing in Rolfe's hammock, brandishing his arms at the ceiling. The hammock tipped, and he tumbled to the floor.

Rolfe stood over him, mimicking Dyce's words in a shrill falsetto. " 'Get out, darling. Save yourself.' "

Orr lunged at the man's scrawny legs, but he passed right through and smacked against a chair. A holograph? Was there no end to the trickery?

Rolfe's projected image skipped away. "Noble, your Dyce. Quite the little martyr. Tell me, why are the virtuous ones always such bores? Could it be, they're too predictable?"

Orr tried to yank off his web specs, but white-hot sparks shot through his skull. He said, "I did the hour. Let me have her."

"Sure, I'll keep my bargain." Rolfed quirked an eyebrow. "As my old pal Sophocles says, 'One word frees us of all the weight and pain of life. That word is Love.'"

Orr couldn't get his web specs off. "Where is she?"

"Relax. Have a snack. She's coming."

Orr tried to stand, then dropped back to the stone tiles. The sim had sapped his strength. Sweat dripped down his chin, and the chilly air turned his breath to steam. Only his quu-suit remained eternally fresh. When the robot trundled in with a tray of ice water and sautéed kelp, Orr couldn't resist the food. How long since he'd eaten? He stuffed his cheeks.

"Ah, the appetite of youth." Rolfe eyed the snack till the last bite was gone.

Orr propped himself up against a chair leg. He saw a ghostly aura outlining the old man's form, a holographic telltale. He signaled his specs to mark it with a tag. Next time, he would know the difference between a holograph and a real person. Rolfe wouldn't dupe him again.

Something squeaked across the floor tiles, and Orr turned. A small hidden door had opened at the back of Rolfe's office, and just inside its frame, he saw a drab young woman dressed in a colorless Cyto uniform. She stood fidgeting, clutching the wall for support, evidently not sure whether to enter.

He said, "Dyce?"

More than two months had passed since he'd seen her in the flesh. He got up and hurried toward her as fast as he could move. She hid her face. Her skin had gone dull, and her short black hair needed a wash. Her uniform, too, was wrinkled and stained. But Dyce had always been such a clean freak.

When he drew near, she shot a timid glance at Rolfe, then whispered, "What are you doing here, Lagi? You're making trouble with my boss. I told you to leave."

Orr touched his dark glasses, praying she wasn't an illusion. His specs picked up no holographic aura. She was solid. His fingers circled her wrist. "I've come to take you home."

She glanced at Rolfe, then hissed from the corner of her mouth, "Go away. You shouldn't be here."

She seemed smaller than Orr remembered, and so twitchy. Her chopped hair hung limp, and there was something anxious about her posture. Her upper spine had developed a stoop. When he drew her closer, she bumped against him and tried to slip something into his hand. He glimpsed the flash of a gold coin. But Rolfe was approaching, so she moved away.

Rolfe said, "Do you want to leave us, Ms. Iakai?"

"No, sir. We're working on the movie archives. They're nearly finished."

Rolfe arched one eyebrow. "You've been riding sims on company time."

"No, I—" Tiny spasms jerked her cheek muscles. "We were installing updates. I had a few minutes to kill, so I—"

"So you violated company policy." Rolfe rested his hand on her shoulder, and his bony fingers closed like a vise. "That's like stealing, isn't it?"

"It'll never happen again, Mr. Luce. I swear." She took an edgy little step forward, then back, then forward again. With Rolfe's grip on her shoulder, she couldn't move far.

Rolfe said, "'He who steals an egg will steal an ox.' I've checked your credit account. You owe Cyto quite a lot of money. It doesn't seem fair of you to pilfer more time."

Orr tried to knock Rolfe's hand away. "Let her go. I'll pay her debts." But again his real flesh passed through the old man's fake projection. He felt confused. What kind of hold did Rolfe have on Dyce?

The old man's mouth widened. "This guy says our wikiverse is addictive. Tell me, Ms. Iakai, is there any credence to that? Do you ride sims because you're a druggie?"

"No sir. No way. He has no business butting in." She kept shifting from one foot to the other like she was wired to an AC battery.

Rolfe winked at Orr. "He says he's your sweetheart. He wants you to abscond with him."

She said, "I'm not going anywhere."

"Good girl." Rolfe released her shoulder, and she almost lost her balance. He said, "Shouldn't you get back to work?"

She took a wobbly step, then halted, looking lost. Her trembling made

Orr burn. All at once, she flung the gold coin at his chest, and he caught it. She said, "Go home, Orr. We're quits. Don't bother me again."

Orr stammered, "You don't mean that." He whirled and faced Rolfe. "I'm taking her away now."

Rolfe made a show of pouting. "But your lover wants to stay here. You should be grateful she has a job, what with her little credit problem."

"I told you, I'll pay her debts."

"Yeah? You just blew all your cash on Cyto minutes. Never asked about the cost, that was reckless." The old man capered around, throwing mock punches. "Sorry, skydiver. You have your own work to think about."

Orr glanced behind him. Dyce was gone.

Gone? He stared at the vacant space where she'd been standing. One second ago, she'd been right there within arm's reach. Now the hidden door had closed, and she was nowhere. He raced after her and beat his fists against the jade-green wall.

Rolfe's robot locked its calipers around his shin, and he kicked at the bristling machine. He made a fist to smash Rolfe's teeth, but what could he do to a phantom? In his fury, he bashed the robot to pieces.

Rolfe scrutinized his busted bot. "Nothing's built to last anymore."

"We had a bargain," Orr thundered. "You owe me."

"Wrong, skydiver. I own you." A contract materialized in Rolfe's hand, and he shook it in Orr's face. "You're going to help me rescue the ecosphere. That's more important than any personal love interest, no matter what you think."

Orr's voice rumbled with a sound that was not in any lexicon.

"Well, don't worry," Rolfe said, as the enormous arched doors fanned open and the two Swiss Army robots rattled in. "You can visit your girlfriend any time in her 'secret haven.'"

Grips. Handhold positions when one diver docks
with another in freefall.

Orr punched Rolfe's holographic nose. "I'll get you for this." Then he darted around the Swiss guards and galloped down the hall.

Rolfe's laughter vibrated through his web specs. "Wear yourself out. Be my guest."

The instant Orr burst out of the Cyto compound into the public tunnel, his specs overloaded with ads from the nearby vendor stalls. Cho's face popped up, too, scowling through clouds of cigarette smoke.

"Cold-hearted brute. Didn't I tell you? Wasn't I right about Rolfe?"

Orr stood reeling in the corridor, disoriented. Dyce didn't break up with him, she couldn't have. She was only pretending. He drew out her coin and held it close to his specs so he could see. It was her plate-gold locket, with their torch song duet inside. *I will always love you.* She'd given it back?

He felt sucker-punched. He clenched the yellow metal in his fist.

Cho said, "She doesn't need you anymore. She has Cyto."

Orr shut Cho down with a blink. He would have yanked the web specs off, too, but the frames had fused into his flesh so deeply, his fingers could no longer dig under the plastic temples. Behind him, Cyto's door was rattling shut. At the last second, he almost darted back into the compound to search for Dyce. But cops were coming, so he ran.

Cho popped back up in his specs. "Better to face the truth. You're nothing to Dyce anymore. You heard what she said."

Orr turned the web specs off. Then he galloped down the hall and took random turns. She couldn't honestly want him to go away. She had to be pretending, acting out some scene. His numb mind couldn't accept any other explanation. And just when he was about to lead her out of this insane mausoleum—

Why didn't you stick with me, Dyce?

Cho whispered through the glass earring, "She belongs to Rolfe now. He offers pleasures you can't begin to give her."

Orr yanked the earring off and threw it in the gutter. His earlobe split, and red streaks branched up the side of his head. His eye socket screamed. The shock to his system made him nauseous, and he leaned against the moldy corridor wall. Inside the mastoid region behind his ear, nanofilaments slowly died and began to flush away in his bloodstream, but he didn't know that. He felt diseased.

When a policeman approached, he ducked into a small workers' cafeteria and got in line for a tray of food. Maybe if he'd been calmer, he would have remembered his lack of cash. But everything he'd counted on as solid and permanent had turned to mist. He couldn't find his footing. He half expected the floor to dissolve.

The automat cafeteria smelled of bug spray. Mechanical scoops loaded up his plate with marinated sorghum croquettes, but he barely noticed. When the cash machine demanded payment, he stood like a halfwit, chewing the corner of his lip.

"Twenty-four dollars," the machine repeated. "Rolfe stole her away from you."

Orr's head whipped around. The cashier screen displayed a wiggling emoticon, and the mechanical voice said, "It's me, Cho. Switch on your web specs."

"Leave me alone." Orr turned his back on the machine.

Through the cafeteria window, he saw more police gathering outside. That locket, thrown back in his face. Worse than a slap. One minute, he thought Dyce must have been warning him away from danger. The next, he felt like a total chump for coming here at all.

Cho spoke through the cash machine again. "Pay Rolfe back. Find his web servers. That's where you can hurt him."

Orr said, "I don't care."

"Then get out of the line." A girl in a Hijab veil stamped her boot behind him. Brown eyes. Orange skirt. Freckles. She was the same girl who'd approached him earlier in the arcade. She seized his hand and yanked him behind the drink machine. "Change your suit. Hurry."

Orr saw the police unholstering their stun guns, and his instinct for survival kicked in. He restarted his web specs and scanned his quu-suit menu. One of the cops leaned through the cafeteria doorway.

"Choose ambient," the girl said. "Hurry. Ambient."

Orr spoke the word, and his suit altered from dark blue to quicksilver. It reflected the surroundings like a fabric mirror, blending him into the background. The girl tugged his hood up over his head and made him hide his hands in his pockets.

She whispered, "Listen very carefully to what I'm about to tell you."

Her veil covered most of her face, but Orr thought he recognized her voice. "Dr. Leo?"

"Christ, am I that obvious?" The surgeon rolled his brown eyes. "I'm supposed to give you a piece of crucial info—"

Everyone hushed when the cop squeezed into the eatery. Leo put a finger to his lips, and Orr jerked his hood lower over his face. When the cop turned his back, Leo poured a mug of hot soup down his collar.

The cop yelped and whirled. "Who did that?"

Leo ducked behind the drink machine and shook with giggles. When the cop turned away again, Leo grabbed a dripping green burrito off the counter and lobbed it. The cop fired at the raining food, and people stampeded.

Orr wove through the scuffling bodies toward the exit. Behind him, Leo got caught in the crowd, and Orr lost sight of him . . . her. Anyway, Orr had no time to contemplate Dr. Leo's bizarre disguise. He checked around for the black crust of mote cameras. They were everywhere.

Out in the corridor, he sprinted for the nearest stairwell. When he dove in, was it fate or lunch-hour traffic that drove him down the descending spiral? Cho's pane opened in his web specs. "Good, you're finally headed in the right direction. I have a hunch Rolfe hides his servers on the Underside."

Orr didn't answer. The crowd shoved him steadily down the heel-strike treads, and the locket sweated in his palm. Shoddy plate-gold. A keepsake from a carnie stall, no wonder she didn't want it. He stuffed the cheap toy in his pocket. And it seemed to him that every noise ever created in Seattle must still be ringing through the hard igneous walls. Drills, hammers, footsteps, people talking, water spurting through pipes.

When a door opened below, a stream of ads blasted him with visions of the Gravity Pilot streaking through the sky. He saw himself, Orr Sitka, tricked out in skintight pants and Tinker Bell boots. Then an icon popped up, a black sun. Cyto. He didn't look away fast enough. The portal expanded to fill his view.

Cho's voice filtered through his specs. "Shut." And the black sun vanished.

But Orr wasn't afraid of Cyto anymore. He'd been there.

Ground speed. Horizontal velocity of Wing diver relative to the ground.

Orr circled down to the lowest rung of the stairs. Water oozed from the walls and wetted the stair treads. The central pole felt slick. But after so many years together, how could Dyce break up with him? Because he was broke, worthless, a dropout. She wanted kids, and he was a poor risk as a father. He fingered the plate-gold locket, hardly noticing where he went.

Cho spoke through his specs. "I've seen Rolfe destroy people before. He's very thorough. You need to accept that Dyce is gone."

At the bottom of the shaft, a door slid open, and a loud racket assaulted Orr's ears. Pumps, machinery, rushing water. The air smelled of slime and wet earth. When the mob herded through, Orr went with them. They probably didn't notice him, though, because his suit was still set on reflective quicksilver.

Cho said, "You want to get even? Trash his servers. Help me stop him before he does this to someone else."

Orr flipped the locket between his knuckles. He was not able to let it go. Never, he swore, would he open that locket. Never again did he want to see their two sappy faces pressed together in the quick-mo stall, singing that corny song. Yet it was the only thing he saw. He couldn't get the wretched lyrics out of his head.

Cho's voice came across like a steel blade. "The man's inhuman. How much proof do you need?"

Water sluiced underfoot, and Orr nearly slipped. The booming noise concussed his jaw. People were grabbing industrial earmuffs and respirators off a rack, so he took a set, too. The respirator had a sour tang. Dozens of hard hats dangled from hooks, along with insulated suits and work gloves. As the people suited up and switched on their helmet lights, Orr realized they were miners.

Cho displayed a local map in Orr's web specs, with a route flashing red. "You want more evidence? All right, I'll show you the addicts. Go straight, then left. You'll see."

Orr didn't care about evidence. He stumbled forward like a man with no head. Maybe he never really knew Dyce. All they had in common was kid stuff. Okay, great sex. And she was so easy to be with. A little sharp-edged, a little hardheaded, but fragile, too. He pressed the respirator to his face.

The hand-hewn rock ceiling sloped in uneven arches, and support beams loomed at head-smacking angles. Water gurgled down the gutters, and overgrown white insects fed on scallops of black mold. Orr's boots skidded. Promise we'll always be together, she said. Sure.

"Not that way. Go left." Cho sounded urgent.

Orr didn't care which direction he took. He wandered on, absently following the overlay of Cho's arrows. When he turned left into a low hall, something peculiar happened to the light. Surfaces sharpened. Colors stood out in grainy brightness, and sounds rang abnormally clear. The hall felt dreamlike. Orr wiped fog from his specs. What kind of pit had he wandered into?

People bunched thicker here. Some wore scraps of cloth, old bedsheets. A few were naked. In places, they couldn't move without squeezing against each other. Their stinking bodies swayed together, mouths drooling, arms reaching overhead.

"Rolfe Luce's victims," Cho said. "Now you see his depravity."

Orr rubbed the back of his neck. These were the addicts? The scene struck him as exaggerated. The men and women behaved like caricatures from a dementia ward. Then he noticed a faint flickery haze outlining each figure. Were his web specs reading a holographic tag, or were his blurry senses deceiving him? He said, "Is this a sim?"

Cho roared, "Have I ever lied to you? I'm your only friend in this place. You have to trust me."

Orr wiped his damp palms on his pants and wandered among the addicts. Some wore antique gaming goggles, and many had old-fashioned cell phones taped to their jaws. Others clutched retrofitted Palm Pilots, iPhones, MP3 players and miniature TVs. Coaxial cables snaked along the floor connecting hardcase routers. No wifi here. Every peripheral device ever tossed on a junk heap had sifted down to this catacomb, to be resurrected and rewired to the web.

Cho still sounded peeved. "You see the devil's harvest. Rolfe steals people's lives. How much evidence do you need?"

Orr thought Cho was trying too hard to convince him. Yet the people's salt-caked eyes held him quiet. After a while, he said, "Your friend, Cho. What happened to your friend?"

Cho took a deep drag on his cigarette, and smoke coarsened his voice. "Yeah, she's here."

Orr didn't want to ask which one she was. He watched the people writhe and twist. If these were real human beings, they needed medicine, food, clothes. Merciful Agugux, they needed care. He felt an urge to do something. But then it came over him—their contortions were not random. He recognized their swoops and tucks. They were crunching their abdomens, steering with their hands and feet. They were skydiving.

The shock made him stagger. In the half light, he tripped over a yellow-haired woman clasping an ancient laptop to her breast. He swung his arms to keep from falling on top of her. But what was wrong with her head?

Thick wires looped from her laptop to an enormous battered game helmet that covered the top half of her skull. The helmet made her look like an alien. Orr knelt beside her, but she was so lost in her fantasy life, she didn't feel him gently tilt her laptop so he could see the screen. And there was the Gravity Pilot sailing through a wall of storm clouds.

Acid burned through Orr's veins. He felt a wild impulse to tear off the woman's helmet and set her free. But instinct warned him that might injure her. He watched her fingers moving and moving over the cursor keys. The helmet hid her eyes but not her mouth. She wore an expression of rapture.

Cho said, "Someday, this'll be Dyce."

Orr patted the woman's shoulder and pictured Dyce whirling in her symphonic sky. Lost. He'd lost her to the web. Then he tugged at the specs sunk in his own inflamed flesh. How fast he'd come to trust their data more than his own instincts. His fingers slid along the edges of the frames glued to his skin. Who was he to think of freeing anyone?

"Help me get justice," Cho growled.

"Revenge, you mean." Orr closed the woman's laptop and drifted on.

12

Hand deploy. Parachute deployment using a pilot chute
pulled out by hand.

Memories. Sometimes Rolfe thought they might kill him. Images, sounds, and smells, not real and yet not false. He shut his eyes and tried to focus on the view of Vera through his ocular. Multivisioning took more effort now than when he was young. His mote cameras showed her stealing into his office. She sat behind his desk like she belonged there. She linked into his hardwired interface, and he ground his teeth, watching her hack the city Geist. She was tracking her skydiver.

Orrpaaj Sitka had gotten lost in the guts of Seattle, and cops were gathering to arrest him. When Vera phuxed their scanners, Rolfe saw how ineptly she covered her digital trail. The Geist would not be fooled. He should have stopped her right then, before the disaster got worse. But memories, what close cousins to dreams.

Rolfe himself had been arrested, twice. Once at age thirteen, for burning his schoolmate's hair. Then again at twenty-five, right after his game, Death Count, made him richer than God. He was caught buying a black-market pancreas, because living on the web as he did, coding new games at all hours and rarely getting up from his chair, his own pancreas had turned to mush. At twenty-five, his blood sugar went hyperbolic.

Through his spy cameras, he watched Vera barrage the Geist with signal noise. Sloppy. The girl had no art. Did she not know the Geist would retaliate?

Rolfe crept through the private back door of his office and approached her from behind. He had to stop her before she ruined him. His hands hovered around her neck. But who was guilty? And of what crime?

When the pancreas deal landed him in jail, he went into a diabetic coma for six days. That seminal experience convinced him, his web habit could kill. All systems crashed. No restart. That low point in the jail cell marked the beginning of his recovery.

As soon as they let him out, he paid full retail for a lawful new pancreas, then refocused on his lifestyle. No more yo-yo diets, weight loss pills, or tummy tucks. He'd been through that shit. He tore himself away from his computer and bought hiking boots. He explored the Olympic rain forest. He summitted Mount Rainier. And he fought like Prince Valiant to limit his daily web time.

Still, his games called him. They reached into his psyche and pulled. When he sank into his old rut again and again, he disciplined himself with his mother's bamboo cane. Yet even his noblest efforts failed. He couldn't quit.

That taught him life's prime lesson: Personal self-control was crap. So he turned to technology, his true-blue companion, and he found his cure for web addiction. A private cure for himself alone, which he never brought to market. He called it the Anabuse Germ.

Five years of hard research led him to the tiny package of microelectronics that finally set him free. One brave night, he swallowed his cure, and the Anabuse Germ soon migrated through his bloodstream to his cerebellum, where it spiraled around his parasympathetic nerve trunk. From then on, every time he entered a full immersive sim, the Anabuse Germ induced projectile vomiting. He had to get up from his computer and walk off the nausea. Sometimes, it took hours. Sometimes he hurled splinters of blood. Needless to say, he kicked the FM habit.

And bulimia brought unexpected benefits. For the first time in his adult life, he shed fat. He fell in love with mirrors and new clothes. As his body slimmed, his personality expanded. He grew jovial, charming. Also, he pursued women. Vera's mother was one of many. A swan-necked beauty with too much free time, she died soon after Vera's birth from an overdose of sedatives. Maybe he was too much for her.

In any case, she left him with a fresh project to occupy his genius, an extraordinary new peripheral device that would one day extend his reach and power in wild new directions. She left him with a daughter.

"*Me?*" Vera squeaked.

"Yes, you." Rolfe lifted her by the collar. "You let my servers crash."

He dragged her out from behind his desk, forced her to her feet and marched her down the hall. Into his private elevator he shoved her, and deep underground they plunged. When they hit bottom, he hauled her to the concrete vault that housed his Cyto web servers. The AC had failed, and thirteen units had melted.

"This is all *your* doing," he roared. "Your screwing with the city Geist caused this AC failure. It's the Geist's revenge."

The hardware looked like Salvador Dalí's dripping clocks. Beyond the wall, Seattle's geothermal plant shot caustic fluid down an injection well to gather Earth's heat. Rolfe had to shout to be heard. "We've lost a terabyte of static content, and I can only guess how many interfaces went down. Want to see the hate mail? My users are fuming. Cyto never goes down."

Vera cupped her hands around her mouth. "Everything goes down, Dad."

Rolfe paced the sweltering vault. The sharp chemical reek burned his nostrils, and his implants could not stanch the perspiration running down his ribs. Even in boxer shorts and Birkenstocks, he felt overdressed. He banged his fist on a dead server. "One job I gave you. The most important job of all. And look."

"We're backed up," Vera yelled. "We have full redundancy. This is not the apocalypse."

But Rolfe was too distraught to listen. He shoved her against the wall. "If you hadn't lost your skydiver—"

"Careful, you'll blow an intestine." Vera straightened her hair. "I found Orr. He'll be back on the job tomorrow morning."

"One disappointment after another, Vera. I had so much hope for you." He ran his hands over the warped units like he was caressing a dead lover. "This is unforgivable."

She said, "You have zero reason to be mad. Cyto's profits are soaring, thanks to me. *Me*, Daddy. People are going apeshit for the new docking sim, just like I told you they would."

"And the ionosphere?" he bellowed.

"You'll have it, Dad."

Rolfe massaged his bald scalp. Somehow in the rush of the moment, he'd forgotten his hairpiece. A major construction loan was coming due on the botanical habitat, and he felt eaten down by time. Eighty-seven years had zipped by, yet his work was not half finished. If only he could count on Vera.

She picked up a melted optic cable. "This is a typical Monday foul-up. We've dealt with hardware issues before. Ten minutes, we'll be live again."

Steam burned Rolfe's lungs and made him cough. He rubbed his chest. Maybe he had a touch of heartburn. "It's the law of gravity," he said. "When you're down, everything falls down on top of you."

Vera blotted her damp cheeks. "I need the aircar tomorrow, so I can take Orr back to work."

Rolfe felt a cramp radiating down his left arm. "Take care of my servers, or I swear to you, I'll . . ."

The pain sharpened, and he bent his arm against his chest. Sweat beaded his face. For a few minutes, Vera stood watching him. Then she got hold of his waistband and helped him walk outside to the cooler air. He leaned heavily against her, and she supported his weight.

"It'll be okay, Dad. You taught me how to manage people. You should trust me."

His eyes shifted back and forth, examining her face. Such perfect cosmetic features. "Trust requires predictability, Vera. And the only predictable people I know are the Dead."

She helped him ease down onto a bench. Then she stood over him, stroking the back of his neck. "I'll set things right, Dad. Soon you'll have everything you need. I promise."

He shook his head. "How did you get to be so worthless?"

Vera faltered backward. He watched through his oc as she circled behind him. Her lips quivered out of shape. When she finally spoke, her voice sounded low and dry. "Are your birds a better fuck than me?"

Rolfe sat on the bench, gripping his chest. "No more games. Get the skydiver now."

13

*Harness. Webbing which secures a skydiver to the parachute.
Alternately, webbing which secures a participant during a sim ride.*

Orr pressed the earmuffs tight to his head. Groundwater blasted down the walls and flooded the gutters. Heavy rain must be falling outside. Pumps boomed through the rocks, and their noise strung Orr's nerves tighter than piano wire. He turned back toward the stairwell. He had to get out of this place. Let someone else find the Cyto server. He barely knew what a server was. Yet no matter which passage he took, the floor seemed to slant ever downward, and the rising water tugged at his ankles. "Dyce," he whispered. But Dyce was gone.

The farther he waded, the more the air stank of ozone and motor exhaust. He could see only a few meters ahead where the light-tube disappeared in a thick miasma of steam. His respirator could not filter out the particulates, and damp soot collected in his bronchial tubes. Behind him, a door slammed. Did he imagine the heavy thud of a lock falling closed?

"Cho, talk to me," he said. But the newscaster had fallen silent. Maybe the signal didn't reach that far down.

Something prickled his neck. He pinched the thing off his skin. A white millipede. Albino, its exoskeleton had no pigment. Orr could see right through its cellophane shell into its milky guts. He flung it away.

Water rose over the tops of his boots, and for one bright instant, he visualized how deep under the Earth he'd descended. Climbing to the surface

222 / M. M. BUCKNER

would take hours, and what if he couldn't find the way? What if the flood trapped him down here. His windpipe squeezed. He yanked off his respirator and sucked for breath.

The stench snapped him back to reality. He coughed and choked and snugged his breather back on. He kept turning, retracing his steps, looking for the stairs. Hot steam blurred everything. He felt waves of heat blowing off an invisible forge, and he stretched out his arms, almost blinded.

The flash flood swirled higher around his thighs, and he groped along an uneven ledge, clinging to the jagged rock and feeling the way with his boots. After a few paces, the floor dropped completely away, and he balanced on the lip of a waterfall. In the gloom, he saw water foaming down a crack in the bedrock. Its force buckled his knees. He took a step backward and smacked against a wall.

"Cho?" he yelled.

Still no answer.

He slid his hands along the streaming wall. Where was the opening? Jets of water drenched his quu-suit. The flood was intensifying. "Let me out!" he yelled. But gravity steered him now. His boot skated off the ledge, and he tumbled.

How far down that underground river did he fall? He bashed against a slotted metal grate. The force of the water flattened him, and he lay trapped under the flood. By main force, he pulled himself up where he could breathe. His knee smarted like the devil, and the ringing metallic blows of the drain pumps made him want to dig fistfuls of flesh out of his head. If he stayed there much longer, the noise might drive him to do it.

Bruised, bleeding, he slid his fingers up the watery stone, seeking anything he might grab. His fingertips crooked around a metal seam. The edge of a door? He pulled himself higher, and his hands traveled around the seam. It was round and shoulder-wide, like the valve of a large pipe. He couldn't find any way to open it, and he had no reason to believe it would lead to the surface, only desperation. After several minutes, he found a recessed panel near the center, probably a reader, but he had no pod or keycard to send it a message. Plus, he didn't know the code.

He banged it with his fist, but the hellish din covered the sound of his blows. "Help!" he called out—and couldn't hear his own voice.

He clung to the metal pipe, and his phobia ran loose. Mineral monsters fevered his mind, and rock geniis sucked him deeper and deeper under the water table. Thousands of leagues under, he snagged between fault lines that crushed him flat but never killed him. His flesh shredded to pulp. His heart shattered, but he could not die. Farther down he kept sinking, into Earth's red core, where molten lava charred his flesh. He rolled his head and screamed.

Then through the howling blast, Cho's voice broke like a clarion. "Sorry, I've been away."

Orr stopped screaming. His web specs flickered to life. He knuckled his ear. "Away?"

"You're on the Underside." Cho's words sifted through his mastoid bone directly to his auditory nerve. "I can't track you there. You have to tell me what you see."

Get me out! Orr couldn't tell if he spoke the words aloud or only imagined them.

Cho laughed. "I found the Cyto servers. They're in the geothermal plant. I knew they had to be on the Underside. I already looked everywhere else."

Orr shut his eyes. *Please.*

"Okay, you have to find an access panel with a biometric reader."

"I found it," Orr shouted into the ocean of noise.

"—should be a small recess, dead center of the panel. As soon as you find it—"

"I found the freaking thing," Orr bellowed.

"—to the panel. Got it?"

Orr wiped his streaming nose. His eardrums felt bludgeoned.

Cho said, "Touch your web specs to the panel. Do it."

Orr pressed his dark glasses against the metal reader. Cho transmitted a code, the panel slid open, and he fell through.

Harsh light made him cover his specs with both hands. He crawled inside, and the panel slid shut behind him. Then, blessed peace, the noise muted to a subliminal thud. Through layers of fluffy clouds, he heard people talking.

"Where's your sound hat, man? You insane? You got blood coming out your ears."

"You're tracking water in here."

"Get the boy some tea."

Orr had fallen into a nest of diggers. Literally a nest. When he could bear to crack his eyelids, he saw a room filled with damp straw. Actually, it was shredded printout. The diggers had wetted the document waste and plastered it around the walls, floor and ceiling as a sound barrier. Some of it drifted in the air like confetti whenever anyone moved, and it morphed the room into a feathery ink-marbled cave. Orr snatched a ribbon of confetti from the air and regarded it with awe.

The diggers fed him kelp rolls and weak tea. Then he curled up in the minced documents and slept.

14

Heading. Direction of forward movement, expressed in degrees.

In dreams, they say, the soul is most vulnerable—although Vera didn't put much stock in hearsay. Soon after the diggers left for work, Vera sent her friend Dr. Leo to retrieve Orr's sleeping body. All along, she'd tracked Orr's movements through the eyes of the city Geist, because of course the Geist watched the Underside, too.

Leo slipped Orr an extra drug to keep him comatose. Then two robot bearers transported Orr through the Underside into the gassy bowels of the geothermal plant—because Cho was right, that's where Cyto hid its servers. Hardware was the only vulnerable point in Rolfe's web-based empire. Of course he kept the location deeply encrypted. And of course he chose a site nearby for his daughter's home base. He needed Vera to guard his treasure.

Next door to the server vault, Vera's bedroom walls bled hot drips of water, and the tapestries did not completely muffle the pumps. Air fresheners couldn't quite stand up to the corrosive stench of fluid the machines piped into the bedrock to capture the Earth's heat, and sometimes the whirl of turbines made her hairs stand on end. But she couldn't object. She knew Cyto's future depended on the web servers.

This one time, though, she needed privacy, so she phuxed the security motes in her bedroom and fed Rolfe a rerun. Then in her muggy grotto, with her dehumidifiers running on max and her AC coughing up gouts of moldy air, Dr. Leo dumped the sleeping skydiver onto her white bed. The surgeon whisked off his Hijab veil and helped Vera unzip Orr's water-soaked quu-suit.

After they stripped him bare, Leo yawned and covered his mouth. "Nice. If you like beefcake."

"Keep your claws off," Vera said.

"Now, lovey, don't be rude. I'm on your side."

Vera would've scatted Leo away, except she needed him. He opened his kit and sorted his scissors and blades. Idly, he touched the tip of a scalpel to check its sharpness. He was going to remove Orr's web specs. For this favor, Vera had to give him a promissory note for a new aircar.

Leo rolled his shoulders and stretched his fingers. "There's a fresh scandal making the rounds. You might find it worthwhile."

"How much?" she asked.

"Your father keeps a nice Pinot in his cellar. One case for little me?"

Stealing Rolfe's wine would be a nightmare. She pinched Leo's bum. "This better be pure gold."

He leaned toward her and whispered behind his hand. "Rolfe's botanical habitat has crashed."

"Hallelujah!" She kissed him on the mouth. "Tell me all."

As Leo plied his knives, he described how Rolfe's sprinklers had over-amped and flooded the conifers. So much bioturf washed away, it clogged the recycling system, and some of the creepycrawlers drowned. Rolfe was pulling out his new hair plugs.

Color Vera pink. She gave Leo a hug. "This time, you've earned your wages."

Leo slitted his eyes. "I always do, love."

After the surgery, Vera bandaged Orr's wounds with her own hands and dressed him in a clean robe. She shaved his fine beard and trimmed his hair short. Leo watched her work. Then he gave her a slap with his head scarf. "God, you're in love with the boy."

She laughed. "This jock?"

Leo said, "You're sick with lust. Be careful, Vera. Don't forget who you are."

"You're just jealous." She shooed Leo out.

Hook knife. Razor-edged knife with a curved blade used by skydivers to cut lines in emergencies.

Alone in her bedroom, Vera sat beside Orr, struggling over what she was about to do. All this second-guessing made her ill. She shut her eyes and reiterated her reasons. Anyone would agree she had the weight of justice on her side. Yes, any impartial observer would agree. Again her compulsive memory reenacted the evidence—the day Rolfe sent her to the surgeons' ward.

She was nine years old when the sawbones cut her open to implant her body mods. The operation phuxed her womb and left her sterile, but Rolfe called that a bonus. As soon as she could stand, he started experimenting to see what her mods could do. At first, just for yucks, he swelled her up to tubby-tub size, then watched her stumble off balance.

"Fatso," he teased. "Blubber butt."

But that game soon bored him. He wanted a perfect daughter, so he made her strip and stand in his steam room to let the mods absorb plenty of vapor. Then he inflated different parts of her anatomy in fine increments, measuring her naked flesh with calipers and adjusting her curvature by degree.

"I'm doing this for *you*," he kept repeating.

Nine years old, she believed him.

He took his time poking her with his pincers and comparing her dimensions to a model he'd designed in his computer. The two of them spent hours cloistered in his steam room, and as he molded her to his new form, she couldn't name the longing she felt. The tingle down her neck. The heat flaring up her frame. Wrong or right, those words failed to explain her fluttering attempts to caress him.

"Stop that." He slapped her hands away. "That's dirty."

Nine years old, she didn't know. She hid her hands behind her back.

After that, they barely spoke during their long sessions in the steam. He put on antiseptic gloves and handled her like a figure carved in wax. Her skin stretched till it ached. Her subcutaneous cells throbbed. As long as she kept still and didn't flinch, everything went fine. But if she moved too close or tried to hug him, he chanted a quote from Edmund Burke, and to help her remember, he punctuated each phrase with a rap across her thighs.

"Restraint. And discipline. And examples of virtue. And justice. These are the things that form. The education. Of the world."

Genuine bamboo, that cane he used to discipline her. As long as his forearm, as thick as his thumb. His mother taught him its value. It was an antique, he told her, a family heirloom. He kept it locked in his desk, and one day, he promised, it would be hers.

A few weeks ago, she jimmied Rolfe's desk and took the cane. Her legacy. At night, she slept with it. Rolfe hadn't discovered her theft yet. Any day he would.

Orr stirred restlessly beside her in the bed, and she stroked his cheek. He would wake soon. She had no time left to question her choices. She got up and changed into a shimmery white gown and restyled her hair. Then she spritzed the room with hypnagogic nerve gas. Finally, she teased Orr's eyelid open and dropped in a tiny wireless ocular. His eye tremored at the foreign object, until the lens merged into his cornea where he couldn't feel it. Very tenderly, she kissed his lashes.

Then she whispered a code, and the sim she'd held so long in readiness began to ping his optic nerve. Half asleep, he drifted through her artificial dream.

"Lie still," she whispered. "You're safe in my condo."

In the sim, he pushed himself up from a nest of satin pillows and stared at his surroundings. No mildewed tapestries. No growling pumps. Her synthesized bedroom appeared bright, dry, and sweetly fragrant. She sat beside him and offered a tray of refreshments. Puff pastries, sparkling water, fresh apples.

He touched the robe she'd draped around his body. "What happened?"

"Eat first. We'll talk later." She fed him a delicacy by hand, knowing the buttery taste would ease his misgivings.

He knuckled his eye sockets. When she tried to nudge another bite of pastry into his mouth, he pushed her hand away and swung his feet to the floor. His quu-suit lay draped over a nearby chair, and his freshly polished boots waited by the bed. He rubbed his eyes again. "The web specs?"

She said, "I had them surgically removed."

"So this is real?"

He glanced around her room, examining her personal belongings as if they held secret clues. She'd reproduced many details of her real condo. Ancient leaves preserved in glass, empty seedpods of long-extinguished flowers, the skeletons of birds. Gifts from Rolfe lined her shelves. Her father collected lost things. She patted Orr's knee.

"You were wandering in the Underside, remember? I brought you here for safety. The Geist can't see us. This is my private space."

He took one of her pillows in his hands and rubbed his fingertips over the embroidery, assuring himself in every possible way that it was real. "Why me, Vera? Of all the skydivers in the world."

She knelt before him like a penitent. "If you could see what's in my heart . . ."

When he reached for his clothes, she gave up trying to explain. Still, she needed to show him the truth. So she launched the second chapter of her sim.

Her bedroom vanished, and his hands lashed out as if tearing at cobwebs. Her artwork swept him back through time to her sessions with Rolfe in the steam room. In those few compressed seconds, she forced him to witness every outrage her father had ever inflicted. Her story buckled and cracked apart. Her recall may have been distorted, probably it was. Still, her simulacra jolted Orr to his toenails. His muscles knotted. His mouth quivered. She could see he wasn't prepared for such knowledge. After her memoir flashed to its end, the sim transported him back to her imaginary bedroom.

She knelt before him and spread her fingers on his thighs. "You see how my father abuses me. I can't stand up to him alone."

Never had she felt so naked. Not with her father, nor with any of the long succession of men and women she'd seduced and exploited, had she ever allowed this intimacy. Maybe she went too far. Orr shrank away from her.

"Have mercy," she said. "Help me."

In the sim, Orr grabbed his boots and searched for an exit. She followed, knee-walking. "You don't know how spiteful he is. If you leave me now, he'll . . . he'll . . ." She sobbed and clutched at Orr's ankles and spritzed more hypnagogic gas. The sim clogged his mental filters so he wasn't able to see her poisonous clouds winding around him. He kept trying to unlock the door.

She said, "Remember what he did to your girlfriend."

At the mention of Dyce, Orr's face darkened. "You're not trapped, Vera. You can leave."

Leave Rolfe? Vera almost showed him what she thought of his moronic advice. She would no more leave Rolfe than the Moon would leave Earth.

She sobbed louder and kept fogging him with gas, hoping he would take pity and yield.

But he didn't. He stood by the door, rubbing his eyes, barely able to keep his balance. Even so, he resisted her touch, and she had to work hard to pull him back toward the bed. She sensed his will weakening, though. She pumped more gas, and he stumbled.

In a drug-thickened voice, he asked again, "Why did you have to pick me?"

She wormed into his arms. Her simulated red hair streamed through his fingers, and her spicy special effects seeped down his brain stem. She watched his expression blur to vagueness. They fell together across the bed, and then she knew she owned him. For a few moments at least, he was hers.

She whispered what she wanted and helped him shed his robe. He responded like a sleepwalker. Soon their bodies slid together and interlocked. When she pushed him down into the pillows, she tried her level best to believe that he liked her.

Hook turn. Sharp turn executed close to the ground.

Vera's capacity for truth had not completely withered. At times, she could still be straight with herself. It wasn't Orr she loved. Not this slumbering twenty-two-year-old with the sweaty hair and sour breath. She loved an impossible ideal—she knew that. But don't all suitors frame their passion in rosy make-believe? Her illusion of love looked so very much like Orrpaaj Sitka that the resonance of his snore set her trembling. She gravitated to the warmth radiating off his chest. She yearned for his salt.

How sweetly he rested beside her. Vera hadn't known such safe confident sleep in years. But of course, she'd drugged him. Lying in his arms, she opened his eye and gently removed the ocular. The sim had done its work. She spread her fingers over his brown nipple and felt the thump of his youth. Then she jacked him off in his sleep to make the illusion complete. Good-hearted boy, he would wake soon. If only he could see her for herself and . . .

His sleep-crusted eyes fluttered open. "Dyce?"

"It's me," Vera said, crashing.

When he saw they were lying naked and slick with cum, he sprang out of bed. She sprang up, too, and wobbled on her knees in the sheets. His face twisted. He didn't even try to hide his regret. She wanted to slice his eyes out.

How could he still be obsessed with the simpering girlfriend? Saint Dyce. She left him for a library job. Never knew what she had. Threw it away. While Vera, Vera bared her soul for him. Made skydives for him. Cherished the clouds he walked on. Did her devotion mean squat? She wanted to eat his heart with her teeth.

But she restrained her fury. Self-control kicked in like an autonomic reflex, and she streamed a soothing tone. "Don't blame yourself, Orr. You only meant to comfort me."

When he backed against the concrete wall, she pretended not to feel the tiny blades carving her insides. She wrapped herself in sheets and hurried away to her dressing room. All right, so he'd slept with the wrong woman. Let him stew in his guilt, let him wallow. She needed him unfocused. She needed him . . .

What Vera needed from Orr was impossible. A vanished delusion. What she needed from him might exist in a different universe, on another time line. Not here. So she tied her hair back and scrubbed her face at the sink. Then she deflated her mods and gazed at her own natural reflection. After a while, she dressed in a simple white suit and returned to the bedroom—to get what was necessary.

He hadn't moved. He leaned against the wall, groggy and sullen. She stood in front of him and rested her hands on his shoulders. "Do you want to go home, Orr?"

He stole a quick glance at her face. She'd used no makeup or mods. She meant for him to see her age. She'd brightened the room light to make it easy. Thirty years old, forty, what would he guess?

"I'm fifty-five," she said, "old enough to be your mother."

The fresh shock made him close down and withdraw deep inside. His body went flaccid, and his gray eyes lost their light. He said, "Nothing is true."

She touched his cheek. "We're both Rolfe's victims. He sent me to trick you again. He wants you to make a skydive from the ionosphere."

Orr's eyes snapped open.

She kept speaking in low bell tones. "We can't escape him, Orr. But maybe there's a way for you to get back home."

He moved past her. "Don't play games. Just say what you want."

Vera breathed through clenched teeth. Stupid boy. Did she have to lead him every step? She tuned her voice carefully. "Maybe if we agree to do this ionosphere dive . . ."

He finished her sentence. "Rolfe will let us go back to Mundo Mountain."

15

In date. Reserve parachute showing fresh pack date on data card.

Hauling Orr home to Alaska felt to Vera like lugging dead weight. She never meant for him to take things so hard. She gnawed her thumb watching him drag his big feet. He bumped his head getting into the company aircar. She thought he would love going home, but he didn't seem to care where he went.

Flying back to Mundo Mountain, she showed him stats about his swelling fan base, and she read aloud some of the texts from his admirers. "It's a good thing we've kept our drop zone secret," she said. "Otherwise, your public would pester you to death." Still, she rarely got him to talk, and when he did, he wouldn't meet her eyes. He slept through most of the flight.

Outside the aircar window, April clouds dimpled and bloomed, but Vera didn't see their beauty. Rolfe kept texting her about the ionosphere dive, goading her with his deadline. His seven fricking days were nearly gone, and she was sick of his bullying.

"*Me,*" she whimpered. "*My* team. *My* work." Her breath fogged the window.

She'd been right about Orr's star quality. Rolfe had no grounds to persecute her. But the ionosphere, yeeze. She did need a miracle. As a last ditch, she'd bribed Red Lips to plant a suggestion: The most media-friendly date for the ionosphere dive would be the summer solstice, the longest day in the year. Rolfe set a high value on media relations. At least that bought her another six weeks.

Vera bumped her forehead against the window glass. Rolfe and his dead-lines. Schedules plucked from nowhere, he talked about his dates like they had force and mass, and he used them to control everyone who fell under his influence. But his timetables had no bearing on anything. Vera could have told him about real gravity. She squinted down through the vapid sky.

Gravity takes her own sweet time, hunting, gathering, stirring her pot. One part cinders, one part ice, a pinch of volatile gas, gravity brews up black holes and blue planets. Mankind's dream to slip her bonds and fly free, weightless, head in the clouds like milky angels—pure crap. Vera enjoyed gravity's weight. Fighting a heavy load made her strong and smart, and that was better than happiness. Joy fizzled. Gravity endured. She turned away from the window and scanned her to-do list.

When they entered the Mundo hangar, she wasn't surprised to see Bettie and Al running up to greet them. Bettie's gray mane swung in damp tendrils, and she'd stuffed her pudgy butt into a pair of workout shorts. Her tent-shaped blouse showed signs of a recent bout of aerobics. Al wheezed through the same fusty asthma mask. When they saw Orr, their warm welcomes ossified. The boy looked rough.

For once, Al spoke first. "Glad you're back, old man." Then to Vera's horror, Al produced a white flapping dove from the sleeve of his lab coat. Animatronic model, naturally. Orr pretended to enjoy the magic trick, but his smile didn't reach his lips.

Bettie said, "You need a cup of tea."

Orr nodded.

Some of the crew came to say hello, but Vera ordered them back to work. They were polishing big curved sections of glass for the geodesic dome, and airborne glass dust scintillated through the hangar. She could taste it on her tongue.

After Orr hung up his raincoat and breather, Bettie put a motherly arm around his waist and guided him through the gerbil tubes to the lab. Al chit-chatted about their ionosphere research, and Bettie held on to Orr's waist in case he tripped. They treated him like a sick man. Vera followed at a distance.

Al babbled technicalities. He said the ionosphere could reach eighteen hundred degrees centigrade, while the layer below, the mesosphere, was a subzero deepfreeze. The more he talked, the more Vera recognized the enormity of her mistake suggesting this dive.

Long hours of work had given the lab a post-tsunami theme. Vera noted the high-tide ring of Post-its, diagrams and miniature Wing models tacked around the wall. She sniffed the strong tannin odor of microwaved tea mingled with baking ceramic. Ants had invaded. Through the window, she saw the construction crane lifting a section of geodesic glass.

Orr stumbled against Bettie's workstation and knocked an iPad to the floor. Quietly, Bettie signaled to Al. Then she pressed Orr gently into her personal chair and straightened his sloppy collar, while Al made tea.

"Maybe this briefing should wait," Al said.

Orr gazed up with sleepy eyes. "No, I'd like to hear."

"Right." Al glanced briefly in Vera's direction. Then he set the kettle brewing. "We have three problems."

One, he said, gases in the upper atmosphere were so sparse, a Wing diver might fall too fast and spin to death. Two, if the Wing hit the thick lower atmosphere at the wrong angle, it might skip like a stone and bounce out into space. Three, the friction of atmospheric reentry might set the Wing on fire.

Vera stood against the window and watched Al's eyes dance behind his wire-rims. Apparently, he got his jollies from engineering conundrums. His revelations were news to Vera, though, and she began to feel sincere alarm. But Orr didn't object. He sat woodenly facing the screen. His suntan had faded, and his new short haircut exposed the shape of his skull.

The designers exchanged glances behind his back. Bettie adjusted one of her hairpins. Al polished his wire-rim glasses on his coattail. They cast accusing frowns at Vera, but what was she supposed to do? Did everything have to fall on her shoulders? Outside, the heavy piece of glass swung in the wind.

Al said, "Tell him about your teacup, Bettie."

"Sure thing, Al." Bettie looped a teacup handle over her thumb. "Ceramic absorbs heat, right? So we thought, hey, a ceramic ablation shell. You know, to burn?" She squeezed Orr's shoulder. "Sweetie, do you need an aspirin?"

When he didn't answer, she smoothed his wrinkled shirt. He'd left his boots in the hangar, and his big toes poked holes through his socks. She stroked his short hair. "An ablation shell absorbs heat and burns away one layer at a time."

He still didn't respond.

"So Al came up with a new synthetic," she said.

"Right, Bettie got me thinking about nested shells of high-temp ceramic micromesh, and I've been testing different formulations, and . . ." Al adjusted the oxygen feed in his breather. "Basically, you'll fly the first part of your ionosphere dive in Bettie's teacup."

Al took Bettie's cup, poured it full of tea and pressed into Orr's hand. "Nothing like tea to restore a man's soul."

Orr stared at the cup, and the two engineers hovered like a pair of nursemaids. Vera turned to the window. Outside, the geodesic glass swung against the crane and cracked. The crew scattered to avoid the falling pieces. The lab's thick window muted the sound. No one in the lab saw it but Vera.

Finally, Orr got to his feet. "Thanks, guys. I—I can't seem to—"

Bettie took the cup from his unsteady hand.

"I just need a little rest," he said. Then he drifted off to his quarters. Vera's knuckles scraped the window as she watched him go.

16

Jumpmaster. An experienced skydiver certified to teach others.

Late that evening, long after Bettie and Al had turned in, long after Vera had retired to her cube for a web conference, Orr made a night dive. His able body refused to sleep any more, and he needed another mode of oblivion. So he slipped out and took the pilotless aircar. The late-shift crew didn't care. No one was watching.

He flew to six thousand meters above ground level, high enough to need oxygen, though he didn't carry any. He didn't take a Sky Wing either. No strobes, chem lights, or laser goggles. No GPS. He didn't light up the drop zone. He switched off his radio and automatic safeties. He considered leaving his parachute behind, only he felt naked without it.

Riding up to altitude, he looked for stars. The sky was clear, but the bright full moon blotted out the firmament. He'd been hoping for one last view of Polaris. The wretched song bounced around his head, *I will always love you.* But Dyce changed her mind.

The moon lit up the mountains like God's own floodlight, and platinum smog shimmered in the valleys, toxic and lovely. Yet Orr couldn't feel the night's grandeur. As he stood in the open hatch, he didn't even bother to check the wind. Dyce had set him free. He didn't owe her any allegiance, right? What he chose to do didn't affect her. He couldn't be unfaithful. He glanced toward the east. *Right?* The doubtful clouds so engrossed him that he forgot to tell the autopilot where to land the car.

Sharp rocky ridges etched lines through the silver mist like stanzas on a sheet of music. Far to the east, amber light stirred over the plexi roof of Unimak Village, but he didn't notice the incandescent haze. He had no cause to blame himself. So why did he feel untrue?

He leaped from the aircar. Maybe he should have forced her to leave Seattle, for her own good. The mountaintops glittered like shards of jet, and he streaked down in a swift vertical track. But what right did he have to force Dyce? Whatever they'd shared was broken. The whole world felt broken. His body whistled toward the Earth, and in seconds, he reached terminal velocity.

Volcanic peaks loomed almost purple in the moonlight. And that time she traded her Game Boy for his medicine. And the way she folded his shirts. And how she trotted along beside him to keep up with his long stride. He didn't notice the mountains or the seconds blasting by.

Out of nowhere, two headlights blinded him. Radiance scattered through the smog, and his body arched in reflex, just as he heard the whine of the approaching engine. It was the aircar. The autopilot was turning slow aimless circles, spiraling down around him like an unmanned motorboat in a black lake. He swooped left to avoid its downward corkscrew of light.

If his helmet display had been live, if his audible altimeter had been active, he would have recognized the hard deck, four hundred meters above the ground. That was the minimum altitude any sane jumper needed to open a parachute. But love was for children. Not for the real world. He saw the aircar crash in a brief orange flare muffling to auburn. And he rifled through the hard deck without a blink.

He was falling fast, over seventy-five meters per second. The valley exploded upward. The end of memory, that's what he wanted. Still, his body sensed the pressure change. Six seconds to impact. Five. He reacted without thinking. He arched and opened his 'chute.

His canopy streamed from its bag and filled with wind. Still plummeting, he felt the brutal opening shock and cried aloud—right before he landed in a tumbling roll down the steep side of a mountain. Loose gravel rained up in a dry splash as he slid headfirst down the slope. He came to rest when his canopy snagged on an outcrop. He didn't know it then, but he'd broken his clavicle.

———

Jump run. Aircraft flight which places skydiver over the drop zone.

Vera found Orr sleeping late the next day in a dust-caked jumpsuit. He was too dead asleep to notice when she rolled him faceup. Only when she undressed him did she discover the livid bruises covering one whole side of his body. What the . . . ? She linked through her motes to browse footage from the previous night. Then she checked satellite scans. Damn him. Her aircar! She bit her knuckles. Then she slid her fingertips over his bruised chest. Poor guy, he must have walked home through mountains.

She washed his face with a cloth and breathed in the familiar oily smell of his hair. She kissed his eyelids. He was practically comatose, he didn't know. She tugged off his boots—phew! She stripped off his socks and dumped the whole mess in the recycle bin. After that, she got bags of ice from the breakroom and piled them on his bruises.

What next? She couldn't call Bettie. Bettie would want to rush him to the Unimak clinic, and the local doctors might postpone their project. So she voned Dr. Leo.

Leo was sleeping late—and not alone. Her call woke him in a pissy mood. He examined Orr via web scan and prescribed orthopedic nanobots to fix his fracture. For an atrocious extra charge, Leo agreed to air-freight the prescription. His brown eyes looked bloodshot.

He said, "Maybe I should come there in person. Your pretty boy may need my healing touch."

Vera kicked at the pile of dirty clothes next to Orr's bunk and watched black ants fly out. Her aircar was smashed. Orr needed a new Wing. No way could she afford Leo's house call. Ironic, the little doctor seemed to forget she'd paid his med school tuition. She counted on his tact, but he always demanded recompense.

She said, "Not now, sweet. When I need you, I'll whistle."

He laughed through his nose. "Poor Vera. How the mighty are fallen. Your boy isn't giving you any dick, I can tell."

She terminated the call.

Then she watched Orr's dive again, more slowly this time. The satellite angle was poor, and cloud cover obscured the view, but the silvered night sky gave her an inspiration. What a terrific backdrop for a sim. Next time Orr made a night dive, she would send holocams.

But as she saw him streak down through the layered night, suddenly she crammed her fist in her mouth. Orr meant to kill himself. Thank God he opened his parachute. Twenty-two years old, he had a ruddy strong will to live. She bit into her hand.

She, she was to blame. She'd made him want to self-destruct. Her mind shuddered. The idea of packaging his death wish as entertainment felt massively corrupt. But packaging passion was what they did at Cyto. She rocked back and forth. She couldn't go soft, not at this late date, certainly not about Cyto.

Jumpsuit. A close-fitting coverall worn by skydivers.

April morphed into May, and Vera was still brooding over what to do. Alone in her private cube, she sat on the floor combing oil through her hair with her hands. The aircar wreckage had left a big blot on her spreadsheet, which Rolfe had not failed to mention. All month, he'd been sending her obscene texts about his money troubles.

Forget Rolfe. She squeezed another drop of vat-grown natural hair oil into her palms, then worked it through her brittle curls. The last four weeks had emptied her. Every hour, she'd been monitoring Orr through her motes and satellites and holocams, praying he would not try to hurt himself again. The lost car didn't seem to bother Orr a bit. On the contrary, it gave him bold new ideas for annihilating his sorrow. He'd been making "stuff dives."

Right, that's what he called this new brand of stunt. Stuff dives, absolute madness. Vera rubbed and worried her hair. She could've grounded him, but she was afraid of what he might do if she pulled his reins too tight. Instead, she made sure his safeties were switched on, and for reassurance, she'd browsed vlogs of other jumpers freefalling with "stuff." Motorcycles, pianos, Humvees. She didn't get the motivation. Did they really need one more way to cock-tease death?

Since the aircar was shrapnel, she allowed the crew to fly Orr up in a construction tractor, and before each flight, she watched him collect stuff from the work site. Say, for instance, a working laser jackhammer.

The morning Orr did his airborne break dance with the jackhammer, Vera nearly tossed her breakfast. But she didn't dare stop him. He was still too near the tipping point. Naturally, he chose a day when gale-force winds were blowing off the Alaskan Gulf. The jackhammer had a pair of thick vibrating handles, and when he dove out, gripping these handles in his elbows, the rotary torque metamorphosed him into a flying drill bit.

Twice the handles slipped out of his arms, and the laser cut random arcs through the sky till he caught it again. When he sailed over the ocean to drop the sinister thing, its beam nearly sliced his thigh open. Vera rubbed and rubbed her long thick hair, remembering.

That dive had reamed her intestinal fortitude, but it only heightened Orr's. The next day, he juggled foil-packs of liquid explosives. Then he somersaulted through loose bundles of rebar. He tried to twirl a forklift over his head, but it fell too fast. Whatever he could scarf from the construction arsenal, he took along for a lark. Vera chewed her knuckles raw, but she also streamed the holos to Rolfe.

Even now, secluded in her cube, she kept seeing Orr's deadly dance with the jackhammer. She squeezed out more oil and kneaded her dry split ends between her fingers. Damage control. If only she knew how. But Rolfe loved the stuff dives. Lately, his cash reserves had taken a rapid and uncontrolled descent, so he actually thanked Vera for creating the stuff dive concept. She didn't bother to set the record straight.

Overnight Rolfe rushed a new jackhammer sim through production, and sure enough, it proved intensely narcotic for Cyto users. Now Rolfe had dollar signs dancing in his eyes, and he rented Orr a new jumpjet full of toys—power drills, jet skis, trash compactors. He even talked about ramping up more web servers to accommodate his growing community. Yeah, let him dream. Vera slid her hands through her hair.

The stuff dives gave Orr a hectic charge. When he wasn't in the sky, he buzzed around the hangar like a quantum particle. He couldn't sleep. He couldn't settle. So Vera had to spoon-feed him game sims to help him relax. And instead of refusing the ocular, he seized on it.

Role-play games offered the best relief. Imperiled utopias. Lairs and lizards. Heroic journeys by ship. The kind of pabulum mothers fed to hyperactive kids. The sims teased Orr's brain and dulled his pain, the standard formula. Already, he'd gotten in the habit of needing them every night.

As of yesterday, Vera started feeding him daytime sims as well—training scenarios for the ionosphere. The summer solstice was still forty-five days off, but she knew how slippery time could be. She'd been scavenging through junkyards for a low-priced space shuttle. Bettie and Al were still agonizing over the new Sky Wing design, and her Seattle code team was working ahead, fleshing out her artwork for the sim. So far, they'd built little more than wireframe, but Orr used it anyway to train.

Vera coiled her hair round and round her hand. She wondered if she was unwise letting Orr practice his moves in web space. The code-heads might leave out something crucial. They'd never seen the sky, and no diver had jumped from the ionosphere. It was all hypothetical. She ran her own research and corrected their code where she could.

Orr never complained. He never mentioned Dyce. Every morning, he packed his parachutes and charged his helmet batteries. Every afternoon, he scraped the muddy pumice off his boots. When all else failed, he plugged his head full of music and ran laps in the hangar. He went through his days on autopilot. Then at night in the funk of his messy room, he enlisted with a massively multiple group of Argonauts to sail the Aegean Sea.

But Vera knew from experience, the longer you live in denial, the more it frags you. Orr didn't smile anymore. He didn't practice sleight-of-hand tricks with Al or warm up Bettie's tea. He didn't sneak out at night to look for stars. At mealtimes, he barely tasted his food.

Vera worked the oil through her roots. She always used her hands to oil her hair. Hands were gentler than brushing. The ancients thought a person's spirit resided in the hair. King Nisus. Samson. Apollo, the unshorn. Rapunzel lured her lover with her hair. Mary Magdalene used her hair to wash Jesus' feet and gain forgiveness. And Brahma's hair, like Medusa's, turned into snakes.

Rolfe said the old myths always reenacted themselves, not in cycles, but in one long braided thread, spiraling through space and time. As Vera massaged her bushy locks, a few loose strands fell out and slid down to the floor. She hated when that happened. She dreaded losing her rich red mane. Tighter, she gripped the wig stand between her knees and stroked the curls with her fingers. Her pride, this wig. She'd styled it years ago from her own youthful tresses.

She lifted a curl to the light and noticed how its color had faded. What she'd done to Orr harassed her. If she'd had the means, she would have relieved his pain. She would've given him new memory stints to bypass every engram of Dyce. Maybe he would have welcomed it. But she'd already meddled too much with his psyche. They barely spoke now. There was an ugliness between them, and it made Vera feel hollow inside. But it was necessary.

17

Key. Signal between skydivers to trigger next sequence in a formation.

Rolfe Luce zoomed from one science archive to another, seeking knowledge more agreeable to his taste. Astronomy incensed him. He resented the fate of aging stars. Yet all the web sites aired the same ugly report: Each time a celestial body grew so massively bright that its luster swelled through the heavens, then without fail, gravity reached out and crushed it into a tiny black ball. The wrongness of that outcome made Rolfe's toes curl. He shook his fist at the skylight over his head. He felt sure the same cosmic injustice had brought on his problems with social workers.

All this time, he'd been martyring himself, rescuing his flooded woodlands, and for whom? For mankind, of course. The next generation. The fucking children! And just when his firs were teetering on the brink of viability, the Pacific Social Workers League started flaming him in their vlogs. They peppered his inbox with insults. They sicced the school board to audit his taxes. And this morning, they issued a parental warning: Cyto's full immersion sims stunted the development of children!

So bloody unfair. And at the worst possible time. This was exactly the reason Rolfe had stopped appearing in public. This and, of course, the rising incidence of disease. Rolfe didn't trust the outside world. He hardly ever left his sterile compound. Too many mutating microbes. Too much unfiltered human breath. Talk about stunted children!

One day soon, he would make his comeback. Oh yes, he would have his say. He would shine again, as bright as any supernova. But he would pick his own moment. Meanwhile, with this parental brouhaha and so many extra palms to grease, Cyto barely finished the quarter in the black. All his hopes were riding on the Gravity Pilot now. He needed the ionosphere dive to be a blockbuster.

With a grunt, he shut down his browser. The damned oc made his eye sting. He'd been wearing it too long without a break, spying on Mundo Mountain. He'd gotten very OCD about tracking his investment, and from what he could observe, things were not going well. It was time to pay a visit and bring his motivational skills to bear. He advised Vera to be ready.

The night before his arrival, he watched her cavorting in her "private" cube, singing off-key as if she'd won some bleeping lottery. Did she think he would come out of hiding that easily? Play on her game board, by her rules—in the flesh? Did she take him for a cretin?

No, the moment hadn't arrived yet for his triumphant return. Only he would control that program, and he'd make sure the media turned out in force to document his brilliance. As for now, he would travel to Vera's little outpost via satellite, in holographic projection.

He met Orr Sitka on the launchpad, under the perpetual work in progress which the crew fabulously called a dome. Muggy May clouds rolled through the geodesic trusses, and mosquitoes congregated. The skydiver wore his hermetic jumpsuit and helmet. Rolfe wore shorts and a tank top. A holograph didn't need special clothes.

He pretended to box Orr's ears. "You're looking trim, kid."

It was true, Orr had lost weight. Meanwhile, Rolfe had gained several kilos. He blamed it on stress. One or two minor food binges, and his metabolic implant flaked out. Abysmal product quality, he would demand a refund. Sure, he knew his bulging eyelids gave him a piggish squint, and maybe his complexion resembled lard. All of this was fixable. He tried to smile.

He said, "You're a phenomenon, kid. Sportscasters analyze your swoops like frigging poetry. They find deep meaning in the way you tuck your chin." Then the jumpjet fired up, and he had to shout over the roar, "Just remember, it's not the critic who counts. Nor the man who stands in the arena, marred by dust and sweat and yada yada. The only one who matters is the guy who buys the ticket!"

Rolfe cackled extravagantly at his own word-play, but Orr's nonreaction disappointed him. No one read the classics anymore.

The skydiver passed his fingers through Rolfe's holographic field, then wiped his glove on his pants, turned on his heel, and mounted the ramp to the jumpjet.

"Cheeky brute." Rolfe followed.

Orr stumbled through the hatch, and Rolfe almost reached to help him. Cyto's prize athlete tripped on a door sill? This did not bode well. Vera was feeding the boy too many game sims. She should have known that would leave him hungover. Rolfe texted a cautionary note to his daughter: *Our Gravity Pilot needs more exercise.*

Holocams followed them inside the jumpjet, along with hundreds of mosquitoes, and Rolfe visualized a bloody zoo of parasites and viruses. Malaria, encephalitis, dengue fever. What a world to live in. He congratulated his own wisdom for traveling in holo.

For this dive, Orr intended to waltz with a kelp baler. The motor-driven contraption squatted inside the fuselage, flaunting its eight nested wheels, each one bristling with tines long enough to pierce a meter-thick stack of kelp leaves.

Rolfe's holographic finger touched the point of a baler tine, gathering data. "This mother is sharp. You really plan to leave the motor running?"

Orr thrust his hand into a grab loop and signaled the pilot to take off. Rolfe eyed him. Prima donna. Celebrity must've fogged his brain.

The baler almost filled the jet's bare fuselage, and the two of them hunkered behind its spiky wheels. The jet engines made a lot of noise, so Rolfe used his implants to volumize his voice. "Have you seen the XS Channel? These stuff dives, you've roused jumpers all around the globe. I mean real athletes, not sim riders."

Orr pressed his shoulder against the steel airframe and squinted through the window. The rain clouds were clotting thicker.

Rolfe kept examining the baler. "Some of your skydiver pals in Australia, they want to meet up with you. I think we should plan a webcast."

The jet thundered, building up thrust. It lifted straight up, then shot forward, throwing Orr into Rolfe's phantom field. The boy sprang away as if he'd touched a necrotic corpse, and Rolfe snickered.

"We could have maybe two billion viewers for your ionosphere jump. *If* we do the right marketing. And one dime out of every dollar goes to cleaning up the ecosphere. Doesn't that make you proud?"

Orr edged closer to the window, and when the jet made a wide turn over Unimak Village, he brushed mosquitoes off the glass and gazed down. Rolfe noticed how tense he was. Athletes were high-strung creatures. Always needed special handling. Sometimes the carrot. Sometimes the stick. Vera should've learned that lesson.

The jet rose above the clouds, and sunlight shafted through the window, spotlighting the baler. When Orr grasped one of the tines in his glove, Rolfe wondered if it might be sharp enough to cut through the Kevlar. Stuff dives made for cool fun on the web, but in real life? Rolfe tapped his teeth and eyed the knife-sharp tines.

The jet was approaching jump altitude, and they didn't have much time left, so Rolfe spoke quickly. "I'm not the one who lies to you."

Orr unhooked the tie-downs holding the baler in place. He opened the hatch, and the blasting wind sucked at his jumpsuit. He switched on the baler's ignition, and the tines spun like eight electric fans. Mosquitoes fled, and holocams tumbled. Rolfe eased away. What kind of mentally unbalanced dolt would skydive with an active kelp baler?

Rolfe yelled, "Your girlfriend's turning into a real computer artist."

Orr whipped around and glared. Rolfe nodded. "Yeah, Dyce. She's creating a whole family tree of little characters, giving each one its own personality and talents. Very original. I may decide to merchandise it."

Orr stood in the open hatch clenching and unclenching his fists. "You stole her life."

Rolfe shrugged. "I made an offer, and she took it. She's happy where she is. You need to accept that."

From the blaze in Orr's eyes, Rolfe knew he'd been doubly right not to come in the flesh. He only meant to encourage the boy, but talking to Orr was like juggling bird's eggs. "You know, you can visit her anytime in—"

Orr lunged into the sky, pulling the baler with him. Rain clouds swallowed him, but Rolfe didn't need laser goggles to see. He watched the whole show via satellite in the comfort of his fur-lined hammock. He also streamed the live recording to Orr's numerous fan sites.

The baler weighed half a metric ton, and sure enough, it heard the call of gravity. Orr drew his body into a tight vertical missile to keep pace with its rapid plunge. Seconds hissed by, and his downward speed increased. His fingers locked fast around the control yoke. When he hit the rain, the bailer swung him around, buzz-cutting the yellow air. Holocams swerved and scattered. He tried to arrest the spin, but the baler outweighed him by too much. He couldn't control it. And he was running out of time.

Rolfe sat bolt upright in his hammock. Was the Gravity Pilot going to off himself in a live webcast? Could this be Vera's bullshit game? Fuck this. He switched to a view of his daughter's private cube. She was clenched up in her blanket, watching the dive through her oc and biting her pillow. She looked ready to spontaneously combust. No, she hadn't planned this.

As Orr and his bailer whistled down between two granite peaks, Rolfe tugged at his toupee. This was his meal ticket punching out. His fir trees. His beautiful green garden. But . . . maybe he could give this disaster a positive twist. He visualized the skydiver splatting into the rocks, blood and viscera fountaining upward. Yeah, he could do something with this. He kept the holocams running.

Orr and the bailer were locked in a runaway spin. If his fingers had been made of steel, he might have held on till his last breath. Fortunately, he was made of flesh, so he lost consciousness, and his hands slid off the yoke. His automatic opening device popped his canopy open ten seconds before he smacked into the ground. Rolfe wrapped himself in his cat hides and shuddered.

For the next two hours, Rolfe used satellite beacons to tag the spot where Orr landed, while Vera led her crew on a ground hunt. They found the skydiver hobbling along a ravine twelve kilometers from the drop zone, a hundred meters from the shattered baler. Rolfe cursed his maker and texted fresh obscenities to Vera. His investment had a fractured ankle and two broken thumbs.

18

Line of flight. Imaginary reference line used in formation skydives.

After that fall, Orr was glad his injuries gave him an excuse to lie in bed. He needed to hide from himself. As the last two weeks of May unreeled, he barely glanced out the window. Gradually, Dr. Leo's nanobots fused his fractures while food trays, ice packs, flying ants, and wadded handkerchiefs collected around his bunk. Vera spiked his protein shakes with painkillers and pro-biotics, and he played sims more and more. Lightweight role-play games with loads of action. Sometimes Vera sat by his bed watching his face, but he pretended not to know she was there.

When the games ended and the anesthetics wore thin, he spiraled back to Dyce. He kept seeing the nervous curve of her shoulders and hearing her last words. He tried to put her out of his mind. She'd made it clear she didn't want him. The more he tried not to think of her, the more she haunted him.

One sleepless night, he hobbled to Bettie's workstation and tried to compose a text message to Dyce. Vera had cut his hair short so it wouldn't fall in his eyes, but he missed having something to run his fingers through. Beyond the window, the midnight sky glowed lavender. The Alaskan days were lengthening, overtaking the night. It was almost June.

Flames fluttered in the kiln. Lab computers hummed. He touched the small disk lying against his naked brown chest. Cheap plate-gold, strung on a nylon cord, Dyce's locket. Inside was the quick-mo chip with their schmaltzy duet, *I will always love you.* The locket, her parting stinger missile. He deserved to lose her.

His bandaged thumbs made him gawky with the stylus. *I need you,* he scrawled. Then he couldn't list a single reason. She burned him down like candle wax, who knew why.

Miniature models of Sky Wings cluttered the counter. He picked one up and rubbed its glassy smoothness against his lips. He'd gotten in the habit of relying on Dyce. Not love, then. Just habit? Whatever the feeling was, it kept tugging, pulling, dragging. His stylus scratched, *Why did things change?*

He pictured her library, not the new one in Seattle but her first one, in Unimak. Her little white desk by the back window near the water fountain, he remembered how tidy she kept it. She said the history of the Aleut nation hid in fragments all over the web and in the library attic, too. She spent three years lacing the old stories together.

Sometimes she would meet him in the village at night, after he'd been skydiving. She would nestle in his arms, smelling of crumbly paper, and she would chatter about some diary she'd found in a cardboard box. Did he pay attention? Not enough.

He held the Sky Wing model up to the light. With his thumb, he tested the sharp leading edge he'd personally helped to define. And there inside the cone was his belly strap. He, Orr Sitka, had added that strap. The great achievement of his life. He dropped the model, and it cracked.

Nothing? Everything? In a century, he felt sure that all he and Dyce ever accomplished would sink out of sight. His world record, broken. Her library, obsolete. Their histories and passions, buried under layers of fresher ones. So why couldn't he get over her?

Dead tea steeped at the bottom of the electric pot, giving off a burnt ether. If Dyce had been there, she would have sorted his thoughts into a T-shaped grid, with check marks and crosses to weight the priorities. He'd seen her do that when they were deciding what kind of mattress to buy for their rented room. Without her, he felt like half a person.

Al told him that love was more than a feeling, it was something you had to do. Orr understood doing. He would've rushed back to Seattle and dragged Dyce away. Only, she didn't want that. And he'd ignored what she wanted too many times.

What do you need? he scribbled.

He got up and found his yoga mat. In the dim light, he did a hundred push-ups. Then he lay facedown and raised his upper body, curving his spine backward in a Cobra pose till he was staring straight up at the ceiling panels. What he did, what he should've done, what he ought to do next—he wanted to stop thinking.

He bounded up and ran in place, punishing his half-mended ankle. His hands sliced up and down, and his bare feet pounded the mat. Breath rasped through his throat. His legs beat a drumroll. But the exercise didn't kill his ache. In his periphery, the screen still glowed, waiting for him to finish his message to Dyce.

19

Log book. Web-based documentation of skydiver achievements.

The next morning, Vera woke to a loud knocking. She'd ordered the crew not to bother her in her private cube. Trust Bettie to break the rule.

"Let me in. It's about our boy." Bettie pounded till the door rattled.

The noise had startled Vera from a hot nap. She sprang up, shoved the bamboo cane under her pillow and opened the door. "Is he hurt? Where is he?"

When Bettie saw Vera, she reeled backward, and her round saucer eyes almost made Vera laugh. Vera had not yet tuned up her body mods. Possibly, she resembled a withered root vegetable.

She'd spent most of the night in pitched battle with her dad. The baler incident freaked Rolfe, so he ordered her to cease and desist with the stuff dives. Now he said they were deranged. The insurance alone was making him bleed out his gums. He repossessed the rental jumpjet. If she didn't cook up a better idea quick, he might yank the whole project out of her hands and give it to his newest boo squeeze—Mrs. Jadri.

Their late-night jag left Vera strung out, and the Prune's early visit did not sweeten her mood. "Is he injured? What? Tell me."

Bettie eyed her flat chest and droopy hips. "Orr's not hurt. He's asleep."

Vera nearly slammed the door on her hand. "Wait outside." Then she stripped and started the shower.

Bettie spoke through the door crack. "I found some of his writing in my delete bin. This breakup with his girl has him spooked. We told him, he needs to accept it, get on with his life. But the message doesn't register."

This was Bettie's big news? Didn't Vera fret about Orr every second? Thin steam jetted from her shower and beaded on her wrinkly skin. Slowly, her pores absorbed vapor, and her mods began to inflate.

Bettie yelled through the shower noise. "Al and I worry he may do something drastic."

"Worry about your deadline." Vera rubbed herself to hurry the process. Gradually, her physique regained its succulent curves, while she agonized over what to do.

Bettie was waiting when she stepped out of the shower. "Body mods. I thought so."

"You should try them." Vera faced her in the buff, pink with heat. She hoped her nakedness would intimidate the engineer, but Bettie eyed her anatomy like she was choosing meat for vivisection.

Vera reached for her clothes. "Get out."

"Admit it, Vera. You're scared, too. I know you're fond of him."

"I can handle Orr."

Bettie grabbed her wrist. "Like you've done so far? He's losing it, Vera. He's not a champion anymore."

Splinter-eyed hag, who did she . . . Vera wanted to . . . She sat down on the bed, tired to death. Everything was turning out wrong. Maybe this game was too big for her.

Bettie draped the sheet around Vera's bare shoulders and sat beside her on the cot. Vera felt the warmth of Bettie's hip and pictured rolls of dimpled cellulite. Bettie was close to Vera's age.

"We love the boy as much as you do," Bettie said. "We have to help him get his focus back."

She patted Vera's hand, and her soft spongy hip mashed closer. Vera felt confused having someone in her bed who didn't want sex. She studied her knees. Beside her, Bettie's thighs spread wide in her frumpy trousers. Normally, Vera would have bristled at the Prune's advice, but exhaustion made her quiet.

"He's lonely." Bettie's fleshy shoulder rested against Vera's. "You know what that does to a person."

Her age-freckled hand squeezed Vera's fingers, and very faintly, Vera squeezed back.

"He's hanging on by his toenails," Bettie whispered. "We think he needs a real stratosphere dive."

Vera snorted one flat note. "We just lost our jumpjet."

"What?" Betty frowned. "How?"

"Don't ask." Vera settled a little closer into Bettie's warmth. "Money's tight, okay? From now on, Orr has to do all his training in the sim room."

Bettie wouldn't give up. "He's made only one real stratosphere dive in his life, and you expect him to jump from the edge of space?"

Creepers, didn't Vera know? Didn't Orr's short time in the upper atmosphere give her night sweats? But Rolfe left her no room to maneuver. She said, "Do you realize the cost of rocket fuel? The carbon penalties are criminal. And what if he breaks another bone? It's an unnecessary risk."

Bettie said, "He can't do all his practice in that ratty sim."

Vera turned on her. "Our training sim is absolutely true to life."

Bettie sniffed.

"But it's perfect," Vera said. "I've consulted meteorologists, aviators, aeronautics engineers. We've animated this sim in higher verisimilitude than ever before in the history of man. Why, the troposphere's a masterpiece. We've added supercell tornadoes, accelerated jet streams, every possible hazard. You've seen Orr go through the training."

"I've seen him black out twice," Bettie said. "I've seen his heart race so fast, you had to shut the sim down to prevent cardiac arrest."

No denying it, Orr had injured so many muscles, Vera finally caved and brought Dr. Leo on site to look after him. Serious payroll expense. Not to mention Leo's snarky comments.

"You care about him, admit it." Bettie stroked Vera's hand. "The pad's finished. We can rent another jumpjet. Forget the dome, we don't need it."

Vera gave her the evil eye, and she gave it right back.

"At least let him take a break," Bettie said. "Let him go home, visit his cousin. Maybe that'll help."

Help? Something had to help soon. Vera felt the Prune's thick fingers warming the back of her hand. They felt good, those fingers. But she couldn't trust them. The Prune had no reason to like her.

"Let him go home," Bettie repeated.

Vera got to her feet and pulled on a fresh white coverall. "I'll think about it."

Main. The principal parachute canopy.

Vera found Orr lying in bed, snarled in a wad of sheets. He smelled like embalming fluid. Evidently, he had helped himself to the crew's stash of homemade pearl millet gin. His eyes were closed, but Vera noticed his lips moving. He wasn't passed out. He was helping Jason and the Argonauts chase the Golden Fleece.

Damn it, Bettie was right. Orr had lost his focus. He no longer moved with the same physical poetry. The nanobots had knitted his bones back together, but his rhythm was off. His reflexes had turned to glue. He wasn't good enough anymore to dive the ionosphere.

Vera swallowed the dregs of her spit and watched him play his sim. Her own grandiose game had brought him to this. She would've paced, but his room was too cluttered to move. Helmets, gym shorts, battery chargers, wet clumps of tea leaves, his junk covered every surface. If she'd had some implement close at hand, she might have thrashed him.

Bettie and her meddling advice. Vera rubbed her temples and thought. Was there any possible way she could wrangle a real stratosphere dive? She subvocalized to her oc, and a spreadsheet beamed onto her retina. Already, her project was cave-diving in red ink, plumbing new trenches in the ruby deeps. By no possible means could she rent another jumpjet. She could barely afford a taxi.

Orr stirred, rustling the sheets. His game action must have been rising to a climax. She sat beside him and stroked his injured ankle. The bandage showed soap rings, and soft black hairs curled over his bare shin. What she wanted, or what he needed—neither of them had a choice.

She shook his shoulder. Dear boy, he needed to get up. She unplugged his earbuds and spoke in a loud voice, "Your inbox is full. You need to clear your inbox."

"I don't have an inbox," he muttered, waving her off.

"Guess again. You have dozens of inboxes linked to your official fan site. Now get the fuck up."

She seized his forearms and hauled him to a sitting position. He was naked.

His young body smelled sour. "Take out the oc. Come on." She coaxed him to pop the tiny lens into her hand. She'd given him several new wireless models. This one looked greasy. She dropped it into a cup of cleaning fluid, then pushed him toward the shower.

"Shave," she said, "and brush your teeth."

While he bathed, she opened her pan, and a 3-D web browser ballooned around her like a spectral blue globe. A comet was circling. She maximized the browser to room-size, and the comet gained definition. Orr returned, wrapped in his wet towel, just as the comet resolved into an animated action figure in lavender-lime pants and winged boots. A cartoon ghost of the Gravity Pilot was sailing around his room.

"Is that a new ad?" He sounded sullen. The browser colored his skin in watery shades.

Vera inhaled the scent of his shampoo. "It's just business."

But the ad jingle was playing, and his forehead knotted. The lyrics didn't promote the Celestia Sky Wing, as she'd told him. No, the jingle offered a one-month free trial of Gravity Pilot sims. Vera should have killed the ad faster. She wasn't thinking. After three seconds, the black Cyto sun swelled and swallowed the room in darkness.

"Shut," she said quickly.

She didn't want him to see the other ads Jadri was running, with a lifelike Orr extolling the splendors of the Cyto wikiverse. They'd made him their puppet. If he heard the drivel they'd put in his mouth, he might go supernova. She minimized the browser and muted the audio.

But even a shallow web cruise brought too many head-on collisions with their marketing campaign. Gravity Pilot ads clogged every web port. As Vera ticked through the layers to reach his inbox, his counterfeit image flashed across her browser like a bad memory. In the room beside her, his real face turned surly.

She said, "Ignore this. Look at your fan mail."

He said, "I've seen the ads, Vera. I know what they say."

She hoped he was bluffing. She let the remark pass. His inbox listed thousands of requests for autographs, hundreds of serious questions about skydiving technique, and video love letters by the teragig.

She said, "People adore you. They memorize your maneuvers. They know your style. You could make a skydive anywhere in the world, and people would recognize you, Orr. Look at this tuberculosis patient. She says you gave her a reason to live. And this ex-con says you reunited his family. And—"

"They're not talking about me." Orr dropped his towel and reached for the ocular floating in the cup by his bed.

Grenades detonated in Vera's small intestine. His sulks jangled her worse than his stuff dives. She searched her pockets for antacids. "If you need sims, ride your training scenarios. You dive from the ionosphere in three weeks."

"You can fake that, too." He dabbed the ocular out of the cup with his little finger.

Obstinate kid. Vera had no clue how to kick-start a twenty-two-year-old mope. She floundered. On the table by his bed, she noticed a locket on a cord. She picked it up. "What's this?"

He yanked it from her hand.

She said, "No need to be rude."

He stood glaring at her, naked, wet, magnificent—and livid. Blocked blood mottled his brown face. Finally, he dropped the locket in a drawer. "You want me to dive. I'll dive. I'm doing my best, Vera."

He pulled on the sweat pants he'd worn the day before. Then he searched under the bed for clean socks, and when he couldn't find them, he tramped barefoot down the hall toward the sim room.

Vera ran after him and scrambled in front to make him stop. "The ionosphere, Orr. You'll dance with the northern lights. You'll fall farther and faster than anyone. You want that, don't you?"

His red-rimmed eyes blinked. "It's the only thing I have left."

Vera wanted to pull her hair. How in the world could she lift his spirits? A trip home, yeah, that might help. Funny how she'd come to trust the Prune's advice.

She wiped a bit of soap off Orr's chin with her sleeve. "By the way, your transit pass came through. Would you like to visit your cousin Gabe?"

20

Malfunction. Parachute failure, either partial or complete.

When Orr's taxi landed on Mount Shishaldin, he felt like he'd traveled back in time. Everything at Pete's old air base looked exactly as he remembered: the hangar, the glass dome, the rusty tower. The same engine oil stained the concrete. The same grime smudged the windows. The retractor motors were still growling, sealing the two halves of the dome, and the air exchangers labored to blow out the hot summer smog, but Orr hesitated in the taxi, blinking at the people who'd come to meet him.

Orr's friends couldn't wait for the haze to clear. They burst through the hangar doors. Gabe Lermontov marshaled the parade, and his three little sons raced ahead, skipping and squealing. While Orr was still in the taxi, Yanny, the youngest, scrambled in and climbed onto his shoulders. Nick grabbed one of his legs, while Ilya, the eight-year-old, took his elbow and tugged him out of his seat. The boys smelled of fried bread and cave mold, the sweet scent of home. Their wiggling bodies plus the ankle cast made it hard for Orr to walk.

Gabe pressed Orr's one free hand between his paws. "Cousin. Good to see you." Then he noticed the taped thumbs. "You're hurt."

"It's nothing." Orr didn't meet Gabe's eyes. The crowd swarmed him.

Gabe's wife Kriis gave him a hug, and her scrimshaw necklace smacked against his nose. She looked plump and shiny in her turquoise-and-pink muumuu, more pregnant than ever. She roughed up Orr's short hair with her fingers. "How's Dyce? Is she with you?"

Orr shook his head and turned to say hello to Pete Hogue. Everyone wanted to hug him. Shep Innoko. Connie Nujuat. Mrs. St. Paul. They asked about his thumbs. The whole seafarm crew had turned out, along with the tribal elders, the chief of police, and the marching drum corps from the Unimak tribal school. The kids carried a handmade banner done in glitter-paint: WELCOME HOME, GRAVITY PILOT.

Orr couldn't breathe. This was worse than the Underside. He felt almost relieved when Vera took charge.

"Everyone, move back into the hangar," she boomed. "The caterers have set up a nice lunch."

Orr didn't understand how she amplified her voice like a public address system. Probably some of that gear implanted in her throat. Vera had a lot of capabilities he didn't understand, but when her voice blasted like that, the crowd backed off. She tried to wrench Yanny out of Orr's arms, but the kid shrieked as if she'd pinched him.

"Give us a minute, Vera." Orr waited till she moved away. Then he returned to the taxi, drawing the little boys with him. "Come on in, Gabe. Kriis."

While Vera corralled the welcome committee into the hangar, he sat alone with his family in the car, silent and weary, trying to coax a sentence out of his head. The boys climbed all over him, roughhousing and pulling his hair. They wore soccer caps with the Gravity Pilot logo blazoned across the front, which he found vaguely embarrassing.

"You look good," Gabe said.

Kriis lifted a sack of homemade biscuits from her purse and pushed them into Orr's hands. "You're thin. You should eat."

He held the fragrant sack as if it were alive.

"Stay with us tonight," Kriis said. "I'll make you kobu tartare."

Kriis's raw seaweed salad was Orr's favorite dish, but the thought of it now gave his mouth an ashy taste. He balanced the biscuits on the seat beside him. When Yanny's sharp little fist punched his chest, he flipped the boy upside down and tickled him. Yanny giggled and fought back.

"Get down. You're kicking too hard." Kriis pulled Yanny to her lap, leaving Orr defenseless.

Orr squared his shoulders and smiled down at Nick, who was still clinging to his leg and gazing up with large brown eyes. "I should have called you," Orr said. "There was—" He almost said "a dead spot," but he'd stopped. "I've been thoughtless. It's unforgivable."

Nick looked confused.

Gabe said, "We wondered if you were okay."

Orr still couldn't face Gabe. *I'm not okay,* he wanted to shout.

But he knew it wouldn't be fair to lay the truth on his cousin. Gabe deserved reassurance, not more worry. Orr studied the toes of his boots. "We're gonna break another skydiving record."

"I heard. That's terrific." Gabe rubbed his moist hands on his shirt. "You're all over the web. People trade slow-mo's of your dive technique. Check out iTube. You're, like, a textbook. They're laying bets on your ionosphere gig."

Young Ilya recited sternly, "The ionosphere is approximately four hundred kilometers high, depending on solar wind conditions."

Nick piped up. "It's ionized gas. My teacher showed us a chart. It's got charged electrons and X-rays and geomag— mag—"

"Geomagnetic storms," Ilya finished.

"We're proud of you," Kriis said. "Yanny made up a song about you. He'll sing it later."

Orr tried to wink at Yanny, but his eyelids didn't move right.

"We watch your interviews." Gabe's laugh sounded tight. "Hey, we didn't know you could talk like that."

Interviews. Orr had seen those computer-generated gab fests on the web. He didn't want to discuss that topic.

Nick tugged his sleeve. "Can I have your autograph?" He offered his soccer cap and a felt-tip marker.

Orr tried to laugh. "You don't need my autograph. We're family."

Nick pushed the marker into his hand. "The kids at school won't believe me. Please."

Orr said, "I'll come to school with you. How's that?"

Kriis whispered, "Don't make promises you can't keep."

Gabe put his arms around Nick and rested his chin on the boy's head. "I got a copy of your Wing docking sim for the boys to play with."

Orr gripped Gabe's arm. "Don't let them touch it."

"Huh?" Gabe and his wife exchanged glances.

At that point, Vera banged open the car door. "The crowd's getting antsy."

Nick pleaded, "Sign my cap."

"Mine, too," said Ilya.

Orr bit his lip. Hastily he scrawled his name across each of the boy's caps. He felt like a fraud.

Gabe scooted out of the taxi. "We know you're busy."

"Thanks for the biscuits." Orr hugged Kriis, then each of the boys. At the last minute, he and Gabe shared an awkward moment of grappling.

Vera separated them fast, and after that, she never left his side. Orr posed for quick-mo's with the mayor and a long line of neighbors. He watched the drum corps perform and listened to the speeches. For the rest of that brief homecoming, Vera made sure he didn't see his family in private again.

Microline. Small suspension line within parachute.

What Vera didn't count on was the unregistered vone Kriis hid in the sack of biscuits. She didn't have time to surveil Orr's every move. Not an hour after they flew back to Mundo Mountain, Orr snuck out of the caldera, linked up with a satellite and voned home.

"Your boss is a tiger lady." Gabe chuckled. "Don't you ever get a weekend?"

"Things are complicated here." Orr tightened his raincoat hood close around his respirator, then climbed up toward the pass. Hot June winds whistled through the mountains, and fluffy pink thistledown blew everywhere. He gazed up at the layered yellow clouds. Low stratocumulus puffs. Higher, solid wings of altostratus. Highest of all, cirrus.

He took a sip of gin from his flask. "I'm sorry about not staying in touch. Tell Yanny I want to hear his song."

"Sure. I'll put him on in a minute."

Orr rolled burning gin around his mouth and swallowed. "I need help, cuz."

Gabe said, "They're keeping you prisoner. What's going on?"

Orr scrambled higher up the slope through a thicket of purple loosestrife. Blowing grit stung his shoulder. He had to bend low and turn his face away from the wind. "I went to see Dyce. Seattle's insane. She doesn't belong in that place. I— I should've made her come home."

Gabe said, "You can't force people to do things your way. Dyce is an adult. She has the right to choose."

Orr sat down at the verge of a high cliff and drank more gin. A hundred kilometers away at the opposite end of the island, Mount Shishaldin rose above his village. He imagined he could see it through the smog, but he was only dreaming.

Gabe said, "People grow apart. They find new interests. Sometimes, you have to accept that love doesn't last."

Orr dug in his pocket for the yellow metal disk. He knew he couldn't force Dyce to love him. In the palm of his glove, the locket reflected dull light. He considered throwing it over the cliff.

"They're using my skydives to addict people," he said. "I think they addicted Dyce."

Gabe said, "Who did? Excuse me, cuz, but that sounds like paranoid delusion. Maybe you've been locked in solitary too long."

Orr upended his flask and drank the last of his gin. He tossed the locket straight up in the air, then caught it. "I have an inbox full of mail to answer. Maybe I should tell everyone the truth about the Gravity Pilot."

"What truth?" Gabe's voice strained to a higher register. "You can't let your fans down. They depend on you. Think how my boys would feel if you dissed their hero."

Orr kept tossing the locket. "I saw the addicts, Gabe, I swear to God."

"Don't go nuclear. Begin at the beginning."

Orr balanced the locket at the brink of the ledge where, any moment, the wind might lift it away. He thought, *Let the wind decide.*

Then in his own lumpish style, he told Gabe what had happened in Seattle. The vone loosened his tongue better than a face-to-face meeting. When he came to the night in Vera's bed, his words funneled. Finally he confessed that, too. He'd been unfaithful to Dyce.

Gabe said just enough to keep him talking. When Orr finished, he was damp with sweat. The wind died down, and thistle seed flecked his raincoat. His flask lay in the rocks where he'd flung it, and the locket still rested on the ledge. Fading sunlight tinged the cirrus clouds in bands of plum and tangerine. Alaska's long summer twilight was coming on.

Gabe said, "You can't expect Dyce to give up her dreams. You've got to reconcile yourself to the way things are."

"Should I tell her, you know, about Vera? Maybe she'll forgive me."

Gabe shook his head. "That's your hurt. You've got to swallow it."

Orr broke off a spear of loosestrife. Gabe was right. Confessing to Dyce would only be unkind. He tossed the purple flower stalk over the cliff. "I still feel like I should do something."

"Leave that place." Gabe's tone lightened. "Come home. I'll fly the bus over right now to pick you up."

Orr scooted closer to the cliff's edge. That was the answer he'd yearned for, and in the same instant, he knew it was wrong. Running home, crawling back into the shell of his old life, would only be another bogus evasion. He wouldn't find comfort there.

Besides, Vera would track him down. Vera. It all came down to Vera. The more he considered his options, the more he realized the Gravity Pilot could never go back to being plain Orr Sitka again. He and Gabe argued and talked till past Yanny's bedtime, so the boy sounded sleepy when he finally sang his little verse.

> *Twinkle, twinkle, Uncle Orr,*
> *Oh what fun to see you soar.*
> *Up above the world so high,*
> *Like a rocket in the sky.*
> *Twinkle, twinkle through the blue,*
> *I want to grow up just like you.*

By the time the call ended, the sky had gone platinum. Pollinating wasps buzzed through the loosestrife, and feral cats meowed. Orr sat dangling his legs over the cliff and thinking about Yanny. Beside him on the ledge, the yellow disk glimmered. It wasn't even real gold.

"Love sucks," he said aloud. Then he picked up a stone and slammed it down hard, smashing the locket in two.

The metal disk sprang open and blurped a single phrase before it died. But the phrase didn't come from their karaoke torch song. It was Dyce's voice. She'd overwritten their duet with a new message. "Orr, you have to believe . . ." And there it ended.

Orr picked up the locket, and it fell apart. He tried to push the pieces back together with his gloved fingertips. He kept clicking the button, shaking it, holding the disk to his ear. Useless. Only those five words. *Orr, you have to believe . . .*

Believe what, Dyce? That love never lasts? That time heals all wounds? That what we shared was just a fool's glitter-paint rainbow?

But his gut told him that wasn't how Dyce would talk. He should have listened sooner. He should have listened. Was she trying to let him down easy—or begging him to come back?

21

Nil. Odds of surviving atmospheric reentry in a Sky Wing.

That same night, in the wee hours, Vera got a call from Rolfe. She was working in her private office. She'd come to rely on the peacefulness of her soundproof cube in the hangar. Crisp dry sheets. Quiet white walls. No mildew, only a few ants. And her favorite part, the locked door. She did her best work there—and her fiercest fretting.

Rolfe blocked visuals when he called. He probably didn't want her to see how much weight he'd gained, but she knew. A person could cover a lot of territory with one spray can of mote cameras. Sure, she surveiled his office. He was prancing barefoot on top of his enormous desk, his white marble altar to himself. He wore a sumo wrestling outfit, and he was going through some weird martial arts routine. She pulled her blanket to her chin and listened to his tirade.

"The Seattle governing body has my testicles in a garlic mincer. They claim we're hogging bandwidth."

"That old saw?" She bit her finger to keep from laughing out loud. Her own anonymous call had stirred up the governing body, just like she'd stirred up the tax auditors and the social workers. She chewed the hem of her bedsheet.

Rolfe's exercise made him pant. "I know it's BS, but everyone wants swag. They're threatening to moratorium our growth."

She curled her toes. "They want bribes?"

"Bonuses, blackmail, compensatory inducements." He high-kicked and fell on his bum. "Ow."

"Dad, you've paid off the governing body scads of times."

He sat crooked on his marble desk, rubbing his backside and wincing. "Not like this. The bureaucrats are getting inventive."

Evidently, out of the blue, Seattle's wifi masters launched a new protocol for tag clouds. Such a crisis. Tag clouds weighted the popularity of web content. Basically, they worked like a people's referendum on which content got first dibs through the public airwaves. And on a technicality, the new protocol had glitched the Gravity Pilot out of first place.

Rolfe griefed that the governing body might use this cynically concocted brick of bullion to snatch some of Cyto's bandwidth. He said, "I'm commandeering your code team for forty-eight hours to fix my tags."

"Criminy, Dad. My ionosphere."

"Check your inbox," he said. "I had to set new spending parameters for your project. Cut some corners, girl. Help me out."

She browsed his spreadsheet, and the new budget made her eyelids roll back. Cut corners? He wanted her to lop off spiral galactic arms. She gripped her mattress. "Daddy, this isn't fair."

He grunted. "Tell me. I got the tax bill today."

Her head sank in her pillows. "How much?"

"I'm thinking Siberia looks good. Tobolsk has a flat tax."

"Come on, Rolfe. It can't be that bad."

Through her motes, she watched him lie on his desk and gaze up at the bogus skylight like a wounded warrior in a tragic Greek frieze. He said, "Ever heard of Syncytium?"

She rolled in her blanket as another game piece dropped into place. "Syncytium, yeah, the new startup. I've seen their ads. You know how to deal with competition."

"They've got this sim of a hang glider flying a hurricane off the coast of Texas. The Cloud Surfer. Total ripoff." He scratched at a new pink skin graft on his chest. "Of course we have to sue."

She wiggled in her sheets. "You always win."

"How's our boy?"

"Never better. He's got the strength of Atlas, the speed of Nike, the courage of—"

"Vera, you are the mother of all lies."

Without a hint of warning, he materialized beside her bed. Right there, in full living color, his holo stood glowering down at her. She sprang up and squeaked a cry. He'd invaded her sanctum? That was just wrong.

He said, "The boy's suicidal, and you play your silly cons. You can't handle him. I should put Jadri in charge."

Vera had to exert all her willpower not to react to his threat. She craved to cancel his signal and void the very whisper of his breath. Nevertheless, she spoke quietly, clasping her hands behind her back. "This is *my* project. *I'll* be the one to finish it."

He sighed. After a moment, he touched her cheek. "I keep hoping, Vera, hoping you'll show me a different face."

His holographic field gave her a mild shock. Gently, he took her in his arms, and electricity tingled her skin. She almost felt the weight of his embrace, and they moved like an old couple dancing a slow foxtrot. She couldn't read him. He seemed empty.

"All right," he said. "One last reprieve for Daddy's little girl."

22

Out landing. Accuracy jump that is off target.

Fifteen days before the ionosphere dive, Orr felt more unhinged than ever. He'd tried in vain to fix the sound chip in the locket. He'd invented a hundred different endings for her phrase. *Orr, you have to believe it's better this way. We've grown apart. We want different things.* A hundred different versions of good-bye.

But he couldn't make himself believe those endings. One more time, he carried his gin flask into the mountains and tried to call Dyce. He couldn't get through, though. Some new "dead spot" kept jamming his secret vone.

"Vera." He spat her name like a curse.

Yet when he returned half-drunk to the hangar, Vera surprised him. She said, "We're getting a space shuttle. Tomorrow, you're going to make a real dive. From the stratosphere."

Vera didn't tell him she'd begged a secret loan from Dr. Leo—at a scandalous rate of interest. She didn't confess the risk she ran by defying her father. Orr saw her anxiety though. He knew she had begun to doubt his skydiving skill. So had Bettie and Al. So had he.

Nevertheless, Vera kept her promise. The following morning, the space shuttle arrived, reconstructed from NASA's junkyard. When Orr walked out across the launchpad, the shuttle gleamed like a castle in the sky. Reconditioned thermal tiles shielded the orbiter, and a fresh coat of brown insulation covered the huge external fuel tank. The twin rocket boosters showed hardly any rust.

The air smelled of bug spray and clean lubricated machinery. The steel tower glistened. And though the geodesic dome was still mostly wireframe, a few glass panes sparkled with dew. Everything had a pristine, first-time luster. The weather itself had turned fine, and a bright blue sky twinkled overhead. Orr mounted the tower's bottom step, groggy from hangover.

He touched a small lump at his chest. Under the insulated layers of his pressure suit, he felt the shape of Dyce's locket, smashed in two, taped back together. Did she want him to come back—or not?

He scanned the sky for clouds, as if some nebulous puff of vapor might help him decode her message. But not a single wisp interrupted the blue frame. There were no mosquitoes, either, nor flying ants. Not a single point of reference marked the view, only solid azure shading to cobalt. So instead of reminding him of great open spaces, the sky closed like a ceiling. Its shimmer hurt his eyes. He darkened his visor.

Holocams snapped pictures of the new beta Sky Wing wreathing his helmet. Furled in a tight flat roll, it refracted blue-green sparkles. This time, Bettie had scrapped the cheap beryllium resins. She and Al had made dozens of improvements in the Wing design, including a handy little connector strap in the underbelly. This would be its premiere.

Orr mounted the gantry tower, sliding his glove along the rail for support. Hundreds of times in the training sim, he'd climbed these steps. Vera's coders had replicated the ring of his boots on the treads and the taste of recycled air in his helmet. This reality did not feel new to him. It felt hackneyed.

At the capsule level, he struggled into the nose cone, and he couldn't help remembering his previous stratosphere dive in *Mister Missile*. Half a year ago, it felt like another life. He slumped in his seat and nearly dozed through the shuddering roar while the engines built up thrust.

The launch went off without a glitch. Perfect trajectory. Flawless climb through the troposphere. Orr felt drowsy and sick. Al, Bettie, and Vera watched from the lab while G's laid him flat in his vinyl seat.

When he broke through the weather into the black heights, his eyes opened. He could sense space widening around him, and he heard its silence, even through the engine blast. He leaned forward to see out the windshield.

But the window framed his view exactly like a flat screen, and when he put out his hand, his glove met the intervening glass.

"Thirty seconds to exit," the AI droned in his helmet. Exactly like in the sim.

Orr held the steering yoke, but the flight was not under his control. The onboard AI steered the shuttle, and after he jumped, the AI would bring the shuttle home. He fondled the lump at his chest. And he remembered the way Dyce tried to slip the locket into his hand at first, like a secret.

When the shuttle reached low orbit, he rose up in his seat, weightless, just as he always did in the sim. It felt like another dry computer run.

"Exit," the AI announced. The hatch sprang open, and he exploded from the cockpit.

He and the shuttle hung side by side in the stratosphere, and Earth's haze billowed beneath, as yellow as Jason's fleece. But the cirrus clouds churned the same way in the sim, and right on cue, sunlight glared accurately from the east. None of it seemed urgent. And why did she hide her message in the locket? She said good-bye in public. She didn't need a secret recording.

Bettie's voice echoed through his helmet. "Orr? You okay?"

Al said, "Why don't you unfurl your Wing?"

Orr didn't feel like talking. Holocams zoomed around him, recording yet another rerun for his fans. Same old monotonous do-over. Same circling thoughts. He'd been through these repeats too often. He felt stagnant. But he wasn't. He was rocketing down.

"You're dropping too fast," Vera shouted. "Unfurl the goddamn Wing."

Five hundred meters he plunged every second. When he hit the troposphere, friction scorched his outer suit, and soot powdered his shoulders. That never happened in the sim. Through long vital seconds, he cupped the brown mist in his glove.

Al wheezed over the com link, "Think, Orr. Your nephews will see this."

Clouds whipped by like sheets of gold. When lightning flashed, he twisted one shoulder to see, and his body made a sudden carving turn. The move felt different in the real sky. The wind buoyed him with palpable force. It felt— good.

He swept out his left arm and changed directions. Then he bent his right knee and skidded sideways. The physical air pushed him around, and the simple maneuvers gave him bone-deep satisfaction.

"Unfurl," Vera repeated. "Now!"

He arched and stabilized. Threads of rain streaked his visor, and all at once, he sensed the Earth's mass pulling like a hand. Gravity. Real, indisputable gravity. This was his own Alaskan sky. He wheeled and danced. He did a somersault. And what a fool he'd been to waste so much time. Whatever Dyce said in the locket didn't matter. He had to go to her, that was all. He had to.

"Berry," he said aloud.

"Idiot!" Vera shouted.

He gazed down at the sawtooth ridges and checked his altimeter. He'd drifted far beyond the drop zone. Holy God, he was way too low. He focused on the fast-approaching peaks and searched for a flat spot, a thermal, anything. There—he saw his chance.

"Ground impact in fifteen seconds," the AI announced.

Orr counted five. The ground rushed up. He saw grain in the rocks. He saw kudzu. Through the com link, he heard Vera groan, "You're killing me."

Then he subvocalized the command to unfurl the Wing. The instant its cone snapped open, he seized the pilot braces and steered for the southern slope. Hot wind lifted him up, one second before impact. He loved that feeling! He skimmed along the slope, two meters above the sunbaked rock. The new belly strap increased his control, and his body hummed like a lyre.

Just in time, he found the strong thermal swell, and he rose. Light-headed with relief, he flipped the Wing in a snap roll. He sailed higher and did a piqué kick. In the sunny fountain of wind, he shot straight up, turning slow pirouettes. *You have to believe I still need you.* That was her message. He had no proof, no solid evidence, only necessity.

Surfing the sun-warmed air, he drew his Wing into a tight fluttery ball and whirled sideways, forward, diagonally. He tumbled in every dimension, and as he clenched himself tight to keep the blood in his brain, his breathy chant sang through the com link, "Hick, hick, hick."

No one had ever performed such a dervish and survived. The Wing revolved so fast, its edges seemed to smear. Later, when the recording hit the web, astonished fans named his maneuver the "GP Gyro." And for years after that, Wing divers in both the real and simulated sky would struggle to reenact it.

Back at base, the crew cheered. Bettie and Al swung each other in a circle, while Vera leaked a micro-moan of hope.

third

INTO THE BLUE DANCE

1

Peas. Small pea-sized gravel used to soften landings in drop zones.

It's difficult to admit how many decades have passed since the Gravity Pilot first appeared. Tens of thousands of unnoticed hours, time out of mind. Yet, even back in Orr's day, professional journalism had already lost legitimacy. In those years, no one liked paying specialists to unearth facts when so many amateurs tweeted their viewpoints for free. Do-it-yourself reality vlogs grew as common as cucarachas, and volunteers posted much spicier tattle than any grim journalist could ever substantiate with data. Well, and even now, who among us can bear the unadorned truth? Better to mute the news and watch opera.

But not Cho Sen Yao. Androgyne, hermaphrodite, slippery sexless retrovert, Cho lived to lay the facts bare. One might almost think Cho waged a private vendetta against fiction.

For a second time, Cho breached Mundo Mountain security. He rode in on a fuel freighter, wearing a full-face respirator and a blue coverall with the name ED stitched over his breast pocket. Under his blue coverall, he wore an orange one with a different name, and under that, a white one—always with a pair of black gloves. He wore half a dozen layers of disguise, and if any mote cameras caught him changing his colors, no one saw the footage. Cho found Orr in the men's washroom.

Orr had just returned from his stratosphere dive. He stood in the shower with shampoo foaming in his eyes, suds dribbling down his loins, water sluicing into the drain. He was singing an old pop tune and framing resolutions about Dyce.

Newscaster Cho had a knack for picking the right moment. "Sitka. Psst. It's me."

"Cho? What the—"

"I talk. You listen. Meet me in the locker room."

Orr rinsed soap from his hair and grabbed his towel. He'd taken to using the crew locker room because he felt more comfortable there, less exposed to intrusions. He found the diminutive newscaster squeezed into an empty metal locker next to his own. When he slung his wet head, beads of water went flying.

"Don't mind me. Pretend I'm not here." Cho wiped droplets off his face. "I came to tell you, Dyce is not well."

Orr rubbed his dripping hair with the towel. "I'm going back to get her."

"You're serious?" Cho leaned out of the locker to see Orr better.

Orr pulled on his briefs and snapped the waistband. "I've got everything worked out. First, I have to stage my death."

"Stage your death." Cho cast a sardonic glance at the ceiling bulb. "This is the bullshit I expected."

Orr zipped up his pants. "When I dive from the ionosphere, I'm going to fake a crash in the ocean."

"You probably won't need to fake it," Cho said.

"I'll hide in the mountains till Vera stops searching." Orr rummaged through his locker for clean socks. "Then I'll go live in Seattle with Dyce."

Cho's elbows banged the locker walls. "Let me etch this into your pea brain. Dyce is an addict. She spends eighteen hours a day in Cyto. She has severe attention deficit, plus social stress disorder, plus a nasty eye infection from the oc. She needs a major intervention."

Orr's mouth set in a firm crinkled line. He knew Dyce needed help. He intended to find her a drug counselor on the web. Cho treated him like a blockhead, and he was tired of it. "I'll get a job," he said. "Maybe I can work in one of those veggie farms. Then I'll look after her. I'll—"

"You'll enable her habit. You've got your head screwed up your backside as usual. She needs to get the hell out of Seattle."

Orr blotted his damp face with the towel. "She likes the city. It wouldn't be fair to make her leave."

"Fair is for fairy tales." Cho pulled a dirty gym shoe out from under his butt. "And let me tell you something else. A recovering addict is a bitch to live with."

Orr tugged a T-shirt over his head. He didn't want to hear any second-guessing. Who else would take care of Dyce if he didn't? Love had to be more than just a feeling, more than words. It was what you had to *do*.

Cho twisted in the narrow locker. "Anyway, you can't live in Seattle. You're too well known. Rolfe Luce will find you."

"That's why I have to die," Orr repeated.

Cho pulled out his tobacco pouch. "Roll me one. It's too tight in here."

Orr sighed. "Can't you survive ten minutes without that stuff?"

Cho made a scornful noise in his throat. "I go cold turkey, more than you know."

Orr fumbled with the illegal cigarette papers. In his mind, he was already stashing food and air in the mountains to wait out Vera's search. When he handed over the abortion he'd made of the cigarette, Cho eyed it, then wadded it into a tiny ball and chewed it.

"Let's say you pull this stunt and pretend to die," Cho began.

Orr slung his wet hair. "I'll be free of Vera Luce forever."

Cho stopped chewing. "Is that so necessary?"

Orr jammed on his boots with a vengeance. "She's a monster."

The newscaster didn't say anything for a while. Eventually, he gulped down the tobacco ball and cleared his throat. "Okay, say you disappear. What comes next? Have you thought that through?"

"I have," Orr said.

Cho leaned out again to take a good look at his face. "You've got a signature style, sports byte. Next time you make a skydive, anywhere in the world, some satellite's bound to record you, and you'll be recognized."

Orr's boot laces went slack in his hands. He'd considered that. He wanted to believe he could wear a disguise and make jumps without drawing attention. But Vera owned his image now. The contract she'd written gave her unlimited rights to record his skydives as long as he lived. He saw only one way to escape.

Cho put his thought in words. "You'll have to quit skydiving."

For several seconds, Orr remained silent, looping his laces in knots. When Dyce asked him to quit before, he couldn't. Forking lines of action branched through his cranium, what he valued, what he couldn't live without. He slicked back his wet hair. "I don't need the sky."

"Right." Cho wiggled in the locker and dug in his pockets. He had to unbutton two more layers of coveralls and reach into a special hidden sleeve velcroed to his underpants. "Pardon my frankness, but your plan is crap. I've made other arrangements."

Orr jerked his boot laces. "The Gravity Pilot has to die."

"We'll discuss that later. First, you need to memorize what I'm about to tell you." The newscaster kept fishing for something hidden in his crotch. He squirmed and twisted in the narrow space and also contorted his mouth. When he finally brought the object to light, Orr saw a soft waxy cube the size of a gamer's die.

"RAM cube. It's firewalled from the web." Cho scooted out of the locker. "Sit on the floor where I can reach you."

When Orr sat down, Cho mashed the cube against the back of his neck. "This has all the instructions you need."

Pilot chute. Small drogue parachute which pulls
main canopy from container.

That night, Orr sat in his bunk, fingering the little gob of memory at the back of his neck and clicking his mental cogs. Many people had called him reckless, but he was capable of reckoning. He drank steadily from his canteen—sweet cold tea, not gin. Give up skydiving? He still didn't want to believe that sacrifice would be required. He tried to fool himself.

In his lap, Al's game pod hummed. Orr had been borrowing it every night, allegedly to play EverQuest, but he was not using the pod in game mode now. He was running searches on the web. And what did he investigate in the sanctity of his bunkroom? FM technology, no less. He had a fantasy—call it a faint hope. If worse came to worst, maybe he could still skydive in the web.

Other divers did it. Top-ranked athletes. All the most important sports meets took place in the web these days because travel was too high-priced. And Vera didn't own what he did in the web. Surely he could find some full immersive sky that was not addictive. Surely in some virtual outback of the wikisphere, he could fly his Wing in peace.

Product brochures, schematics, user reviews, he found oodles of info about full immersion. He read that the earliest FM came online in the 2020s, submerging its users in a three-dimensional world of vivid graphics and audio effects. 3D/2S, pundits called it, because it fired only two senses, sight and sound. Haptic tech, the touch sense, was too crude to fool anyone, and forget about smell or taste. Turns out, 3D/2S left the user's disbelief tragically unsuspended.

Around 2044, the industry launched an intense X prize competition to find a practical direct-to-brain illusion of taste, smell, and touch. Their first imitations of olfactory stimuli were to real aromas as carburetors are to human lungs. But after months of fMRI mapping, EEG measuring, and live brain tissue sampling, web techs finally cracked the alphabet of human neuropeptides. It was all in the brain juice, the electrochemical sparks. Once they deciphered the enzyme code, transcribing the five senses became trivial.

Sure, there was slippage. Neural pathways weren't fixed, they moved. For the calculations to work, the engineers had to ignore cerebral drift. Doesn't everyone? The first genuine FM device transmitted a one-way signal of simple smells and vibrations through a game helmet the size of a small child. FM 2.0 expanded to include tastes, temperatures, and surface textures. Plus you could wear it like a pair of spectacles. FM 3.0 created a near perfect illusion of solid reality. It streamed input through a contact lens called an ocular—simple, easy to maintain, stylish. Mass marketing of the oc brought Cyto to life.

Cyto. That name, like a curse. Orr held the little pod screen close to his face to view an angry mother's vlog. She claimed Cyto spiked its sims with extra voltage to increase the addictive crave. Worse, Cyto targeted its ads at teenagers, the most emotionally sensitive animals on the planet. And hers was not the only vlog spreading this point of view. Orr browsed dozens.

After a while, he lay back in his bunk and pondered. Cyto. That recurring nightmare. Somehow, he and Dyce had to get free. Still, he wasn't ready to give up skydiving. Not yet. He had a right to more good years in his sport. There had to be other web skies besides Cyto . . .

He noticed something odd on the ceiling over his bunk. Besides the usual beetles and flying ants, he saw a glittery crust. He'd seen that before in Seattle. Mote cameras.

His features warped into a bitter mask. "Do you hear me, Vera? Are you watching? I have no secrets."

But he did. He was hiding something huge. He'd never been good at acting, but he would learn. It was necessary.

Pin. Closing device of parachute container.

Next morning, Orr showed up in the lab, clean, combed, and wide awake. For the first time in days, he viewed the world without the intervening frame of a hangover. Pearlescent sunlight filtered through the kudzu that now draped one half of the lab window, and stiff breezes stirred eddies in the volcanic grit outside. Ragged yellow smog rushed through the caldera, casting quick blue shadows over the launchpad, and the dome supports made a lattice of triangles that dissolved and reappeared in the mist. How had he allowed himself to miss this beauty?

Al clapped him on the back. "Splendid dive yesterday. We looked for you after, to celebrate."

Orr rubbed his nose. "I, uh . . . went to bed early."

Bettie was so glad to see him, she got up and rolled her chair across the floor. "Have a seat. You earned it." Bettie never gave her ergonomic chair to anyone.

But Orr rolled the chair back to her. "Thanks, Bettie. I'll stand."

Owlish Al, curmudgeonly Bettie. Orr read their affection in the weary droop of their eyelids. All this time, they'd been working without rest—for him. Gratitude welled in his throat, and he pretended to check the kiln.

The baking ceramic smelled like hot lava, and scattered through the lab were several new small-scale Wing models. Orr noticed Vera's lucite calendar taped to the window. Only two weeks remained before the ionosphere dive.

"It's time I stopped goofing off." He gave his sheepish smile. "Could you please tell me again about the teacup?"

"Absolutely." Bettie hurried to display a diagram of the ablation shell on her screen. She moved so quickly, her arms jiggled. "This small miracle will keep you cool when you reenter the atmosphere."

The diagram showed a cutaway view of eighteen concentric porcelain spheres nested together with layers of insulation between. She and Al had elaborated the drawing a good deal since the last time Orr saw it. He ran his thumb over the screen, reading the specifications in a soft whisper.

Al nudged in between them. "The insulation absorbs temperature shocks, you see? Each layer will ablate in seconds, but that's all you need. You'll be falling fast."

Orr cocked one gray eye wider. "Ablate means 'to burn,' right?"

"You've been reading my reports." Al seemed delighted. He clicked his stylus over the screen and rotated the view. "For the ceramic shells, we've developed a synthetic kaolin."

Bettie pushed Orr down into her chair, then stood behind, squeezing his shoulders, while Al trotted back and forth, lecturing. "We added silica, of course. And feldspar for the flux. We've ordered eighteen isostatic press molds to fabricate the ceramic layers. Then we'll harden them off with low-temperature bisque firing."

Bettie said, "You're talking too fast, dear. Slow down."

Al unclipped a second stylus from his coat pocket, forgetting the one he already held. "The final firing will come in the sky, as it were. That's where the bisque will harden into true porcelain."

Al chuckled at his modest joke, but Orr was only half listening. *All this for me?* He wondered at the enormity of Bettie's and Al's kindness. He'd been too self-absorbed to see it before. *For me?*

Al clicked for a data pane, and parabolic green lines multiplied over a dense grid of numbers. Orr couldn't make heads or tails of the screen, but Al said, "You see? It's like magic. When you hit the atmosphere, the intense friction heat will vitrify the ceramic. Carbon-based impurities will burn out, and sulfates will decompose, producing gases. So we designed these vents."

"Vents." Orr titled his head sideways.

"Yes, and the feldspar will react with the decomposing minerals." Al was so excited, he twiddled his styluses like a pair of chopsticks. "After about forty seconds, the outer layer will form liquid glass."

"It'll melt," Bettie translated.

"Yes, it will melt away, exposing the next layer of insulation, which will burn. Then the next ceramic layer will vitrify. And so on. Like the skins of the onion, you see?" Al seized the gray box clipped to his belt and pumped up his oxygen feed, while Bettie smoothed a curl behind Orr's ear.

For the moment, Orr couldn't think in language. He felt their kindness bearing down on him like a debt. Who was he, to deserve such friends? And if his plan worked, what poor coin would he use to repay them?

"We predict approximately four minutes for the entire shell to ablate," said Al. "That should be enough time for you to safely reenter."

The engineers stood gazing at their data like a couple of proud parents. Bettie said, "Well, what do you think?"

Orr blinked at the intersecting green lines. Then he swallowed the hard lump in his throat. "Can we put all this in the simulator so I can practice?"

Bettie and Al traded smiles. "We'll need to render a few graphics."

Orr swallowed again. "Let's do it."

2

PLF. Parachute landing fall, a safe way to touch down under canopy.

V era literally clapped her hands when she heard Orr speak those words. Spying from her soundproof cube, she watched Al and Bettie hug him. Orr was back on track again. Back in the game.

That same day, while the engineers set to work on the digital mockup of the ablation shell, Vera got busy, too. She downloaded specs for Orr's new spacesuit. The ionosphere required a higher order of protection, at a much higher order of cost. But cash-flow issues had forced her to put the spacesuit on layaway, another bitter injustice marked down to Rolfe's account. For now, she would have to simulate the suit from schematics on the manufacturer's web site.

Over the next week, Vera beat a path between her cube and the launch-pad. The old NASA shuttle she'd bought with Leo's loan stood naked in its gantry, minus its tank and boosters. She had zero cash to pay for another practice launch. So she measured and holographed every square centimeter of the shuttle cabin and fed the data into her model. The space launch would be critical, so she wanted the shuttle in Orr's training sim to be one hundred percent accurate.

Her Seattle code team put in astronomical hours to flesh out her graphics. Oh yeah, she tyrannized them. Nothing but the best would do for her Gravity Pilot. Plus, she was killing two birds. She would reuse the graphics later in Cyto's next new megahit—Ionospheric Freefall.

For the first time, Orr took an interest in the coding. Every day, he checked the updates and gave Vera notes for revisions. He also spent hours researching other web skies. He seemed as determined as she was to make their ionosphere sim the most accurate ever, and before the program was half finished, he entered the sim to practice gearing up. Of course Vera linked in to watch. So did Bettie and Al.

First, Orr had to slip a condom over his penis with a tube leading to a urine bag taped to his leg. Doing this in the sim, where everyone could see, made him blush scarlet. But he couldn't risk an untimely squirt of piss shorting his suit's electronics. FM effects were brutally precise when it came to electrical fires.

Then he slithered into the clammy nanogel leotard that coated his skin like slime. The nanogel absorbed his excess body heat so the spacesuit wouldn't poach him. Over the leotard, he wore a close-fitting pressurized coverall lined with inflatable bladders. In case of a runaway spin, the bladders would swell up and squeeze off blood flow to his legs and keep more blood in his brain. Theoretically, this would prevent him from blacking out.

Next came the airtight exterior spacesuit, hardened to cold and cosmic radiation. The helmet enclosed his head like a clear bubble. On top of everything, he had to hook up his parachute rig, life vest, gear belt, emergency oxygen cylinder and, of course, his Celestia Sky Wing.

His outfit weighed thirty kilos, but Vera restyled it to be streamlined and close-fitting. Above all, her Gravity Pilot needed to look sexy. Suiting up took Orr a full hour, but he repeated the routine for days till he could do it blindfolded. Gear, at least, was something he understood well.

Once he was dressed, he practiced sealing himself into the mocked-up ablation shell, then launching and falling. A hundred times he did this. The shell spun him in every dimension, like a gyroscope on LSD. The first time Orr tried it, he threw up. After that, he rode the sim on an empty stomach.

To remain conscious during the spin, he learned to inflate the bladders at just the right time, and he also practiced an old pilot's trick called the "Hick" maneuver. It was the same technique he'd used in his GP Gyro stunt. What he did, he curled his toes and clenched every muscle in his lower body, abs, glutes, quads, and gastrocs, to keep as much blood as possible in his head. "Hick, hick, hick" was the sound that hissed out of his straining throat when he breathed.

He rehearsed with the bladders and the Hick maneuver till he was able to stay conscious for a full three minutes of violent spinning—a small triumph—although Al wasn't completely sure that was long enough.

At about a hundred and twenty kilometers above ground level, Al said the teacup would probably encounter enough friction to burn away its first outer insulation. Al used the full weight of the web's computing power, but his predictions remained inexact. More than once, he reminded them that no one had ever done this.

Once the insulation burned off, if the underlying ceramic had the tiniest microscopic flaw, Orr would blossom into a fiery shooting star. That happened several times in the sim, so Al kept tweaking his recipe.

Somewhere around eighty-five kilometers, Orr would either be a smoldering cinder, or he would hatch out of his melting ceramic shell and punch into the deep-freeze mesosphere. That's when he had to unfurl his Sky Wing.

In his first record-breaking dive, he'd boinged up to the lowest part of the mesosphere. No skydiver had ever touched its roof, much less crashed in from above. The mesosphere's plunging cold could snap his Sky Wing into a million itsy bits if he didn't unfurl it fast enough.

Both designers had serious misgivings that the dive was feasible. They slaved night and day to enhance the Wing design, but nano-resins had limits. Al timed Orr's moves to the microsecond. He needed to be faster. Vera wanted to install an AI chip, but Bettie didn't think that would gain them any speed.

Assuming a best-case scenario, Orr would shriek down through the mesosphere at eyeball-slicing speed. Gases at that height were too thin for steering, so if he lost control, the sim predicted a stochastic process of branching realities. Four times in practice, he broke up in pieces. Three times, he flashburned. Twice, his body froze and shattered. Only once did he come through the replicant mesosphere unscathed. And then he still had the stratosphere to face.

If Orr had been less physically fit, those practice runs might have bent him. Vera knew he suffered. After one of the flash-burns, she had to ice him down for an hour because his body temp spiked so high. The freezing-shattering event left him with severe bruises. She learned not to underrate the psychosomatic power of full immersion.

She suggested installing navigation jets, but Orr absolutely refused. He said that would blow the concept of a pure skydive. He assured everyone that in the real mesosphere, he would track straight down without spinning. As for the stratosphere, he'd been there before. Twice. But Vera could not forget it nearly killed him.

Post dive. Recap discussion after skydive.

Vera rose before dawn every morning to spy on Orr's workout. He'd let himself go slack, but he did know how to train. She watched him go through a curious morning ritual. He would stand at the hangar windows, facing east and breathing great lungfuls of air as if he were gulping sunlight. After this peculiar ceremony, he ran laps and lifted weights. No more gin toddies for breakfast. He drank protein smoothies.

After his workout, he spent mornings cruising their wireframe sky and reviewing the finer points of the coding. Afternoons, he rode the half-built training sim like a fiend. Sometimes he got Al to help him recalibrate the FM projectors. He'd become a perfectionist again, which surprised and pleased Vera. Inside his skydiver mind, something had flexed and quickened. Her boy had his focus back.

Often she snuck out of her cube and watched him doing his mat work in the hangar. Robots flared welding torches in the background, linking sections of truss for the never-ending construction of the dome. Crew workers tromped in and out, trading insults and smelling of muddy rain. Orr concentrated on his workout. He warmed up with deep Pranayama breathing and yoga-pilates combinations. Then he stripped down to his gym shorts and did slow-motion isometrics. Of course Vera watched. He had latissimus dorsi like Michelangelo's *David.*

Abs tight as granite, back like a plank, thighs from God, the boy was gorgeous. She watched him push up from the floor in a slow-mo count, till he balanced on his rigid fingers and toes. Then he held the position for half a minute before gradually lowering, then rising again. His only sounds, heavy sighs. His expression, inward.

He did twenty different styles of calisthenics, with and without free weights, all deathly quiet, serious and slow. He told Al he'd developed the routine from a patchwork of bodybuilder web sites. With each move, he focused on one muscle group at a time. Now and then, he counted aloud, chanting the rhythm of his breath.

Even if he noticed the crust of mote cameras Vera had sprayed in the hangar, she knew he didn't care. Nothing existed beyond the edge of his mat. He was living inside his fiber and ligament, in the leverage of his hinged bones. From measured contraction to gradual release, his limbs swept through their full range of motion like galaxies circling heaven. Then he laced on his shoes to run laps.

"Can I join you?" Vera asked one morning. She'd downed an adrenaline tab in preparation.

His glance brushed over her running togs but didn't rise to her face. His nostrils fluttered in and out. She knew he didn't like her anymore.

She jogged in place to warm up. "Need to clear my head, you know? The sound effects are giving me spasms. My team can't get the level right."

He nodded, then took off, so she bounded after him. He'd established a running track inside the hangar. It wasn't marked, but everyone knew where it was, and no one violated its imaginary border. Toolboxes, power cables, tractors, and crates were parked carefully out of his lane. Vera huffed and panted at his heels.

She said, "Maybe you could help with the clouds? We're rendering them in fractal geometry, but I don't know, they look fake."

"They *are* fake." He rounded the corner and disappeared behind a stack of trusses. At the next turn, he slowed to let her catch up. "I'll help, Vera. I'm trying to make the sim better."

"Believe me, I'm grateful," she said. "I need this sim to be miraculous. You know my reasons. But—" She almost hesitated to ask. "Why do you care so much?"

He rubbed his nose. "If I live long enough to retire, you know? This sim may be the only place I can still dive."

"Retire? You?" Vera laughed.

"You're right. I probably won't live that long. But now, I need to sprint." Then he left her like a stone leaves a slingshot.

Later, she peeked in on his sim practice. Actually, she watched him dangle in the sim room harness while he imagined himself whizzing through suborbital atmosphere. He could have done his training in his bunk, using an ocular. But the sim room's FM projectors made the experience much more intense. Plus the suspension harness gave him freedom of movement so his body could experience the tangible maneuvers he would have to make in the sky.

Vera sat cross-legged, listening to the small noises he made and watching. His smell saturated the air like animal musk. She liked the sim room. It was the only place where she could be close to him. He avoided her in the break-room and the lab. Went out of his way so their paths didn't cross in the hangar. He would never like her now. But in the sim room, absorbed in his sport, he didn't know how close she sat, and he didn't feel her fingers touching his legs. In the sim room, she could still dream.

Bettie had him hooked up with biofeedback pads to make sure he didn't go into seizure, lung collapse, cardiac arrest, or any other unwholesome state. Did people ever die in FM? Yes, they did.

Vera thought about this as she gazed up at his moisture-beaded thighs. He wore gym shorts, and a sweatband circled his head. His damp shoes and socks tilted in an aromatic heap by the door. Again, she noticed how the lines of his body swelled like epic verse. Beefy carnal sonnets. Lyric quatrains of flank steak and tenderloin. Some might call it depraved for a woman her age to fall for a boy like him, but they were either hypocrites or corpses.

3

Relative wind. Apparent wind felt by diver in freefall, caused by diver's airspeed.

Eight days before the ionosphere dive, Orr seized an opportunity to sneak off into the mountains. Cho had given him a new industrial-grade vone, supposedly hardened against all types of interference. Orr still couldn't get through to Seattle, but at least he could call his cousin. They'd been talking about once a week.

Cool moisture kissed Orr's bare hands as he hiked up the pass. He enjoyed the flinty feel of the rock and the reflections in the rain pools. Pink thistle heads swayed in the slanting light. Mid-June, the summer solstice was near, and Alaska's midnight sky glowed dusky rose.

He slipped off his respirator and took a breath. He couldn't taste any toxins, only ocean brine and fragrant thistle. He gazed straight up and tried to conceive the distance to the ionosphere. Anticipation made him rise on the balls of his feet. Higher than any skydiver had ever been, what would it feel like?

Infinity pulled at his inner strings, and he knew he'd been born to sail that sky. Only . . . he had to give it up? No more clouds and winds? No rain storms? "Vera," he growled. She destroyed everything. He started coughing then, so he snugged the respirator back on.

When Gabe answered his call this time, he asked as usual, "Have you talked to Dyce?"

"Sorry. Still no answer. I'll keep trying."

In the high mountain pass, Orr gazed toward Seattle. The ocean lay as flat as slate. It looked almost solid enough to walk across. "Maybe I should go right now—"

Gabe interrupted. "Stick to the plan, cuz. Everything's ready. The room, the clothes. As long as you're still sure."

"Sure?" Orr whistled. How could he know for sure?

He scanned the ridge lines. Under the blushing midnight, the summits glowed bronze, and fluffs of fog lazed in the valleys. He studied the high cirrocumulus clouds and . . . was it his imagination, or did he see a star? A tiny twinkling pinpoint. So much twilight filled the sky, he had to look away and glimpse it side-on. Venus? He kicked at the gravel scree. "How are the boys?"

"Aw man, they love your stuff dives."

"I wish you'd believe me, Gabe. Sims are addictive."

"Cuz, I'm just not seeing that. Mildly habit-forming, maybe. Kriis and I ride your sims every night, and we're not showing any symptoms."

Orr threw a rock. It bounced off a boulder and ricocheted down a cliff. The star overhead was moving. A satellite then, not a celestial body. He lay on his back in the gravel and watched it flicker through the haze. Mostly, he tried not to think about his decision, but sometimes, it came down on him like a ten-ton avalanche.

Gabe lowered his voice. "Did you and the nicotine freak ever agree on the plan?"

"Yeah, finally," Orr said.

Gabe grunted. "By the way, I looked him up in Face. His profile's thin. Like almost not even there. What if he made up this whole story?"

Orr squinted at the satellite. Its twinkle barely showed in the crimson sky. He watched the clouds sweep east, and he searched high up for the place where he used to imagine Agugux. His famous Unangan Creator, just a myth for children? He didn't want to believe in a world where everyone lied like Vera, and where every offer was an underhanded plot.

"Dyce," he said. "Dyce is real."

Gabe remained silent for a moment. "But this crazy dive. So many things could go wrong. Can you . . . do it?"

The sky was turning lilac and magenta as the short arctic night rounded to dawn.

Orr said, "I need to try."

4

Reserve. Emergency parachute used if main parachute fails.

O nly seven days to go. Enough time to make a world, but Orr did not feel ready. Outside on the pad, cranes were lowering the shuttle's rebuilt fuel tank into place and connecting a pair of secondhand boosters. Inside the sim room, he and Vera hung static in the artificial storm. He wore a computer-generated version of his Celestia Sky Wing, and she wore a plain coverall. They were doing final revisions. He didn't enjoy working in such close quarters with Vera, but he had to. Around them, lightning fanged and thunder echoed.

Orr shook his head. "This air's too dense. At this altitude, it needs to be thinner."

He'd gotten very frank about criticizing Vera's background design. He said her smog felt gooey, which it did. While he talked, the lightning revealed a hectic expression on Vera's face, like a woman running on speed. He wondered if he looked the same.

She texted her code team: "Make the air thinner."

They felt the tactile parts per billion bump down a point or two. Then Orr flew his simulated Wing in a quick circuit to test the change.

"A little better," he said.

She crossed her arms. "What else is wrong?"

He analyzed her thunderheads. "They're dry."

"Yeezes, my thunderheads?"

He waited till she texted the coders. "Make the clouds wet."

As they watched, new incremental shadings appeared. The outlines blurred with fractal droplets. An ambient smell emerged, imitating rain. Orr tilted his head, appraising the effect. He never felt completely satisfied.

But Juho Fagerholm dived artificial skies. So did Banda Rat. Even the Olympics took place in the web. If he kept finessing the details, surely he could get used to this knockoff sky. The complete loss of his sport was not acceptable. He needed this last figment of hope.

Inside his Wing, he made a frame with his thumbs and fingers, like a photographer sighting a shot. "See how those air pockets collide? That should happen faster."

Vera rolled her eyes and texted the coders, "Speed up air pocket collision."

They watched the currents accelerate. Algorithmic vapors puffed out and mushroomed.

"Let's recheck that jet stream," he said.

Vera spoke a command, and they dropped out of the web sky into the swinging harnesses of the sim room. The abrupt bright light nailed their dilated pupils. Wicked sting. They both blinked and squinted.

Orr said, "Why did you do that? We're not finished."

"It's nearly midnight. I'm ordering lunch," she snarled. "My blood sugar is, like, fictional."

Orr followed her to the breakroom, hating the lovely sway of her hips. Distance, that's what he dreamed of. Light-years of time and space between himself and Vera Luce. But for now, there was a play to enact. So he sat at her table and wolfed down vitamin tabs with his health shake. Vera took some pills, too. He didn't think they were vitamins. He noticed a fresh wound on one of her fingers.

A couple of crew workers came in for tea, and Orr made a joke about the dome. They laughed. Orr had fun with the crew, but Vera mostly ignored them. He felt her watching his face, so he shifted and brushed crumbs off his shirt. She'd styled herself in the old youthful twenty-something disguise, like on the first day they met. But Orr remembered her real face. He thought she probably did the youth thing out of habit.

"Will we be ready in time?" she asked.

The extensor muscles in his forearms clenched as he screwed the cap on his vitamin bottle. He rubbed the side of his jaw. "There's one more thing—um—the shuttle launch. I haven't practiced that enough. Al and I want to move the FM projectors out to the real space shuttle cabin to make sure the sim matches up."

Vera's mouth twisted. "Not necessary. I measured that myself."

"We'll double-check!" He hadn't meant to raise his voice. He took a breath and spoke more calmly. "We'll do it tonight. It's the best way to make sure the program is accurate."

She searched his eyes. He felt blood heating his face, so he bent under the table to fiddle with his boot.

She said, "It'll burn a lot of time, but . . . all right. I need this sim to shine."

"Yeah, keep the users happy." He got up and dropped his dish in the chute, then returned to the sim room to help Al move the projectors.

5

Rig. Full set of skydiver gear.

Six nights before the ionosphere dive, Vera sat in her soundproof cube and wiped sleep from her eyes. Something in her oc had interrupted her bleary dreams. Jadri's voice.

"The Australia Skydive Club has challenged Orr to a tournament. Rolfe wants us to set it up."

Jadri sounded awful. They both blocked visuals. It was the fag end of the night, and neither of them wanted to bother about makeup. Vera's quiet haven felt as stale as a locked closet. The only light came from the radium dial of her antique alarm clock. Redundancy. She could not afford to lose track of time.

She rubbed almond-scented lotion up and down her legs. Her strokes made a soft liquid sound in the darkness. She felt good about her ionosphere sim—and even better about Orr. He'd grown lean and hard over the last few days. He hadn't been sleeping much, but Vera didn't think he needed sleep. His inner battery radiated heat. And his skills? She had watched droves of other Wing divers, kids in Australia, Finland, the north Greenland coast. As far as she could tell, Orr aced them.

She stroked her legs up and down. "We haven't even finished the ionosphere, and already Rolfe's onto something else. Typical. So when does our lord master expect this command performance?"

"In three days," Jadri said, "for publicity."

"Three days? You mean—*before* the ionosphere dive?" Vera guffawed.

To be blunt, she wanted to bite the head off a small living animal. How dare Rolfe distract her boy this close to his perilous dive? With so little time left, he needed every second to train.

"It's just a webcast," Jadri said. "No one has to travel."

Vera threw her lotion tube against the wall. Then she turned on the light. Flying ants awoke and circled up from the floor. "Where does Rolfe expect these skydivers to meet? Even in the web, they need a sky."

"Cyto?" Jadri sounded tentative. "I know what you're going to say. Our Gravity Pilot sims are getting stale."

"Moldy. Expired. Those sims are so overused, people have pet names for the clouds." Vera rummaged through a drawer by her bed for a small broken sliver of bamboo. When she found it, she stuck it in her mouth like a toothpick.

"But Vera, what can I do?" Jadri said. "All the other skies are copyrighted."

"Poor lamb." Vera pictured Jadri's scarlet lipstick smeared down her chin.

Jadri said, "Don't play the crown princess with me, Vera Luce. It's not like everything's gnarly keen at your end either. I've seen the daily rushes. Your boy does marginally okay in the training sim, but darling, he has to dive from the authentic sky, in his own fragile flesh, in a real-time worldwide webcast. If he bites it, your career is pish."

Jadri's words made her clamp down hard on her bamboo splinter. "Has Dad seen the rushes?"

"Through his pan," Jadri said. "You know he never goes full immersive."

Somewhere in Seattle, Jadri was lounging in her own hard cot, going over the same dates and budgets and rating points that kept Vera electrified every night. And she'd sent Rolfe only the best of Orr's runs, not the disasters. She and Jadri were both standing against the bullet-pocked wall, and they knew it. Orr's dive had to succeed.

If only Orr could practice again in the real sky. Earlier that day, Vera had asked her dear friend Leo for another loan for shuttle fuel, but Leo turned feisty. Said he couldn't give her any more unsecured credit. Said he wanted equity in Cyto. She had to sign over some of her own personal shares.

"He—he's not eating," Jadri said.

Rolfe. Vera knew who Jadri meant. Rolfe and his fasts. Vera lay back and touched the low ceiling with her fingertips. Ants scattered and hissed. She'd sprayed insulation foam over every one of Rolfe's motes. Now, she wanted to bury her head under her clean white sheets and sleep there till the stars rained down, and never have to go back to Seattle.

Three days? She hugged a pillow. Often she'd sensed how time mimicked gravity. Time pretended to be constant and predictable, always exerting a steady pull, always in the same direction—but that was a trick. When you least expected it, time and gravity swerved. Unseen forces stretched and warped them till you couldn't tell when from where. But Vera had a hunch she was approaching terminal velocity.

That night, one of her ulcers started bleeding. Jadri said it was Banda Ratulangi who'd challenged Orr to a "boogie." Banda Rat, Olympic medalist and president of the Australian Skydive Club, had seen Orr's stuff dives on the web. In her vlog, she called him one crazy yobbo and said it was high time he met the Aussies. The tournament she dreamed up in his honor involved a lunatic pastime called blade running.

In this party game, Wing divers ran a slalom course of moving "blades" suspended in the sky from helicopters. Random-number generators controlled their GPS coordinates. And not only did the blades constantly change position, they also warped the air currents moving around them. Burbles and gusts formed unpredictable patterns, and since the blades were constructed from nanocarbon razor wire stretched harp-wise on steel frames, any head-on collision would slice a diver to ribbons. Consequently, blade running demanded both exceptional steering skill and utter insanity.

Vera chewed her toothpick. She wasn't surprised to hear that Rolfe adored the concept. He'd ordered Jadri to build a brand-new FM sky with blades—in three days! Vera had to give the woman credit, Jadri had already hired a secret off-the-books team of freelance coders based in Lapland, and she'd paid them triple fees under the table to finish the sim in time.

The Lapps were plagiarizing snips and snipes of FM skies from all over web space to patch together the backdrop. They didn't have time to build anything from scratch, so they extrapolated blade-running scenes from videos, graphic novels, and Saturday morning cartoons. Controlling the wind effects around the blades was the fiddly part. They didn't waste time on helicopters. In web space, the blades could float free.

Jadri said, "Vera, you have to lend us some of the effects you've built for the ionosphere."

"Leak our magic before the product launch? You're joking."

"Throw me a crumb. I'll give you producer credit. You might win an Ennie."

Vera ground her teeth. "You can have some lightning."

"And, um . . ." Jadri spoke in a whisper. "Do you think Rolfe will show up? I mean, he's the head of the company. It would mean so much to our ratings."

Vera gave a laugh. "You know what a lily-liver he is. Maybe he'll send a holo."

"A holo? I can't fool media professionals with a holo."

Vera kneaded her pillow. Jadri was flailing. She'd lasted longer than most of Rolfe's mistresses. Sometimes Vera tried to imagine them kinked up together in Rolfe's leopard skins, reenacting the *Kama Sutra*. She could have told Jadri, that investment would not pay off. Too bad, though. She still needed the woman's marketing skill.

"I'll ask him," Vera said, knowing full well how Rolfe would answer. It would take more than a blade-running boogie to lure the lord of Cyto from his hole.

Jadri said, "Thanks, darling. I could kiss you."

"Soon, darling, you will."

They ended the call with artificial sweetness, and Vera chewed her bamboo toothpick to shreds.

Rigger: Certified professional parachute packer.

Orr knew nothing about the Lapland coders, of course. Secluded at Mundo Mountain, he remained totally fixated on the plan he and Cho had concocted. He kept mum, stuck to his training routine, and waited out the time till he could act. But when he heard Banda Ratulangi wanted to dive with him, he almost dropped a barbell on his toe. Banda Rat, the Olympian? He felt shock that she remembered his name.

Time seemed to quicken after that. Jadri's work-for-hire coders rushed through their gawky pastiche of a sky, and as a grace note, they glossed the whole burlesque with sparkle effects and background music. It wasn't Shakespeare, but the blades would draw realistic spurts of blood if a diver grazed them.

Four Aussies signed up to compete—Banda and three other members of her Olympic team. Also two Finns and a stunt diver from eastern Siberia. Eight contenders in all, five men, three women. Orr might've guessed Vera would try to rig the international panel of judges. He could've told her that was no-go.

On boogie day, Orr sat in the space shuttle cabin waiting for his cue. He and Al hadn't found time to move the FM projectors back into the sim room yet, so he had to enter the boogie from his pilot seat in the shuttle nose cone. Hair uncombed, barefoot, wearing nothing but a pair of old shorts, he reclined in the vinyl seat and gazed straight up through the windshield at towering cumulonimbus clouds.

Then Jadri signaled "Go," and everything brightened. He materialized in the simulated staging area, geared up in his shimmering silver jumpsuit, with his Celestia Sky Wing furled around his helmet. When the other jumpers linked in, he greeted them with respectful handshakes and a few shy words. He felt ill at ease among these titans of the sport. They were his heroes. Most of them had competed for years. They had thick dive logs and cases full of trophies. Next to them, he felt like a cartoon action figure.

He had never run a blade course, and with zero practice, he could not expect to do well. Swooping through mobile slalom gates was not at all like freeflying through open clouds. He'd prepared by viewing the same vlogs Jadri's code team used to animate the phony sky, but with his work schedule, he had very little time to devote. Everyone at Mundo Mountain grumbled about Rolfe's harebrained publicity lark.

Orr watched Banda stretch her hamstrings and joke with her friends. The Australians wore Celestia Sky Wings, too—that was heartening. He watched the Finns check each other's gear. They wore Cielo Wings, another top brand. He felt outclassed. He lowered his eyes and stood with his hands clasped over his peter, waiting for them to trounce him.

The judges set up a simple contest. Each diver would make two runs through the course, and only the best score would count. The judges would rate the contestants on speed, style, and proximity to the blades. Missing a gate cost two full points. Steering within a meter of a blade added a bonus point, but touching a blade knocked a point off. Also, each touch incurred penalty damage to the diver's gear and/or person which, depending on the severity, might affect his steering through the rest of the contest. For instance, a full-on collision scored death.

In honor of Orr's media celebrity, the other jumpers let him go first. This was not to his advantage. He stepped to the edge of the "dive platform"—Jadri's coders hadn't bothered to simulate an aircraft. He squinted into the patchwork sky and counted the dancing blades. There were eight pair, eight gates, but he couldn't see them well in the fuzzy clouds. He glanced over his shoulder at Banda. Sure enough, she was scrutinizing his every move. He stretched out one arm to get a feel for the wind. Wind? The imitation air felt like syrup.

"Yio'kwa." He unfurled his Wing and dove.

The simulated wind didn't move right, and there were aberrations in the cloud graphics. As he approached the first pair of blades, a phony gust drove him sideways. He went wide and missed the first gate entirely. Pathetic. He could almost hear the Australians cracking jokes. He swooped for the next gate.

Wind anomalies plagued him. Digital seams and defects littered the slap-dash sky. Soft air pockets morphed into hard bumps, and he struggled to hold his line. The second pair of blades bounced away just as he approached, and he had to execute a hammerhead stall to get back on course. Long seconds ticked by. Drastic penalties. Then another blade leaped right in front of him. He braked hard and went high, but just as he vaulted over the top, the blade's upper neck slashed the trailing edge of his Wing.

His Sky Wing damaged? That could never happen in real life. In the sim, though, the Celestia's glossy cone fluttered, and his steering went loose. If not for his belly strap, he might have lost it. He did, in fact, lose a foot. Blood streaked behind him like a crimson smoke trail.

The rest of his run was grim. With his punky steering, he couldn't risk shaving close to the blades. He missed four more gates, and his speed was so slow, the judges didn't write it down. With only one foot, he landed on the platform in a mortifying tumble.

The wiry blond Siberian went second. A well-known movie stuntman, he wore a custom acrobatic Wing called a Zlin. He had no more blade-running experience than Orr, but he'd made thousands of zany circus dives. He started out well. Orr admired his hook turns. But the crude wind effects bolloxed him. He shredded himself against the harp strings of gate number seven. Siberia was out of contention.

Banda went third, and she also had trouble in the substandard sky. Orr sat cross-legged inside his droopy Wing, squeezing his bloody ankle and watching her intricate tango. Banda was good. The same irregular currents batted her Wing around, but she compensated. Orr rocked forward. His triceps flexed and lengthened as he visualized flying along beside her. She made a clean run. When she returned to the platform, her teammates slapped her buttocks and yelled flattering expletives, but she was not happy.

Orr swallowed his bashfulness and hobbled over to congratulate her. His damaged Wing trailed behind him. "That was excellent. Especially the way you—"

"Wind's bodgy." She slung her helmet down. "Person could get their arse carked."

Orr balanced on his one good leg, working up the courage to speak again. "I guess you're used to better sims than this. Web diving, it's pretty good fun?"

She loosened her neck gasket. Up close, she looked older than Orr had expected, maybe forty-five. She had a strong stocky build, and her fair cheeks showed a tinge of sunburn. "Yeah, I dive the web. No choice. You have to dive artificial if you want to compete."

Orr hopped a bit to keep steady. "But . . . you get to like it?"

"Never. It's perfect junk." She moved to the edge of the platform and flung an impolite gesture at the blades. "This course is a no-hoper. But they're all junk. Sims make you feel closed in, right? And there's that furphy background buzz."

Orr cocked his ear and noticed the electronic hum. He'd been hearing the FM projectors all along, but now they seemed to drown all other sounds.

Banda drew her sleeve across her cheek. "Worst thing about sims is, there's no fucking gravity."

She and the other Australians bunched in a tight huddle, and Orr moved away. He knew she was giving them pointers, and it was bad form to eavesdrop. He crouched at the far edge of the platform, and his wilted Wing draped over him. No gravity. He pondered Banda's words.

When the other Aussies made their runs, his body twitched and swayed along with them, but he was running on reflex now. He didn't want to think anymore. The Aussies cleared every gate, but they all came back with blood on their Wings. Obscenities buzzed around the platform thicker than holocams.

The two Finnish girls looked like wrestlers. Thick, brawny, and flat-chested, they paced around, gulping energy juice and shaking their limbs. Orr almost asked if they'd met Juho Fagerholm, but their pugilistic scowls held him off. When they made their runs, his shoulders tucked and turned, unconsciously copying their lines. They went for speed. They steered tight close lines through the course, but one Finn lost a finger, and the other sliced off part of her Wing. Jadri hadn't sprung for a Finnish language filter, but their curses needed no translation.

Everybody agreed the sky was messed up, but no one wanted to be first to lodge a protest. Too much machismo in the air. Too many fans watching. When the judges posted the first-round scores, the fliers from down under slammed the top four spots, and of the remaining contenders, Orr came dead last.

Rip cord. Handheld cable used to release reserve parachute.

Halftime. Vera squeezed her eyes shut and rubbed her head. Beside her in the cot, Leo stifled a snicker. "Looks like a fiasco, love."

"Shut it." She pinched his leg. She didn't really like Leo anymore.

They were watching together from her soundproof cube in the hangar, and the little doctor had her hooked up to an IV cocktail of antibiotics to clear up her ulcers. Her room smelled like an apothecary.

She texted Jadri. *Tell me this isn't going out live.*

It is, Jadri texted back. *Got any hemlock?*

Vera called up the Gravity Pilot ratings. Unfortunately, their web audience was growing. Rolfe had not deigned to make a public appearance, of course. Still, he'd promoted the spectacle to the nth degree, and this was embarrassing. If Orr blew the tournament, nobody would tune in to watch his ionosphere dive.

What the hell was Rolfe thinking? Jadri texted.

When Vera didn't answer, Jadri whined through her earbud. "Should I run the ad now?"

"Negative," Vera shot back. "This is the supreme worst moment to advertise our Gravity Pilot."

Jadri's voice blistered her eardrum. "We can't have dead air."

Damn Rolfe. This tournament was turning into one regal clusterfuck. Their webcast showed the skydivers milling around on their "platform," snarking about Cyto's cheap graphics. Not good. Their show needed a rousing halftime diversion.

Vera had to admire Jadri's presence of mind. The woman slotted a docudrama on skydive fatalities. Midair smashups, entangled water landings, ground impacts at terminal velocity; that twenty-minute bloodfest took their viewing audience to another plane.

"Good stuff." Leo eyeballed the exploding body parts through his oc. "We should sign up Banda Rat for a sim. She's great on camera."

"*We*? There is no *we*." Vera shrugged away from Leo's massaging hands and focused on Orr.

He stood at the brink of the ersatz platform, balancing on one foot and dangling his grisly stump over thin air. His helmet hid his face, and his damaged Wing flopped and fluttered.

Vera bolted from her cot. The dear boy needed a friend. She ripped the IV out of her arm, shoved Leo aside, and ran out into the hangar. Somebody's respirator hung on a nail by the airlock. She grabbed it, cycled outside, then sprinted to the gantry tower, holding the respirator in one hand.

She didn't wait for the elevator, she took the stairs, and by the time she staggered up to the space shuttle cabin, her lungs were burning. Inside, Orr lay in his pilot seat, eyes shut, body rigid. She glanced around the quiet cabin. The six FM projectors made a tiny whirring sound. Al had positioned them behind the wall panels so as not to distract Orr from the illusion of his training sim. Vera sat down and caught her breath. Then she spoke a few commands and popped into the sim dressed as Orr's coach.

"We can call this off," she whispered.

He gave her a tight head shake.

"We're with you," she said. "Bettie. Al. Me. We're here."

He lifted his stump. White bone and gristle stuck out from clots of torn flesh, and blood pooled on the platform beneath. He said, "You should be pleased. This is what people pay to see."

Vera jerked back from the blood. The amputation was a graphic effect, not a physical injury. Still, it prodded her pain centers. Orr's darkened visor hid his eyes. He kept cocking his ear, listening to some noise in the background.

When he spoke, he sounded like a man choking on a mouthful of earth. "This is no substitute for skydiving."

Vera sensed agony in those words. She popped out of the sim and caressed his actual foot, still whole and healthy. He flinched and jerked it away.

Orr's second run showed a miraculous transformation. No surprise, he'd learned a lot from watching. Evidently, he'd memorized the anomalies in the sky. Everyone knew the boy had talent. Vera sat beside him in the shuttle, stroking his forehead and watching the webcast through her oc. He ran the gates clean, though his injury handicapped him and slowed his time.

When he landed on the platform, Banda walked out and smacked her knuckles against his. "That was a bonzer run. You've got style, Orr Sitka."

Orr took off his helmet and blinked. "Thank you."

Banda pointed her index finger like a pistol at his heart. "You're on my radar, kid."

That was the high point. Banda Rat praised the Gravity Pilot. Vera tagged that byte for instant replay.

But Banda's compliment did not improve his score. Every contender rated better the second time through the blades. The Australians held their own, and Banda carried off the purse. Orr took fifth place. Jadri laid in a soundtrack of applause, which mainly just amplified the furphy buzz in the background.

6

Risers. Straps connecting parachute harness to suspension lines.

Why, Daddy? Why did you set me up to fall?

Rhetorical question. Vera knew the truth. Rolfe needed to see her suffer. No, she wasn't making this up. Rolfe was heinous. He'd invested millions in the Gravity Pilot, and if the project didn't meet its numbers, his net worth would tailspin. Yet he played his tricks anyway to watch Vera sweat.

She stood at attention in his office, choking down her spit and reliving Orr's humiliation at the boogie. Naturally, Rolfe had dragged her back to Seattle. No holograph this time. The physical smell of him hovered like a fog. Even disinfectant sprays could not conceal the mold-sweet reek of his flesh. He sat behind his enormous desk, his white marble monument to his own ego.

"Fifth place." He howled at the joke. "That's pitiful."

She watched him puff out his chest. Oh yes, she had honest cause for grievance. While he reveled over Orr's defeat, she tallied her accounts.

"What kind of medal do you win for fifth place?" He tipped back in his chair and propped his bare feet on his desk. "Must be tinfoil and candy, like those coins they give kids at holidays. Only they melt, don't they?"

He found this hilarious. He threw back his head and cackled. His new black hairpiece drooped over his scalp like a dead crow, and he'd gotten bone thin, not just from fasting. Vera suspected lipo. Scratchy water noise buzzed from his webcam view of Victoria Falls, and the chilled air stiffened her nerve.

She beamed a spreadsheet to his oc. All the financials flashed red. The projected web audience for the ionosphere dive had dropped to less than a million, and she'd lowered sales projections by eighty percent. She said, "Too bad, you'll have to cut back on birdfeed."

Rolfe browsed the report. "Your numbers are off. We'll have half the human race watching our show. Disaster always draws a crowd."

Vera felt a bright-white headache circling her cranium. "You deliberately sabotaged my project."

"Why would I? I have more to lose than you do." He bared his front teeth. "You're coming unglued, Vera. Please don't force me to put Jadri in charge."

She felt her eyelid spasm. "Jadri won't take the job. She knows a train wreck."

He tilted his chair farther back and crossed his ankles on the desk. "Ah, but money, sweet Vera. Money's the root of all loving kindness. Jadri will do what I say."

"Jadri plays on my team now," Vera bluffed.

"No, kid. You and me, we're the team. Use your logic. This sets us both up for success."

"Liar."

He gave her a pouty look. "I'm not the one who lies, princess. I'm the one who loves you."

His overstretched lips buckled and cracked. Vera loathed his mouth. She wanted to reach out and pinch it shut. He said, "You've got the slutty lust for your skydiver, and it's twisting your judgment."

She leaned across his desk till they were so close, she could smell his meaty decay. She said, "You envy my friendship with Orr."

Rolfe made a tsk-tsk sound. "The worst lies are the ones you tell yourself. They're like dope, they make you stupid. Face it, the boy doesn't like you."

Vera hot-flashed. Her arm swung out in a wild roundhouse punch which connected with Rolfe's ear. His chair toppled backward behind the desk, and from the sound of the impact, she thought he might have cracked his skull on the stone tiles.

"Daddy?" She raced around the desk and found him sitting cross-legged on the floor, smirking.

He batted his lashes. "Gotcha."

Hatred filled the back of Vera's head and seeped forward like a flood of hot rainbows till she thought the dams in her brain would burst. She turned away, took ten shallow breaths and reminded herself what was necessary.

Then she faced her father again. "Orr dives from the ionosphere day after tomorrow, and we've got international media flying in. Will you at least send a holo?"

"Holo, nothing. I'll be there in person."

"But—in person?"

He smiled. "Do you think I'd miss the big show?"

Vera gave her finest rendition of outrage. "You don't need to babysit. I'm perfectly capable—"

"Oh, I'm coming." He snickered. "Like a train wreck."

She turned away and bit her thumb to keep from grinning.

7

Rotate. To reposition a Sky Wing one hundred and eighty degrees.

Late that same night, Orr tossed in his bunk at Mundo Mountain. He wadded his sheet and flung his pillow to the floor. Banda's words kept coming back. *No gravity.* That's why his Wing didn't move right in the artificial wind. He'd been stupid to think a sim could replace the sky. "Dumb, dumb, dumb." He thrashed his heels against the mattress.

But . . . what if Banda was wrong? That cheap blade-running course, sure, that was garbage. But the sim they'd built for the ionosphere was a masterpiece. Even Bettie admitted it was a work of art.

He rose up on a shaky impulse of hope, drew on his sweatpants, and headed outside. Floodlights brightened the caldera. The space shuttle glowed like a beacon. The late shift was hastily reconnecting umbilicals and replacing damaged tiles. His ionosphere dive was less than forty-eight hours away. He didn't bother with a raincoat, or even a shirt. He jogged across the launchpad in his respirator.

Gritty wind sandblasted his bare chest, and low-hanging smog radiated shades of sodium. Robots crisscrossed the pad hauling tools and weed-eating kudzu. Orr scaled the gantry ladder. Inside the shuttle, he sank into his seat and cued up the ionosphere sim. The FM projectors purred to life. He skipped the launch, tabbed through various chapters and played Troposphere. He wanted to body-dive through weather. With a one-two blink, he materialized in the sky.

Air masses collided and flung him backward. He rose on thermal currents, then sliced sideways. The clouds felt velvety wet and buoyant. Vapor streaked his faceplate, and wind sang over his clothes. Every sensation seemed absolutely genuine. He spread his arms and flew joyfully through the . . .

He flared and stalled. He turned a slow cartwheel, analyzing the move in parts. He carved an arabesque. He did a standup, then a back loop. He vaulted through the nimbus. How many hours had he and Vera worked on these wispy vapors? How lovingly they'd sculpted these wind shears. Now he surveyed his creation and told himself, this is good. But he was lying.

On he flew, straining to sense the difference between up and down. There were forces, yes, caused by his own reeling movements. At one point, he glimpsed a faint ghost of the shuttle cabin where he was sitting. He closed his eyes to make it go away.

Back in the fractal clouds, he steered a slow spiral and concentrated on his weight-bearing skeleton. One vertebra at a time, his mental attention moved down his spine. Where was that force acting at a distance, that invisible hand guiding him down the sky curve? He couldn't feel it. He had no mass. Every point of reference evaporated.

"Stop," he said aloud.

The wind died. The clouds went as flat as photographs. He hung motionless, somewhere in the margin between two frames. In his bones, he knew that if he hung there a million years, he would never feel the Earth pulling him home. There was no gravity.

For a few more minutes, he continued to deny the evidence. No gravity, that could be a good thing, right? No time limit. No danger of smashing into the ground. He wanted to keep hoping. He wanted to, but he couldn't.

He rubbed his knotted hair. Without gravity, his skills and choices wouldn't mean anything. His dives would be an endless series of do-overs where every mistake was forgiven. Instinct told him he would hate a sky without consequences. He needed the end in sight.

Twenty-two years old, he didn't often think about dying. The end seemed remote, inconceivable, something that happened to others. He had no wish to die. But as he hung arrested in the blurry ghost overlays, he recognized that death was a guiding force. It made him focus on what he had to do. No one could live in the clouds forever. Even Thunderbird needed to land. Otherwise, there was only this safe static midpoint of nowhere.

He blinked the exit code and sank back in his seat. Banda was right about sims. They were perfect junk.

8

Running. Flying a Sky Wing in the same direction as the wind.

Mundo Mountain, June 20, the eve of the great event, and Orr felt superglued to the vinyl seat in the space shuttle. The FM projectors whined softly, battering him with images from on high. Since the blade-running boogie, no one had time to move the projectors, so he practically lived in the shuttle cabin. He'd rehearsed the sim so often, he thought tomorrow's dive might feel like a rerun. He was in an unstable mood.

One smoggy thought kept cycling through his head: It wasn't fair that he had to give up skydiving. He'd worked so hard for so long, and didn't everyone say he had natural talent? If only he'd met some other sponsor, made some other deal. If only Dyce hadn't . . . He bumped his knees against the console. He didn't mean to blame Dyce. Two things he needed, only two. He gazed up through the windshield. Why did he have to choose?

While he sat deliberating, the crew hopped around Mundo Mountain like microwaved grease. Bettie ran system-wide diagnostics, and Al kept a constant check on the weather. Technicians scrambled up and down, X-raying every nut, bolt, thermal tile, and O-ring, while robots sawed kudzu off the gantry. Vera worked in the lab calibrating the holocams. She said Orr's ionosphere dive would be the priciest show Cyto had ever produced.

He clicked his touchscreens on and off. He was not calm. Rings of moisture darkened the underarms of his T-shirt. His hair had grown long again, and it hung plastered to his forehead. He hadn't spoken to Cho Sen Yao in days. What if the plan had changed? What if he screwed up? So many un-fixed details. Anything might slip out of place, and then . . . Someone opened the shuttle hatch, and his head jerked around.

Vera climbed in beside him. Vera, the very last person in the universe he wanted to see. She said, "You've done this a hundred times. You know it cold."

He lifted his shoulders, then let them drop. *Go away,* he wanted to tell her. His damp hands slid over the armrests of his seat. Then he swiveled toward the back of the cabin. In the aft behind the passenger seats sat a furry brown sphere the size of a weather balloon. It was Bettie's teacup. Thick straps moored it in place. Orr studied it with heartache.

In the morning, Rolfe Luce would arrive—in the flesh. The old man had paid a lot for this party, and he expected a ringside ride-along. Vera said he was braving the germ world merely to steal her thunder. At the same time, she seemed giddy about his visit, like a child hoping her popa would show up for a birthday. Her ups and downs made Orr's eyes glaze.

Naturally, Vera would ride the shuttle, too. Father and daughter both wanted to eyewitness Orr's giant leap. Orr wondered if Vera knew yet about the other surprise guest, the one Cho had orchestrated behind the scenes. Probably not. He certainly wasn't going to tell her.

After the big show, the passengers would touch down in Seattle just in time to see Orr land outside the city gate. Jadri had planned a fancy gala, and Orr wondered how long the spectators would wait when the Gravity Pilot failed to appear.

"You've done a good job," Vera said. "You're ready."

He turned to face the heavens. Midnight. Through the shuttle wind-shield, amethyst clouds rolled across the sky. The sun had sunk to its lowest point, just below the arctic rim, and air pollution did amazing things to Alaska's summer nights. He gazed at the clouds as if he might never see them again.

Vera patted his hand. "Do you need anything?"

He glanced down at her fingers. Vera had introduced him to Banda Rat. She'd bought him this space shuttle. She'd made him famous. Maybe he owed her something for that, but still, her fingers burned his skin like ice.

She said, "The ionosphere, can you believe it? We're nearly there."

Her voice harassed him. If only she would be quiet. She wore full makeup, but what he saw was her middle-aged face. He longed for her to leave, but she seemed to need being near him. They both knew this would be their last night at Mundo Mountain. He eased his hand free.

"I adore you," she said.

That tipped it. He got up. "I'm going for a walk."

He didn't mean to hurt her, but he couldn't be responsible for everyone's pain. Right now, he needed solitude. Outside, he strolled around the caldera in his respirator and sweats, inhaling the rosy night sky. He climbed up to the berm where Vera crash-landed from her first skydive. He stood on the spot where her parachute nearly dragged her over the cliff. He saved her life that day. That ought to be enough.

Frankly, he didn't want to waste another thought on Vera Luce. He was pining for the sky. He felt he'd already lost it. Sitting on the rocks, he watched low-hanging stratus clouds change shape, and he grieved.

But athletes had short careers. Steep rise, steep fall, everyone knew that rule. He'd been luckier than most. Luckier? Anyway, he'd had his time, and now it was nearly finished. Dyce needed help. Dyce, his best friend. She had no one else to depend on. He loved her, yes, he still believed that. They'd shared so much history. Surely, they had a future, too. Earnestly, he swore to himself that he was doing right.

He got to his feet and marched back to the hangar. Dawn was near, and many difficult tasks lay ahead.

9

Stabilizer. Small flange on Sky Wing designed to reduce air vortices for more efficient flight.

W hat a grand morning!"

Rolfe gazed out the hangar window, admiring the details of his new property and rubbing his hands together. He felt his face glowing from a recent cosmetic skin peel. Around his neck, he wore a small electromagnetic field generator that, according to the brochure, would zap infectious microbes on contact. Also, he'd dosed his immune system with heavy antivirals and stuffed his pockets full of germicide wipes. He'd planned a long time for this moment. No way would he miss Cyto's greatest show on Earth.

News reporters were snapping stills and quick-movies, so he sucked in his belly and puffed out his chest. The Great Rolfe Luce in the flesh? Yeah, that was news. This was his first real public appearance in eons. He wore his favorite slinky purple coverall and sparkle-studded flip-flops. On his bald head, a vintage green beret. When the reporters started asking questions, he radiated charm and tossed off cavalier gems of insight. What fun, just like the old days with Death Count.

Vera greeted him with a peck on the cheek, and he felt her squeezing his arm to make sure he was real. Oh yes, he'd come to her turf in his own physical bodkin. Vera's bullshit didn't frighten him today. He gave her a hearty hug.

Not only did he arrive in solid corpus, he also brought a surprise. Dyce

Iakai. He'd decided to take Dyce up in the shuttle to watch her boyfriend dive. Actually, the fan base had decided for him. Thousands of Gravity Pilot groupies had been blasting the Cyto portal, insisting their hero needed his ladylove for inspiration. Rolfe had no idea who started up the rumor, but he liked giving motivational surprises.

The sky overhead burned a flagrant aquamarine, which stung Rolfe's eyes. Morning sunlight never had been his friend. Gazing out the window, he saw the half-completed dome framing geodesic facets of the infinite, and he had to grip the sill to keep steady. Too much open space played tricks on his equilibrium.

Mrs. Jadri was serving local delicacies and cocktails to a small Mongol horde of reporters. Dr. Leo was there, too, passing out media kits and raving about Cyto's brand-new summer line-up. How the little drag queen did vamp in his golden veils. Acted like he owned the fricking company.

Conversations echoed off the metal walls. Twelve national web channels and four international ones had turned up to cover the event live. Rolfe strolled over to mingle and glad-hand. He arched his back and lifted his chin, playing to the cams.

And Dyce? Where had she slipped off to? Rolfe spotted her standing half in shadow behind a construction tractor, evidently trying to shrink out of sight. The poor girl had faded. Rolfe had taken her to a spa for a makeover, yet an escapee from a malaria ward would've presented a healthier glow. Flimsy little figure, gray-tinted glasses, librarian to the marrow. And that curve in her spine, pitiful. Even her swanky new quu-suit couldn't disguise her bad posture. Rolfe hoped his surprise would not backfire. He really did want to make the skydiver happy.

Thirty minutes before the final countdown, Mrs. Jadri whispered in his ear that their web audience had spiked to a billion, and more viewers were linking in by the second.

"Huah!" Rolfe twirled Jadri in a tango, dipped her backward over his arm and gave her a theatrical kiss. Then he winked at Vera. "Didn't I tell you? They're hoping to see our guy go down in flames."

Vera crossed to the food table and downed a fistful of roasted faba beans. Rolfe watched her fidget. There was no satisfying Vera. He rubbed his hands together and tallied his sales. A billion viewers. This would put his habitat back in business.

At a certain moment, the reporters' noise swelled to a crest, then hushed as Orrpaaj Sitka made his entrance. "Ah," Rolfe murmured. The Gravity Pilot stood resplendent. His silver spacesuit reflected the popping camera lights, and the unfurled Sky Wing wafted around him like an aura. Very cool effect. Rolfe applauded longer and louder than anyone.

The bright lights made Orr's visor go black, and this gave him an air of mystery and romance, which Rolfe totally loved. All over the planet, teen-aged girls would be creaming their panties. Cha-ching!

Then Rolfe noticed Orr fondling something at his chest, something hidden under the folds of his suit. Probably some lucky charm, some superstitious native crap. Naturally the boy would be nervous.

Mrs. Jadri gave a signal, and Orr did something with his chin. Instantly, the Sky Wing furled up into a tight glittery cowl around his helmet, astonishing everyone. It was a cheesy stage trick, but Rolfe cheered and whistled.

Vera stood close beside the skydiver, straightening his cuffs and brushing nonexistent lint from his sleeve. She treated the boy like her own prize pet. Rolfe didn't like the way she hogged the limelight. It was time to drop his own bombshell. He led his surprise out from behind the tractor.

When Orr saw Dyce, he took one step, then stopped. Rolfe relished the drama. The boy's dark visor hid his expression, and he had a way of quieting his body language to cover his feelings. Still, there was electricity in his stillness, and even the reporters knew something unusual was going down. They parted to make an aisle between the two lovers, and Rolfe guided Dyce by the elbow, like a fricking father of the bride.

Her short black hair had been professionally styled, and her tinted glasses camouflaged her eyes, but the skin at her temples showed fine white stretch marks. She walked with an uneven step, ducking her head between her rounded shoulders. Rolfe wished she wouldn't tremble so much. When she approached Orr, her whole body palsied. She mumbled so low, Rolfe had to key up his hearing aid.

"Orr, are you real?"

"My God, Berry." Orr tugged off her tinted glasses. Flecks of dried blood clogged her tear ducts, and her right cornea had hazed over with a snowy film from wearing the ocular too long. Rolfe cursed the beauty salon for not doing a better job on her eyes.

She jammed her shades back on. "Please, Orr. Don't look at me like that."

She shifted from foot to foot. When Orr embraced her, she resisted at first. Then she flung her arms around his waist. His heavy gear got in the way. Finally, he tore off his helmet and rested his cheek against her hair. Rolfe listened in.

"I got your message," Orr whispered.

She quaked in his arms. "You must despise me . . ."

He stopped her with a kiss. "We're mates. Always. No matter what."

At that point, Rolfe maneuvered Dyce toward the cameras. "Friends, it gives me great pleasure to introduce the Gravity Pilot's sweetheart. Ms. Dyce Iakai."

The reporters swarmed her. They demanded to know her favorite song, her birth sign, who designed her clothes. Rolfe smacked his lips. A little extra spice for the fans, yeah, he'd timed it to perfection.

Naturally, Vera butted in and ruined the moment. She shoved the reporters away and hauled Dyce to the locker room. Dr. Leo came strutting up, posturing like an usher, and said, "Follow me, Rolfe. I'll show you where to go."

Leo announced that all the passengers had to put on flight gear. They didn't need the sophisticated outfit the Gravity Pilot wore, but since they were flying to the ionosphere, federal aviation law required them to wear pressurized spacesuits.

In the locker room, Leo gave everyone chewable mood enhancers to take the edge off their pre-trip jitters. Rolfe washed his down with a cup of purified water, and when Leo offered him a few extra tablets, he didn't say no. He wanted to enjoy this ride.

They returned and paraded through the hangar, carrying their helmets. Rolfe loved the way his shiny astronaut suit showed off his slender form. Holocams flitted around like champagne bubbles, and he felt luminary. Oh yes, he'd chosen his moment well.

Bettie led Dyce by the hand, while Mrs. Jadri herded the reporters behind a cordon. Vera stayed glued to her skydiver. At the airlock door, Rolfe climbed on a crate to make the impromptu speech which he'd carefully prerecorded in his oc. With so many worldwide webcams zooming around, who could blame him? Of course, he did notice Vera shaking her head, pointing at her wristwatch. Killjoy, she never approved of anything spontaneous. He amped up his microbe shield and ignored her.

"Friends, a famous athlete once said, 'Perfection is not attainable, but if we chase perfection, we might catch excellence.'

"I don't have to tell you, we live in an unstable world. Fifty years ago, people could sit on a balcony overlooking Puget Sound and enjoy a nice cup of Ethiopian coffee while reading a newspaper printed in New York State. They could munch a bite of toast from Yunnan Province with jam imported from Auckland, then wipe their greasy lips on a disposable paper napkin made in New Delhi. And to transport that little snack, they buggered the sky.

"What goes up must come down, and that world had to crash. Now we know better. We've localized. We've got scientists and engineers chasing brave new solutions, and we're going to clean up the atmosphere. That makes me absolutely ecstatic to be living in these times. I have to tell you, what goes down can rise again. We can soar like angels.

"Now the Gravity Pilot, he's pursuing that eternal dream. He *lives* to fly, so he risks too much, cares too much, practices too hard and gives up too many pleasures to keep perfecting his skill. You could say he's a fanatical fool. But he's one of the happiest men alive.

"As the blind lady said, 'One cannot consent to creep when one feels an impulse to soar.' We need to soar, every blessed one of us. And that's what our Cyto wikiverse is all about—a chance to be like the Gravity Pilot and lose ourselves in the chase for perfection.

"Now let's put our hands together for Orrpaaj Sitka. We've got a really big show planned for you today. So sit back, relax, and let's see what the boy can do."

10

Stall. Loss of lift during forward flight; may result in a crash.

Nobody spoke as they cycled through the airlock—four people bound in forward momentum. Orr felt a chuffle of fear as he guided Dyce by the elbow. She walked unevenly, squeezing his hand, and he crooked his arm around her bent spine. The bubble visor made it easy to see her infected eye.

"Who's that redhead?" she whispered. "Is that Mr. Luce's daughter? She's beautiful."

Orr sucked air through his teeth. "That's Vera."

Holocams from sixteen channels circled like a flock of winged ball bearings. Close to a thousand lenses were recording. Mrs. Jadri said their webcast would have a record audience. Orr never used to worry about what lay ahead. He used to feel exhilarated before a dive. Six months ago, he would've been bouncing on his tiptoes. But now he ushered Dyce across the pad with a sense of onrushing doom.

Overhead the blue sky shimmered through the arc of steel frets, and the shuttle stood waiting in its gantry, clamped to its enormous fuel tank and boosters. Foursquare, they crammed into the elevator's open cage and rode up to the highest platform.

Rolfe said, "Will this old crate get off the ground? Looks like something from a flea market."

Vera grinned. "NASA's finest."

Orr gave the orbiter one last visual scan. The Smithsonian Museum had scraped off the insignia when they junked it. Nameless now, its yellow tiles still showed the scratch marks. He found that fitting. Already, his muscles were flexing, priming for flight. He raised his eyes to the clear shining blue, and he swallowed.

One by one, they loaded into the passenger cabin, and the bug-eyed holo-cams swarmed in to roost. A few mosquitoes slipped in, too, but Vera chased them out with bug spray. When robotic arms sealed the cabin hatch, Orr heard the heavy thunk of the lock.

In the dimness, his visor cleared to transparency. The narrow cabin was tilted straight up, like a bus turned on end, so moving required effort and care. The passengers had to cling to handholds and pendulum into their seats. Dyce slipped, and he caught her.

He said, "You okay?"

She squeezed his arm, and the force of her grip surprised him. He could read the pain in her face. He helped her into her couch.

"I love you," she said.

He mouthed the words back at her. Then he tightened her safety belt. She winced a little when he adjusted her legs, but she seemed preoccupied, staring off at nothing. Frightened, he thought.

Down in the aft end, beneath the couches, the large brown ablation shell rested under its tie-down straps like a sleeping Gulliver. All at once, Dyce twisted in her seat and studied it. "Tell me about that brown ball, Orr. I want to know everything."

He butted his helmet against hers. "You do?"

He was about to explain the ceramic layers when Dyce started reciting the story of Bettie's teacup. She grinned. "I'm linked to your official fan site. They've posted every detail on the web. It's so cool."

He watched her eyes unfocus and her smile blur. When her attention drifted back to her oc, he clenched his jaw and said nothing.

Then Rolfe reached down to touch the ablation shell's furry insulation, and Vera tugged open its hatch. "Want to look inside, Dad?"

Orr watched the old man strain to lower himself till he could peer through the small opening. Inside were the restraints and padded lining that would keep Orr's spine from snapping in the centrifugal spin. Rolfe wrinkled his nose and grunted, "Straight out of bedlam." Vera laughed and closed the hatch.

Orr's heavy gear bogged him down in the cramped cabin, but he helped everyone buckle into their safety harnesses. Then he double-checked Dyce's belt latch. She fingered the controls on the front of her spacesuit. "Don't worry about me. I'm running queries to figure out how everything works."

Orr's throat tightened. He touched his visor against hers and whispered, "Be brave, Berry."

When everyone was secure, Orr climbed up to his seat in the nose cone and belted into his couch. For a moment, he lay facing the daylight, breathing. There was no future, no past, only what he had to do now. He set one of his screens to display a rear view of the cabin so he could keep an eye on his passengers. Sitting with his back to everyone, he saw Dyce staring into space like a glitter-eyed child. He yearned for this unholy circus to be over.

Over the com link, Rolfe let out a guttural belch. "Sorry. Too many damned faba beans. That's the last time I eat native food."

Vera pointed to the holocams collecting on the walls. "Make nice, Dad. We're live."

Orr saw Rolfe stretch his neck and gulp, trying to swallow. When he said his helmet fit too tight, Vera made a joke about the size of his ego. Then she winked at Orr and gave two thumbs up.

Again, Orr twisted in his seat and gazed at Dyce. He sent a wordless prayer to Agugux, then flipped a switch to start the preordained sequence. The final countdown began.

Swoop. Aggressive dive or landing technique.

Thirty seconds before ignition, the onboard AI took control, and the three main engines ignited. The cabin shuddered in place till the engines built up to one hundred percent thrust.

"We're committed for takeoff," Orr announced.

A fiery plume thundered down the flame trench, and Orr concentrated on his touchscreens. The AI showed all systems green. The shuttle separated from the gantry, and shock waves buffeted the cabin. When the shuttle slipped two meters down, Rolfe yelped.

Orr said, "It's okay. It's normal offset thrust."

The ablation shell rocked in its tie-downs, and Rolfe laughed, letting off tension. "Some carnival ride." Then he burped again. His face looked clammy. "What genius decided to serve faba beans for breakfast?"

"Dad, the cameras," Vera said.

Slowly, the shuttle rocked back into place, and the heavy ablation shell grated a few centimeters in its straps. Orr watched the countdown ticking on his screen. Next, the solid rocket boosters lit up, and the shuttle took off.

"Yee-haw." Rolfe slapped his armrests.

Dyce gripped her belts and tucked her legs under her seat. Her eyes had a distracted shine, but she nodded when Orr turned to check on her. She said, "I'm fine, babe. I'm having fun."

Orr kept her centered in his view screen. "Hold on for rollover."

The outside view flipped over as the shuttle pitched upside down. Seats tilted, harnesses swung. Everything revolved, and holocams bashed against the windows. Rolfe threw up in his helmet.

"Dad?" Vera reached across the aisle and squeezed his arm.

He sputtered, "Was that a normal rollover? It felt strange."

Orr said, "It's routine procedure."

The upside-down position turned their faces into masks of divine comedy, and the remains of Rolfe's puke dribbled inside his visor till his filtration scrubbed it clean. The ablation shell bucked in its straps. Rolfe twisted and eyed it. "If that thing comes loose, it'll pulverize us."

"It won't come loose," Vera said.

Dyce rocked in her harness with eyes shut tight. Orr wanted to get up and verify her belt buckles again, but his console demanded attention. Was luck still with him? He couldn't remember the last time he felt its feather weight riding his shoulders. Right luck. And right *doing*. In his mind, the two values pushed apart like the polar ends of magnets. He kept checking to make sure Dyce was okay.

Outside, thunderheads engulfed them. Orr watched the vapor stream over his windshield. So much for their fine weather. He activated everyone's laser optics, and Dyce finally opened her eyes to peek out the window. The clouds gave them a bumpy ride. When lightning flashed, Dyce jerked back from the glass. Orr kept everyone in view.

Rolfe said, "This is a little more fun than I bargained for."

Next to him, Vera was hyperventilating. Or humming? Orr never could understand Vera Luce. Half the time, lately, he suspected she was living through some make-believe drama in her own mind.

They were still climbing through the clouds when warning lights flared across Orr's touchscreens. The AI spoke in clipped computer English: "Weather Alert. Category three cyclone approaching. Wind impact in ten seconds."

Dyce looked at Orr. "Cyclone?"

Vera said, "That's wrong. We checked the weather."

Rolfe made a grab for Vera's faceplate. "What have you gotten us into?"

Orr kept a close watch on his passengers as they felt the first jostle of wind. Rolfe and Vera knocked heads, and Dyce shrank into her harness.

Orr reached back to give her knee a reassuring shake. "We'll be above the storm in eight seconds. No worries."

She nodded. "I believe you."

The next bump came harder. The AI warned, "Brace brace brace!" In the same instant, everyone saw a flash and heard a loud rolling bang. Gale-force winds shook them like cracked ice in a cocktail mixer.

"Son of a bitch," Rolfe fizzed through his teeth.

Orr checked his readouts. "Lightning struck a fin, but it's okay. We're shielded." He watched Dyce's reaction when they broke through the ceiling into the quiet stratosphere. She'd shut her eyes again. He strained to reach her gloved hand. "Berry, relax. It's all right."

As they rose higher, Rolfe and Vera pulled themselves to the windows to see the storm below. Orr studied it, too. The cyclone's spiral arms wheeled across the Gulf of Alaska, reaching from the Aleutians to the Washington coast. Bright veins of electricity scattered over the cloud tops, but they were safe above it now.

Rolfe turned to Vera. "Where the fuck did you get the weather report?" His cheeks had gone dark olive, and over the com link, Orr could hear him belching again.

Vera said, "You're the one who set the damned launch date. Who plans a space launch based on a media campaign?"

Two minutes into the flight, explosive bolts released their spent booster rockets, and the view revolved in a blur as the vehicle rolled upright. Everyone settled back in their couches, and after that, Orr thought Dyce looked a little more relaxed. The main engines roared louder, and the com link fell silent.

Then a lurid red light flooded the cabin. The flare lasted only a few milliseconds, almost like a hallucination. Except it happened again. And again. The sky strobed crimson.

Dyce sat up in her seat. "Is it a solar flare?"

Orr said, "High-altitude fireworks. They're called sprites, I think. They're caused by electrical discharges from the storm."

Rolfe clutched his belts. "Can they hurt us?"

Orr said, "Not likely."

The shuttle was flying at a slight nose-up angle, so everyone had a good view when another set of red sprites flashed out to starboard. What registered were the afterimages in their retinas, because the flashes were so brief. Orr kept his eye on the screen view of his passengers.

Dyce clung to the window frame. "They're pretty."

"Bloody gorgeous," Rolfe said. "Let's put sprites in our sim. Make them different colors. People love special effects."

Vera stifled a groan.

Gassy indigestion puffed out Rolfe's cheeks, yet Orr noticed how he still hammed for the holocams. In a phony highbrow accent, he said, "Buddha taught us that life itself is but a flash of lightning." When he belched again, he tried to cover it with a laugh. "I prefer to think of life as a giant leap in the air. Up up up to the highest possible apex, the crowning achievement, the bright fleeting vision of glory."

"Yeah," Vera muttered under her breath, "then down down down to irrelevance."

When the main engines died, Rolfe almost jumped out of his seat. Vera chuckled as more bolts exploded, and the enormous empty fuel tank fell away, exactly as it was meant to do at this point in the launch. She smirked at Rolfe. "Everything's A-OK, Captain America."

"Right, I know that," he said.

Orr watched Dyce curl against the window to take in the view. She definitely seemed more confident. The onboard engines fired, and the shuttle pitched higher, heading for the ionosphere. They were dead on course, all systems go. Orr rolled his shoulders to loosen up. He was not used to having passengers, and the responsibility stressed him. *Don't question your luck. Accept it,* Mr. Bobby said. Again, Orr streamed a silent supplication to the eastern sky, half doubting half hoping that Agugux might hear.

He was still mouthing his prayer when a brilliant purple flash sheeted across the sky far above. He peered up through the windshield and said, "That's gotta be ELVES. They're sort of like sprites, only higher."

Dyce said, "Whatever they are, I like them." Her hands fluttered against the window glass.

Vera said, "ELVES stands for 'Emissions of Light and Very low frequency Electromagnetic pulse Sources. See, Daddy, I did my homework."

Orr watched Vera in his screen. She knew about ELVES? Well, sure, she'd burned a lot of midnights researching the atmosphere.

Rolfe watched the upper sky. "They're harmless, right?"

Orr said, "They're way higher than we are."

But Vera teased, "We'll find out soon, Dad. They erupt in the ionosphere, and that's where we're going."

Then a fang of blue lightning split the sky off their port side, and for an instant, they were blinded. Orr said, "Wow. That was a blue jet. First one I ever saw."

Dyce pressed her nose against the window. "Space lightning. Awesome." When a second blue jet struck dead ahead, she pointed. "There's another one." She actually giggled.

Vera said, "Sprites, ELVES, blue jets. Looks like we're getting the whole show of upper atmosphere lightning."

Orr swiveled and met Vera's eye, but he had no idea what she was thinking. All around them, scores of blue bolts forked up from the storm clouds toward the ionosphere above.

Rolfe moved back from the window. "Tell me we're safe."

Orr hesitated. "Blue jets can be intense, but the AI will steer us clear." He kept watching Dyce, but she was craning to see the pretty blue bolts of energy.

"Approaching exit altitude," the AI announced.

Orr unbuckled his harness and rose out of his seat. It was time. He tried to clear his mind, but never in his life had he felt so stiff and wary. He glided through the passenger cabin toward the ablation shell. Passing Dyce, he mouthed another, "I love you." Then, as he'd practiced a hundred times, he released the tie-downs and rolled the shell into its jettison tube.

Vera said, "Will you be okay out there?"

Rolfe coiled in his harness. "What if we have a problem? I don't think you should leave us alone in this storm."

"You can trust the AI." Orr opened the shell's hatch. One more time, he turned to face Dyce. When she blew him a kiss, he pretended to catch it in his glove. He said, "I'll meet you in Seattle, babe."

He was just about to climb into the shell when a blue jet struck the nose cone. He heard a scary pop and saw a flash. Next, the cabin lights went dark, and outside, the Earth and sky spun around. They were rolling upside down again. Except, this rollover was not standard. This was not in the flight plan. Rolfe flung out his arms and screamed.

Orr sailed back to the nose cone. He climbed into his seat and checked the readouts. In the flattest tone he could muster, he said, "We've lost the AI. We're going down."

Terminal velocity. Speed at which friction balances gravity, creating a constant rate of fall.

Dyce saw the Earth swing past her window. The whole sky was turning. She felt her insides rise up and float loose. The shuttle pitched and spiraled, and her head banged the glass. She couldn't see Orr's face, so she listened for his voice. When his baritone dropped to bass, she understood their flight had gone critically out of control.

He said, "We're reentering the atmosphere at the wrong angle."

Bright orange sparks flew past the window, and Dyce queried her oc for data. She speed-scanned old videos about atmospheric reentry. Heat shields. Ceramic tiles. Aerodynamic friction. She skimmed through the figures and graphs. They were going to explode into a ball of flames?

Her boss, Mr. Luce, threw up again. Between bouts of retching, she heard him say, "This can't be."

She felt the same shock and disbelief. Her mind couldn't accept that any second she might burn to death. But blisters were forming in the window glass. She searched the cabin walls for an escape pod, an emergency kit, anything she'd missed earlier. She scanned through her oc, but this rebuilt shuttle was not listed on any public web site.

Across the aisle, Vera grabbed her father's flailing arms. "Calm down, Dad."

"Bullshit," the old man railed. "We're gonna cremate."

Wispy black cinders curled from the walls, and Orr said, "The controls are locked. I can't reset the angle."

Dyce watched him stab at his screens. But she knew more about computers than he did. Maybe she could find a work-around. She unhooked her belt and dropped out of her harness. She felt stronger now. Adrenaline zipped through her bloodstream.

When the shuttle tossed her sideways, Orr said, "Don't be crazy, Dyce. Get back in your seat. You'll get hurt."

Grains of smoke spiraled through the cabin, and heat bubbled the walls. She grabbed the back of Orr's seat, and he caught her around the waist. "Berry, please get back in your safety belt."

"Let me help, babe." She studied the displays on his screens. The data in her oc showed NASA's original cockpit design, but this one didn't match up. They'd rearranged the console. She scrolled for a user's guide.

Orr turned to Vera. "The ablation shell. It'll carry two people if you squeeze."

"Right." Vera unbuckled her belt.

Dyce glanced at the ablation shell. Two people? How were they supposed to choose? Who planned this expedition? Mr. Luce was peeling out of his harness and mumbling, "My forest. It's not half ready. I have to get back."

Dyce watched him slither down and open the shell's hatch. When he wormed inside, Vera said, "I'll climb in there with you, Dad."

Dyce's mouth dropped open. "We didn't even draw straws."

She felt Orr gripping her waist. "Stay with me, Berry. Help me steer."

Steer? She tried to make Orr see what the Luces were doing, but he wouldn't leave his touchscreens. Did he mean to sacrifice himself? But he was worth more than all of them. A loud pop ripped through the cabin, and she broke free of his grip.

"Berry, no!" He stretched to catch her, but she dodged away and shot toward the ablation shell.

"I have to, babe."

New waves of smoke mushroomed out of the walls. She saw Mr. Luce struggling to close the hatch. He looked panic-stricken. When Vera tried to squeeze in beside him, he pushed her out.

Dyce blinked. He pushed out his own daughter?

Vera said, "Daddy?"

He said, "There's *NO TIME*."

He would've shut the hatch, except Dyce butted in and wedged herself in the opening. "Orr!" she called. "Hurry, I'm holding it for you."

"Bimbo." Vera arm-locked Dyce's helmet.

Mr. Luce pulled at her legs and bellowed, "Get in or out! We have to close this hatch!"

Dyce clung to the rim, braced her knees, and forced the hatch wide open. This one thing she could do. "Orr, hurry."

At last, she saw him gliding toward her. Her own wild Aleut. She felt her heart booming against her ribs, but it was all right. She'd kept the door open for him. She eased her hands off the hatch and caught one last glimpse of his eyes as he slid past.

Then he turned and said, "Get in, Vera. Save yourself."

Dyce lost her bearings. Orr wanted to give his place to Vera?

Vera sounded surprised, too. "You want to save *me*?"

"Yes," he said. "You."

Sparks boiled through the smoky cabin, but Dyce saw the intimate look they exchanged. She felt her universe imploding. Orr and Vera? No, it couldn't be. They had to be acting out some play.

Then a new thought altered her frame of mind. Was it possible? She glanced at the melting walls with a bright gust of hope. "Is this a sim?"

Vera seized that moment to slam the hatch in her father's face. "Game point."

Half a second later, flames blossomed through the cabin, and everything went white.

11

*Track. Skydiver body position used to achieve maximum
forward speed.*

On those days when your dreams fade, and you lose all the games
you were ever good at, and everyone you know decides not to like
you anymore, have you ever thought that very soon, any minute,
with one kiss so tender you can feel its warmth on your lips, you will wake
up and find that all along you've been a hero in disguise?

"It's a lie," Vera said aloud.

Her neck hurt. One whole side of her body felt bruised. She was lying on
the floor of the shuttle cabin, wedged under one of the seats. Outside, the sky
shimmered royal blue. She crawled to the window. Shreds of smog streamed
through the caldera and swirled around the launchpad. The space shuttle
stood in its gantry tower, snorting steam. The robotic arms had shaken it
hard, but it had never moved from Mundo Mountain. The girlfriend guessed
right about the sim.

Vera noticed the cabin door gaping open. Quickly, she glanced around, but
Orr and Dyce were gone. She sank on her knees. Orr was gone. She couldn't
pretend to be surprised. She had hoped she might inhale the scent of his curly
hair one last time, but now a white void opened up in her mind. He was gone.

Throttled choking sounds came from inside the ablation shell. Sighing, she
pushed herself up, crawled down to the aft and opened the shell's hatch. Her
father was still cuffed to the padded lining. He was writhing and gyrating in

multiple dimensions and vomiting in his helmet. The coward thought he was riding down to rescue his peacocks. Didn't have time to save his own daughter. She undid his neck seal and let his helmet drop. She needed to see his face.

When his fingers strained for something to catch hold of, she moved beyond his reach. He batted and kicked against his shackles. She listened to him gag. She watched his mouth stretch out of shape. She watched his blasted eyes.

He was dry-heaving, pumping his stomach inside out. The Anabuse Germ, what a bitch. She used her sleeve to wipe his chin. Next, she unzipped a pocket concealed in the leg of her spacesuit, a long slender pocket custom-designed to hold one special instrument. She pulled it out and felt its heft. Smooth and fibrous, as long as her forearm, as thick as her thumb. The cane. With one quick move, she struck him.

He made a loud barking noise, then drooped lifeless. But he'd only fainted. She unhooked his restraints and dragged him out. He weighed almost nothing. She stretched him flat and snugged a small travel-size gamer's crown around his head. Soon he would wake up, and the sim would go on.

"I won," she whispered, hardly able to believe it. Ah, sweet justice, she knew this sugar high wouldn't last, but for the moment, its froth tasted righteous on her lips.

"As Socrates says, 'Nothing is to be preferred before justice.'"

Vera flinched at the unexpected voice. In the far corner, she saw a spot of orange light balloon outward, then materialize as a tiny holograph about ten centimeters tall. It was Dr. Leo.

"Congratulations, dear. Now you're free to reign over Cyto." He swished his gauzy veils. "Ah, the riches, the glory, the bliss."

Vera clicked her front teeth. "How did you stow away?"

"Little me? I rode in on a holocam." He danced across the cabin, gyrating his hips like a miniature belly dancer.

She said, "Whatever you think you know—"

His laughter cut her off. "I know everything, sweet. I know you've already hired a dozen other athletes to play the Gravity Pilot. Oh yes, he'll rise from the ashes, and fans will spin new episodes of his adventures. No doubt, we'll see him skydive from Mars to Pluto soon."

Vera swatted at Leo, but he danced away. "You've sold the habitat to a group of bird hunters, am I right? And the parental warning is history, too. Bandwidth hassles, melted hardware, they were only girlish pranks after all."

"Shut it, Leo. You have nothing to do with this."

"I wonder, do you really believe that?" He swirled his chiffon skirts. "Anesthesia's fine for surgery, love, but not for your waking life. You need me to sign Rolfe's death certificate."

Vera felt her father stir in his sleep. She touched his hand.

"Admit it, weren't you going to ask me?" Leo's pixie eyes sparkled. "Of course you couldn't kill your father. He means the world to you. But you don't dare let him out of that sim, either, not after this naughty joke. This time, you've gone too far."

Vera fingered her cane, but what could she do to a holograph? Truth was, she did need that death document.

Leo bounded up and perched on Rolfe's chest. "I know you, princess. You'll tube-feed him with your own hands. Wash him, swaddle him, force the insulin tabs down his throat. Ages from now, he'll still be tumbling down in his teacup, spinning his guts out in Cyto Cyto Cyto."

She shivered, realizing the power Leo held over her. Leo, her dearest friend. She said, "What's your price?"

He curled in the hollow of Rolfe's belly and toyed with his gold necklaces. "We can leave that till later. We have loads of time now to arrange our schedule of payments."

"Go away," she said.

"I'm not even here, love. But trust me, I'll watch over your precious cargo. I've persuaded a couple of your robots to crate Rolfe up and ship him to a discreet location. I'm always thinking of your interest." Leo puckered his lips. "Kiss kiss."

His holograph flashed bright, then vanished. Vera knew he was probably still lurking. When the construction bots arrived then to bear her father away, she didn't try to stop them. She sat in the empty shuttle, listening to his groans, and her victory washed over her like cold dark vapor.

Outside on the launchpad, she heard a noise. She scrambled to the window and saw a taxi landing. She sprang to her feet. Maybe Orr hadn't left yet. She banged her shin climbing out of the shuttle. Twice, she nearly lost her balance running down the gantry steps. Her boots pounded the concrete pad, and her pulse pounded in her ears. Maybe she still had one more chance to see him.

12

Updraft. A rising current of air.

Orr sat inside the hangar, cradling Dyce in his lap. She'd been knocked unconscious during the final moments of the sim. He opened her helmet visor. "Berry? Can you hear me?"

Already, a bruise was coloring her temple. He used the folds of his Sky Wing to fan her face. What if she had a concussion? What if . . .

"She'll be okay," Bettie said. "Give her time."

He loosened her neck seal. "She tried to save me. She would've given her life for me."

Bettie brought a flask of water, and Al located a blanket. "We aired the phony skydive," Bettie said. "The whole world just saw the Gravity Pilot flame out in the atmosphere."

Al nodded as he tucked the blanket around Dyce's shoulders. "We fed those reporters so much gin, they stumbled out of here like zombies. They don't know what they saw."

Bettie dabbed cool water on Dyce's temples and said, "Jadri rushed off to some party she's throwing in Seattle. And the crew's gone, too. I personally authorized their first furlough in weeks. You should've seen them clear out."

"Thanks." Orr gently lifted Dyce's head and slipped off her helmet. The very weight of her body felt precious to him. Tenderly, he opened her eyelid, popped out her ocular and flung it away. Never before had he understood how much she loved him. He rubbed her hands and kissed her cheeks. He listened to her breath.

"Is Cho here?" he asked.

Bettie grunted. "Lord knows where that creature might be."

Cho Sen Yao had a mania for conspiracy. Weeks earlier, he'd roped Bettie and Al into airing the fake webcast to cover Orr's escape, but Cho never liked the final death scene. He said it complicated the plan too much and wasn't necessary. Orr held firm, though. To get free of Vera Luce, the Gravity Pilot had to die.

He kept rubbing Dyce's cold hands. Bettie gave her a whiff of ammonium carbonate. Gradually, she roused. Her left eye gleamed bright black, while the right one remained clouded.

"Lagi?"

"Berry."

She threw herself at Orr, and they connected like yin-yang spirals. He kissed her brown throat, her familiar ear. His dearest friend. He would nurse her back to health, he swore it. They would build a home, a family. He saw their years stretching ahead. "I love you," he breathed. And once again, after a long absence, he sensed a feather lightness beating at his shoulders. He squeezed her frail body as if he might never let go.

Bettie and Al traded winks. Then Bettie held out a bulging gym bag and a tea thermos. "Get moving, kids. Time flies. I packed some food."

Al opened the airlock. "Taxi's waiting. Better hurry."

They were all flabbergasted when Vera Luce came hurtling through the airlock. She tore off her helmet and stood panting, glaring at them. As soon as she caught her breath, she said, "The whole flight was a sim. That's why you moved the FM projectors to the shuttle. You planned this, all of you."

Orr's vision of the future crumbled. He saw there would be no escape. With leaden moves, he pushed to his feet. "I lied to you, Vera."

She unzipped her spacesuit. "My father's still out there. He doesn't know the exit code. You meant for *me* to end up like him."

Orr lowered his head. "Not forever. Just long enough for us to get away."

She wrenched off her gloves. "Are you blind? You could've ruled the sky, but you've thrown yourself away for this. . . ." She gestured at Dyce. "This web junkie."

Al glared, and Bettie tried to intervene, but Vera shouldered them aside and kept talking. "How could you sacrifice the ionosphere?"

Orr knelt and propped Dyce up. She seemed wooly-headed, and her eyes didn't focus quite right. He knew her bewildered brain was searching for its ocular. He watched her rub her temple like she was trying very hard to remember something or someone who had passed away. He held her in his arms and combed her hair with his broad blunt fingers. Two things he loved, but he'd made his choice.

"It's over, Vera. I won't skydive again."

Dyce raised her eyes. "Lagi, what are you saying?"

Vera clutched his sleeve. "You don't mean that. You think you're happy now, but later, you'll realize what you've lost."

Orr pushed Vera's hand away. "You cheated Dyce and me. You used us. Admit it."

Vera seemed to struggle. In a ragged voice, she said, "Orr, you have to believe . . . I've never been your enemy."

He stood his ground, waiting for her to go on, though he knew nothing she said would be reliable. She wiped sweaty makeup off her cheek with the back of her hand. Her eye shadow had congealed in ridges. "Yes," she muttered, "*I* did it. Everything. *Me.*"

Then she sat down heavily on a crate of geodesic glass panes. She looked hollow and used up, but Orr felt no impulse to console her. She dropped her gloves and continued in a low tone. "A taxi's waiting outside to take you to Australia. You'll change your looks, get new IDs. For the first month, you won't leave your room for any reason. A few friends will know where you are, but no one else. Otherwise, the media will hound you."

"But . . . Vera?" Orr gave her a fuddled frown. "That's Cho's plan. How did you find out?"

Vera reached inside her spacesuit. She rifled through an inner pocket, twisting and stretching, digging deep to find some hidden object. At last, she pulled out a tobacco pouch. Orr watched, bewildered, as she rolled a cigarette and licked it with her tongue. She lit up, inhaled, and blew a smoke ring. She said, "Damn, I've been needing that."

He said, "Cho?"

When she answered, her voice sounded deeper, harsher—almost, but not quite, masculine. "It's me, sports byte. It's always been *me.*"

Winds aloft. Wind speed and direction at skydiver exit altitude.

Maybe Vera really was the mother of all lies. Orr felt appalled to see her buxom curves deflate. He went squeamy when her face shifted around. She pried off her dark red hairpiece, and under the wig, her thin frizz lay plastered to her skull. Last, her irises faded from green to black. Ninety seconds it took for her mods to complete the changeover, and Vera Luce transmogrified into Cho Sen Yao. Which one of them was real, Orr couldn't begin to guess.

She took another long drag of smoke, then gazed hungrily at the butt between her naked fingers. "You can't imagine how much I've missed this."

Orr saw the scars on her hand. "The gloves," he said. "Cho never took them off."

Vera inhaled another deep puff. Then questions tumbled out of Orr's mouth so fast, his words collided.

"Why did you . . . ? How long . . . ? Why?"

"You know why." Vera pointed her thumb outside, where her father lay folded in a shipping crate, still plunging through his never-ending sim.

Orr squeezed Dyce to his chest. He didn't want to look at the woman sitting before him. She had the face and body of Cho now, but her voice sounded like Vera, and something in the way she clicked her front teeth reminded him of Rolfe Luce. Her mascara was running, and her hair stuck out like wire.

Bettie touched Orr's arm. "The taxi."

Vera got up and physically barred the airlock. "Orr's not leaving yet. There's one more thing he needs to do."

Bettie wheeled and raised her fist. "It's what we planned. Orr and Dyce get new lives. Don't screw this, Vera—Cho—whoever you are."

Al picked up a wrench. "We won't let you trick them again."

Orr didn't say anything. He knew the desolate old woman couldn't stop him. This sad game she'd been playing, how could she live with herself?

Then to his surprise, Vera's deformed lips parted in a smile. "Did you forget we have the space shuttle fueled for launch?"

Orr went taut. Al turned to Bettie. Bettie dropped her thermos of tea. "You want Orr to launch for *real*?"

Vera laughed. "Hell, I've already paid the insurance."

Al scratched his white hair with the wrench. "But the ionosphere? It's not necessary now. We're not entirely certain it's possible."

Vera lifted her chin. "Orr can do it."

Bettie's eyes narrowed. "It's a trap. The satellites will see."

"No way," Vera said. "For one night, I can phux the satellites. This dive will be private." Then she turned to Orr and opened her hands. "It's yours, Orr. The aurora borealis. Just like I promised."

Orr no longer noticed her misshapen features or her false glassy eyes. He didn't hear Bettie's protests or Al's wise caution. The ionosphere. He could do it.

"Say yes," Vera whispered. "You were born for this."

Even now, he could feel the magnetized solar winds sweeping around him, stirring bright veils of radiance. Down through the aurora borealis he could streak, farther and faster than any human had ever gone. He could absolutely do it. He could fly like Thunderbird.

Vera stretched out her hands. "You're ready. This is your time."

"You'll record me," he said.

"I won't. I swear on my life." She stood tottering over him, grasping the air for balance. Her shattered face glowed with expectation. "Remember when you told me how it feels up there? How the whole universe comes inside you? Your body doesn't exist. Your name, your life, all that sinks away, and your spirit opens wide. You can have that feeling again, Orr. This is the one pure thing I can do for you."

Outside the hangar window, the sky was shining. Orr gazed down at Dyce and felt the warm weight of her body curled in his arms. Her eyes were quiet and full. She smiled up at him. She said, "Whatever you want, babe."

And once again, after a long absence, he sensed a feathery lightness beating at his shoulders. He bent to kiss her hair.

Vera said, "I know you, Orr. You need this dive. You can't quit now."

"You're wrong." He laughed. "I can."